Ruby Basu lives in the bea̶ her husband, two children, the world. She worked for and policy lead in the Civil ̶e̶r̶v̶i̶c̶e̶.̶ ̶A̶s̶ ̶t̶h̶e̶ ̶s̶e̶c̶o̶n̶d̶ of four children, Ruby connected strongly with *Little Women*'s Jo March, and was scribbling down stories from a young age. She loves creating new characters and worlds.

A one-time legal secretary and director of a charitable foundation, **Susan Meier** found her bliss when she became a full-time novelist for Mills & Boon. She's visited ski lodges and candy factories for 'research', and works in her pyjamas. But the real joy of her job is creating stories about women for women. With over 80 published novels, she's tackled issues like infertility, losing a child and becoming widowed, and worked through them with her characters.

SAILING TO SINGAPORE WITH THE TYCOON

RUBY BASU

CLAIMING HIS CONVENIENT PRINCESS

SUSAN MEIER

MILLS & BOON

First published in Great Britain 2023
by Mills & Boon, an imprint of HarperCollins*Publishers* Ltd,
1 London Bridge Street, London, SE1 9GF

www.harpercollins.co.uk

HarperCollins*Publishers*, Macken House, 39/40 Mayor Street Upper, Dublin 1, D01 C9W8, Ireland

Sailing to Singapore with the Tycoon © 2023 Ruby Basu

Claiming His Convenient Princess © 2023 Linda Susan Meier

ISBN: 978-0-263-30650-7

08/23

MIX
Paper | Supporting responsible forestry
FSC™ C007454

This book is produced from independently certified FSC™ paper to ensure responsible forest management.
For more information visit: www.harpercollins.co.uk/green.

Printed and Bound in the UK using 100% Renewable Electricity at CPI Group (UK) Ltd, Croydon, CR0 4YY

SAILING TO SINGAPORE WITH THE TYCOON

RUBY BASU

MILLS & BOON

For my special assistant, Toffy, as promised.

CHAPTER ONE

DEEPTI ROY PUT her suitcases in the cabin that would be her home for the next thirty days.

When her friend Alex had told her he would be head chef on a super-yacht that would be sailing from Southampton to Singapore, and suggested she should join him as a crew member, she'd jumped at the chance. Singapore had been top of her list of places to visit ever since she'd fallen in love with it when watching some of her favourite Asian dramas. But, more than that, she needed to get away from England—and running away to sea had sounded perfect.

With its twin beds with a small desk in between, enough storage, an *en suite* bathroom with a shower and even a tiny window, her cabin was more spacious and well-furnished than she'd originally imagined. But it was probably in line with what she should have expected after she'd toured the rest of the yacht.

When she'd been standing on the dock at Southampton and caught her first view of *Serendipity*, she'd stood in open-mouthed awe. She imagined her response had been similar to how the passengers had felt when they'd first seen *Titanic*. She only hoped her voyage would have a better outcome—although, with how her life had been going recently, she should probably expect the worst. The only stroke of luck she'd had recently was the timing of the journey—she'd read March was one of the best times of year to visit Singapore.

No... Deepti deliberately turned her thoughts away from the direction they were headed. Although things had imploded spectacularly recently, she still had been given this opportunity to work with her friend. She suspected he'd called in significant favours to get everything sorted out for her to become crew at such short notice and she would be grateful for their friendship for ever. She wouldn't let him down.

As soon as she'd unpacked and freshened up, she would head to the galley to report for duty. She could just about remember where she was from Alex's tour of the yacht when she'd first got on board.

Even though she'd known they would be sailing in a top-of-the-line luxury yacht, Deepti had still been unprepared for its splendour. With five upper decks and one deck below the waterline, *Serendipity* was almost as large as a cruise liner, with exquisite and expensive equipment, furnishings and décor, and top-of-the-range water toys for entertainment.

Alex hadn't shown her the very top deck because it belonged to the owner—she would probably never have a reason to go onto that deck. Below the owner's deck, the upper deck had been turned into a business suite with a board room, conference room and the owner's offices.

The main deck below that had the state rooms for the guests. She hadn't wanted to leave the stunning main salon with its full-height, sliding glass walls which opened on three sides. There were plush white sofas with accent cushions in blue and yellow on one end, next to an outside side deck with more seating and a bar. At the other end of the salon was a large twenty-seater dining table.

Alex had specifically pointed out a large mirror behind the dining table. He'd pressed a secret panel on the floor and the mirror had slid open to reveal a small galley. It was a secondary galley, mainly used for food service, but Alex had explained she would be based there primarily when she was making her desserts. Inside the galley was a small lift which took them directly to the lower deck, with the main galley and some crew quarters on one side.

On the other end of the yacht from the crew quarters there was effectively a beach club with an indoor swimming pool, steam room, sauna, rooms for beauty therapies and a gym, the ceiling of which was the underside view of a glass-bottomed outdoor swimming pool on the deck above.

She hadn't been to that deck, since Alex had explained it was for guests—Deepti would have no reason to go there.

Rather than take Deepti to the lowest deck, where there were more crew cabins, the laundry and storage, Alex had ended the tour on the deck above it so he could introduce her to some of the crew, and then he'd taken her to her cabin.

She quickly unpacked her belongings then made her way to the galley, luckily easy to find, since she knew it was on the same level. Alex was talking to the head steward. When Alex had introduced her to Deepti earlier, Deepti had noticed a closeness between the two of them.

Now, as she watched them interact, their body language and the way they looked at each other made it clear there was something romantic between them. It also explained why the head steward had agreed to the unusual sleeping situation, whereby Deepti effectively had a cabin to herself, whereas she would usually have had to share with the other assistant chef or a member of the steward crew.

When she left, Deepti raised an eyebrow and smirked. Alex smiled but didn't say anything, and Deepti didn't press. Alex had been through so many bad relationships and, although misery loved company, Deepti would much rather her friend was happy with a new romance than wallow with her in their tragic love lives.

Deepti's insides clenched, which was becoming an automatic response any time she thought about her ex-boyfriend. She needed to concentrate on looking forward. At some point, she would need to think about getting her career back on track and clearing her name but, for now, she was working as crew on a super-yacht and needed to give her current job one hundred per cent.

'We're going to get underway around twelve and my current instruction is to serve lunch at one p.m.,' Alex said. 'There will only be two for lunch in the main dining room—Mr Di Corrado and his assistant.'

'His assistant is eating with him rather than us?'

'It's a working lunch. The nanny will have lunch with us after she's fed the children, and then both will have dinner with crew.'

Deepti nodded. 'I see. So, the nanny eats with us but the assistant eats with his boss.' Deepti didn't know whether that was an unusual arrangement, but the assistant and nanny were probably in a peculiar position on a yacht: not a crew member but not exactly treated as a guest either. It almost felt as if she were in a period drama, with the upstairs-downstairs division. This voyage was going to be a unique experience.

'So what do you need me to make for lunch?' she asked.

Alex referred to his notes. 'Mr Di Corrado hasn't requested dessert, and the crew will have fruit and yoghurt, so why don't you start thinking about what dessert you want to serve for dinner? There will be four for the main dining. No particular dietary requirements indicated.'

'Four.' Deepti furrowed her brow. 'How can there be four? You said it was only the owner and his assistant for lunch. What will the other guests be doing for lunch?'

Alex gave a belly laugh. 'The other guests will arrive by helicopter in the evening.'

Deepti rolled her eyes in an exaggerated manner. 'Of course—this yacht has a helipad. I should have guessed. The lifestyles of the rich and famous.'

'I would have thought you'd be used to this lifestyle.'

'Me? Definitely not. Not even my clients have this level of luxury.' Deepti's smile faltered. 'Ex-clients now, I guess.'

'Sorry, Dee. I shouldn't have said anything.' Alex's face fell, so she hastened to reassure him.

'No, don't apologise. I can't bury my head in the sand and pretend I didn't get fired.' She tried to give a nonchalant shrug but assumed, from Alex's sympathetic head tilt, she hadn't been successful.

'Have you had any more thoughts about what you're going to do about your work back home?' he asked.

She sighed. 'No idea. My head's been in a whirl, trying to decide what to do for the best. This opportunity has come at the perfect time for me. You are my saviour.' She put her hand to her heart.

Alex grinned and playfully rubbed her head. 'Anything for you. Always. You know you're like a sister to me.'

'Ditto,' Deepti replied. 'Like a brother, that is. In all seriousness, thank you. I don't know what I would have done without you or Mum and Dad.'

'How did your parents react?'

'As expected, completely supportive. I went to stay with

them for a few days to get away from London. Which is for the best,' she added with a laugh, 'Because I had to stop my mum marching into my boss's office and demanding justice for me.'

'That does sound like her.'

'I just hate letting them down.'

'Deepti, you didn't do anything wrong. Your mum's right—this is a complete injustice. Anyone who knows you can see that.'

Deepti clamped her lips together to hold in her emotions. After having had her integrity and honesty questioned by the people she'd worked closely with for seven years, all her working life, it meant so much to have the absolute confidence of Alex and her parents.

How had her life imploded so completely in such a short time? Only three weeks before, she'd been working on a proposal she'd expected would land a huge client and all but guarantee a promotion. Instead, she'd lost the deal and then, barely a day later, an existing client had switched to a competitor. She'd consequently lost her job mere days after her boyfriend of almost a year had broken up with her.

This opportunity to spend a month at sea was a lifeline before she sorted out what she was going to do in the future. If she had any hope of getting back into the financial sector, she needed to find out how the deal had gone so sour. And, if that wasn't possible, what could she do instead?

The loss of her career was a much more significant blow than her relationship ending. That hadn't come as such a shock. Although they'd been together for almost a year, it had never been a grand passion. For her, it had been about companionship rather than love. The only thing surprising about its end was the timing.

'I know my ex is involved somehow,' she said. 'It's too much of a coincidence for him not to be.' She waved her hands in front of her face, as if trying to brush away her thoughts. 'Anyway, I need to get some distance and clarity if I'm going to have any chance of sorting out what happened.'

'I always thought he was a creep,' Alex said.

'Really? You met him once about six months ago for two hours.'

Alex shrugged. 'I did tell you I thought you could do better.'

'You did, but you say that about most men I've dated.'

'And I've been right so far.'

'Perhaps I'm just a terrible judge of character,' she said, not sure she was joking.

'You can't be that bad, Dee. You chose me as one of your best friends.'

'True,' Deepti replied with a grin. She could always rely on Alex to raise her spirits. She reached out and covered his hand for a brief moment. 'Thank you, Alex. You're always looking out for me.'

'Always will. You know there's Internet access onboard if you need it? There's a sign-up sheet in the crew lounge.'

'I guess I will have to brush up my CV.'

'What will you do if you get interviews?'

'Cross my fingers they'll do them by video. If worse comes to worst, I could always stow away on the helicopter. But I can cross that bridge if and when it comes. For now, there's work to be done.'

She grabbed Alex's hand. 'Thank you for suggesting this and arranging for me to join as crew. I know you went out of your way. It's exactly what I need right now.'

'As I said, anything for my best friend.'

'Okay, before we get too mushy, you should give me my orders. No desserts for lunch, but I'm sure there's still lots to do.'

A prolonged blast from the yacht alarm jolted Deepti.

'Ah, that means we're about to set sail,' Alex explained. 'If you want, you can go to the beach club sea terrace and watch as we leave England.'

'I'm good, thanks,' she replied. Then, giving a mock-salute, she said, 'Goodbye, England. See you in a few weeks.

'Come on, tell me what to do. I'd better get a move on if we're going to have lunch ready in an hour.' She pulled up her sleeves, ready to begin her new adventure.

'Ahoy, Matteo. *Bon voyage.*'

Matteo Di Corrado shook his head at his executive assistant's effort to use sailing terms for her parting words as they signed off from their video chat. It was a shame she was staying to hold the fort in his London offices but she had told him she didn't want to sail for a month. He couldn't blame her. It wasn't his first preference either. Not at this time.

He stood up from behind his desk and turned to the large glass doors which opened onto an aft deck. He placed his palm on the access panel then, once the glass doors slid open, he stepped onto the deck. There were four areas, each with a table surrounded by six arm chairs. There were no decorative comfort features. It had been designed as an outdoor breakout area for when the yacht was used for conferences in the future, not for relaxation—unlike his private deck on the level above, which had a large hot-tub surrounded by loungers that were almost drowning in throw cushions.

With his arms folded, he watched as the coast of Southampton faded further into the distance…finally. The original plan had been to set sail that morning, but he'd taken the red-eye flight from New York and had had an early-morning meeting in London. Then another last-minute early meeting had delayed his travel down to Southampton, which meant the captain had needed to reassess his plans, and they'd departed late.

He ran a hand across the back of his neck. He needed to be at the top of his game for the complex discussions he'd be having in the afternoon's meetings. Then the guests would be arriving in the evening for business talks over dinner, and would be staying on board for further talks as they made their way to their first stop in Lisbon.

He was used to being on the go, jetting across continents at a moment's notice, but this kind of hectic schedule was one of the main reasons he'd bought *Serendipity* and converted a deck into a business suite. He needed the change of pace which, hopefully, this voyage would provide.

He breathed in the sea air and experienced a moment of calm. The cold breeze ruffled his hair, blowing his fringe into his eyes. He ran his fingers through his hair. The added benefit of working on the yacht was he wouldn't need to look and dress immaculately, the way he would in the office. His executive assistant had even commented she had only seen him in a polo shirt when he'd been on the golf course.

Naturally, he had a smart suit, shirt and tie hanging in a cupboard in his office, and a whole row in the walk-in robe which was part of his owner's suite. He would change before his afternoon meetings but otherwise he planned to stay in his casual clothes. It would be an interesting experiment, whether how he dressed affected his productivity.

Serendipity was making good progress towards the

open waters. Although it wasn't strictly the yacht's maiden voyage, it was his first time using it as a floating place of business. He had always wanted to reduce his reliance on air travel; working on board the yacht would also give him unprecedented privacy, particularly with early stage negotiations, when he didn't want the business world to get wind of his plans.

But he hadn't expected to put those plans into action so soon. The situation with Bella and Leo had accelerated matters. His niece was the reason he was being forced to sail to Singapore in the first place. Bella categorically refused to fly, and there was no other easy way to get her from England to Singapore, where his parents were waiting for them.

His jaw tightened as he recalled his parents' refusal to fly to London so they could take the children on the yacht, which he'd put at their disposal. Instead, they'd come up with multiple excuses why it wasn't convenient for them, causing Matteo to adapt his plans to take the children to Singapore himself. He shouldn't be surprised; his parents constantly disappointed him. They had shown their true colours when they'd chosen to side with his brother over him. Matteo pressed his lips into a tight line, as he invariably did whenever he thought about what had happened.

Thankfully, his thoughts were interrupted by the intercom, signalling his temporary assistant needed to speak to him. They quickly went through the arrangements for his afternoon meetings.

'If that's all, Mr Di Corrado, I'll double-check that the video-conference room is functioning properly.'

'Thank you, Jack. And it's all right to call me "Matteo".' Matteo inwardly sighed at the look of surprise the assistant gave him. 'We're going to be working closely on this boat for weeks. There's no need for formality.'

Jack gave a brief nod of acknowledgement. 'There's a few hours until the meeting. Would you like anything to eat or drink?'

'No, thank you.' Matteo indicated his assistant could leave, then turned his attention to his computer screen. Without looking away, he added, 'Can you check that everything's in order for our guests' arrival? I've already confirmed the helicopter with the captain, but could you liaise with the head steward about everything else?'

'Of course, sir.'

Matteo could only hope Jack was a quicker study than his apparent inability to follow the instruction to call him by his first name would indicate, because he certainly didn't have time on this trip to break someone completely into his way of working.

But perhaps he was being harsh. To accommodate his executive assistant's wish to remain in England—Matteo would do anything to accommodate her, as he wasn't prepared to risk losing her—he had exchanged assistants with his company vice-president for the duration of the trip. The vice-president was from an older generation and probably insisted on honorifics. It could take Jack time to get over that habit.

Matteo turned his focus back to the spreadsheets on his screen. Within minutes, concerns about his temporary assistant and his niece and nephew were put to the back of his mind as he worked through the data.

Not thirty minutes had passed before there was an urgent knock on the door and Jack came back into the room.

'Sir, Tracey needs to speak to you. I'm afraid there's a problem,' the assistant said.

Matteo frowned, trying to recall who Tracey was. When a lady came in carrying Leo, he realised she was the children's nanny.

'Bella's missing,' Tracey said. 'I left her playing in the play room while I put Leo down for his nap and, when I went back, she wasn't there.'

Matteo stood up immediately. 'How long ago was this?' he asked. 'Have you alerted the crew to look out for her?'

Tracey shook her head. 'It's only been five minutes, but I thought you should know immediately.

'Well, she can't have got far,' Matteo said. 'Jack, please alert the captain so he can implement any search protocols. Tracey, you should return to the play room and stay with Leo while we search.'

'You're going to search for her?' Jack asked, his voice rising in surprise.

Matteo didn't bother with a reply. Of course he was going to look for his niece. He had arranged for the whole yacht to be child-proofed as soon as he'd found out he would have to take Bella by sea. There was no access to the yacht exterior or dangerous engine rooms without additional security—either his handprint or a code—so there was no way Bella could have made it out on deck.

But, if Bella had managed to slip past her nanny, there was no telling where she could be on an eighty-metre boat. How could Tracey have left Bella on her own in new surroundings? Hadn't his parents done the proper checks when they'd hired this nanny? How difficult could it be to look after two children when one of them was practically a baby?

He had no idea what involvement his parents had had with employing a nanny for the children; he hadn't spoken to them for over six years. All communication about

bringing the children to Singapore had been through in-
termediaries. Six years later, he still couldn't wrap his
head around the fact that, despite acknowledging what
his brother had done was wrong, his parents had chosen
not only to keep in contact with but actively support him
rather than take Matteo's side. He'd been betrayed by his
whole family.

He could admit, he had no interest in talking to his parents when he handed over the children; he didn't want to
see them at all. But at least that was still weeks away. Right
now, he needed to concentrate on finding Bella.

Matteo spent twenty minutes searching the lower main
deck. The VIP guests' suites were large but there weren't
many places a child could hide. The port-side rooms had
been converted to the family rooms with the children's
and nanny's bedrooms, a play room and a large entertainment suite. The crew was searching their quarters and
the yacht's exterior, unsuccessfully so far. Bella wasn't
anywhere.

His face was steel as he strode to the main deck. With
work piling up and an imminent meeting, the last thing
he needed to do was look for a missing child. If Bella was
playing a game of hide and seek, she was doing very well.
Since she barely spoke, he wasn't expecting her to answer
him, but he called out her name anyway.

CHAPTER TWO

AFTER LUNCH AND clean-up were over, Deepti was working in the small galley off the main dining room, putting the finishing touches to a variety of *petits fours* she'd made for dessert for the evening. She wanted to get an idea of what was popular with the guests and crew. As she was about to put the final touch of an intricate decoration on one of them, she heard movement behind her but she didn't look up, assuming it was one of the crew checking on preparations for that evening—they'd been coming in and out all afternoon.

Unusually, she sensed the visitor silently stand opposite her.

'What are you doing?' a young child's voice asked.

Not expecting that sound, Deepti squeezed her piping bag a little too tightly and too much frosting escaped, drenching the dessert. Turning the pastry in her hands, she chewed the inside of her cheek. She couldn't see an obvious way to salvage the mess. She grimaced. It wouldn't be wasted—she was sure some crew member would be happy to eat it—but she couldn't afford to make mistakes, particularly not on her first day. Hopefully, no unexpected guests would be helicoptered in that day, so there would still be plenty of her *petits fours* to go round.

While she put down her piping bag and wiped her hands

on a towel at her waist, Deepti observed her visitor. Large, round brown eyes stared back at her. Deepti had no idea how old the child was, but the little girl was adorable, with those eyes and her curly brown hair. But her face was so sad. Deepti resisted an urge to give her a comforting cuddle.

She'd had very few dealings with children in her twenty-eight years. As an only child, Deepti had had no nieces or nephews to spend time with, and none of her friends were yet at that 'having children' phase. From her limited knowledge, Deepti didn't think a young child should be wandering freely round a large yacht. Where were her parents?

'Hey, have you got lost? Are you looking for your mummy and daddy?' she asked in her normal voice. Then she paused a moment. Didn't people usually speak to children in a high-pitched tone or was that just for babies? She had no idea how to engage with kids.

'No. What are you doing?' The girl repeated her earlier question.

'I'm decorating the desserts for dinner this evening.'

'Why?'

'Because they look pretty this way, don't you think?' Deepti picked up one of her perfectly decorated *petits fours* and turned it round for the girl to see.

'It's nice. Can I help you?'

Deepti looked at the remaining *petits fours*. She could spare one. She'd made enough individual pastries for each guest to have four, but hopefully at least a couple of guests wouldn't eat all their share, and she was sure the owner wouldn't count how many she'd put out to notice some were missing. And this way there would be an even number of desserts: it was one of her quirks that she preferred numbers to be even when they could be.

Perhaps if she could get the child to concentrate on the decoration she could ask her some questions and find out who she belonged to. And perhaps, if Deepti was really lucky, the girl's parents would be happy to have a badly decorated piece if their daughter had created it.

'All right, then. Let me put this tray away,' she said, and suited her actions to her words. 'Why don't you sit over here, sweetie? What's your name?'

'Bella.'

'Okay, Bella. I'm Deepti.'

'Dippy.'

Deepti sighed. It wasn't the first time her name had been pronounced that way. At least Bella wasn't doing it deliberately to tease her.

'Deep-ti,' she enunciated. 'But you can call me Dee.'

She placed a towel around Bella's clothes to work as an apron. Then, on a plate, she showed the girl how to squeeze out the frosting. While Bella was decorating, Deepti asked her where her parents were.

'In the sky.'

'They're on a plane?' Deepti asked, surprised the girl was on the yacht when her parents were flying.

She was caught off-guard when Bella's face crumpled and tears started to fall. She took a step forward and then paused. Was it right for her to go to the girl? She wished she had more experience to know the appropriate thing to do in these circumstances. Then Deepti shook her head. Forget appropriateness. She couldn't watch a little girl cry in front of her and not offer her comfort.

'Oh, sweetie. Don't cry,' she said, stroking the girl's back. She looked around the galley and found a kitchen roll. She broke off a sheet and used it to wipe the tears. 'It's going to be okay, sweetie.' Or perhaps she shouldn't have said that. You weren't supposed to say things you didn't know you could deliver, were you? Or did that only apply to doctors and the police? Deepti had never felt so out of her depth as she did at that moment.

She closed her eyes. All this second-guessing wasn't simply because she hadn't dealt with children before. Ever since she'd worked out her ex-boyfriend must have been involved in her losing the deal and her client, she'd known she'd put her trust and belief in the wrong person. When she couldn't trust her instincts, when she couldn't trust her judgement, how could she trust herself? The unfortunate legacy of their relationship.

She grabbed the damaged *petit four*. 'Here, Bella. What do you think of this? It's a bit of a mess. Do you think you can fix it? Look.' Deepti started scraping the frosting off the pastry with her finger. Bella stopped crying as she watched her, carefully reaching out to touch the frosting.

Deepti also had the ingredients ready to make dinner rolls with her. Bella couldn't do too much damage if she helped with preparing the dough, and while she was occupied Deepti could try to find more information.

'Who's looking after you on this boat?' Deepti asked while they were sifting the flour.

'Uncle Mayo.' Bella scrunched her face up. 'And Tracey.'

Deepti couldn't remember being introduced to a Mayo or Tracey but perhaps they were part of the engineering team rather than the stewards. She needed to find Alex and ask him to contact this Mayo.

She moved towards the door, then halted. She probably shouldn't leave Bella alone in case she hurt herself or even wandered off again. But, if she didn't let someone know Bella was with her, there could be two worried guardians on the yacht.

She'd heard a lot of activity in the crew quarters and outside the boat when she'd brought the dessert from the main kitchen to this side galley. Perhaps they were searching for this little girl.

Should she take Bella out and look for someone from the crew? Deepti looked at her as she played with the mixture. It seemed a shame to interrupt her when she looked as if she was enjoying herself. Surely a member of the crew would come round soon?

A few minutes later, she thought she heard movement in the next room, but no one came through to the galley. Thinking it could be a deck-crew member who wasn't aware there was a room behind the large mirror, Deepti moved to the dining area doorway to ensure she kept her eye on Bella.

'In here,' she called out before moving back to help Bella with her mixing.

She turned to greet the visitor. Suddenly the very small galley felt even smaller. Deepti swallowed, craning her neck to look at the man.

He was tall.

Most people were tall compared to her, at five foot three, but even so he was tall—at a guess, a few inches over six foot. Thank goodness the ceilings in the yacht were incredibly high. Although he was wearing a polo shirt, it wasn't the standard one that was the crew's uniform, nor the shirts that designated the people working on the bridge.

She definitely hadn't been introduced to this man earlier in the day. There was no way she would have forgotten him. He was probably the most stunning man she'd ever seen in the flesh. She couldn't stop staring at the perfection of his features: a strong jaw; straight, almost arrogant nose; dark-brown eyes that could have been staring deep into her soul.

She licked her lips, her mouth suddenly dry. He exuded power and control. This was obviously a man who was used to being in charge. And equally obviously, with his unblinking stare, someone who was not happy.

'Bella, everyone has been looking for you,' he said. 'What are you doing in here? You're supposed to be in your room.'

The man hadn't raised his voice but Deepti automatically stood in front of Bella, as if she could protect her from his displeasure.

'Bella, honey, do you know who this is?' Deepti asked the girl.

'Are you suggesting I...?'

Deepti barely spared him a glance before turning back to Bella. 'Sweetie, do you know this man?'

The girl nodded. 'Uncle Mayo.' Although Bella didn't appear scared of Mayo, she wasn't rushing to greet him either.

When Deepti went to speak to Mayo, he had his back to her. 'I've found her,' he said, speaking into his phone. 'Let the steward know so he can inform the others. No, no. That's okay. She should stay with Leo. I'll bring Bella down to her.'

'It sounds like people have been looking for you,' Deepti said, stroking Bella's hair. 'Are you ready to go back with Uncle Mayo?'

Bella shook her head vehemently. 'I want to stay here.' She glared at the man, who had finished his call and seemed to be glaring back. Deepti expelled a breath as she looked from Bella to her uncle. There was an unusual family dynamic between them but it was none of her business.

'I want to help Dippy,' Bella insisted.

'Dippy?' The man quirked an eyebrow.

'Deepti.' Suddenly something clicked. 'And your name probably isn't Mayo…'

'No, Matteo.' There wasn't even the hint of a smile at his niece's amusing mispronunciations.

Matteo? She hadn't heard that name mentioned as part of the crew. The only Matteo she'd heard of was the yacht's owner, Matteo Di Corrado. She looked over at the powerful, controlled man standing across from her. Of course it would be him. That was exactly how Deepti's luck had been going for the last few weeks.

'Hi, I'm Deepti. I'm the assistant chef, sir.' She went to stand beside Bella and put her hands on her shoulders. 'I hope you don't mind, we thought it would be fun if we did some baking together.'

'People have been looking for Bella. Didn't you notice the crew calling for her?'

Deepti gulped. She could say anything to justify herself. She hadn't known what the best thing to do was. He was rightfully angry his niece had been missing but she wanted to point out Bella had been safe. She could only hope her error of judgement didn't cost her this job. The last thing she needed was to be fired from two jobs within weeks of each other.

She gently pressed Bella's shoulders. 'Perhaps it's time for you to go with your uncle back to your room.'

'But I want to carry on helping you,' Bella said.

'Is it possible, Mr Di Corrado—sir…' Deepti began.

'Matteo,' he bit out.

Deepti cleared her throat to speak again. 'I could take her back to her room once we've put these rolls into the oven.'

He frowned. Deepti didn't need to be a genius to read Matteo's expression. He was not pleased. From everything she'd heard about the owner of the boat and the company he owned, he was an extremely successful businessman. And an extremely busy one. He probably hadn't wanted to spend time chasing after his niece.

She bit the inside of her lip. 'Bella, sweetie, I think you need to go back with your uncle now. I'm sure we can do some more baking another day.' Deepti reached over to remove the tray from Bella but was completely unprepared for small arms to grab her around the waist and hold on tightly.

'No, stay with Dippy,' Bella whined.

Deepti noticed Matteo's eyes narrow. Why was he suspicious of her? She hadn't done anything to encourage Bella's actions.

'Sorry, sweetie, I do need to go back to work.'

'Yes, Bella. Come along. Tracey's waiting for you.'

Deepti lifted her eyebrows at his tone. If she didn't know exactly how to speak to children, she at least knew barking orders at them wouldn't help the situation.

Much as Deepti didn't have a problem with having Bella stay with her for a while longer, she wasn't going to argue with the yacht's owner on her first day. Her soul would be crushed beyond repair if she got fired from another job.

'Why don't I come with you to find Tracey?' she offered to Bella. 'Then maybe I can speak to your aunt about you coming to be my helper another day?'

Bella's mouth trembled but, instead of throwing a tantrum, she gave a tight nod. Deepti breathed a sigh of relief.

'Tracey's her nanny, not her aunt,' Matteo said, looking at his watch. 'I have a video conference that should have started five minutes ago. Can you take her down-stairs on your own?'

At Deepti's nod, he gave her the code for the entrance to the lower state rooms, which would now remain closed to prevent any further escapes. Without saying anything else, not even a 'see you later' to his niece, Matteo left the galley.

Deepti breathed deeply a few times, as if trying to re-gain the oxygen Matteo's presence had seemed to suck out of the room.

She turned back to Bella with a bright smile. 'Are you ready to go downstairs?'

Bella nodded and stood up, then giggled. 'You look funny with all the flour all over your face.'

Deepti laughed without humour. Of course she would have flour on her face when she met an incredibly gor-geous male for the first time. At least she wouldn't have to worry about being attracted to him. Even if he weren't her boss, she wasn't interested in romance or relation-ships. What was the point when she had incredibly bad judgement when it came to men? She would never be able to trust how she felt any more. She would rather be alone than end up getting hurt over and over again.

CHAPTER THREE

BY SEVEN O'CLOCK the following morning, Matteo had already finished a session in the gym, followed by a quick swim, and had completed an hour of work. He stood up from his desk, ready for his first cup of coffee. His brows drew together when he realised there were no coffee-making facilities in his office suite. Since Jack wasn't around to ask, Matteo walked round the deck, checking whether a machine was hidden in some corner, without success.

Although there was a kettle in his suite, instant coffee was unappealing. He supposed it was natural some adjustments would have to be made since he was working on a yacht—he couldn't expect everything to be as organised as his usual routine demanded. But, as far as he was concerned, having the means to make his coffee was non-negotiable. He didn't have the time or patience constantly to contact Chef or a steward whenever he wanted a cup.

Although, he wouldn't object if Chef delegated that task to his assistant. Matteo paused as the image of Deepti from yesterday came to mind, her standing in front of his niece in full protective mode, her fierce stance slightly diminished by the flour on her cheeks and across her forehead. He'd had to physically restrain himself when his hand had instinctively reached out to rub his thumb across her face.

Strangely the flour had only highlighted how stunning

she was. For a moment, he'd even forgotten why he'd entered the galley. He'd stood there unblinking until the sight of Bella happily playing with the dough had caught his attention.

For obvious reasons, he hadn't had much to do with Bella or Leo since they'd been born, and had limited his contact once he'd found out he would be responsible for getting them to Singapore. But he'd been told by Bella's care-givers she had withdrawn into herself after her parents had died. He'd been advised it wasn't unusual, in the circumstances, but it was something that he, or rather his parents, would need to keep an eye on.

So to have seen Bella happily working with Deepti and talking to her, when she'd barely said two words to anyone else, including her nanny, had roused his suspicions. He wasn't sure what he was suspicious about, exactly, but it wasn't beyond the realms of possibility Deepti had specifically targeted the girl as a way to ingratiate herself with him. He wasn't a particularly vain man, but he knew his wealth and his looks drew women to him, and it wouldn't be the first time it had happened.

But he was getting ahead of himself. He would wait to see whether there was anything to his suspicions. If there was, Deepti would find out soon enough he wasn't interested in a dalliance with anyone, and definitely not a member of his crew. And, if she was hoping for more, for a relationship of some kind, she'd picked the wrong candidate.

He decided to go downstairs to the dining area where breakfast would soon be laid out for the guests, hoping the coffee was ready and available. At the entrance to the main state room, he could already see there was nothing visible on the buffet table, but Matteo could hear some movement in the galley. Was it Deepti? He hurried in that direction but came to a halt when a different crew member walked out of the galley.

'Oh, Mr Di Corrado, I wasn't expecting to see anyone. Can I help you with something?'

Matteo didn't know who this steward was, but he didn't have to be a genius to tell there was a flirtatious undertone to her simple words.

He pressed his lips together. 'I'm looking for freshly brewed coffee.'

'Oh. I'm sorry, I don't know where that is. I'm only here to set up the tables, and Chef hasn't sent up anything for breakfast yet. It's going to be at least twenty minutes until we start bringing things up. I'm sure if you call down to the galley someone will bring you a cup. Or I can go downstairs and ask Chef.'

'That's fine, thank you. I'll go down and ask Chef myself. Carry on.' He gave a brief nod and then turned to go back into the foyer.

'Mr Di Corrado, there's a service lift in the adjacent galley which will take you directly to the main galley below. It's probably the fastest, most direct way to get there.'

Matteo nodded in acknowledgement then went over to the lift she'd indicated. She looked as though she was getting ready to join him in the small lift, but his intentionally fierce expression must have caused her to change her mind. Was this something he needed to bring up with the captain, or was he just in a bad mood because he hadn't had his first cup of coffee yet?

Thankfully, he could smell the fresh brew as soon as he entered the main galley. The chef was giving instructions to a man as he went through the dining plans. There was no sign of Deepti, not that Matteo was particularly looking for her. He cleared his throat to announce his presence.

'Mr Di Corrado. Did you want to approve the dining menu?' Chef asked.

'No, I'm looking for coffee.' Matteo had already started to regret his impulse to go searching for a coffee himself. He should have stayed in his office and called down to the chief steward. But he liked order, and he liked his routines, and part of his routine was a cup of fresh coffee in the morning.

A buzzer sounded and, seconds later, Deepti came into the galley.

'That's the rolls ready,' she called out, coming to an abrupt halt when she noticed Matteo.

'We'll deal with these, Dee. You stay with Bella,' Chef said to her, putting a mug of coffee in front of Matteo.

Dee? There was an obvious close relationship between Chef and Deepti. But that was none of his business—he didn't have a fraternisation policy for the crew. Then he recalled exactly what Chef had said.

'Bella?' Matteo looked sharply at Deepti, who had sudden colour in her cheeks.

Why was Bella with Deepti again? Did Deepti have some scheme that involved his niece?

'Oh, please don't worry,' Deepti said. 'Bella didn't run away. Tracey brought her to me. Apparently, Bella asked to see me when she woke up.' She put a reassuring hand on his arm.

The jolt from the unexpected contact was greater than the hit from his first sip of coffee. He moved his arm so quickly, Deepti flinched.

'Where is Bella right now?' he asked.

'Um…' Deepti swallowed. Was that a sign of nerves or guilt?

'She's sitting in the crew lounge,' she continued. 'She's not alone; there are crew with her. I only left her for a moment because I knew the timer was about to go off. And I finished my meal prep before she joined me, so there won't be any delay to the guests' breakfast.' She spoke in a rush, casting nervous glances at the head chef.

Matteo shook his head. He wasn't accusing Deepti of abandoning his niece: in fact, it was the opposite. Deepti had been recruited to his yacht to carry out a job, and that job wasn't being a babysitter for Bella for the whole day.

'Make sure Bella goes back to Tracey soon. I presume you have other work to keep you occupied.' His tone was harsher than he'd intended.

Deepti flushed then looked at the ground. 'Yes, Mr Di Corrado.'

Matteo grimaced. She'd taken his tone as a chastisement when he'd been trying to make sure his niece wasn't disturbing her.

Why was Bella so drawn to the woman? Were they actually strangers? Something didn't add up. Experience had taught him people weren't to be trusted without question. Was Bella's attachment to Deepti wholly coincidental, or was he correct in suspecting it was part of some scheme? And, if it was a scheme, what kind could it be? How would befriending his niece give Deepti an advantage—unless, as had happened in the past, it was a reason to get close to him?

'Is there anything else, sir?' Chef asked. 'We have a note you'll be taking breakfast in your office. Is that still your instruction?'

'Yes.' He drank down the rest of the coffee and placed

the mug near the dishwasher. He glanced at his watch. He was already half an hour behind on his day, all because he decided to get his own coffee. 'Please also ask the head steward to arrange for coffee-making facilities to be placed in the outer office.

'Of course, sir,' Chef replied.

'Deepti, take me to Bella. She needs to go back to her nanny now. Don't indulge her,' Matteo said.

Deepti's eyes widened. She looked behind her in what he assumed was the direction of the crew quarters. 'I can take Bella straight back. I'm sure you're busy, Mr Di Corrado.'

'Matteo,' he bit out. Why was she wasting his time arguing? If getting close to him had been her plan, she wasn't doing a good job of capitalising on her friendship with Bella.

'It's breakfast time in the crew lounge,' Deepti said hesitantly. She was trying to communicate some message with the look she gave him. He narrowed his eyes. He didn't have time to mess around. If she had something to say, she should just say it.

With an angry sigh, he opened his mouth to repeat his request.

'It's breakfast time,' she repeated before he could speak. 'The crew are eating now.' She flashed a quick, nervous smile, as if she was worried she'd said something out of order and feared reprisal. He closed his eyes briefly when her meaning became clear. His presence in the crew mess could be awkward. As the owner, he could technically go anywhere he wanted on board this yacht. Deepti had tried to be careful with her warning that he would be going into a space where the crew should be free to relax, and definitely eat breakfast, without him disturbing them.

He took a few seconds to observe Deepti as she finished

with whatever she had been making in the oven. She was an interesting contradiction—in some ways unassuming, but not afraid to stand up to him when it came to Bella, and also not afraid to hint at how something he was planning to do might not be appropriate. She wasn't fawning on him, that was for sure. He could probably disregard the notion she had a scheme to get close to him.

He couldn't quite define the emotion he experienced at the moment—it was most likely relief.

'Very well,' he said. 'Take Bella back to her room. Then ask Tracey to make an appointment with my assistant. I want to speak to her.'

'Of course, Mr Di Corrado.'

'Matteo,' he said again as he was leaving the galley.

Bella was starting to be a problem. She couldn't expect Deepti to be at her beck and call. And Tracey needed to be able to look after both her charges without assistance. Or maybe that was the issue. Perhaps he should employ a second nanny specifically to look after Bella.

By the time he got back to his office suite, his assistant was at his desk, waiting to go through the agenda. The first meeting with his guests would be in an hour. He had a lot to get through before then…and he was ready for his second cup of coffee for the day.

CHAPTER FOUR

LATER THAT EVENING, while the guests were at dinner, Deepti completed all the prep work she could do for the following day's meals. She'd promised Bella she would pop in to spend a little time with her before she went to bed, and if she was going to keep her promise she needed to finish up in the galley quickly.

After this evening, she probably needed to start keeping her distance from Bella. She wasn't on board to be her babysitter, as Matteo had made abundantly clear. She grimaced as she recalled how she'd annoyed him that morning. She couldn't afford to do anything to jeopardise this job.

It had been a completely lucky break when Alex had called her with the offer— a month away from her troubles to regroup and decide what to do next. How to clear her name was the priority. But that wouldn't be possible if she was sent off the yacht at the first port they docked at because she wasn't spending her time on her work, or because she simply irritated the yacht's owner.

Sometimes, when Deepti saw the lounges and bedrooms, she forgot she was on a boat. They were bigger than the rooms in her parents' house. Her entire London flat could probably fit in the main salon. The playroom and children's bedrooms were cheerful, with their vibrant, primary colours. Deepti had assumed Matteo wouldn't care much about the children's area, but the amount of toys and play things available showed he'd spared no expense in making sure the children would be comfortable during the voyage.

Deepti spent an hour playing with Bella before the little girl fell asleep on her lap as they were reading together on one of the bean bags in the playroom. Deepti lay there for a while, unsure whether to take Bella to her room or wait for Tracey to return. From the awkward position she was in, she probably wouldn't be able to get up without waking Bella, so she remained seated, holding the little girl closer.

She heard a noise in the foyer and looked up to see Matteo enter the state room. The previous times she'd seen him, he'd been dressed casually in a polo shirt and chinos, and he'd been a walking Adonis in those simple clothes. But in a form-fitting, superbly tailored jacket, he looked as if he had walked straight off a catwalk. It was all she could do to stop herself whistling in reverent appreciation.

Suddenly, she became aware of him calling her name. 'What? Sorry.' She tore her gaze from his broad chest and looked down at Bella instead to gather her thoughts.

She became acutely aware of how awkward she must look, splayed out on the bean bag. First, flour on her face, now this. She should probably reconcile herself to never looking her best in his presence.

'I asked where Tracey is,' Matteo said.

'In the bathroom. I told her to take a wash after she put Leo down for the night. When she gets back, I'll help her put Bella down and then go back to my duties.' Not that she had anything left to do that night, but she didn't want to give him the slightest reason to think she was shirking her work. 'Tracey shouldn't be too long. Shall I ask her to find you when she's out?' It was really difficult to maintain a dignified attitude when she was splayed on a bean bag with a child covering her.

He waved his hand. 'There's no need. I spoke to her earlier. How long have you been with Bella?'

'About an hour. After I finished prepping for tomorrow.'

He narrowed his eyes.

Deepti worried her bottom lip. Had she said something wrong?

'Normally, what you do with your free time is up to you. However, I would like to speak to you this evening—about Bella. When do you think you'll be free?'

'Tracey shouldn't be too long. I'm sure I'll be able to leave here within half an hour.'

'Good. I'll speak to you then.'

He was almost at the door before Deepti remembered to ask where he would be. Her shoulders sagged in relief when he told her to go to the upper-deck lounge. She didn't really want to be seen by any of the guests—there was a strong possibility some of them could be from the financial sector. She couldn't take the risk of bumping into anyone who might know her, or even of her.

If Matteo found out she'd been fired from her previous job, and under a cloud of suspicion for unethical behaviour, he might be unhappy to have her employed on *Serendipity* when there were business guests coming and going.

He nodded and left. Almost immediately, her thoughts started whirring with concern about what he wanted to speak to her about. The only thing she knew was it couldn't be anything good.

Twenty minutes later, she was making her way to the upper deck, taking the crew stairs to avoid all the guests. Once she reached the floor, she listened carefully for any sounds before going into the foyer, in case Matteo was with someone.

She knocked on the door of the outer office, but there was no response. She cautiously opened the door and walked inside. Both the outer office and the main office were dimly lit and quiet. There was no sign of Matteo or his assistant Jack.

She glanced at her watch. She had told Matteo it could be half an hour before she was able to come up so, since she was early, he could still be socialising with his guests.

She went back out into the foyer. Across from the offices was the main business suite she'd seen on her first day. The door to that side was closed and there didn't seem to be any lights on to indicate someone was waiting there.

She stood in the foyer for a few minutes and then remembered he'd asked to meet her in the upper-deck lounge, which was a room off Matteo's office. She went back through the offices to a salon which had a large L-shaped sofa across from a wall-mounted television. It was probably the most snug room on the boat with, unexpectedly, a lot of space taken up by a staircase which she assumed gave direct access to the owner's deck.

Although the lights were on in the lounge, it was empty. She called out in case there was a hidden room but, when no response came, she turned to go back to the foyer and was almost through Matteo's office when she heard a voice.

'Deepti. There you are.' She whirled round at the deep voice behind her, almost tripping over her feet in her surprise.

'I didn't mean to startle you,' Matteo said, putting a hand on her arm to help steady her.

Every nerve in her skin flared into high alert. 'I'm fine,'

she said, moving away. He must have come down the stairs without her hearing, but she knew his sudden appearance wasn't the reason for her heightened response to his touch.

'I wasn't expecting you to be down here,' he said, leading her to the staircase and putting his hand out to request she should go up ahead of him.

'Isn't this the upper-deck lounge?' she asked, puzzled, indicating the room they were in.

He didn't answer and she didn't press. She would need to check what the decks were called with Alex or another member of the crew, so she didn't look so incompetent in the future.

'Take a seat,' Matteo said, gesturing to the sofas and arm chairs surrounding a dark-wood coffee table.

Deepti had never thought of furniture as gendered before, but she would have known instantly the room was for a man. There were no scatter pillows or purely decorative pieces on the sofas, and the coffee table was bare, not even an artistically placed photobook in view. There was a decanter and Scotch glasses on a bar made of glass and aluminium. Every instinct told her the modern décor should clash with the older-style coffee table and seating, but it didn't at all. Whoever had designed and decorated the interiors on *Serendipity* was a genius.

'How about a drink?' Matteo asked, once she had chosen to take an arm chair.

Deepti took a deep breath. 'Of course, what would you like?' she asked, getting ready to stand to carry out her crew duties.

Matteo laughed, the sound making her heart do little flips. Deepti's eyes became round. Where had her reaction come from?

'I can pour the drinks,' he replied. 'You don't need to

wait on me. You're off the clock now. Stay where you are.
Would you prefer a soft drink? Or the wine fridge is well
stocked, and there appears to be Scotch or brandy.'

'I'm good, thank you, sir.'

Matteo looked over at her. 'What is it with people not
being able to call me by my name?'

'Pardon?' She wasn't sure she'd heard him correctly.
Alex had pointed out the level of formality on yachts varied between owners and, since none of them had ever
crewed for Matteo before, they were all learning his pref-
erences as they went.

Her slight discomfort came from recalling how Alex
had mentioned Matteo's earlier command to call him by
his first name had been to her specifically. At that time,
Alex had teased her that he hadn't asked anyone else to
call him Matteo. Being asked to call someone by their
first name wasn't something to make a big deal of. She
always called her bosses by name and, although she initially maintained a level of formality with her clients, she
used their first names too whenever they invited her to.

The lighting in the room was low but enough to illumi-
nate Matteo at the bar. She couldn't take her eyes off his
strong arms and elegant hands as he moved efficiently to
pour his drink. The image of his arm gathering her around
the waist and drawing him to her popped into her mind.
She coughed to dispel the image. She needed to get her
thoughts and reactions under control.

It was the room: the atmosphere was too romantic for
her liking. And romance was the last thing on her mind,
particularly after the way her last relationship had ended.
This was a work meeting, after all. Would he think it was
strange if she asked him to make the lights brighter?

Luckily, without her having to say anything, Matteo increased the light as he came to sit across from her.

'Was Bella okay when you left?' he asked.

'Yes, still sleeping peacefully. I hope you don't mind that I spent time with her. I promise she wasn't in the way, and I did get all my work done.'

Matteo pressed his lips together. Did that mean he did mind?

'You've probably heard the situation with Bella and Leo,' he said, staring at his glass as he twirled the liquid in it.

'I know they're your niece and nephew and you're taking them to Singapore. But that's all,' she answered truthfully.

'But you've no doubt noticed Bella doesn't speak much.'

Deepti shrugged. 'Not really.'

'Hmm.'

What did that sound mean?

'You haven't noticed?' he asked, sitting forward with a curious expression.

'To be honest, I don't know how much children are supposed to speak. I mean, she is quiet, but she can hold conversations and sometimes, when we're playing a game or talking about her favourite shows, she can be quite chatty.' Deepti puffed out her cheeks—she had never expected to be having the same conversations on repeat as much as she had with Bella.

'That's unusual.'

'Pardon?' Deepti asked.

'From what I've been told, Bella hasn't spoken much to anyone since her parents died. It's unusual that you say she talks to you.'

At first Deepti bristled at the implication she was lying

about Bella chatting to her, then her mouth fell open as she realised the full extent of what Matteo had said.

'Her parents died? The poor mite.' She was quiet for a moment, thinking about the children who would have to grow up without their parents. Little Leo probably would have no memory of them. And now their uncle was taking them to their grandparents in a new country. No wonder the little girl had burst into tears when Deepti had asked about her parents.

'Oh, so that's what she meant by her parents being in the sky. I thought she meant they were in a plane.'

'Bella won't fly at all. Not since her parents died. I wonder whether sky and flying and heaven have become confused in her mind in some way.'

Deepti didn't respond. She was no child psychologist, so she wasn't going to offer an opinion. Her heart went out to the children, and to Matteo too. As Bella was his niece, it meant Matteo's brother or sister had passed away. She covered her mouth briefly. 'I'm so sorry for your loss.'

He waved away her condolences.

'You appear to be one of the only people Bella engages with,' Matteo said.

'I don't know why. Do I resemble one of her parents?'

Matteo's laugh was grim. 'Not even remotely. Bella looks like her mother. She was very beautiful.'

'Okay,' Deepti replied. Her lips twitched… Had Matteo meant to insult her own looks? 'What was she like before her parents died? Was she quiet then?'

'I don't know. I wasn't in touch with them.'

'With your brother?' She figured he would have mentioned if Bella's mother, who was very beautiful, had been his sister.

'That's right.'

His curt response warned Deepti not to question that further, but she couldn't deny her curiosity was aroused. There was silence for a few minutes as Matteo took a few drinks from his Scotch.

'Bella likes your company,' he said finally, putting his glass down on a coaster on the coffee table. 'She hasn't responded to Tracey the way she has to you, and it's making things difficult for Tracey to balance taking care of Bella and Leo at the same time. I would like you to consider being Bella's companion until we reach Singapore.'

'Her companion?' Deepti beamed. What a relief she wasn't in trouble for spending time with Bella, but instead was being invited to spend more time with her. 'I'm very happy to spend time with Bella when I'm not on duty.'

Matteo swallowed and blinked a couple of times. He shook his head, as if clearing some unexpected, unwelcome, thought. Then he said, 'No, I'm not asking you to take on additional duties. I know you passed the background checks I required for all crew, since you're sailing with children on board, so there's no concern there. I did consider hiring another nanny to take sole care of Bella but there would be a risk Bella wouldn't respond to a new person either. I already know she likes you. It makes sense for you to become her companion.'

Deepti expelled a breath. She wouldn't know how to take on that role. Just because Bella had spoken to her the last couple of days didn't mean she would continue in the future. It could be the baking that engaged Bella. She said as much to Matteo, adding that she didn't have any qualifications to be a nanny.

'Maybe Bella is just enjoying the baking with you, but I doubt that's all, since you've been together when you're not in the kitchen,' he replied. 'And I'm not asking you to be her nanny, but her companion. Bella needs a friend right now. You can be that friend.'

'But I can be her friend and carry on with my work as assistant chef. I'm sure Alex wouldn't mind.'

Matteo's jaw tightened, making her worry about contradicting him further. 'I would prefer you concentrate on Bella. I already spoke to Chef and he is fine with you taking this role. He has asked whether you can continue to assist with desserts and pastries, and I'm sure that will be no problem for me, but if it does turn out to be too much work for you, you can let me know. I understand you're *cordon bleu* qualified as a pastry chef, so it would be foolish not to use your talent when I'm entertaining guests. When there aren't any guests on board, I don't need desserts.'

Deepti nibbled her bottom lip. It was true she did have a qualification, but she was certain Alex hadn't informed Matteo that she had never worked as a chef or in a kitchen in any capacity before.

She'd already been terrified of messing up as an assistant chef and now she was being asked to take on a completely different role, one she had no qualifications or experience for.

She didn't have any other arguments, apart from her intense worry that she would fail at the role. She didn't know whether her self-worth could take losing another job, especially not immediately after having been fired from the previous one.

'I've also asked Chef and the head stew to add another assistant chef once we get to Lisbon, so you don't need to worry about your duties being a burden on the others.'

'It sounds like you've thought of everything. I'm guess I'm not really in a position to say no.'

His face hardened. 'No! You *are* in a position to say no.

I'm not forcing you to take this role. You were hired as a galley assistant—if you want to keep your current job, that's acceptable and understandable.'

'Then what will you do about Bella and Tracey?'

If it was possible, his face got even tighter, as if he were sucking lemons. 'We will have to manage somehow. It's not something you would need to worry about. In any event, my parents will need to consider the situation once we get to Singapore. I'll send them a message.'

Deepti was struck by his unusual choice of words—sending a message rather than speaking to them directly. There was something more to the situation. But it wasn't any of her business, unless it was relevant to the issue of Bella.

'Would it help if I understand some of her background? What happened to her parents?'

Matteo didn't reply immediately. He drank more of his Scotch. She was sure he was swallowing down some indefinable emotion with the alcohol.

'I hope you understand, it's a family matter. I don't think it's necessary or appropriate to go into details unless you accept the position.'

'Understood,' Deepti replied. 'And I appreciate you haven't tried to guilt-trip me into taking on the role,' she added without thinking.

Matteo blinked in surprise at her response. Had she been too flippant?

'Bella's a five-year-old girl,' Matteo said after a minute. 'She deserves to have a companion who likes spending time with her, not someone who is acting out of guilt or financial motives. That's why I asked you and didn't simply hire someone to join the yacht.'

Colour rushed to her cheeks. She was on the precipice

of annoying Matteo and she couldn't afford to do that. She felt stuck between a rock and hard place. She was crewing as an assistant chef, a role she had no experience in, and now she was being asked to take on a different role as a child's companion—another role she was supremely unqualified for.

Whatever she decided, it could end up badly for her. She couldn't bear to make any more mistakes. But could she trust herself to make the right decision?

CHAPTER FIVE

THE FOLLOWING DAY, Matteo stood on the deck watching the helicopter take his guests back to shore. The meetings had been successful, and being able to conduct them without any interruptions and in complete privacy had provided an added benefit. So far, conducting his business on *Serendipity* was working out well. Now he had a clear day free from meetings before they docked at Lisbon that evening.

Matteo knew his assistant was inside, waiting to go through some papers with him. If he'd begun straight away, he'd have been able to accomplish a lot before taking a break for lunch. Instead, he was on deck thinking about his conversation with Deepti the previous night.

He'd given her until the afternoon to make her decision. What would it be? He could understand her wariness at taking on a role for which she had no experience but he wasn't asking for a childcare expert, only someone to be a friend to Bella. Someone who Bella could, hopefully, open up to. From what he'd observed, Deepti was the natural choice.

And if she didn't agree? He'd told her he wouldn't force her and that was true. But he'd never said he wouldn't try to persuade her to change her mind. He'd already countered most of her objections when offering her the job, but he needed to think about additional inducements. He couldn't explain why, but he was certain that an increase in salary wouldn't be a sufficient incentive.

'Mr Di Corrado?' his assistant called, coming onto the deck. 'An email has just come through. I think you should take a look…'

Matteo nodded and made his way back inside. It was better to concentrate on work rather than think about Deepti—about what would persuade Deepti to take on the new role.

By the time he stopped for lunch, Matteo had caught up on most of the work that had been delayed from the previous day while he'd searched for Bella. Usually, when he was in his London office, his executive assistant brought him lunch to eat at his desk, but part of the reason for him to trial running his business from the yacht was to introduce more balance into his working life. He decided he'd take a proper break and eat in the main dining area. He assumed food would continue to be served there unless his assistant had told them to stop.

He would ask Deepti to join him for coffee after lunch so he could ask her about his job offer. It would be more convenient for him if he didn't have to make time during his hectic afternoon to schedule an appointment with her.

When he got to the main salon, he heard a noise from the galley. He walked over to see who was in there, when a steward came out with Bella. He felt relief it wasn't the flirtatious steward but it was a shame it wasn't Deepti. It would be convenient if he didn't have to send for her. He had no interest in Deepti beyond that—he was used to working with very attractive people.

He walked over to the buffet to see what dishes were on offer. Bella started helping the steward lay the table. She looked comfortable and happy, putting the cutlery down carefully, then straightening it.

Had he made a mistake? Was Bella happy to be with anyone and only acting out against Tracey? He had been sure there was something special between Bella and Deepti.

'Bella, where's Tracey?' he asked.

Bella gave him a quick glance then continued her task.

'Tracey went to put Leo down for his nap,' the steward replied.

'And she left Bella with you?' he asked with a frown.

'Ah, no.' The steward was interrupted by Deepti coming out from the galley, carrying a tray.

'Here it is, sweetie. A special meal just for you,' she called out before stopping short when she noticed Matteo. 'Sorry, I didn't realise you would be eating in the dining room today.' She put the tray on the buffet then went to stand next to Bella. 'Hey, poppet, why don't we go back to your special room and eat there?'

Bella shook her head. 'I want to eat here.'

Matteo noticed that, besides cutlery for him, a place had been set with a child's fork and knife.

With a nod towards him and Deepti, the steward left.

'I'm so sorry, Matteo,' Deepti said. 'I hadn't got the message that you were eating in the main dining room today. Bella said she wanted to eat her lunch like all the important guests,' Deepti said, giving him the sweetest smile as she repeated what his niece had said. 'And I assumed it would be empty. We'll leave you to eat in peace.'

Matteo looked at his niece, who was already climbing onto a chair next to him.

'It's fine, Deepti, she can eat here.'

'Are you sure?'

He bit down his impatience. Why did she need the reassurance? He caught the tightness in her eyes. She was really anxious about disturbing him. Was he that scary? 'Honestly, Deepti. It's fine.'

Her smile of relief was like the sun coming out on a cloudy day, which was a ridiculously fanciful simile—he had no idea why he'd thought of it.

'Thank you,' Deepti said. 'Shall I have your tray sent to your office?'

That would be the wisest choice. He could work while he ate and try to catch up on lost time. Deepti placed a reassuring hand on Bella's shoulder as she waited expectantly for his reply. He presumed she would stay with Bella while she ate, which would save time again.

He sat down. 'I can eat here too.'

Bella clapped her hands. 'Yes, Uncle Mayo and I eat like the important people.'

His look of shock was reflected in Deepti's expression.

Admittedly, he hadn't spent much time with the girl before, but this was the first time she'd acknowledged him in a friendly manner.

Bella patted the seat next to her, so Deepti carried Bella's tray over. 'Would you like me to bring the dishes over?' Deepti asked him.

'That's fine, I can serve myself.' He walked over to the buffet and started piling food onto his plate. 'Shall I get you a plate while you help Bella?'

Deepti looked horrified. 'Oh no, thank you, sir.'

So it was back to 'sir'… Rather than remind her to use his first name, he asked, 'Have you had lunch? Isn't it your break?'

'Yes, but I'll eat later. Once Bella's back with Tracey.'

'There's plenty of food here.'

'But that food's been made for you and Jack.'

His jaw clenched. She was being unnecessarily obstinate about something insignificant, but it wasn't a battle that was worth his time to fight. It was clear Chef was preparing different meals for him than for the crew, but that wasn't necessary, when there were only five people who weren't crew on board and two of those were children. He would have a word with the captain and head chef when he had some free time.

'Do you want to watch *Pets in Petland* with me, Uncle Mayo?' Bella asked.

'It's a kids' programme,' Deepti explained when he turned to her. 'I watched a few episodes yesterday. It's very good.' There was laughter in her tone which suggested the opposite.

He couldn't help returning her grin before saying, 'I'm afraid I have a lot of work to do once I've finished eating.'

Bella looked crestfallen. 'Daddy was always busy too.'

He felt a stab of some undefinable emotion go through him at hearing his brother referred to as 'Daddy'. After that, Bella only spoke to Deepti. Although Deepti did keep trying to bring him into the conversation, Bella refused even to look in his direction.

'Why don't we watch some of your pets programme in the evening, just before bed time?' he found himself saying. 'If you want, we can watch it in the big cinema room.'

Bella smiled and clapped her hands again. 'Yay.'

His face broke into a grin when he caught Deepti's expression of admiration. He stopped smiling immediately—there was no reason for him to be pleased by her approval. 'Please do join us for food,' he said and then, being completely underhand, he said, 'Bella, don't you want Deepti to eat with us?'

'Yes,' Bella answered. 'Dippy is an important person like Uncle Mayo and me.'

He gave Deepti an expectant look. His lips twitched; he was sure she rolled her eyes before she walked over to fill her plate. And he was sure she was getting a small measure of revenge when she encouraged Bella to tell him, in minute detail, about some of her favourite episodes of the pet show.

They were about to start their coffee when Tracey arrived to take Bella downstairs for her nap. He signalled to Deepti to remain seated when she was about to leave too. It was a good opportunity to ask whether she had made her decision.

'I'm happy to help out as Bella's companion,' she said, slowly. 'If you're sure you are happy to hire another assistant chef, then I'll take on the job.' She paused, then she jutted out her chin in a gesture of determination. 'On one condition.'

Matteo raised his eyebrows. She had a condition for *him*?

'And that would be?' he asked.

Deepti rested her chin in her hands. 'Bella enjoyed having lunch with you. It seems to me that it could help if you spend more time with her. Well, her and Leo. I think you should play with her or read to her when you can. I know it will be difficult when you have visitors, but perhaps around her bed time. That's my condition.' She'd spoken quickly, in a rush to get her demands out without interruption.

Matteo pressed his lips together. No, he didn't think that was a good idea. Bella was a constant reminder of his brother's betrayal. She looked exactly like her mother. But that wasn't the problem, because Matteo hadn't spent much time thinking about his brother or sister-in-law in the six years of their estrangement.

The problem was he was busy. Several deals were at a critical stage and being on the yacht instead of flying, while having its advantages, also meant some things had to happen at a much slower pace.

'You've already agreed to watch *Pets in Petland* with her,' Deepti pointed out.

He still had no idea what had possessed him to do that—he had planned to go on land once they docked that evening. But there was something about Bella's crestfallen expression. Whatever had happened between his brother and him, hadn't been Bella's fault. She was an innocent child. If Deepti thought it could help, then he was willing to give it a try.

'I'll make time to spend with Bella. But you'll need to be there too.'

'Oh, I don't know if that's necessary,' Deepti began.

'Before you came into the dining room, Bella didn't engage with me at all. It would be helpful if you could be there, at least to begin with.'

Deepti stared at him intently, not saying anything. Then she nodded. 'Of course; that makes sense,' she said.

'So we have an agreement?' he asked, putting out his hand.

'We have an agreement,' she replied, clasping it.

He flexed his hand after releasing hers, still feeling that brief warmth. Making time for Bella would have the added advantage of inevitably getting to spend more time with Deepti.

But not because of her beauty, or at least not just because of that. She intrigued him and he wanted to know what it was that was catching his interest. He had discarded his earlier theory that she was using Bella to get closer to him, but that didn't mean she didn't have some other agenda. He trusted his instincts and they were telling him there was more to Deepti than met the eye. It was for that reason he wanted to get to know her better.

CHAPTER SIX

A FEW DAYS LATER, Deepti was putting the children's lounge back in order after a day of playing with Bella. She had no idea why any room needed so many scatter cushions, but Bella liked making forts with them, so at least they served some kind of purpose.

She was probably the most exhausted she'd ever been. Who could have guessed that looking after a five-year-old was so much work? She laughed to herself—parents and care-givers everywhere would probably roll their eyes at her naivety.

Once she had finished, she sat in front of the bookcase to select a couple of books to read with Bella before she went to bed.

It had been less than a week but they had already settled into a decent routine. The only negative point was Matteo's failure to fulfil his side of the bargain. She'd been able to understand and make excuses for him while they'd been docked at Lisbon and he had been staying on land for various meetings, but since they'd set sail again she couldn't deny she was disappointed—for Bella's sake. Personally, she wasn't expecting to see him, so it didn't matter that she hadn't spoken to him since she'd agreed to take on the role of Bella's companion.

And the good thing about being constantly occupied

was that she didn't have any time to think about the mess back home. One day she would need to start looking for a new job, and hopefully find a way to clear her name, but she still had a little time before she needed to worry about that. She was too bruised to deal with that at the moment.

She still couldn't understand, couldn't believe, what had happened. She'd worked in that job since she'd graduated from university—she'd done her graduate training programme there. She'd thought a promotion to director level would be her next step. Instead she'd lost a deal, which would have cost her a bonus, and immediately afterwards a high-value client had left and she'd been fired under the guise of restructuring. Colleagues with whom she'd worked closely had been ready to rush to judgement, with the inference she had acted unethically. One of her biggest mistakes had been putting her trust in the wrong person: her ex-boyfriend. It wasn't a mistake she wanted to repeat.

'Has Bella already gone to sleep?' Matteo's deep voice broke into her thoughts.

Her breath caught when Matteo's broad frame filled the doorway. She licked her lips, her throat suddenly dry.

'No.' Her reply came out as a croak. She coughed then said, 'Tracey's giving her a bath. You're right on time to read a bed-time story with her.'

He didn't acknowledge her comment but took a seat next to her on the sofa.

'Is that what you're reading with Bella this evening?' Matteo asked with a slight quirk of his lips.

Deepti looked down at the book she was reading. She'd brought it with her to read while she babysat the children later that evening but had picked it up while she'd waited for Tracey to finish. 'Absolutely! Have to start her on the classics early.'

He stifled a laugh. 'That's a classic, is it?'

She shrugged. 'Well, it's a classic of its genre.'

Matteo held out his hand. With a puzzled frown, she handed over her book, assuming he wasn't asking to hold her hand, although she'd been tempted to pretend she didn't understand his gesture.

'"A gripping psychological thriller with twists you'll never see coming",' he said, reading the cover blurb. 'Is it any good?'

'Well, I haven't got very far yet, but I've loved all her other books, so I expect it to be excellent. I'm looking forward to getting stuck into it tonight.'

'Is that your plan for the evening? A quiet night reading?'

'That's right,' Deepti replied. 'The crew are having their weekly fun and games night on the lower deck but I'm babysitting.'

'Don't you want to join them?'

'Somebody has to stay with the children, and Tracey hasn't had the night off since we got to Lisbon.'

Before they could talk further, Bella rushed into the room and climbed onto Deepti's lap. Deepti gave her a quick cuddle then moved her onto the sofa to sit between Matteo and her. She handed him a large selection of children's books. After Bella had read three books with Matteo and Deepti, she was dropping off.

Deepti took her to tuck her up in bed. When she returned to the living area, she was surprised to see Matteo still there, leafing through her book. She'd expected him to leave as soon as Bella was asleep.

'You know there's a library on board?' he said after she sat down.

She grinned, 'I did not know that. But why should I be surprised when you have a spa with massage rooms downstairs?'

He ran a hand over his face. 'When I bought this yacht, it was with the intention of spending a considerable proportion of the year on board. I don't know... I'm always on the go. I wanted to get some peace. But, at the same time, I can't simply leave work for weeks at a time. This was a way of getting some balance—more important than ever. Life can change quickly.' He opened his eyes suddenly.

It took a while for Deepti to respond, her mind still processing Matteo's admission. Even though the companies she'd worked with were billion-pound corporations, she hadn't usually engaged with the most senior executives on a day-to-day basis, and definitely not on a social level. She couldn't imagine anyone she'd liaised with in her field giving up the hustle culture for the slow serenity of sailing on a yacht, regardless of how huge the yacht might be.

'Are there children's books in your library?' Deepti asked.

'I'm not sure. I wanted the children's things to be contained in their suite.'

'Well, Bella loves the books you have for them. She loves to read. Did she read a lot with her parents?'

'I don't know.'

'I guess liking books is something we have in common, as well as baking.'

'It is interesting that she opens up to you,' Matteo remarked.

'I'm glad she does. But I don't know why. Maybe it's because we're almost the same size,' Deepti replied with a grin. 'She may think I'm a little kid.'

'You're nothing like a kid,' Matteo declared.

Something flared in his eyes, as he stared directly into hers, that made her think he wasn't talking about her height. She blinked to break their connection.

'For all I know,' Matteo continued, 'She could always

have been quiet. The main thing is she seems to be happy spending time with you. And what about you? Are things working out for you?'

'Yes, so far so good.'

Again, there was the smallest hint that there was a story behind his brother and him. She didn't know Matteo that well, barely at all, but she couldn't imagine him being the kind of person to have no relationship with his nephew and niece without a good reason. But maybe she was giving him more credit than he deserved. The reality was, she didn't know him that well at all; they'd only met a few days ago.

They were quiet for a moment. Matteo's lips quirked. 'Thanks for not scolding me for not keeping to my part of the agreement.'

'You're a busy man. And you were here today, so it doesn't strike me that you're deliberately shirking.'

'I'm going to adjust my schedule to include time with Bella. It's just going to take a little time.'

She gave a nod of approval. 'I understand. It sounds like you have a lot on and, from what I can gather, you weren't expecting to have to take Bella by sea.'

Matteo stretched his neck. 'The way this conversation is heading, it looks like it needs some wine. I'm guessing there isn't any in the children's suite. I think I'll go up to get a bottle,' he said, standing up. His polo shirt lifted up slightly, exposing a taut stomach and abs. Deepti couldn't tear her eyes away until he asked, 'Do you prefer white or red?'

'Oh, none for me, thanks. I'm not sure it's a good idea for me to drink when I'm babysitting.' It was probably also not a good idea to have alcohol when she was already having a strong physical reaction to him. 'You don't have to keep me company. I'm sure you have more important things to do.'

Matteo looked at her with an inscrutable expression.

'Okay,' he said, then left the room.

Okay? What did okay mean? He hadn't wished her goodnight. Did that mean he was planning to come back or had he momentarily lost the courteous manner she'd observed up to that point?

She couldn't decide whether she wanted him to return or not. They hadn't spent much time together before, but she'd enjoyed chatting with him this evening and watching him while he interacted with Bella. And she couldn't deny he was very easy on the eye.

As long as that was all it was—an objective acknowledgement that Matteo was an attractive male. She wasn't interested in him for a relationship. She wasn't interested in relationships at all—not after what had happened with her ex-boyfriend.

It wasn't that she was heartbroken after her boyfriend had broken things off, but they'd been together for almost a year. She'd trusted him and it was now clear her trust had been misplaced. She couldn't imagine being so foolishly trusting again. If she could spend that much time with someone and not pick up on what he was really like, what did that tell her about her ability to trust her own judgement? She wouldn't risk putting her trust in the wrong people again, so romance and relationships were out of the question.

Not that either was in question with Matteo. He was her boss. Well, not technically: he'd told her when she'd taken the job as Bella's companion she was in his parents' employment, the same as Tracey. But that was besides the point.

Matteo was an attractive man. She could see that objectively, and it would remain objectively. Why was she even thinking of Matteo and romance at the same time? There was no indication he was interested in her or wanted to spend time with her outside their time with Bella. And she didn't want a relationship either so why were her thoughts even going in that direction?

The only reason she was in Matteo's company was because she was Bella's companion and that should be the only thing of importance. If things didn't work out, it wouldn't be fair to expect Alex to fire the new assistant chef simply for Deepti to get her old job back, so things had to work out.

Deepti stretched her legs out on the sofa, settled back against the arm and opened her book.

Less than ten minutes later, Matteo came back into the room.

'Am I interrupting?' he asked.

'I thought you'd left to get a drink.'

He held up a bottle. 'I brought it with me. But, if I'm disturbing you, I can go back to my rooms.'

'No, of course not.' She was about to put her legs onto the floor when Matteo held up a hand, suggesting she didn't need to. He took an arm chair opposite her.

'My assistant has joined the crew's games night. Are you sure you don't want to go? I can stay here. I'll even forgo the wine.'

'Oh, thank you,' she replied. It was an incredibly generous suggestion, since it would restrict what he would be able to do. 'I'm fine staying here. Why don't you join them?'

He gave an embarrassed shrug. 'This is the crew's free time. I don't want them to feel uncomfortable or on edge because the owner's there.'

Her mouth dropped open at his explanation—she hadn't expected him to think about the comfort of the others. There was no reason for her to be that surprised—he'd shown how thoughtful he was when he'd asked her to be

Bella's companion and hired an assistant chef so Alex wouldn't be under-staffed.

She wanted to get to know this gorgeous, considerate man better. To cover that alarming thought, she cleared her throat and said, 'That's probably a good idea. The crew could feel like they'd have to let you win all the games.'

'Believe me, nobody would have to *let* me win.'

She answered his wide grin with one of her own. They stared at each other for a few seconds before Deepti forced her gaze to the floor. She was tempted to tell him she'd changed her mind—not because she wanted to join the games but, with seeing Matteo as an attractive male, she wasn't sure whether being alone with him was the most sensible thing.

She sat up, suddenly feeling awkward, having her legs stretched out in front of him. He was her sort-of boss; it wasn't proper for her to sit in such an informal position. As long as she remembered he only saw her as a sort-of employee, everything should be okay.

'Why don't you have a soft drink to keep me company?' Matteo asked. 'There should be a drinks fridge somewhere in this room.'

Deepti grinned. 'There is.' She indicated the cupboards behind the dining table. 'It's hidden in one of those, but the drinks are more suitable for children.'

'How about some juice, then? Or I'll get you something from the upstairs bar.'

'I'll get some juice,' she said, starting to rise.

'You stay where you are. I can get it. Despite what you and the crew seem to think, I'm quite capable of getting things for myself.'

'I very much doubt anyone thinks you're incapable of anything. But we all have our roles to do.'

Matteo didn't respond as he poured a drink then handed it to her.

'That's an interesting point you make,' he said as he sat down.

'Is it?' She was just stating a fact.

Rather than continue on that topic, Matteo started talking about the planned stops for the rest of the journey, which led to a chat about places they had visited and a wish list of countries to travel to. The conversation flowed easily without any awkward moments.

Perhaps an hour later, Matteo pulled his phone out of his trouser pocket. Deepti couldn't help warming at his thoughtfulness at turning off the sound and putting it on vibrate so the ringing didn't wake the children.

'Please excuse me,' he said, taking a glance at the number. 'This is our California office. I'd better take this call.' He answered and immediately asked the caller to hold before turning back to Deepti. 'This will probably take a while, so I'll wish you goodnight.'

'Night.' Deepti forced out a breath after he walked out of the room. Spending time with Matteo had been an unexpected treat. He was nothing like the ruthless businessman she'd imagined when she'd first looked into him. It wouldn't be a hardship to spend more time with him, particularly since this evening had shown that she should keep her attraction under control.

The next day, Matteo made his way to the lower deck after he'd finished his afternoon meeting. He had promised to spend time with Bella, as a condition of Deepti agreeing to be Bella's companion, and he wouldn't be keeping his end of the deal if he only saw Bella for a few minutes in the evening when she was tired and ready for bed. He'd asked Jack to rearrange meetings so he had an hour each afternoon to spend with Bella while they were on board.

And it would be good to observe Bella and Deepti together closely. He wanted Bella to open up to someone but he needed to be careful she didn't form too close an attachment to Deepti. Their time together would end as soon as they reached Singapore.

He could hear laughter coming from the wraparound deck that surrounded the children's suite, so he made his way there. Bella was in the kids' pool with Tracey while Deepti was sitting on a lounger to the side. He went over to her. She must have heard him approach because she lifted her finger to her lips and indicated a sleeping Leo in her arms.

Leo's head was resting on Deepti's chest, making Matteo acutely aware of her curves displayed by her bikini top.

He hastily looked over at the pool. 'Why isn't he in his bed?' he whispered.

'We haven't had a chance to go back in yet. Bella loves being in the water but she refused to go in unless I stayed here with her.'

'You aren't swimming?'

'I was, but when Leo got tired it made more sense for Tracey to stay in the water with Bella because she's got safety training.'

When he glanced at Deepti again, he had a strong urge to hand her a towel or dressing gown. She was far to enticing for his peace of mind.

Instead, he sat on a lounger and watched Bella interacting with Tracey for a few minutes. Bella wasn't as free and easy as she was with Deepti, but she wasn't ignoring Tracey, which was an improvement from before.

Although Bella strongly resembled her mother, when

she laughed she was the spitting image of his brother. He couldn't help remember the two of them as young boys, playing with and splashing each other in the pools when they'd been on holiday. They had been so close once upon a time, spending as much time as they could together, even after his brother had left home for university. But his brother's actions had ripped them apart.

'Did you want something?' Deepti asked, drawing his attention back to her.

'I was hoping to spend some time with Bella.'

'Now?' Deepti's eyes widened but she quickly recovered from her surprise that Matteo wanted to spend time with Bella during the day. 'She's been in the pool for a while, so she could be ready to come out now, but I wouldn't count on it. Your niece is definitely a water baby.'

'I'm not in a hurry,' he said, taking the lounger next to her.

'You could always get changed and join them.' Something in her tone made him look at her expression. What did that smile mean? Did she want to see him in swimming trunks?

He was already having a hard enough time not staring at Deepti in her bikini. He swallowed at the idea she might be attracted to him and wanted to see him bare-chested. Perhaps a cool dip in the pool was what he needed right now.

'Uncle Mayo!' Bella called, running over and throwing cold, wet arms around him. It was the first time she'd been physically affectionate to him and a lump formed in his throat.

'Hello, Bella,' he said, a little stiltedly. 'I came to see if you wanted to play something or watch your pet programme.'

Bella nodded shyly.

'I should get Bella dry and dressed first,' Deepti said, gathering Leo up, ready to hand him to Tracey.

They all went back inside.

While Deepti was helping Bella wash and change, Matteo went to look at the cupboards surrounding the fridge, and thankfully found a coffee machine. He brewed a pot and put the carafe on a tray with cups, cream and sugar, remembering at the last minute to add a third cup for Tracey.

Tracey came into the living room first. 'Leo's down for his nap. Since Deepti's been staying with Bella, I've been going to the crew mess while he's sleeping, but if you want me to stay here...?'

Matteo shook his head. 'Not at all.'

He was more than happy to be alone with Deepti and Bella.

After spending almost an hour with Bella, Matteo needed to return to work. For the first time in a long time, the pull of the challenge and excitement of work wasn't as strong as the fun he'd been having with Deepti and Bella. 'Deepti, perhaps you can come to see me once Bella has gone to sleep?'

He felt a momentary pang of guilt at her look of alarm as she asked if there was a problem. Nobody wanted to do a bad job, but Deepti's reactions translated into a fear, which suggested she'd had previous experience that made her worry more than most people about her performance.

'Not at all,' he replied. 'We should have a catch-up about how things are going with Bella. It's difficult to talk properly when she's around—unless Tracey has the evening off again?'

'No, she doesn't. I'll see you later.'

* * *

Later that evening, Matteo turned off his computer and leaned back in his chair, crossing his legs and putting his hands behind his head. Despite taking time out of his day to spend with Bella, he had accomplished everything he needed to, and it wasn't even eight o'clock. When he was working in his offices, it was rare that he finished work before ten. Between his executive assistant in London and his assistant on the yacht triaging anything that needed to be brought to Matteo's attention, work was being efficiently delegated, and he was the one benefiting most.

He heard a light knock before Deepti entered the room.

'Sorry, there was nobody in the front office. I didn't know whether you were still working or not. Bella's sleeping; is this a good time for you or I can come back when it's more convenient?'

He stood up. 'Perfect timing. I've just finished.'

He strode towards the lounge which gave access to the owner's suite. Deepti followed him as he walked over to the small dining room with a round table set for two.

'I was about to have dinner.'

She looked confused 'Oh, okay. I can come back in an hour or two, then.'

'Have you eaten?'

'Not yet.'

'Why don't you join me?' He reached the small dining table. 'There's plenty of food.'

'I can eat after we talk.'

He smiled. 'I told Chef you would be joining me.'

She still hesitated. Was it because she didn't want to eat with the boss or because of him personally?

'You'd be eating the same thing in the crew's mess,' he

pointed out. 'What difference does the location make? We can talk while we eat so it's a working dinner.'

'Of course; that would be more efficient.' She sat down.

'Is red wine okay for you?' At her nod, he opened a bottle to let it breathe.

As he took the seat opposite her, she gave him an expectant look.

'So, do you have any specific questions about Bella?' she asked.

Matteo cleared his throat. He didn't have any questions about Bella. He could see for himself how she was improving. But he'd enjoyed talking with Deepti the previous evening and wouldn't mind her company again.

If he'd been on land and needed some company, he would have invited one of the many women who showed their interest in him out for a meal or to attend an exhibition or show. But he wasn't asking Deepti to dine with him as a substitute date. Although, he did admit, there was something about her that made him want to know her better, something more than looking at a beautiful face.

He caught her questioning look. 'Do you think Bella is settling down more?'

Deepti frowned. 'She seems fine to me. Quiet…but happy to play. Loves to swim. She's talking more to Tracey and seems happy for Tracey to help with washing and brushing.'

'That's good.'

'But I honestly don't have any experience of children. Bella talks about the nursery she used to go to for some mornings, and her friends, but she rarely talks about her parents or what she did with them. I don't know if that's unusual. And I don't know whether I should be bringing it up. I mean, you hardly mention your brother. If it's difficult for you to talk about him, it must be for Bella too.'

Matteo pressed his lips together tightly. 'My brother and I weren't close in recent years,' he said in clipped tones. 'In fact, I hadn't seen him since before Bella was born.'

He watched an interplay of expressions on Deepti's face but she said nothing, just carried on eating her steak and potatoes. He admired her restraint. It was unusual for him to bring it up at all, knowing that it would invite questions. But he felt an inexplicable compulsion to talk to Deepti about his family.

Every day, they got closer to Singapore and the moment he would see his parents again. His shoulders tightened. He honestly didn't know how he would react when he saw them. He couldn't understand the choice they'd made, which made a close relationship with them again unlikely.

'Would you like some dessert?' he asked.

'Sure.' When he gave her a plate but didn't take any for himself, she asked, 'Aren't you having any?'

'I don't really eat a lot of sweet food. Is it good?'

She shrugged. 'Well, I like it. But it sounds immodest to say it's good when I made it.'

'You made it? Why are you working in the galley?'

'I'm not really but I asked Al…um…the chef if I could make the desserts for the crew occasionally even though my main role is to be with Bella. I know you didn't want dessert unless you had guests, so maybe I shouldn't have made them for the crew if you're not going to eat them. I can mention it to Alex.'

Again, there was the undue nervousness about whether she'd done something wrong.

'I don't want to deprive the crew of desserts,' he said. 'And, since you made this, I'll have to try some now.' He took a mouthful then practically moaned as the food melted on his tongue. It was amazing. Among the best desserts he'd ever tasted.

He loved sweet foods, perhaps a little too much, so he tried to eat them in moderation. But knowing Deepti was talented enough to make such exquisite food was going to make it difficult to keep to his resolve.

'This tastes like it was created by angels,' he said.

'Thank you!' Deepti's face brightened at his praise, making him think of sunlight again.

'Your *cordon bleu* qualification is well deserved. Did you work as a pastry chef in restaurants? Where did you say you live in England?'

'Um… London.' Deepti's voice was higher pitched that usual. He couldn't work out what about his question had unnerved her.

'I haven't worked as a pastry chef before,' she said.

'I see. Were you a sous chef?'

Her smile this time was forced. 'No. Actually, that reminds me, I need to speak to Alex.' She stood up. 'Goodnight.'

She hurried off before he could say anything. Matteo narrowed his eyes. Why was she being so evasive about working in a restaurant kitchen? Hiring decisions were left to the captain and heads of department, and he trusted them to do all the relevant background checks. There shouldn't have been any reason for her to be nervous about his questions.

Had his instinct on the first day been correct? Was there another reason Deepti had taken a job on *Serendipity* and got close to Bella?

And why did he hope he was wrong?

CHAPTER SEVEN

DEEPTI HAD SPENT a lovely morning wandering around the small Italian town of Fiore. Walking down the narrow, cobblestone streets and looking at the mediaeval architecture, she felt as if she were in an EM Forster novel. Like most of the crew, she'd been surprised when Matteo had opted to anchor out at sea, and take the tender to Fiore rather than dock in one of Italy's bigger ports, but it was an unexpected treat.

And now she was getting hungry. The only difficulty was choosing which of the amazing restaurants to eat at.

'Deepti.'

Her heart leapt at the deep, gravelly voice she would recognise anywhere now. Had it really only been a week since she'd met Matteo?

'Matteo. I didn't expect to see you here. I thought you said your business was in the city.' They'd spoken briefly that morning when they'd travelled together to shore on the tender from the yacht but other members of the crew had been present so it had been a brief conversation.

'It was. My meetings are finished. I always come for a visit when I get the chance. My grandmother grew up in this town.'

'Oh, that's why we stopped here. I did wonder why you didn't choose one of the larger Italian harbours.'

He didn't make any comment but asked where Bella was.

'She's with Tracey. I think they've come to town but I haven't been with them this morning. It's my day off, so I thought I'd spend it exploring, and I can't expect a five-year-old to want to walk for hours. It feels like ages since I've been on land. It's funny how quickly you can get used to being at sea.'

He inclined his head in agreement. 'Have you been to Italy before?'

'Oh, yes, plenty of times. My mum loves Italy. We used to go all the time when I was in high school. But we always stayed near the main tourist areas.'

'Where are you about to go now?'

Deepti looked around her. 'Actually, I was going to find somewhere to eat. Can you recommend a place? They all look amazing to me.'

For a moment, Matteo said nothing but stood staring at her. He had that same inscrutable expression. Would she ever know what he was thinking? It was a strange dichotomy, knowing he was such a frank and open person in some ways.

This was completely unlike her. She was lying to him every day, or at least hiding the truth. But she couldn't give up the enjoyment of spending time with someone who didn't know the truth about her job; someone who wasn't going to judge her or believe she was at best unethical and at worst a criminal.

'Never mind,' she said when he still didn't reply. 'I'm sure all of them will be great. I'll see you back on the boat.' She started to walk towards the tavernas.

'Just wait.' Matteo put a detaining hand on her arm. 'I'm taking a break for lunch. I have a reservation. It's a bit of a trek, but well worth it.'

'Oh, is it quite popular, then? Do you think I'll be able to get a table?'

Matteo rolled his eyes. 'Yes. Because I'm asking you to join me.'

'Oh, no, I don't want to spoil your lunch break.'

'Not at all. I wouldn't mind the company.'

Deepti still hesitated. She wanted to spend time with Matteo, and that was concerning. It had only been a month since she'd broken up with her boyfriend and, although he had been far from the love of her life, she shouldn't be interested in someone new already, should she? She tried to reassure herself that wanting to spend some time with someone for interesting conversation was nothing to worry about, and definitely didn't mean she was looking for a relationship.

Perhaps it was her forced proximity to Matteo that was causing these unwelcome feelings of attraction. She really should refuse to join him. In fact, she should go out of her way to avoid spending much time alone with him. She stuck out her chin in a gesture of resolve.

'Deepti, please would you join me for lunch?' There was an almost pleading expression in his eyes.

'I would love to,' she replied, her resolve immediately disappearing. She mentally rolled her eyes at how pathetic she was acting.

They'd been walking for five minutes when Matteo suddenly stopped.

'As I said, it is a bit of a trek to get to the restaurant. We can either keep following the road round, or we can take this path, which is a shortcut.'

Deepti looked around, not really clear what path Matteo was referring to. Her nose crinkled.

Matteo laughed. 'All right, it's not really a path. It's a

little overgrown.' He moved the branches of a large bush to the side to reveal a dirt track. 'It can be steep, so we can use the road is you prefer.'

'I don't mind the path, but won't your suit get muddy?'

'I don't have any meetings this afternoon. But I always keep a spare suit in all my offices.'

Deepti's lips quirked. He mentioned having multiple offices, no doubt in multiple countries, as if it was a usual occurrence. She was used to working with CEOs and CFOs of some major companies, but she suspected Matteo was in a different league entirely.

'Then lead the way,' she said, throwing her arm out in front of her.

Matteo had warned her the path wasn't easy, but that had been an understatement. He was solicitous of her, holding back branches to avoid her being scratched, but the uneven and stony ground, together with the steep incline, was tricky to navigate. She focused her attention on not tripping over.

Although Deepti knew Matteo was adjusting his speed to accommodate her, she still struggled to match his pace with the incline. Suddenly, he turned round and walked back over to her, holding out his hand.

'Here, let me help you—we're coming to the hardest part now. But we should be there soon. I promise you that it will be worth it.'

The smile that he gave her made the difficulty of the path worth it. Without thinking, Deepti put out her hand, instantly feeling secure as it was enveloped by his larger one.

Finally, the path came out at a narrow road with a group of white stone houses in the shadow of fruit trees. The road had a view of the coast, and in the distance she could see *Serendipity* at anchor.

She began to let go of Matteo's hand but had to give it a tug to release it fully. Or had she imagined the resistance? She sneaked a look at Matteo.

He seemed startled. He cleared his throat. 'Right. It's that place over there.'

He strode across to one of the buildings which had some tables outside. The same large crowds that she seen on the street below were not gathered outside the restaurant, and there was no visible menu outside.

As soon as they set foot inside, Matteo was welcomed by an older lady with silver-streaked brown hair. Her greeting was warmer than Deepti would have expected if Matteo had been simply a regular returning customer; it was the kind given to a much-loved family member.

Matteo and the owner conversed in Italian for a few moments before he turned to introduce Deepti.

'Welcome, Deepti,' the lady said, speaking in fluent English. 'Any friend of our Matteo is very welcome here. Are you happy to sit outside?'

Deepti smiled her agreement, recalling the amazing view as they'd come out of the bushes.

As they took their seats, Matteo explained there weren't any menus since the owners decided what to make based on what fresh produce they got in the mornings. 'Let them know if you have any dietary requirements, of course,' he said, 'But usually I trust their recommendations. They haven't let me down yet.'

'Okay.' She looked around at the view. 'It's so peaceful here. But out of the way. How did you find it?' she asked Matteo.

'My family have been coming here for years. The restaurant has been in the same ownership for generations.'

It was interesting how Matteo clearly felt a connection

to this place, where his grandmother had grown up, and yet she got the impression there was something slightly frosty about his relationship with his parents. She wondered if she would ever know what was behind it.

'How lovely to have a genuine family business. You started your company, I understand?'

'That's right. There was no expectation for me to follow in my family's footsteps, but a family business was a goal at one point. I did hope my bro—'

He broke off. 'What about you? Any chefs in your family?'

'No.' She examined her fingers so she wouldn't have to look at him. 'Both my parents are accountants so I guess I did follow—' She clamped her mouth tight before she revealed they all worked in the financial sector. She still didn't want Matteo to know she'd been fired. She'd already been judged by so many people she worked with, it was refreshing to talk to someone who didn't know about that part of her life, so they couldn't judge her on what had happened.

She'd noticed his suspicious look when she'd prevaricated about her job experience before she'd come on the boat. Hopefully, the worst he would think was that she'd got the job through her friendship with Alex and would not delve too deeply into it. It wasn't unusual for junior crew members, particularly assistant chefs, to have limited experience before taking on the role. It wasn't as if she was completely unqualified as a pastry chef.

And he hadn't cared that she was totally unqualified to be a care-giver to Bella. Although his phrasing it as her being Bella's companion meant the only qualification she needed for her role was for Bella to enjoy spending time with her.

He was quite different from the man she'd thought he

was after their first meeting. She'd assumed he was cold and unapproachable, maintaining a clear distinction between himself as the owner of *Serendipity* and the crew. In fact, he was almost the exact opposite. W,henever he kept his distance from the crew she could tell it was because he didn't want to make them uncomfortable.

She'd made assumptions based on her experience of the people she'd met as part of her previous job. But, although Matteo was clearly a successful businessman, he was a good employer who cared for his staff and was kind and generous. It was as if his attitude to Bella, when they'd initially met, was the aberration.

But now he was adapting to Bella, the same way Deepti was, which made Deepti wonder again what the story was behind his attitude to his parents and brother. But she couldn't ask him for more details. And she couldn't expect him to be honest with her when she was being anything but honest with him.

Gradually their conversation turned from work to more personal topics. They talked about books again, which segued into a chat about how they spent their spare time. Deepti loved getting a chance to open up to him and have him reciprocate. But it took an intense effort to concentrate on making coherent responses when all she wanted to do was stare at the male perfection sitting across from her.

Shadows from the afternoon sun delineated the sharp cheekbones of his classically handsome face and drew her eyes to the full temptation of his lips. But it wasn't just his physical attributes. He was intelligent, witty and surprisingly charming. Exactly the kind of person she would want to date in any other circumstances. If they'd met in England, would he have invited her out? Once upon a time, she would have accepted without hesitation.

She immediately discarded that fanciful notion. They would never have met in England. It was only a quirk of fate that they were in each other's company at all. But for the first time in months, or perhaps even longer than that, she felt genuinely happy. She was exactly where she wanted to be.

Finally, they finished their meal. As Matteo paid, he said, 'I don't have any meetings until this evening. Would you like me to show you round this town some more?'

'I would love that!' Deepti replied, excited that she would get to be with Matteo for a little longer. Then it clicked that he probably wasn't suggesting an outing for the two of them alone. 'I'll text Tracey to ask her to meet us somewhere with Bella and Leo. Bella would love to spend time with you during the day.'

Matteo's expression was startled, then he blinked and said, 'Of course. We should head back down the hill, then.'

He put a guiding hand on the small of her back. Something intense flared through her at the simple gesture.

CHAPTER EIGHT

MATTEO STRETCHED AND got up from his seat. It had been non-stop meetings since they'd set sail from Italy four days ago. Having most of his meetings by video conference, and only meeting in person when privacy or networking was the priority, had increased his efficiency tenfold. The decision to incorporate this floating office into his business practices was working out well.

From a work perspective, the whole sailing experience seemed to be working out well too. And his decision to ask Deepti to be Bella's companion was also working better than he'd expected. He'd enjoyed that brief time he'd spent with Deepti in Fiore, and he could see why Bella had formed at attachment to her.

Matteo forced himself to call Jack in so they could talk through the final arrangements for the next day's work. Once that was done, Matteo was effectively finished for the day. In the past he would have ploughed on—there were always more deals he could be working on.

Instead, he went out to his deck, where the dry heat of the Egyptian desert hit him immediately as the yacht began its slow, incredibly slow, passage through the Suez Canal towards Port Said.

He didn't have any in-person meetings scheduled for when they were in Cairo so he had initially planned to stay on *Serendipity* to work. But, with the amount of progress he'd made, he could take a day off to explore the city.

Matteo heard steps behind him. Without turning, he instinctively knew it was Deepti. How was he already so attuned to her?

'Sorry to disturb you,' she said. He stifled the ripple of awareness that went through him at the sound of her soft, low voice. 'Jack said it was okay for me to come through.'

Matteo looked at her and gave a brief nod, then turned back to his view. Deepti came to stand next to him, resting her hands on the rail. She sighed deeply.

'Is something wrong?' he asked.

'No. Not at all,' she replied, shaking her head slowly as she looked towards the banks. 'It's just so still. Not that the journey has been choppy at all, but the complete nothingness around us…' She shrugged. 'Sorry, ignore me. I came to give you an update on Bella, since it's my evening off.'

They'd continued their daily updates whenever he wasn't entertaining guests in the evenings, even though he could see for himself that Bella was enjoying her time with Deepti and was much happier in herself. He found himself looking forward to their catch-ups.

It turned out Deepti was just as much a companion for him as she was for Bella. On future trips on *Serendipity*, he would need to think about bringing someone along for company, although he couldn't imagine not getting bored with them in a way that hadn't happened with Deepti.

'Do you have anything planned for the evening?' he asked when she'd finished her update. He turned round so he could face her and leaned back, resting his elbows on the railing.

'Nothing specific.' She quickly removed her hands from

the rails and straightened but continued to stare straight ahead.

He waited for her to tell him more about her plans and was surprised when she remained silent. It wasn't unusual for them to chat generally after they'd finished talking about Bella. They often shared a bottle of wine as they discussed current events, literature, the arts or sport. Deepti was an interesting and thought-provoking conversationalist.

On a couple of occasions he had found himself wanting to get her opinion on some work ideas he had—and he had never wanted to share that part of his life with people outside the business—but Deepti actively changed the subject when he mentioned business. He didn't expect her to have subject knowledge of the world of finance, he just wanted to get her common-sense thoughts.

Even though they'd barely known each other a week when they'd had lunch together in Fiore, it had felt like a date. He had even been tempted to tell Deepti about his estrangement from his family—to explain, perhaps justify, why he wasn't close to Bella and Leo.

What was it about her that made him feel he could trust her with his story? There was something calming about her; he felt relaxed when they talked—as relaxed as he could be when his body went onto high alert whenever there was any contact between them. And the attraction was growing, perhaps because of the way he felt when they talked.

Being attracted to Deepti, opening up to her, was unexpected...and unwelcome. He didn't want to open himself up to any woman. Not when the evidence of his greatest betrayal was travelling with him to Singapore.

He pressed his lips together. He couldn't really see Bella

that way. She was an innocent child and in no way responsible for the actions of her parents. He almost regretted that he hadn't had a relationship with his niece and nephew before their trip.

When Bella and Leo had joined Deepti and him in Fiore, he hadn't anticipated how bittersweet it would be to show the children some of the places their father had played as a child. Memories had rushed in of the times when the two brothers had been so close; when he'd believed nothing, and no one, could come between them and break their bond. Or perhaps the distance had started before then and he just hadn't noticed. He had been so busy trying to establish his business, he'd been oblivious to many things.

The residual anger he usually experienced when he thought about his ex-fiancée with his brother didn't come this time. Instead, he felt sorrow. He knew now that his ex-fiancée hadn't been the right person for him, but it had taken too long for him to learn that. He'd only known Deepti a week and he felt a stronger connection to her than he'd ever felt to the woman he'd thought he'd marry. But the lasting legacy of his fiancée's betrayal meant he would never be able to trust someone enough to enter into a real, emotional relationship with them.

Deepti pressed her hand on his but didn't try to break the silence that had fallen between them—a small gesture but indicative of how empathetic he'd come to know Deepti to be. The warmth of her hand echoed a similar warmth growing in the region of his chest.

'Anyway, I'll leave you in peace,' she said, about to walk away.

Instinctively, he reached out and grasped her wrist.

'You haven't seen the library yet, have you?' he asked. 'If you don't have any plans now, why don't I show you?'

She opened her mouth then closed it again and simply nodded. He smothered a grin. He could tell she'd been about to tell him she could find the library herself if he gave her directions—it was her default response. He wasn't sure whether it was because she thought he was too busy to spend time with her or whether there was another reason.

He led her out of the lounge, across the foyer. To the left was his bedroom, but he purposefully ignored the temptation to take Deepti in there, and went to the room opposite instead.

'Ta dah!' he said as he walked into the library and swept his arm out. The room was wall-to-wall bookcases extending to the ceiling. There was a rail running across the length of one of the shelves for a ladder to slide across.

'Wow!' Deepti laughed reverentially. 'I feel like I just stepped into a fairy tale.'

'What?'

She was walking next to the shelves, running a hand across the books, occasionally selecting one and pulling it to read the back cover.

'Oh,' she said. 'There was just a scene like this in an animated film I watched with Bella, appropriately.'

He blinked, giving her a blank look.

'The character had a similar name,' she explained.

'I see,' he said, not sure he really did.

Deepti giggled. 'We really have to diversify your taste in movies. I feel like you're missing out a lot.'

He quirked an eyebrow. 'Really?'

'Trust me,' she replied with a cheeky grin.

His smile fell. It was such an innocuous phrase—'trust me'—but something he found hard to do, particularly when it came to attractive women. How was he supposed to trust anyone when the woman he'd been supposed to marry had betrayed his trust so indelibly?

Since that time, he had never let any woman get close to him. In a matter of weeks, Deepti had slipped past his first line of defence. Perhaps it was because there weren't many people on board he could, or wanted to, spend his free time with. He needed to restrict how often he was alone with her.

He'd been about to ask Deepti to join him for a drink once they'd finished in the library but he changed his mind.

'I'll leave you to enjoy the library,' he said, deliberately ignoring the disappointment on her face.

He couldn't allow Deepti to get closer to him. She wasn't a colleague and, even though he wasn't technically her direct employer in her new role, while she was on the yacht, she was under his overall charge, like all staff and crew. In other circumstances, she could have been a friend but, whatever she was, she was totally out of bounds.

Two days later, Deepti was sitting out on the main deck reading while *Serendipity* was moored in Port Said. The majority of the crew, including Deepti, were being given time off while they were in Egypt. The previous day, she'd gone with Alex, his girlfriend and the replacement assistant chef for a quick trip around the port.

That morning, since Tracey was still working, Deepti had offered to help her out. Although they'd only been on the boat for a couple of weeks, Bella had already warmed to Tracey. But she'd still been surprised when Tracey had turned her down, explaining that she was worried that Matteo's parents would think she was incompetent if she couldn't look after the two children on her own.

Watching Bella happily leave the yacht without her that morning, Deepti reflected that, at this rate, she was the one who probably wouldn't be needed soon.

When she found out Matteo had arranged to meet Bella and Leo to be their guide around Cairo, she was relieved Tracey had refused her offer. Part of Deepti desperately wanted to explore with them but, even though Tracey urged her to join them at the time, she came up with an excuse. It didn't seem wise to join them when she was thinking about Matteo so much.

She hadn't seen Matteo since the night he'd showed her the library—not to speak to, anyway. For the last couple of days, she'd taken an early-morning swim in the outside pool. She was convinced Matteo had been exercising in the gym below. She didn't know for sure that it was him, but her instinct had said it was, and it gave her a sense of connection that the two of them were alone, together, out there.

And that feeling was alarming.

She missed him and it had barely been forty-eight hours. She had to be sensible. He was spending time with Bella and Leo, not with her. And their evening catch-ups were about the children. Although lately they'd spent most of their time together discussing anything and everything else.

Maybe she was enjoying adult conversation rather than Matteo himself. She discarded that reason immediately. She got plenty of adult conversation with Tracey, Alex and the other crew members.

There was no explanation for why she liked being with Matteo—apart from his amazing looks. Perhaps she really was just that shallow. Deepti laughed to herself. She'd taken loads of pictures of Matteo and the children and might have sneaked a surreptitious photo of Matteo on his own. If his looks were all she cared about, she could stare at a photo.

She wasn't the only person on the yacht who appreciated Matteo's face and physique. He was a regular topic of conversation in the crew mess. If only Deepti could take a leaf out of Tracey's book. Tracey was completely unaffected by Matteo.

What was wrong with her? Less than two months ago, she'd been in a relationship with someone else. Granted, her feelings for her ex had been lukewarm at best, but she had trusted him.

How naive she'd been. Not only had his attachment been a pretence, but he'd obviously done something to get the deal she was after which had led to the client being lost. She wasn't a believer in coincidences. If she could be with someone for almost a year and not really know them, how could she trust her judgement about anything, or anyone, else?

'Why do I suspect your thoughts are worth more than a penny?' Matteo's deep voice caused Deepti to jump, making her book fall off her lap.

Matteo walked forward, picked it up then he glanced at the cover and frowned.

She grabbed the book out of his hands. It wasn't one of her usual reads, being a non-fiction book about finance which she'd seen in the library. Luckily, it would be difficult for Matteo to comment on her choice without coming across as judgemental, but she wanted to avoid any risk he would talk about it.

'I didn't realise you were back,' Deepti said.

'It was getting too hot for the children.'

She wanted to snatch off the linen bucket-hat he was wearing, to release his wavy hair, but it suited him so ridiculously well. Her eyes raked over the rest of him, down his navy-blue T-shirt stretched tightly against his broad chest to his strong, tanned arms and lower... Her mouth went dry—Matteo in cargo shorts which stopped just below his knees was a sight to behold. She had never thought of muscular calves as particularly sexy before but her body's reaction, every nerve-ending taut and on edge, told her differently. She needed to get away.

'Okay. I'll go to Bella now,' she said.

'No need,' he replied. 'Tracey's trying to get both of them down for a nap. And it's your day off.'

'But I have nothing planned, so I don't mind.'

Matteo frowned. 'I thought you had something on.'

She had initially intended to spend her time exploring Cairo, but having an empty boat had also been a good opportunity to catch up on emails and start thinking about her work situation—there were only a few weeks left before she would be heading back to England—but it had been too disheartening and she'd chosen to read instead.

'I decided I was too lazy to go ashore,' she replied.

The look he gave her was sceptical. She didn't blame him. Who would be too lazy to explore Cairo? 'I've been to Egypt before.'

'You didn't mention you've been to Cairo before,' he said, furrowing his brow.

'Giza. But it's all the same, isn't it?' Deepti closed her eyes tight with mortification as he looked taken aback. She really was bad at prevaricating. 'Anyway, I think I'll go and wash the heat off me.'

She went back to her room and sat on the bed. She had to get her body under control. Her intense attraction to Matteo was inappropriate. What she felt wasn't real. She could trust her emotions.

CHAPTER NINE

THERE WAS NO one around in the children's play areas or bedrooms when Matteo was finally free to visit. He'd had business guests for the last week, which meant he hadn't been able to spend time with Bella.

He was surprised by the fact he'd missed her. The little five-year-old girl was worming her way into his heart. And her brother was exceptionally cute too.

And it had been too long since he'd chatted with Deepti. He should have suggested continuing their catch-ups even when he had guests on board. He missed their chats.

He wondered whether it was solely due to enjoying the company of a beautiful woman. She wasn't like the women he typically dated. Even so, if they'd met under different circumstances, he would have asked her out. But that would have been a bad idea, because he rarely dated the same woman for more than a few weeks—he would have missed out on getting to know Deepti better if he had opted for a couple of nights in her bed.

Concerned at the direction of his thoughts, he left the children's living room and crossed the lobby to the port-side state rooms. He tried calling Deepti's and Tracey's phones but his calls went to voicemail.

He went down to the lower deck in case they were in

the beach club. As he was walking past the gym, the door to the cinema room opened and Deepti walked out.

'Oh, hello,' she said. His face brightened at the sight of her smile. 'I saw you'd rung, so came out to see what you wanted.'

'I was looking for Bella. She's not in her room.'

'Oh, no, we're in here. We've watched a few episodes of *Pets in Petland* and were about to start a film. But I can bring her out.'

'No, that's fine, I can join you.'

They walked into the cinema room. The seating was arranged on three levels with two large body-length sofas on each level. Each sofa arm had a cup-holder and tray for a snack. Bella was curled up on a sofa at the back. A carelessly folded throw next to her indicated Deepti had been sitting next to her.

'Deepti,' Tracey said, while she lifted a sleepy Leo in her arms. 'I'm going to put this little one down for the night. I'll come back in an hour for Bella.'

'Oh, I can take her back.'

Tracey cast Matteo a look. 'No, that's fine. I'll see you in a bit.'

'Uncle Mayo. Come sit here!' Bella called enthusiastically, patting the sofa next to her.

'Okay, princess,' he said. He sat down, then took his shoes off so he could stretch out his legs. 'What are we going to watch?'

'We have the cartoons you downloaded for her the last time we docked,' Deepti said. 'Or there's a film with talking animals, or one with talking tools, or one with talking cars.' Deepti bit her lip as she tried not to smile. Her expression told him that she wasn't particularly looking forward to the films.

'Animals,' Bella said.

As Deepti loaded the film, she looked over Bella's head at Matteo and whispered, 'Escape now. You really don't have to put yourself through this.'

Matteo grinned. He shook his head and settled back on the sofa. Bella nestled closer to him. He put his arm around her, bringing her in for a cuddle, and pressed a soft kiss against the top of her head. If someone had told him, even two months ago, that he would choose to watch a children's movie instead of working, he would have laughed at them. But now he wanted to spend more time with this sweet child and her brother before they had to part in Singapore. He hugged Bella again at the unexpected twinge of sadness that he wouldn't see her as much in the future.

He was sure his parents would be wonderful guardians for Bella and Leo, and it was in the children's best interests to stay with them. His parents might not have supported him over his brother, they might have disappointed him and they might not have been there for him, but he knew they loved their grandchildren. He knew they had visited Bella and Leo in England every few months, and his mother had stayed with them for over a month to help out when Leo had been born. He knew because his parents had sent him a message each time they were in England, wanting him to meet up with them—messages he always ignored.

'Uncle Mayo, look there,' Bella said, bouncing up and down while pointing to the screen. He turned his attention back to the film.

Bella made it through almost fifty minutes before falling asleep. Deepti paused the film and stood up.

'I'll take her to her room.'

'I can do that,' Matteo replied, whispering back.

Deepti opened her mouth, no doubt to argue with him, but they were interrupted by Tracey, who'd returned to collect Bella, as she'd told them she would.

Once they were alone, Deepti seemed nervous.

'I'll clear all this away,' she said, pointing to the snacks and blankets.

He caught her look over at the screen where they'd paused the film.

He narrowed his eyes. 'You're going to finish watching it, aren't you?' he asked, his lips quirking.

Deepti giggled. 'I'm quite invested in it now. I'm not sure I can wait until Bella's ready to watch it again.' She gave him an embarrassed shrug.

Without replying, he sat back on the sofa and indicated she should press play.

'Really, you're going to watch it too?' Her look was sceptical.

'What can I say? I want to find out how it ends. And I may not be there when Bella finishes it.'

'I guess, if you don't have anything better to do.'

Matteo looked at Deepti intently, not sure why he didn't leave. He had a thousand things he could be doing in-stead—there was always work to do—or he could watch a film suitable for adults, or he could read. But, at that moment in time, none of the options sounded *better* than spending his evening next to Deepti, even when they were watching a kids' programme.

He turned to the screen and said slightly curtly, 'Let's start.'

Slowly, and without being consciously aware, as they watched he moved closer to Deepti on the couch. Or had she moved too? He was resting his arm along the back of the couch and Deepti was leaning back, almost touching him. The temptation to move his arm slightly so it dropped across Deepti's shoulders was powerful.

He didn't know if the gesture would be welcome. He wasn't sure whether it was appropriate, even though he wasn't technically her employer. That thought was enough for him to abruptly move his arm off the back of the sofa.

As far as he could recall, Deepti had initially only signed up to crew until they reached Singapore, which had worked perfectly with the change of her role to that of Bella's companion. He had no idea what her plans were after they reached their destination.

Deepti sighed, bringing his attention back to his surroundings. The film had ended.

'What are you doing after we get to Singapore? he asked.

Deepti looked at him in surprise. He supposed the question had come out of nowhere.

'I'll probably fly back to England.'

'You're not staying to crew on the yacht?' That was good news.

'No. This was only temporary.'

'What will you do back in England?'

'Look for another job.' She smiled but she didn't hold his gaze. Again, it was quite clear that she was withholding something from him. Rather than pursue that line of questioning, he asked her about her plans for the next few days instead—so he knew when he could spend time with Bella.

Although it had started as a condition to get Deepti to take on the role of companion, the time he spent with them was one of the highlights of his day. He would miss them once they got to Singapore.

Deepti looked as though she was getting ready to leave.

'It's still early. Why don't we watch another movie?' he

suggested. 'We could even look for something that doesn't feature talking inanimate objects or animals.'

Deepti hesitated for a moment. Then, taking a noticeable breath, she said. 'Sure. Why don't you choose? Anything but horror.'

That was a shame. Horrors were the perfect films to use to get up close to someone. He scanned through the available options.

'How about a thriller, then?' he suggested. 'You love reading them. Do you like watching them too?'

'I do,' she said, with a slightly surprised but happy expression.

Why did she seem pleased he'd remembered what genre she enjoyed? He would have remembered that about anyone. His eyes widened at the realisation that that wasn't true. It was the kind of detail he didn't bother noting most of the time, let alone recalling. So why did he know so much about Deepti?

'Matteo...' Deepti's voice broke into his thoughts.

'Hmm?'

'I said the film's ready.' She tilted her head. 'Is everything okay?'

No, everything wasn't okay. He was unsure of himself, which made him uncomfortable. There had to be a simple explanation for his growing interest in Deepti but, until he worked out what it was, the best thing for him to do would be to find an excuse to leave.

She was still watching him intently, a curious half-smile playing on her lips. He sighed deeply—she was so beautiful. He was only watching a film with her, after all. There was nothing to worry about with that activity. They could maintain their distance even if they shared the couch.

'Ready when you are,' he said.

They both leant back on the sofa. Within minutes, instead of keeping his distance, Matteo spread a throw over both of them.

It took a Herculean effort to resist holding Deepti, particularly when he heard her gasps and quickening breath when something unexpected happened on screen.

When the film finished, Deepti lifted her face to look at him.

'That was so good!' she exclaimed. 'I never expected that. Did you?'

Matteo shook his head. If he'd been paying full attention to the film, he probably would have seen the signs, but he'd spent as much time watching the varied expressions cross Deepti's face as he had watching the film itself. He felt he knew exactly what had happened based on her expression.

She was still looking up at him, the light from the screen playing across her delicate facial bones. He slowly started to bend his head.

A noise from the door snagged his attention.

'Oh, sorry, Mr Di Corrado, I didn't realise you were still in here,' a crew member said. 'I was just doing my rounds to check everything is in order.'

'Everything's fine,' Matteo replied, watching Deepti hastily pick up her stuff and leave the room.

He grimaced. Could she tell he'd been about to kiss her? And was she as disappointed by the interruption as he was?

CHAPTER TEN

THE NEXT DAY, Deepti had the afternoon off to explore Abu Dhabi. She, Matteo, Tracey and the children had disembarked from *Serendipity* when it had docked that morning and gone straight to the hotel they were staying at instead of sleeping on the yacht. After accompanying them to their suite, Matteo had gone to his first business meeting.

Once they'd freshened up in the hotel, Tracey asked Deepti to leave her alone with the children, and they would all meet up again for lunch.

Deepti decided to visit Capital Gate. Although she tried to absorb the skyscraper's unique leaning design and intricate diagrid architecture, it was difficult when she was alone with her thoughts. And she couldn't help replaying what had happened in the cinema room the previous evening.

Had he really been about to kiss her? He'd been staring at her intently. But perhaps she'd had popcorn on her face, or her eyeliner had smudged, or he was going to remove an eyelash. There were hundreds of reasons he could have been looking at her. And perhaps he'd been moving his head to get a better look.

Thank goodness she hadn't given in to her urge to stand on tiptoes to bring his head even closer. She would never know what would have happened if they hadn't been interrupted. But she should be grateful they had been. Her life was already too complicated.

When she finally arrived at the restaurant for lunch, she was surprised to see that Matteo had joined them. As they ate, Bella told them about her morning. Occasionally Deepti would meet Matteo's gaze and smile, affectionate, contented smiles because of Bella. Who would have thought that this little chatterbox at the table had barely spoken to anyone when their journey had started?

Once they had finished eating, Tracey had told them she was taking the children back to the hotel.

'Mr Di Corrado, since you said you don't have any afternoon meetings, why don't you show Deepti around? She hasn't been here before.'

'Oh, that's not necessary,' Deepti replied hurriedly.

'Happy to,' Matteo said at the same time.

'Okay, I guess,' Deepti said, giving Tracey an assessing look. Tracey couldn't possibly be matchmaking, could she?

'I have to make a quick call,' Matteo said. 'But we can go after that.'

'Tracey, what are you up to?' Deepti asked when Matteo had moved away to make his call.

'I don't know what you mean,' Tracey replied with an innocent expression. But she couldn't help a mischievous smile.

'Why are you trying to make Matteo spend time with me?'

'Am I?' Tracey's high-pitched voice betrayed her.

'Tracey, you can't possibly think something's going to happen between me and Matteo?'

Tracey shrugged. 'I think Mr Di Corrado could do with relaxing more. He enjoys spending time with you. You can help him relax.'

Deepti narrowed her eyes. 'I didn't realise you know Matteo so well.'

'I don't. Not as well as you. But then, he's never asked me to call him Matteo.' Tracey raised her eyebrows as if she was making a meaningful point. Deepti sighed. Why did people keep bringing up the name thing?

'Anyway,' Tracey continued, 'It's all sorted now. I'll see you back at the hotel.'

'If—'

'Don't worry—I will call if there are any problems. Enjoy yourself.' She waggled her fingers then she helped Bella onto the buggy board behind the pram and walked off.

Deepti stared after her, shaking her head. The last thing she needed was a matchmaker. Perhaps she should make it clear to Tracey she wasn't interested in any kind of romantic entanglement—not even with someone as gorgeous as Matteo.

'Have the others left?' Matteo asked when he came back to their table.

'Yes, just a few minutes ago. Shall we go?' she asked, heading towards the exit.

'Is there anywhere particular you want to go first?' he asked when they were standing outside the restaurant.

Deepti shook her head. She could sense Matteo looking at her but she didn't turn her head. She was stiff and awkward, trying not to think about the previous night or what Tracey had said. And standing so close to him wasn't helping the whirl of confusion in her head.

'Would you like to go shopping or to a museum?'

'Actually, I think I might join some of the crew for a few hours.'

'Sure—where are you meeting them? I'll walk you there.'

Of course, since Deepti had only just come up with that idea, she had nowhere to suggest.

'I'm still waiting for Alex to text me the details.' She glanced at him briefly, catching his puzzled expression. As a naturally honest person, it wasn't surprising she was so bad at lying but now, instead of trying to deflect attention from herself, she'd probably increased it.

'I see. I'll walk with you until you hear back from him. The Heritage Village is very close to here, or there's a mall too. Why don't we head in that direction until you hear from Alex?'

They walked in silence for a while. For the first time since she'd taken on the role of Bella's companion, she felt uncomfortable.

She wasn't a fool. She knew she and Matteo had been getting closer; it was probably inevitable with the amount of time they'd spent together. And she had obviously always known he was an attractive man. That was simply an objective fact. But she hadn't really believed that he was attracted to her too. And a one-sided attraction was relatively safe because it wouldn't go anywhere.

Rationally, if he had tried to kiss her in the cinema room, he would have addressed it in some way, wouldn't he? It must have been her imagination, or at most wishful thinking.

'What's wishful thinking?' Matteo asked.

Deepti closed her eyes, cringing at the realisation she'd spoken out loud. Hopefully, it was only the last part he'd heard. She quickly cast around in her mind for a credible response. 'Oh, living somewhere like this permanently.'

'Of all the places you've visited, you want to live in Abu Dhabi?' He raised an eyebrow.

'Maybe not here specifically, but somewhere with warm weather.' She mentally rolled her eyes as she came up with that excuse. 'What about you?' she asked, trying to deflect the attention from herself. 'You can live anywhere. Why do you have your main base in London and not Singapore, since you have family there? Or you could have chosen Tokyo or even New York, Paris or Frankfurt. I would love to live in any one of those cities if I had the choice.'

'I have ties in London.' He shrugged. They walked together in silence for a few minutes until he stopped and turned to her, asking, 'Do you know much about finance?'

'Why do you ask that?' She avoided his gaze, feigning an interest in one of the buildings they were passing.

'You were reading a book on it the other day and you just named the main financial cities. Not many people outside finance would know them.'

'Oh, I'm excellent at general knowledge quizzes,' she replied with absolute truth.

'Really? Me too. There are some great places for pub-type quizzes here. Perhaps we should go tonight.' Her heart flipped as his excited grin made the corners of his eyes crinkle.

'That would be fantastic! I bet some of the crew would love to go to.'

Matteo's smile fell but he hurriedly said, 'Of course. If Tracey wants to go, I can also organise a babysitter in the hotel. Let me make a couple of calls.'

Deepti walked away from him to gather her thoughts. Matteo was a gorgeous man, and not just in terms of his looks. It was only natural that she would be attracted to him. It made perfect sense that she was falling for him.

But he was out of her league, not that she was looking for a relationship. After what had happened with her ex, she doubted she would ever trust her own judgement about men.

What did she really know about Matteo? He was kind, he was caring, he was attentive, he was passionate—she knew that much. Or maybe she was wrong about that. Although she didn't think she was. But it didn't matter. A relationship with Matteo wasn't possible. Which was fine, because she didn't want one.

She groaned inwardly, trying to control her overactive brain from obsessing over something that was never going to happen.

When she'd stayed on board *Serendipity* while the others had toured Cairo, she'd given into her curiosity and done an Internet search on Matteo. And some of the sites she'd found—particularly those which loved to dish the dirt on the love lives of the rich and famous—suggested he didn't have long-term relationships. He was often referred to as a commitment-phobe.

Having a relationship with Matteo would be a fantasy on so many levels. She wasn't free to indulge in a romance—not when her life was so complicated. She needed to sort herself out before she could move forward.

No matter how far away her troubles seemed when she was walking along the beach in Abu Dhabi, they would still be there waiting for her when she got back to England. Tempting as it was to draw a line behind her and look for work in a different field, she couldn't let her name and the reputation she'd built up just disappear.

She jumped when a hand touched her shoulder.

'I'm sorry,' Matteo said. 'I didn't mean to startle you. You were miles away. You didn't answer when I called your name.' He turned her to face him and put both hands on her shoulder, staring at her intently. 'Are you sure everything's okay? You seem to have a lot on your mind.'

'I guess I do.'

'Anything I can help you with?'

Ironically, if she could have told Matteo the truth, he probably would have been able to help her with his expertise. But she still couldn't bring herself to admit her past failure. And what if he didn't believe that she had acted innocently, but thought that she was actually guilty of what she'd been fired for? She didn't know how she would feel if he wasn't on her side and, despite only knowing him for a short time, she valued getting to know him and wanted him to have a good opinion of her.

There were only a few weeks now until they reached Singapore. She would cherish the time she got to spend with him and protect her heart.

'It's nothing important. I'm realising how close we are to Singapore. Getting to crew on this yacht is a once-in-a-lifetime opportunity. I can't believe it will end soon. But I'm going to soak up every second until then.'

She lifted her face to the sun and closed her eyes. After a couple of seconds, she realised how ridiculous she must look and hurriedly dropped her head and opened her eyes.

Matteo was standing next to her, his head facing up to the sun with his eyes closed, a small smile playing on his lips.

Deepti sighed deeply. Her heart was already in so much trouble.

Later that evening, Matteo and Deepti were in a sports pub listening intently to the questions, as the quiz was getting to a crucial stage. The competition was really between two teams, one of which was his. Although Alex, the head steward and two other crew members had joined them at the pub to form a team, it had really been a two-person show with Deepti and him.

Thank goodness he'd agreed to be on her team. Initially,

he'd suggested that they should be on separate teams, to challenge her boastful comment about being excellent at quizzes. She'd pouted and he'd caved, which was a good thing, because he probably would have been losing otherwise. But he didn't usually give in to people's small manipulations that way.

As well as vast general knowledge, Deepti could discern patterns and make connections faster than even he could. He was fascinated by the way her mind worked.

Although, truth be told, he was finding himself fascinated by everything about her. She was so different from the women he usually dated. She fell firmly into the danger zone of women who wanted, or needed, to be in relationships. And he was definitely not that kind of man.

It was lucky they'd been interrupted in the cinema room before he had managed to kiss her. That would have been a big mistake.

Had she even realised that had been his intention? She hadn't said anything about it on their walk that afternoon, and he had no plans to bring it up. But then, she'd been unusually quiet and a little reflective. There had been something on her mind.

He silently observed her as she laughed and joked with the crew members who'd joined them. With Chef, she was completely at ease. But that made sense; they were long-standing friends and she openly admitted he was the reason she'd got the job as assistant chef.

Whatever had been on her mind earlier that day seemed to have been put behind her now. He wished she had opened up to him about it. She wasn't being completely open with him and, although she was entitled to keep things private, he couldn't help suspect there was something behind her evasiveness.

He tutted his frustration. He was spending too much time thinking about Deepti. He shouldn't be this interested in her. She would be gone from his life soon. The hollowness in his chest showed it would be a good idea to limit their interactions going forward to when Bella was around.

When the pub quiz host announced that their team had won, Deepti stood up and cheered and then threw her arms around him. He stood frozen by the unexpected gesture, causing Deepti to stiffen and draw back quickly. He was about to draw her back to him when Alex came over to hug her. Matteo frowned. He knew they were close but was there something more between them? Not that it was any of his business if there was, but before that evening the only interaction he'd seen between them was as friends, so he had assumed that was all they were.

A bottle of champagne and a gift certificate was brought over to their table. They decided to finish the champagne there rather than take it back to the hotel. At least the other team members agreed with him that Deepti deserved the gift certificate since she'd been the obvious MVP.

'We're going to join the others clubbing. Why don't you come with us?' one of the crew said as she finished her drink.

'Oh, not for me. I'm not a big dancer,' Deepti replied. 'I think I'll head back to the hotel.'

'What about you, Mr Di Corrado?'

'I'll go back to the hotel with Deepti. Thank you all for inviting me,' he said to the crew. It had been years since he'd been clubbing and, though he enjoyed dancing, he didn't imagine it would be fun without Deepti.

He went outside with some of the others who wanted to find a taxi to the club. Deepti had gone to the bathroom, so Matteo kept an eye on the door. She came through the door with Alex, who had one arm around Deepti and the other around the head steward. When Alex leaned over to kiss the steward, Deepti moved out from under his arm, giving the two of them space.

Matteo couldn't explain why he felt such relief at the unspoken clarification that Deepti and Chef weren't a couple.

This was getting ridiculous. Deepti was an attractive woman, nothing more. There was nothing special about her. Perhaps after they returned to their hotel suite he would go to one of the bars to see whether he could find alternative company.

He dismissed that thought almost as quickly as it had arisen. He wasn't after female company generally—that and Deepti weren't interchangeable. He wasn't interested in spending time with anyone else.

'Are you ready to head back now?' Matteo asked Deepti. 'I can call for a car.'

Deepti gave him a sweet, almost sad smile. 'I was thinking I may take a walk along the beachfront. It's well-lit and the hotel's only a thirty-minute walk.' She turned to Alex. Matteo was sure she was about to ask him to accompany her.

'That's fine. I'll walk with you.' As Deepti opened her mouth, he held up his hand. 'I could do with some fresh air too.'

She gave him a brief nod, then turned to say her good-byes to the rest of the crew. Alex whispered something in her ear, which made her give a shocked laugh and playfully push on his arm.

They walked along the beach road in companionable silence for a few minutes until Deepti said, 'You're quite the quiz maestro. I have to admit, I was surprised.'

'Surprised? Why?'

'I don't know. I never thought it would be your kind

of activity. But you've constantly challenged my preconceptions.'

Matteo stood still. 'What preconceptions did you have?'
he asked, intrigued.

Deepti came to a halt too, then turned to look up at him.
'I don't know. Taking part in a pub quiz just isn't something I imagined you would spend your free time doing.'

'It has been a while since I've taken part in a pub quiz,
but I often enter charity quizzes.' He smiled. 'Growing up,
Luca and I were quite the team. We had complementary
interests and skills, which helped.'

'Do you always win?' she asked.

'Generally.'

She beamed at him. 'Of course you always win. I don't
know why I asked. Are you both quite competitive, then?'
She must have realised she'd referred to his brother in the
present tense because her smile faltered and she bit her lip.

'Yes, we both liked to win. But we weren't usually in
competition with each other.'

Apart from over women, apparently. Matteo paused.
Before that caustic thought had crossed his mind, it had
been the first time he'd spoken and reminisced about Luca
without the sting of betrayal and anger. He swallowed. It
had also been a long time since he'd used his brother's
name—referring to him as 'my brother' made it easier to
maintain the distance in his thoughts too. But Luca's name
had slipped out so easily while he'd been talking to Deepti.

For the first time since Luca had passed away, all he
felt was an overwhelming sense of loss.

She crooked her head, waiting for him to speak. When
he didn't, she gave him a small, shy smile before leaving
the path and walking on to the sand, towards the water.
She stood peacefully, looking out at the darkness.

He studied Deepti's profile in the moonlight. What was it about her that put him at ease? She was so breathtakingly beautiful. Not supermodel, magazine-cover beautiful but, in his opinion, every single facial feature was perfect.

His eyes rested on the contours of her full lips. What would she do if he cupped her chin to turn her mouth up to his? Would she move away or would she rise to meet his lips?

He swallowed and moved his gaze towards the road, watching the lights of the cars pass.

'Matteo, is everything all right?' Deepti put her hand on his arm.

'It's fine. We should go.'

He shook off her hand and hurried forward. In his haste as he moved away, he tripped over his feet. He could have stopped himself from falling if he hadn't sensed Deepti's hands reach out to grab him. Trying to avoid her touch, he continued to fall. His weight and momentum were too strong for her restraining efforts and she toppled over with him.

He managed to land on his back, so she fell directly on top of him rather than onto the ground. His heart was racing. He groaned as his body reacted immediately to her movements when she continued to wriggle against him in an effort to get up.

'Could you stop that please?' he said stiffly.

She stilled immediately. 'Sorry.'

'It's okay.' He desperately wanted to put his arms round her and gather her even closer to his chest. He wanted to turn her onto her back and kiss her until she moaned for him.

Instead, he closed his eyes to gather his peace. Then he helped Deepti sit up, the new position doing nothing to help his equilibrium, but, once upright, Deepti was able to climb off him.

She held out a hand to help pull him up.

'Probably not a good idea,' he said, refusing her offer. 'I'll only make you fall over again.'

Deepti cleared her throat and walked a few steps away.

Matteo stood up and brushed the sand off his clothes. He couldn't believe he'd tripped. He had a great sense of balance. It was because of Deepti. She constantly had him off-kilter and confused.

He wanted her. He wanted to sleep with her. That was out of the question while she was Bella's companion. Even their almost-kiss in the cinema room had been wrong.

But when they arrived in Singapore she wouldn't be under his charge any more. He could ask her whether she wanted to get together with him before she left for England.

But he had to be clear exactly what he was offering her. He would love to spend more time with her, and he very much wanted to make love to her. But there would be no question of a relationship. It would be a brief affair, a fling at most. She'd already told him she was planning to return to England soon after they got to Singapore. He couldn't see a reason to ask her to change her plans.

As long as she knew he would never have romantic feelings for her, for anyone ever again, then they could have a few days of string-free fun together.

As he watched her walk ahead and away from him in the moonlight, an unexpected heaviness filled his chest and he couldn't help feeling it was the prospect of saying goodbye.

CHAPTER ELEVEN

IT WAS HARD to believe they'd already been at sea for over a month and there were now only a few days left until they reached Singapore. Life on a luxurious super-yacht was the definition of smooth sailing.

As Deepti was heading to Matteo's lounge to give him an update on Bella, Jack met her in the foyer to let her know Matteo was waiting out on his deck.

While they'd been at sea over the past week, Matteo had been busy with business meetings, and had had guests on board, so it would be the first time she'd seen him since they'd left Abu Dhabi. Although, Matteo had been a prominent feature in Deepti's dreams since that day.

She kept replaying the fall on the beach. If it had happened like in one of her beloved Asian dramas, when Matteo had fallen, taking her with him, she would have accidentally landed with her mouth on his. She laughed at the image—if only reality could be as simple as that.

He wasn't smiling when she walked out onto the deck. Deepti looked down, unable to meet his gaze, wondering if he ever thought about that night.

'Is this a good time?' she asked, for something to break the silence.

He nodded, still unsmiling. 'Tomorrow we're going to reach Malaysia. The *Serendipity* is going to anchor off a private island owned by my friend. This will be our last catch-up of the trip.'

She frowned. The catch-ups hadn't been necessary for a while. Why had he chosen that day to stop them?

'I asked Chef to send up some food,' he said, gesturing towards a table which had a charcuterie board, platters of fruit and cheese and a tiered stand with macaroons and *petits fours*. 'I hope it's okay to offer the desserts you made.' His smile brightened his face and lightened the atmosphere. 'Take a seat while I pour the drinks.'

She quickly gave Matteo a rundown of what she and Bella had been doing for the past week.

'She seems to have coped well with the sailing, but I think she's ready to be on land now,' Deepti said to end her update.

'And what about you? How did you cope with sailing?'

'It's been fine. I mean, this yacht moves so smoothly, it's hard to believe we're on water, even when it's at anchor. Has it been a successful trip for you?'

Either he hadn't heard her question or he ignored it.

'This was your first sail, wasn't it?' he asked.

'It was.'

'Did you enjoy it? Do you think you'd sign on to crew again?'

Deepti didn't know how to answer. She loved sailing but she'd joined the crew to escape from the past for a few weeks, not to make it a career path. 'Never say never.'

'So what is your plan when you return to London? You said you wanted to find a new job, but you didn't say what. I assumed you would work as a pastry chef, but is that the case?'

Deepti shrugged. She didn't want to lie to Matteo but she didn't want to spoil her last few days by bringing up the past. How could she trust that Matteo wouldn't judge her the way her colleagues had—people who had known her for years—when she had only known him a few weeks?

And it would be difficult to explain the situation without bringing up her ex-boyfriend. Even if, by a slim chance, Matteo believed she hadn't been at fault for losing the client and deal, he might still judge her as having been unwise to trust her ex-boyfriend. The past few weeks—getting to spend time with someone who had no knowledge of her previous career, her ex-boyfriend or the troubles he'd brought on her—had been a joy. What benefit would there be in telling the truth now?

'How long are you planning to stay in Singapore?' he asked.

Deepti tilted her head. Something was going on with Matteo—there was an intensity and a quiet pent-up emotion. She didn't know what could be causing it. And she didn't know whether it was her place to ask. It was a strange position to be in—not exactly his employee or colleague but also not quite a friend, and definitely not a lover.

She decided to take his question at face value. 'I haven't booked my return ticket yet. Alex suggested I wait in case there were any delays along the voyage. But I have a long list of places I want to visit, so I'll probably stay a few days. How about you? Are you working while you're there or will you spend time with your parents?'

'Working. My parents and I... We're not close.' His whole body had become rigid and his shoulders were tight.

'You seem tense,' Deepti said. 'Has it been a while since you've seen your parents?'

Matteo pressed his lips together and the muscle in his

jaw tightened. Deepti cursed inwardly that she'd ruined the mood by asking the question directly.

'Six years,' he replied curtly.

'Oh, that's how long you said it had been since you saw your brother,' she said, then froze. There had clearly been an issue between Matteo and his brother, and now it sounded as if it had repercussions for his parents as well.

Matteo inhaled sharply. 'Yes, we stopped talking at the same time. They took my brother's side.'

'I see. That must have hurt.' She stared at him without blinking. If he didn't want to say anything else, if he didn't want to give any explanations, that would be fine. She wasn't going to pry or ask any questions.

'It did,' he said. 'This wasn't a situation with ambiguity. My brother had an affair with my fiancée. I found out when they told me she was pregnant. My parents agreed what they did was wrong, but they refused to break off contact with them, even though the alternative was to lose me.' He clamped his lips together and looked away from her.

Deepti blinked. She shook her head then blinked again. Had she heard him correctly—Matteo's fiancée had cheated on him with his brother? And his parents had sided with his brother. She didn't understand how they could do that.

She wanted to wrap him in her arms and protect him from the world and anybody who'd ever hurt him. Instead, she reached for his hand and held it between her own. 'I am so sorry that happened to you.'

'It was a long time ago.' He sounded as if he was brushing off her concern but he put his free hand over their clasped ones.

'I don't think there's a time limit on how much that must have hurt you.'

'With hindsight, I know Lauren—my ex-fiancée—wasn't the right person for me. I should have realised I'm not the marrying kind. Work will always be my priority. And, before you ask, there was no need for a paternity test; there's no chance Bella's mine.'

The thought hadn't crossed her mind. But now she was curious.

As if to answer her unspoken question, Matteo said, 'I was so busy building up the business, I barely had any time to spend with Lauren. There was no way I could have got her pregnant. That should have been a sign that everything wasn't right but I ignored it.

'She was exactly the kind of woman I thought would make the perfect CEO's wife. We'd been together for a couple of years and asking her to marry me seemed like the next logical step. At that young age, I thought marriage and children were the boxes I needed to tick to be successful in life.' He gave a bitter laugh. 'I know better now. I'm never going down that road again.'

When Matteo mentioned not being the marrying kind, it caused an ache in Deepti's chest. She could understand the betrayal could make him wary. What her ex had done had made her feel as if she couldn't trust anyone again and it was nothing compared to what Matteo had experienced. But Matteo deserved to be loved and to find someone who loved him deeply in return.

She shook her head. This wasn't about Matteo's future relationships and what she wanted for him. It was about his past.

'You were very close as brothers before, weren't you?' she said. 'I can't imagine what that was like for you, to find out.' And for him to treat Bella as an innocent child, and not the living reminder of having been cheated on, made her admire him even more.

'I was close to Luca. He was my best friend as well as family. We did nearly everything together. I wanted him to join my business and work with me to get it off the ground. Instead, he went after my fiancée. It was a huge betrayal. And I ignored all their attempts at justifying what they did. The sad thing is, I always thought one day we'd reconcile. That our brotherly bond would be stronger than what happened and all it would take was a bit of distance, particularly when I realised Lauren wasn't right for me. But I left it too late. I never thought we'd run out of time.'

Without saying a word, Deepti opened out her arms. Matteo expelled a sharp breath and walked into the comfort she offered.

He held on tightly; she didn't even attempt to let go until he was ready.

When they finally did pull apart, still holding each other but with space between their bodies, there was the sheen of moisture around his eyes. She reached out, but at the last second she avoided wiping his tears and touched his hair, moving his fringe to the side unnecessarily, leaving her hand cupping the side of his face.

They gazed into each other's eyes without saying a word. Almost in slow motion, Matteo leaned forward and planted a quick kiss on her lips so fast, it was over in the blink of an eye, and yet Deepti's whole body fired into life at that brief connection.

She swallowed. Matteo was holding his breath, waging an inner battle with himself. She'd wanted this for so long. Perhaps it wasn't the best time, coming after such an emotional revelation, but she had to seize the chance.

In a moment of perfect synchronicity, they moved closer, their mouths seeking and finding each other's, clinging and devouring, the touch of their tongues sending spirals of desire right through her.

Without warning he broke off and pushed her gently away, his breath fast and heavy. He walked away without a word.

CHAPTER TWELVE

DEEPTI COULDN'T IMAGINE a more idyllic setting as she helped Bella build a sandcastle on the pristine, white sandy beach of a private island near Malaysia. They were spending their last couple of days here before arriving in Singapore. If only her mind could be a quarter as peaceful as the gentle ocean waves lapping against the shore.

Since they hadn't been able to dock near the island, they'd had to anchor *Serendipity* some distance away. To get to the island, she, Tracey and the children had been dropped off by the yacht's speedboat straight after breakfast.

They'd been playing for a couple of hours, and now the children were getting hungry, so Tracey suggested they head back to the yacht. Deepti was about to page the yacht to get one of the watercrafts out to collect them when Tracey put a restraining hand on her arm.

'Just wait,' Tracey said. 'It looks like someone is coming.'

Deepti followed the direction of Tracey's gaze. Her throat went dry as she recognised the imposing outline of Matteo silhouetted against the horizon. He was followed by two people carrying picnic baskets.

'Hi,' Matteo said, as he approached them. 'I thought it would be nice if we all had lunch together. Chef has prepared something amazing for us.'

Bella ran over and threw herself into his arms. He pressed a quick kiss on the top of her head. Holding hands, Matteo and Bella helped lay out the picnic blanket and take the dishes out of the basket.

While they ate, Deepti casually tried to glance at him. She didn't want to get caught staring, but she was down-fallen to find out he'd never looked in her direction any-way.

Had he thought about last night at all or had he man-aged to put it behind him already? He had seemed as into their kiss as she was but then he'd all but pushed her away. She'd stayed where she was on the deck for ten minutes after he'd gone, hoping…wishing…he'd come back.

She sighed. Why was she sad? Matteo had been right to stop things when he had.

He had barely said two words to her since he'd arrived on the island. Was he purposely keeping his distance? Was he worried that she would read more into the kiss than the culmination of a mutual attraction? She knew it wasn't going anywhere. They would reach Singapore the next day and she would return to England soon after-wards. What was the point of giving in to the attraction when there was no way to act on it?

If only their kiss hadn't been so perfect, hadn't made her long for more. Hadn't started her wondering what might have been.

After they'd finished eating, Bella grabbed Matteo's hand and took him to the dunes they'd discovered earlier. Deepti's heart twisted when she heard Bella's easy laugh-ter. He was such a kind and loving uncle. She could now understand his initial distance towards Bella and Leo— their parents had betrayed him in the worst possible way. Looking at the way he was interacting with them now, and how comfortably Bella leaned against Matteo while she showed him her discovery, she could see no resentment at all towards the innocent children. The only emotion evident was deep affection, even love.

At least he was able to open his heart to some people. She hoped it meant he would be willing to listen to his parents in time. Although she understood how he felt and was completely on his side, he'd spoken about having run out of time with his brother—she hoped he would feel differently about resolving things with his parents.

And maybe one day he would be ready to open his heart to a woman again. He deserved to be loved by someone wholeheartedly and without reservation. Deepti rubbed her chest as she felt a pang, knowing she couldn't be that woman. Why did she have these feelings about Matteo? What was it about him that made her long for things which were impossible?

Were her feelings about Matteo caught up in the general confusion that her life had been in over the past few months? She'd thought she was in a stable job with good career prospects. She had thought she was in a stable relationship. Neither of those had been true. She seemed to be making one mistake after another. How she could she trust what she was thinking, what she was feeling, now?

Matteo had been betrayed by people he'd loved. It didn't take a psychologist to see that experience had made him wary and mistrustful. How could she ask him to trust her when she hadn't been open with him?

Her reasons for not telling him about being fired from her job had always been weak. She'd initially convinced herself she didn't want him to know because he was her employer and she didn't want to risk getting fired from another job. The truth was her reasons were based in protecting herself from the humiliation of what had happened. People who'd worked closely with her for years had been so ready to believe the worst in her. Why should she expect Matteo to believe in her when he'd known her a far shorter time? She couldn't expect the same unquestioning loyalty from him as she had from her parents or Alex.

And why did it matter if he didn't believe her? But it did matter...a lot.

'Me and the kids should head back. I'll put them down for their naps,' Tracey said as she cleared away the lunch plates. Deepti started gathering things too.

'You don't have to come, Dee,' Tracey said. 'Didn't you say you wanted to explore the island? I'm sure it's safe for you.'

'I can stay with you, Deepti. I've been here a couple of times. I don't mind showing you around,' Matteo said.

That didn't sound like the most sensible idea. With her thoughts in such turmoil, not to mention her jumbled feelings, she knew that it was safest for her heart if she wasn't in his company as much.

'Oh, that's okay, thank you,' she said. 'I may as well return with you all.'

'That would be a shame, Dee,' Tracey said. 'The kids will be sleeping so there's nothing for you to do on board. And why waste the opportunity of being on this beautiful island rather than being cooped up on the yacht?'

Again a variety of emotions warred for supremacy. Ultimately, she only had a limited amount of time to spend with Matteo. She could control her feelings and simply enjoy his company.

'Okay, I guess I will stay, since you're planning to come back after the children's naps.' She turned to Matteo, shielding her eyes from the sun as she lifted her head.

'You don't have to stay. I'm sure you've got a lot of business to deal with.'

Matteo grinned. 'No. I made such great progress, I've decided to take the afternoon off.'

Deepti blinked. 'A day off? Are you sure the markets will survive?'

Matteo grinned. 'There's only one way to find out.'

They all went to the island jetty. Next to the waiting speedboat was a jet ski on which Matteo had come over from the yacht, while the crew had brought the picnic in the speedboat.

'Do you have your swimming costume on?' Matteo asked after the speedboat left.

Deepti nodded.

'There's a place I'd like to show you, but it will be faster if we go round the island on the jet ski rather than go on land.'

Deepti eyed the single jet ski. She hadn't been on one before so part of her was glad she wouldn't have to control the machine herself. On the other hand, sitting behind Matteo with him between her knees and her arms around his waist, her greater concern was whether she would be able to control her own reactions.

They took the jet ski to the other side, which had a small beach which led quickly into lush vegetation.

'It's through this forest,' Matteo said. 'It can be a little dark once we're in, but I promise the journey will be worth it.'

She could sense his supressed excitement about their destination. 'Lead the way, then,' she said, repeating the arm gesture she'd made when they'd been about to take the hidden path in Fiore. She wasn't sure if he remembered but he reached for her hand.

'To be safe,' he said.

After walking for about ten minutes, Deepti could hear thundering. She couldn't quite define the sound, but it was calming rather than frightening.

'Almost there,' Matteo said, tugging her hand slightly to make her walk faster.

The thundering got louder and she could smell fresh water. When they reached a clearing, Deepti inhaled sharply as she took in a mesmerising cascade of crystal-clear water flowing down a straight drop into a turquoise pool.

Matteo had seen the waterfall before. But seeing the different expressions chase across Deepti's face made him look at it again, as if seeing it for the first time.

When he'd first decided to take her there, he had imagined various ways she would react to the site, but Deepti throwing her head back and laughing deeply and uninhibitedly was a delicious surprise.

His lips twitched, even though he felt as if he'd missed the joke. Then as she carried on giggling without saying anything he understood she was experiencing pure joy. His smile grew wider and he gave in to his impulse to pick her up and twirl her around. She threw her arms around his neck.

'Is this the first time you've seen a waterfall?' he asked.

'Actually, no. I've been to the Niagara Falls. That was impressive, but this actually took my breath away. Is it natural? Something this perfect can't be man-made but I can't understand how there can be a waterfall practically in the middle of an island when there doesn't appear to be an obvious area of elevation or any rivers inland.'

Again, her mind completely captivated him. 'What is going in that beautiful head of yours?'

His question seemed to fluster her. Or was it his compliment?

'The topography of the island is fascinating.'

'The topography? If you think that's interesting, do you want to go for a dip?' Matteo suggested.

'Sure?' Her expression was dubious but he knew she wouldn't turn down the chance to swim in the plunge pool.

He tried not to watch as Deepti threw off her top and shorts. But he failed and his eyes followed her lithe figure as she ran to the edge of the pool.

He expected her to move close to the shallowest area, to where the water met the land, and dip her toe in to test the temperature but, of course, she didn't do the expected.

She looked over at him, calling out, 'Aren't you coming in?' before she took a running leap into the water.

He waited for her to resurface, which she did with a whoop.

'How is it warm?' she asked, laughing as she scooped water in her hands before letting it run through her fingers. Her reaction was exactly what he'd been waiting for. Despite the beautiful scenery around him, it was her glorious smile that captivated him. His eyes homed in on her mouth, on those lush lips that tasted so sweet. He shook his head to clear the memory.

'No idea,' he said. 'I could ask my friend, if you really want to know.'

'I kind of do. As long as it's not artificially heated. If it is, then let me remain in ignorant bliss.' She giggled. 'Aren't you coming in?'

He wasn't sure that was the wisest move to take but he couldn't resist the chance to be in the water with her. He removed his shirt and shorts and folded them neatly, putting them in a pile on a rock. Then he picked up Deepti's discarded clothes and did the same.

When he turned back to the pool, Deepti hastily lifted her gaze. He smirked at almost catching her staring at his backside.

Following Deepti's lead, he jumped into the pool, purposely trying to make the biggest splash he could. He surfaced to Deepti's wide-eyed, disbelieving face.

'I can't believe you did that!' she exclaimed, and he knew he could expect retaliation.

They played in the water like a couple of school children—carefree and relaxed. He had meant to keep a physical distance between them at all times but his body wasn't paying any attention to his brain.

Following his lead, they swam closer to the cascade, basking in the spray. Wading over to where she was treading water, he took her into his arms. Deepti clearly guessed where he was heading and tightened her arms around his neck. When she wrapped her legs around his waist, his body jerked to life. He gulped and forced his feet to move forward, knowing that being plunged under the cold, rushing water was exactly what he needed at that moment.

Matteo put Deepti down on the ledge behind the drop. He watched her as she soaked in the view.

With wet hair plastered to her head, and not a trace of make-up, she was still stunning. Her sheer, open joy and wonderment at what she was seeing animated her face. He desperately wanted to kiss her again.

They still hadn't spoken about the previous evening. He was still processing why he'd opened up to her in the first place. The only people who knew about the past were his family—the people directly involved in it. He'd never shared the truth with anybody. Why Deepti?

He'd had brief, pretty meaningless relationships over the years. A physical relationship was nothing unusual. Kissing Deepti didn't have to have a special meaning but it had felt different.

It was too loud to talk near the waterfall. They had been in the water longer than he'd planned, but for a brief moment he wished their idyllic time didn't have to end.

They should start making their way back to the beach. They stood there for a few minutes more before Matteo held out his hand to help Deepti back under the cascade and into the pool. Deepti swam over to the side near their clothes but, instead of climbing out of the water, she leaned back against the bank.

He waded over to her.

'We probably should get out and get back to the yacht,' he said.

She nodded but didn't say anything. She just stared at him. He moved closer, until their bodies were almost touching. He waited, giving her the chance to move away if she wanted to.

She didn't. She licked her lips and swallowed.

He put his hands on the bank on either side of her shoulders and waited again. When she remained still, he stepped forward again until their bodies were finally in contact, the heat emanating from the contact rivalling the source of the thermal waters.

Slowly, he bent his head closer. She lifted her mouth to meet his questing lips. They kissed hungrily until he tried to break away. This time, Deepti didn't let him go. She made a murmur of protest then moved up against him and held his head down to hers. He hoisted her up and she wrapped her legs around him as he carried her onto the bank and laid her down.

Their kisses became deeper and more passionate, and rational thought only prevailed when he felt her hand on the waistband of his swimming trunks. If he didn't put a halt to things right then, it would lead to the inevitable conclusion. And he didn't want to make love to her in the open, regardless of how romantic the setting was.

He pulled away and sat up, breathing deeply, trying to get the air back into his lungs. He laughed at Deepti's instinctive grunt of protest. She reached out for him again. He pressed a quick kiss to her lips.

'We have to stop,' he said.

'Why?'

He didn't know why the single word, a mix of question and protest, made his chest tighten but the urge to throw caution to the wind was strong. He turned away so he couldn't be tempted. 'I don't have any protection with me, for one thing.'

He heard her gasp and sensed her sit up. 'I don't have any with me either.'

She reached over for her clothes and handed his to him. 'You're right. We should get back to the yacht.'

He didn't want this to be the end of their physical relationship. He liked spending time with Deepti but he had never tried to deny he was very attracted to her. Back in England, he would have invited her out for dinner. He would have set the boundaries then, making it clear that the most he could offer her was a short affair, a fling. He was too broken and bruised to offer her anything more. Would that be enough for her?

Deepti was too open and kind. He would inevitably hurt

her. And, to his surprise, he actually cared about hurting her. He hadn't cared about anyone for a long time.

'We need to talk,' he said.

Although Deepti knew Matteo was right, and they needed to talk, she wished it wasn't necessary.

They left the waterfall and walked back to the jet ski. She sat behind him and wrapped her arms around his waist. It felt like the end of something beautiful. As they moved off, she rested her head against his back and willed herself not to become emotional.

When they got to the beach, they sat on the blanket left there from that morning. Matteo's expression was a grim mixture of anger and regret.

Deepti's first inclination was to brush off their embrace, to tell Matteo it didn't matter. She wanted to protect herself from further pain. But that would be a lie—it did matter. And, just as it had hurt her when he'd pushed her away after they'd kissed for the first time, it hurt her again now that he'd stopped things from going much further— even though the rational part of her brain knew it was the wisest decision when they didn't have any way of having safe sex. But was that the only reason he'd stopped? She couldn't help feeling there was more to it.

She sighed. Why couldn't things be simple? If they'd met anywhere else, they could have acted on their attraction without worrying about the circumstances.

Deepti scoffed. They moved in completely different worlds. The chances of them having met anywhere else was miniscule. Even on the yacht, there wouldn't usually be much interaction between the owner and her as assistant chef.

If Bella hadn't found her that first day and somehow become attached to her, then she wouldn't be on this island half-naked next to Matteo minutes after the most passionate embrace of her life.

She realised her mind had wandered when Matteo cleared his throat and then said, 'About what just happened—it was a mistake. I shouldn't have done that.'

Why did hearing that feel like a knife to her heart?

'I understand,' she said, looking anywhere but at him. He was right: they shouldn't have kissed. She was Bella's companion, and it was inappropriate for her to kiss Matteo. If only she'd brought a cardigan with her, or something more substantial than a coverall; she suddenly felt chilled and needed to get away. She stood up, trying to gather the last remaining items they'd brought out.

'Can you sit down please?' Matteo asked. 'I'd like us to talk here, in privacy.'

Deepti's eyes widened. There was more to say? She sat down again but kept a safe distance from Matteo's magnetic warmth.

'It's important to be open and up front from the start so there are no misunderstandings,' Matteo said.

'Absolutely,' Deepti agreed, while reflecting she'd never had such a conversation in the past. She couldn't imagine him wanting such a conversation up front was going to herald anything good. Usually, she started dating without any discussions about expectations.

'You're a beautiful woman. I can't deny I am very attracted to you.'

Deepti's spirits rose at his simple statement…then came crashing back down. 'But…?' she prompted, knowing one was coming.

'But, while we're on the yacht, it's not appropriate for us to have an affair.'

She wanted to protest that they literally weren't on the yacht, but she knew that wasn't what he was talking about. Then she paused and tilted her head. Was he implying that things could be different once they reached Singapore, or was she reading far too much into a simple, declarative statement?

'We're only on the yacht for another night,' she pointed out.

Matteo grinned. Her heart needed to get used to him doing that—its constant flipping couldn't be good for her. 'That's right. And, once we've dropped Bella and Leo off with my parents, you won't be working as her companion anymore.'

'And would things be more appropriate then?' She spoke slowly. She didn't want to invite rejection but she wanted to be crystal-clear she knew where she stood.

Again, that devastating grin with his adorable dimples appeared. 'I think they would be.'

Deepti lost the ability to talk. She couldn't even remember how to breathe. Matteo was agreeing to a relationship with her once they arrived in Singapore.

'I want to be clear what I'm offering,' Matteo said. 'I don't do relationships.'

Deepti's heart dipped, but she could understand why Matteo wasn't keen on relationships after his experience with his fiancée.

'So what are you offering?' she asked.

'A brief affair or fling while you're in Singapore. You said you were flying back in a few days. Why don't we spend time together until then?'

'And after that it will be over,' Deepti said. It was a statement, not a question; she wanted to make sure everything was spelled out.

'That's right. I don't want to lead you on, making you believe this is the start of something long-term, or love and marriage are in the future, because that's just not possible.'

Deepti was silent, digesting what he was saying. Really, it was what she'd been expecting, but the little hope which had been alive in her that this was the beginning of something real, not the end, shrivelled completely at the stark reality.

She liked Matteo. He was the most attractive man she'd ever met. She enjoyed spending time with him. Every nerve in her body was urging her to agree to his terms and spend a few blissful days in his arms and in his bed. But a quieter, more rational part of her knew she would be in danger of falling even more deeply for him if she agreed to their fling.

It would be safer for her heart if they left things the way they were. The only question was, did she want to be safe?

CHAPTER THIRTEEN

DEEPTI STOOD ON deck with Alex and other members of the crew as *Serendipity* sailed into Keppel Bay.

They'd finally reached Singapore.

Conflicting emotions warred within Deepti: excitement at the prospect of finally exploring a country she'd dreamed of visiting for years; dread at the idea she would soon have to return to England and face her future; sadness at having to say goodbye to Bella and Leo; complete confusion at the situation with Matteo.

She'd tried to keep herself busy since they'd left the private island and returned to the yacht. Any moment she hadn't been occupied, she'd been thinking about Matteo's proposition.

Why was this a difficult decision? She liked Matteo and she was incredibly attracted to him. She definitely wanted to sleep with him. What was preventing her from saying yes?

He'd made it clear that a short fling was all he would offer, which was perfect for her, since that was all she could deal with until she managed to get the rest of her life sorted out.

And, after he had been so open and honest with her about his fiancée and his brother, she understood why he didn't believe in long-term relationships. He'd been betrayed. There was no other way of putting it. She couldn't imagine going through what he had. She'd found it hard to trust anything after what had happened to her, and it was nothing in comparison to what had happened to him.

After the betrayal he had experienced at the hands of two people he had loved unconditionally, of course he wasn't ready to give his heart to someone new.

She hoped one day he would be ready. She'd seen how he'd spent time with Bella and Leo, even though Bella was the physical representation of that betrayal. He had a limitless capacity to love and he deserved to find someone worthy of loving him in return.

And that wasn't her. Though she would never, could never, cheat on someone, she wasn't going to tell Matteo the whole truth behind why she was on *Serendipity*. She was still lying to him, hiding a core part of herself. She was in many ways no better than the people he'd trusted before who'd let him down.

In a few hours, unless she agreed to his suggestion that they have a brief affair before she returned to England, she might be saying goodbye to Matteo for good and she would never see him again.

She rubbed her chest, as if trying to ease the heaviness inside her at the prospect of never seeing Matteo again.

If she did want to agree to having a fling with Matteo, telling him the truth at this late stage could ruin things. She enjoyed being with him without the weight of her past and the fallout of her ex-boyfriend's actions affecting their time together. If a long-term relationship had been a possibility, then maybe she would have told Matteo the truth, but he had made it clear they could only have a fling. He'd told her he wasn't the marrying kind so there was no real reason to tell him what had happened.

Bella calling her name, excited that the yacht had docked, brought her back to reality.

As they disembarked, she came face to face with Matteo. He briefly inclined his head but there was no outward indication that anything had happened between them on the island. But what did she expect? They were surrounded by people. He couldn't very well bring up their kiss in front of everybody.

A car was waiting for them and soon they were crossing Keppel Bridge towards the main part of Singapore, heading towards Matteo's parents' house. Even though he was seated in front of her, something in his posture suggested he was feeling tense.

As she got out of the car when they arrived, she walked up to Matteo and briefly pressed his hand, before moving to Bella to help her get ready to meet her grandparents.

A maid opened the door to them and a distinguished-looking older couple came out to the foyer while Deepti was helping Bella take off her jacket. She would have known these were Matteo's parents anywhere. He'd inherited his father's height and strong jawline, and his mother's cheekbones and wavy hair.

'Matteo,' the woman said, holding out her arms to him.

'Mother,' Matteo replied, remaining where he was.

Deepti watched the sadness cross the woman's face as she put down her arms. She could understand why Matteo wasn't rushing to embrace his parents, but she could also imagine how his mother felt, losing one son and being estranged from her only remaining child.

'Bella, do you remember your grandparents?' Deepti asked, bringing Bella forward, since the little girl had hidden behind her. 'I think you last saw them when Leo was born. Say hello, sweetie.'

Bella shook her head and hid her face on Deepti's leg.

'Why don't we go through to the drawing room?' Matteo's father suggested. 'We can get something to eat and drink.'

Bella snuggled further into Deepti's side.

'That would be very nice,' Deepti responded with a welcome smile as they all followed the parents.

'Let me introduce you,' Matteo said, once they were seated. 'Deepti, these are my parents. Mother, Father, this is Deepti Roy, Bella's companion. I sent you a message about her.'

'Yes, of course,' Matteo's mum said. 'Thank you for stepping in to help out with our Bella. It was reassuring to hear she was okay for the journey.'

'Excuse me for interrupting,' Tracey said. 'Is there anywhere I can change Leo? And he should probably take a nap soon.'

'Of course,' Matteo's mother said. 'Why don't I show you his nursery? And I can show you your room as well. Bella, do you want to come with me?' She put out her hand.

Bella crawled onto Deepti's lap and began to suck her thumb. Deepti threw a worried glance at Matteo—Bella had never done that before.

'I want to see your room, Bella,' Deepti said. 'Why don't we go with Tracey and Leo?' She realised immediately that Matteo would be left alone with his father. She didn't want Matteo to be uncomfortable, but she didn't want to over-step the boundaries of whatever was between them.

She hadn't anticipated Bella's behaviour regressing. Perhaps she should have given more thought to what could go wrong with the handover.

All she'd thought about was Matteo's proposition. Even now she was thinking about giving him her answer. Was that the person she'd become? But what choice did she have? She couldn't stay with Bella for ever.

She left Tracey trying to put Bella down for a nap and went back to the drawing room. Matteo was standing near a cabinet while his parents were seated. His body was facing away from them. She almost shivered from the coolness in the atmosphere in the room.

'Ah, Deepti, come in. Sit down, please,' Matteo's father said as she walked in. 'We've been discussing this situation with Bella. And I would like to ask you to stay on for a few days to help Bella with the transition. Tracey said Bella opened up to her after you'd been interacting for a few days. Hopefully, Bella will open to her grandma and me.'

'Please do agree,' Matteo's mother said. 'We can have a guest room prepared for you. And you would have your evenings free. It would be the same arrangement you had on the yacht.'

Deepti cast a glance at Matteo but his expression was inscrutable. She took a deep breath. Now she had two offers to consider—this was no time for her to be indecisive.

This time, the answer came easily to her.

'Thank you for the offer,' Deepti said. 'And I'm very happy to help Bella with a transition, but it can only be for a few days.'

Another glance at Matte showed his jaw clench and he walked to the window, turning his back on the room.

'I'm very happy to stay here overnight,' Deepti continued. 'But after tonight I don't think it's a good idea for me to be in the same house. The whole point is for Bella to get used to me not being around.' She took a deep breath to steel her nerves. 'Matteo, perhaps you could help me organise a hotel room? Maybe where you're staying?'

Matteo turned back to her, his eyebrows raised in a question.

She smiled shyly at him. It was really difficult to convey her answer to his proposition when she was the centre of attention of his parents. It went without saying that he wouldn't want his parents to know about their fling.

'I'm sure I'll be able to sort out a room for you,' he told her, flashing a bright grin. 'I should head off now. I'll let you know if there are any problems. Why don't I contact you later this evening? We can sort when and where we'll meet tomorrow.'

Deepti nodded, biting her lip to contain the happiness bubbling inside her at the prospect of her fling with Matteo.

'Matteo, aren't you going to stay for lunch?' his mother asked, sounding slightly upset.

'I'm afraid I have a meeting soon and I need to get to the office first.'

'Uncle Mayo, will you read my story tonight?' Bella asked, coming into the room, followed by an apologetic Tracey.

Deepti could tell Matteo was torn. He didn't want to disappoint his niece but the tension between his parents and him was palpable.

'Can't I read your story tonight, sweetie?' Deepti asked Bella.

Bella pouted. She'd got used to her uncle being part of her bedtime routine. It was probably going to be just as difficult to transition Bella off Matteo.

'Why don't you come for dinner, Matteo? Then you can read to Bella.'

Matteo visibly stiffened at his mother's suggestion. Deepti's heart went out to him. She understood the betrayal he must have felt when his parents had supported his brother. But Matteo had admitted himself that he'd always thought he would reconcile with Luca, who it was clear he'd loved very much.

'I'm afraid I have a dinner meeting, mother,' Matteo answered.

Deepti was torn. She supported Matteo and how he felt unquestioningly, but at the same time Bella was a five-year-old child and shouldn't be caught in the crossfire of Matteo's fraught relationship with his parents.

'Tracey, I think Bella would like a snack,' Deepti said, wanting to get the little girl out of the room for the rest of the conversation.

'Good idea,' Tracey replied and then excused herself.

Once Bella was out of earshot, Deepti turned to Matteo to ask when he could spare some time for a video call.

'Video call? Matteo, surely you can make time for dinner?' Matteo's father said, putting a comforting hand on his wife's shoulder.

'It's impossible, I'm afraid.' He stared directly at his father.

'Your mother will be disappointed. She was planning to make your favourite dishes.'

Matteo didn't respond. Deepti started shifting weight from one leg to the other in an effort to ignore the uncomfortable silence that had developed. She cleared her throat. 'Is that a no for the video call?'

For a moment, Deepti thought Matteo wasn't going to answer her. Then he gave her a tight smile and nodded. Looking at his cold, aloof expression as he stared at his parents, she missed the carefree, smiling man she'd got to know and like.

Had she made a mistake agreeing to having a fling with

Matteo while they were in Singapore? Not because she didn't want to make love with him but Matteo had a lot to deal with without trying to navigate a temporary sexual relationship. And she didn't want to be simply a distraction from his frustrations.

Hopefully, tomorrow they would get the chance to spend some time alone and would be able to talk freely.

But, right at that moment, tomorrow felt a million hours away.

CHAPTER FOURTEEN

NOT AN IMPATIENT man by nature, Matteo stood at the entrance to Hort Park, waiting for Deepti and the children to arrive. It was typical of Deepti's empathy for her to suggest they meet in a public place rather than his parents' house. He knew it wasn't the proximity to his office that had been behind the suggestion.

He thought about how he'd felt the previous day, seeing his parents for the first time in years. He'd expected their meeting to be stressful. And it had been. He was the one who'd cut them off completely once they'd chosen to keep in contact with Luca—at the time, it had been one betrayal heaped on another, and the last straw for him.

They'd reached out to him on a number of occasions over the years but he'd rebuffed their advances. His parents were understandably wary of where they stood. He should probably let them know this time he was ready and willing to talk. It wasn't going to be an overnight reconciliation, but he was more open to hearing their perspective, although he might never understand it.

But for now he wanted to put the past, and the difficult conversations that were ahead, out of his mind and enjoy his day with the children and his evening with Deepti.

Matteo turned when he heard Bella calling out his name and saw her running towards him. Matteo was surprised to see Tracey with them. Deepti hadn't given any indication that she would be joining them. But, when he heard the reason Tracey had offered to join them was so Deepti could leave with Matteo rather than drop the children back, he was undeniably grateful to her. Again. He had to admit, he'd had several occasions to be grateful to Tracey over the past few weeks for giving him opportunities to spend time alone with Deepti.

His lips quirked. Had his parents unwittingly hired a matchmaker to be their nanny? He didn't care. Today, it simply meant that he and Deepti could start their fling a few hours sooner than planned without a stressful meeting with his parents to contend with.

Hoisting Bella on to his shoulders, they walked through beautiful, manicured gardens before reaching the Nature Playground. Bella laughed with delight as she explored the tunnels of the Magical Woods and climbed Log Valley.

He adored spending the time with the children; it was one of the highlights of his days. When he'd initially agreed to accompany them to Singapore, he'd expected to hand them over without any problems. Now, he wasn't looking forward to saying goodbye. He would miss them so much. He was still satisfied his parents were the best guardians for Bella and Leo since, as retirees, they could be there for the children. But he would keep in regular contact and find time to visit Bella and Leo whenever he could.

They spent a few hours in the Nature Playground then took a look at the Butterfly Garden before his parents' car came to collect Tracey and the children. Once they had driven off, he turned to face Deepti.

'Well,' she said, twisting her hands in the front of her T-shirt. 'What now?' She glanced at him from under her eyelashes, a gesture he was sure she was making from nerves, but which he found surprisingly seductive.

Tempted as he was to rush her back to the hotel and into his bed, he reached for patience. It was her first time in Singapore and, without the children, he was sure she would want to explore the country.

'Would you like to get something to eat?' he asked. 'Or is there somewhere specific you'd like to go?'

Deepti didn't answer immediately. He got the impression she was weighing up options in her mind.

'There's so much to see in Singapore,' she said. 'But, actually, can we go to the hotel? Your parents said they'd arrange to send my luggage there and I want to make sure everything's okay. I'd like to freshen up before we go anywhere.' She looked down at her top which had the evidence she'd spent the day with sticky hands.

During the drive to the hotel, Deepti chatted about everything she wanted to see and do on what she called her 'touristy to-do list'. He couldn't hide his smile at her attempt to ignore the heightened tension between them. He leaned forward to brush her lips with his, intending it to be a light touch, but she put her hand behind his head, deepening their kiss, testing every ounce of his resolve not to get her into bed the moment they were at the hotel room.

When the were finally checked in, Matteo opened the door to Deepti's room and waited for her to enter ahead of him. He furrowed his brows as he looked around. Perhaps he should have organised a suite for her too. It was a pretty basic room with a king-size bed he was deliberately keeping his attention off, a large three-seater sofa he was also keeping his attention off and a desk. Immediately his mind conjured an image of Deepti hoisted onto the desk with her legs wrapped round him.

He cleared his throat and walked over to join Deepti by the window. The view of Singapore's cityscape on this floor probably wasn't as good as from his suite but it seemed to be absorbing her attention. Was his presence making her uncomfortable?

'Shall I leave you to freshen up?' he said. He gave her his room number. 'You can call me when you're ready or come up.'

She gave him an absent nod.

'Is something wrong, Deepti?'

'Nothing's wrong. It's just...' She straightened her shoulders. 'When I told your parents I wanted to stay at the hotel with you, I was trying to tell you I agree to the fling.'

Matteo laughed heartily. 'I understood.' He walked over to her and drew her into his arms. 'And I'm very happy.'

'Then why did you get me this room?' she asked, her confusion evident.

Matteo grasped both hands in his and drew them to his lips, kissing one after the other.

'I want you to have your own space if you want it. I hope we send our time together, but I don't ever want you to feel you have to be with me if you want some peace or you're not in the mood.'

Deepti quirked an eyebrow.

'For company,' he added hastily.

He bent to kiss her, intending it to be light and quick, but the sensation of her soft lips pressing back created a hunger and his mouth moved urgently over hers, demanding, and receiving, a reciprocal passion.

Reluctantly, he pulled away. 'I'll leave you to freshen up.'

Deepti grabbed his hand. 'No point freshening up yet,' she muttered as she started fiddling with his shirt buttons.

Matteo suddenly forgot how to breathe. He'd imagined wining and dining Deepti, followed by a slow, sweet seduction, but she always threw out his well laid plans with even better ideas of her own.

He lifted her off her feet. She automatically wrapped her legs round his waist, bending her head to meet his eager mouth. He carried her over and placed her on the bed. She kept him cradled between her thighs as her hands went to his shirt, nimbly undoing the remaining buttons.

He wanted this. He wanted this more than he ever remembered wanting something before. But he knew what would happen if he made love to her then—he would never leave the bed. The most Deepti would get to see of Singapore was the hotel and the most she would get to sample of the cuisine was room service.

He gathered both her hands in his. Taking deep breaths to calm his racing pulse, he said, 'We need to stop.'

Deepti went very still. 'Not again! Why?'

He explained his concerns.

'I see,' she said. She rested back on her elbows. Then with a cheeky grin she grabbed the bottom of her T-shirt and pulled it over her head. 'I'm not in the mood to go sightseeing right now...'

She undid the button on her shorts. His mouth ran dry and he swallowed convulsively. He'd known how passionate she could be from her previous responses to him but he'd never expected this assertive sexuality. He was a lucky man.

'Don't let me stop you going, though,' she said, looking up at him through her drooping eyelashes. 'I'm just going to stay here. On this incredibly comfortable and reassuringly firm bed.'

When she slowly reached behind her to unclasp her bra,

he growled and stalked towards her, halting her. He fully intended to unwrap the rest of this gift himself.

He knew when he was beaten, and this was a fight he was happy not to win.

CHAPTER FIFTEEN

THE NEXT DAY, Deepti was sitting in a restaurant staring out at the view of Marina Bay. She'd been so enthralled by the architectural splendour of the Helix Bridge with its steel and glass arches that she hadn't noticed Matteo was twenty minutes late until a waiter came to take her order for the third time.

She fiddled with her phone. Should she send him a text, letting him know it was fine if he couldn't make it? She wanted him to know that she had no expectations of the fling—she didn't need him to cut short meetings or change business plans to spend time with her.

She put her phone back down. It had only been twenty minutes. If she texted him now, she could appear impatient and, since he couldn't read tone from a text, her message could come across as passive aggressive.

In thirty minutes, she would leave and buy some street food. She wanted to spend time with Matteo, naturally, but there was still a lot of Singapore she wanted to explore. She was happy to stare out of the window for a while longer, as it would give her a chance to think through what she should do about Bella.

That morning had not started well. When she'd arrived at Matteo's parents' house, Bella had refused to come out of her room or talk to anyone until she'd heard Deepti was waiting for her in the foyer. Her grandparents had been at their wits' end, desperate for some reassurance that things would get better.

In the end Deepti had persuaded the children and grandparents to spend the morning at Marine Cove Playground. Although Bella had been enjoying herself, the adults had initially clearly been tense, watching for any negative reaction from her. But, by the time she'd finished playing, there had been a subtle shift in Bella's attitude towards her grandparents. She still wouldn't speak to them but she'd listened to them when they'd explained what was around and she'd accepted food from them.

Having no end date for Deepti being around wasn't helping Bella settle in. The little girl would keep expecting Deepti to go round. Deepti decided to book her flight home for the end of the week. That would give Matteo's parents a definitive deadline for the transition.

She really wanted Bella to be happy with her grandparents but there was no denying she would miss the little girl once she left. Perhaps she could speak to Bella's grandparents about keeping in touch, or at least occasionally hearing how Bella was doing.

Not only was she not looking forward to saying goodbye to Bella, but she also wasn't looking forward to ending her time with Matteo. But it was better if it happened sooner, when they were enjoying their brief moments together and she could remember it was only a fling, rather than later, when she would fall more deeply for him than she already had.

'Sorry I'm late,' Matteo said as he came up to their table. Deepti's eyes widened when he pressed a kiss on her lips before sitting down. In any other circumstance, it would be a typical gesture between a dating couple. But they weren't dating. She didn't really know what they were.

'Are your meetings going well?' she asked.

'As well as can be expected. The usual last-minute attempts at renegotiation. A few meetings that I probably didn't need to be involved in.'

Deepti grinned, 'I guess it's hard to relinquish control when the company's your baby.' Her smile faltered as Matteo's face became a stone mask. She hurriedly changed the topic of conversation. 'Have you been here before? The view is amazing.'

They continued to talk about non-contentious topics as they ordered and waited for their food to arrive.

After she'd finished eating her entree, she looked up from her plate to see Matteo with a broad grin.

'What?' she asked. 'Do I have sauce on my face?'

'No. It looks like you were hungry?'

She saw that he still had half his meal left.

'I guess I'm not much of a conversationalist when there's food around.'

He grinned again. 'I had noticed. When we had lunch for the first time together in Fiore, you let me talk for the majority of the meal. You only started chatting once we were on dessert.'

Heat flared in her cheeks. 'Sorry, I didn't mean to be rude.'

Matteo pressed his lips together. 'That's not what I meant at all.'

Deepti didn't respond but turned to stare out of the window instead. She sensed Matteo continue to stare at her for a few moments before he started eating again.

Matteo didn't say anything more. After he finished eating his main course, he excused himself to make a call.

When he returned to the table, he asked if she wanted a dessert. When she refused, Matteo signalled for and paid the bill and they both stood up ready to leave.

Meeting for lunch was turning out to have been a really bad idea. When they'd spent time together before, she'd been Bella's companion. There might have been an attraction between them but they hadn't acted on it.

Now that they'd started this fling, things were different. A meal in their hotel room made sense, as they'd had the previous evening, but eating out for lunch was too much like dating.

And they weren't dating. They weren't at the beginning or the discovery stages of a new relationship. What they had would be over in a matter of days. She took a deep, shuddering breath at the stark reminder of what having a fling meant.

'Have you decided where you want to go this afternoon?' Matteo asked as they left the restaurant. He reached for her hand.

The previous evening, when they'd finally left her hotel room and gone to Suntec City to watch the laser show at the Fountain of Wealth, it had felt natural walking hand in hand, or with their arms around each other. But today it felt wrong. Too little compared to what she really wanted.

She pulled her hand away under the guise of taking out her phone and scrolling through the list of places she wanted to see, trying to decide where to spend her afternoon.

'Yeah, I thought I'd start with Merlion Park, because I have to see the Merlion. It is the national personification of Singapore, of course.'

'Of course,' Matteo repeated with a serious expression, teasing her as she read off her list.

She gave him a poke in the ribs then continued, 'After that, I think I'll go to Gardens by the Bay to see the flower dome, and I must see the super-trees. I've seen the photos and I still can't comprehend what they're like.'

'Good choice.'

'You've been?'

He nodded. 'Shall we go?'

She blinked, 'Pardon? Aren't you waiting for your car to be brought around?'

Matteo smiled, then reached out for her hand again, bringing it up to his mouth for a kiss. 'No, I'm coming with you. I've taken the afternoon off.'

'What?' she asked in astonishment. 'I thought you had loads of meeting today.'

'Jack is rearranging things. This past month has shown me I don't need to be at every meeting, so I'm going to delegate. There's no time to lose. There's so much for me to show you.'

Deepti wanted to cry. Every time she steeled herself to accept scraps of Matteo's attention, he showed her how caring and attentive he could be, making her long to ask for a future together. To ask for the impossible.

She was trying so hard to live for the moment, but that had never been her personality. She was the kind of person who liked to make plans for her future, lead with her head. She'd been determined not to waste their limited time together wishing things could be different but to enjoy the moments while she could. Now her heart was moving her into dangerous territory.

'I'm going to organise my return flight for the end of the week,' she said, needing to voice the definitive end of their fling.

Matteo paused and turned her to face him. 'When did you decide that?'

'This morning.' She explained her need to give a final date to help with Bella's transition. She didn't mention her own need to put an end date to this fling. A time when she would know it was over for good.

'I see. If you have any problems arranging your flight, Jack can help you.'

Deepti forced out a long breath. She hadn't expected him to fall on his knees and beg her to stay for longer, but obviously she'd hoped for a slightly bigger reaction to her announcement than that.

Having waited until he could find a secluded spot as they went along the Changi Coastal Walk, Matteo groaned when Deepti broke their kiss and pushed him away from her. He grabbed her round the waist and pulled her back into him, making her squeal. If only there was a bed nearby: he wanted her beneath him.

'Matteo, people can see you.'

He looked around him at the other visitors along the boardwalk.

'Let them,' he said, cupping her face in his hands and covering her mouth with his She actively participated in their kiss for a few moments then pulled and tried to get away a second time. When he went to grab her again, she giggled and swerved out of his reach.

'Come on, Matteo. We still have lots to see before we need to leave for your parents. Here—you can hold my hand,' she said, putting hers out for him.

Matteo made a face, which made her laugh, but he enveloped her slim hand in both of his. Not for the first time, he was regretting his resolution to make sure Deepti didn't miss out on seeing everything on her 'touristy to-do list'.

Over the past couple of days, they'd visited museums, galleries and more gardens. Watching Deepti's expressions had been more interesting to him than the attractions themselves, although seeing the places through Deepti's eyes, like at the waterfall, was like seeing them for the first time.

That morning they'd woken up early to go to Mount Faber Park so they could watch the sunrise together before he went to his office. Each of those moments with her took his breath away.

And at all of these places, apart from the Buddha Tooth Relic Temple, he sought out quiet, private areas where he could give in to his urge to kiss her until she was as breathless as he felt.

He had never been prone to public displays of affection before; at most his dates got his elbow as support when he was escorting them round. With Deepti, he hadn't been able to resist, taking every opportunity to sneak a kiss.

'We could be late for my parents,' he said, as they continued to walk. 'We could go back to the hotel first.'

She paused, biting her lip. He grinned. He loved that she was seriously thinking about his suggestion. She had thrown herself wholeheartedly into their fling, meeting his passion with an intensity of her own. His face fell when she shook her head.

'No, we can't be late. I promised Bella we'd be round a bit earlier today. And I don't want to have to come up with two believable excuses to give your parents for our lateness, particularly why we're both late and arriving exactly at the same time.'

'Then tell them the truth. You can say we're late because I was having my wicked way with you,' he replied, pulling her back to him and wrapping his arms around her.

'Matteo,' she said, using the stern tone he'd got used to whenever he'd sneaked kisses from her when they'd been with Bella or his parents.

He was going to miss that tone when she was gone...in only a few days. He went still. It didn't matter how much fun he had been having, they'd made an agreement that it would end once she left Singapore. He turned away from her.

If Deepti was surprised by his sudden change of mood, she didn't say anything but, as they continued walking, she would gaze over at him, her expression a mix of understanding and resignation.

They had spent an idyllic few days since arriving in Singapore. He'd visited Bella every evening with Deepti. What his parents thought about them arriving and leaving together, he didn't really care, as long as they didn't make Deepti feel uncomfortable in any way.

Deepti always joined his parents for a drink after putting Bella to bed, in a similar way to the updates she used to give him. His lips quirked. He was certain his parents didn't have the same ulterior motive he'd had.

So far, they had refused his parents' invitations to stay for dinner, but he knew he a proper conversation with them was long overdue. He didn't mind if Deepti was part of the conversation—in fact he would prefer it—but he knew his parents wouldn't be comfortable discussing family truths in front of someone they considered a stranger.

In some ways, since they'd only known each other for a month, Deepti was still a stranger to him. But she was someone he had wanted to get to know better almost from the first moment he'd met her. In another world, they probably wouldn't be ending their fling so soon, but they'd set out the parameters at the beginning. He couldn't ask her to change them now...could he?

Deepti had booked her return to England. The date co-incided with his departure for Dubai. What would Deepti think if he asked her to go to Dubai with him so they could spend a few more days together? It was a tempting thought. But was there really any point when they would simply be prolonging the inevitable?

But they had agreed it was a fling, and Deepti had never brought up the idea of continuing their relationship back in England. In fact, Deepti had made it quite clear that she wanted nothing to do with him once it had ended—she'd not even shared her plans for getting a job. He was tempted to offer help finding her a position to tide her over, some-thing he had never offered anyone before, and something he had never previously considered before.

But one week was too short, even for a fling. He em-ployed extremely competent people who could easily carry out the work he kept taking on himself. In fact, his busi-ness was at the stage where he could step back and take on a caretaker role, perhaps even look for a new venture—maybe take the yacht and sail round the world. Perhaps he would bring up extending her stay once they left his parents.

The evening with Bella went well and it was looking in-creasingly as if there would be no need for Deepti to delay her return on Bella's account. So, the only option was to ask Deepti to delay her return on his account.

He brought it up later that evening when they were tak-ing a walk along the bay before dinner. She let her hand fall out of his and stopped walking.

'Why?' she asked.

He frowned. She wasn't exactly leaping up and down with joy at the prospect of extending their fling.

'If you still don't have to rush home, I could show you some places in Dubai we didn't get a chance to see on the way up, and then we can take the yacht to Egypt.'

'I've already booked my return,' she replied.

'That's not a problem,' he said. He could organise the changes to her airline ticket. If necessary, he could charter a private jet to get her to England. In which case, he could probably go back with her.

'It's a bit out of the blue.'

He rubbed his neck. She was going to turn him down but hadn't definitely said no yet. He turned to look at the water. It didn't matter if she didn't want to continue their fling. It had always been time-limited. The more time they spent together, the greater the risk she would develop feelings for him.

He'd already made major changes to his schedule and plans to fit in more time with her. If he let it continue, then she would keep trying to burrow her way into his heart, and he wasn't going to let that happen. He would always be grateful to her that she had helped him have a relationship with his nephew and niece. And the doors of a relationship with his parents were ajar. But he didn't do love and he didn't do romantic emotions.

'It does make more sense for you to keep with your timetable,' he said curtly.

Deepti laughed. 'Have you changed your mind already?'

He tilted his head. 'What?' She was keeping him off-kilter and he didn't like it.

'Are you un-inviting me from Dubai?' She was still smiling but it didn't reach her eyes and he couldn't read the emotion behind it.

'Of course not. I would love you to join me,' he said, simply and honestly. 'There is no pressure. If you've already started making arrangements for when you're back home, then I completely understand that you don't want to make any last-minute changes.'

She expelled a breath like a sigh. And she had the same slightly lost, slightly hurt expression as always when the subject of her plans back home came up. He wanted to offer to help with whatever problem she was facing. He wanted her to know he was on her side.

But that wasn't part of their agreement. He wasn't her partner. He wasn't even her boyfriend. After this fling ended, they would be nothing to each other.

CHAPTER SIXTEEN

DEEPTI PUT DOWN the book she was trying to read and then stretched out on the sofa area of the guest-floor deck. She couldn't really concentrate anyway and was feeling at a bit of a loose end. They'd been back on board the yacht for three days.

In the end, rather than fly to Dubai and join the yacht there, Matteo had decided to sail to Dubai.

Before she'd agreed to extend their fling, they'd considered the impact delaying her departure could have on Bella. Since Matteo knew Deepti well enough to know there was no chance of her staying in Singapore and not spending time with Bella, they'd decided she would leave on her planned date. Instead, Matteo changed his arrangements.

It was odd being back on *Serendipity* and not spending the day with Bella. Saying goodbye to her had been even harder than she'd expected. Even though it had only been a few weeks, she'd grown very attached to the young girl which, based on her previous limited experience with children, was something she would never have expected when she'd first agreed to be Bella's companion.

If Deepti had this much trouble saying goodbye to Bella, how badly would it hurt to say goodbye to Matteo when the time finally came? And, unlike with Bella, Deepti doubted he'd agree to have video chats with her so they could keep in touch.

In the end, it hadn't been difficult to agree to his offer to extend their fling, even if it was only for a few more days. And this time she knew the reason wasn't because she was putting off returning to England. She liked Matteo, loved being in his company. She wanted to spend as much time with him as possible before they had to part for good. Soon all she would have would be her memories and she was determined to make as many as possible.

Matteo had suggested she move into his suite of rooms, but she asked to stay in her former bedroom. Sharing a room, even for the few days it would take to reach Dubai, would have been too much like a real relationship—and she needed to constantly remind herself they were having a fling. It was easier to protect her feelings if she had a separate room like she'd had in the hotel.

They had less than seven days left together. She was going to make every one of them count. But she was absolutely determined not to delay her return to England once they reached Dubai. Not only did she have to start putting the pieces of her life back together, but she also had to protect her heart.

And, the closer she became to Matteo, the stronger grew the feeling of guilt that she was lying to him, and that didn't sit well with her at all. Particularly when Matteo had been open and honest with her about how he'd been betrayed in the worst possible way.

It made complete sense that he found it difficult to trust people, especially on a personal level. But she wanted him to trust her. And how could she expect that when she had been hiding the truth about her past and her future? Was there any really good reason to hide it?

Although they had only known each other for such a short time, in many ways Matteo already knew her better than anyone else did. She had to believe he knew her well enough to know she would never have betrayed someone's trust, not on a personal or professional level.

Their fling would soon be over, and she could save herself the potential hurt if the conversation didn't go the way she planned, but she wanted him to know the truth. She didn't want there to be any secrets between them, on her part. She wanted him to know he could trust her—as she, against all odds, had learnt to trust him.

It was all very well in theory to make the decision to tell him the truth, but how did she bring up something like that? Perhaps after dinner, when they were sitting out on the deck, sharing a glass of wine in the hot tub.

She imagined how that conversation could go.

Oh, by the way, Matteo, I actually work in the financial sector and I know a lot about your business and the kind of deals you've been working on. I joined the crew of the Serendipity *when I was fired from my job because I didn't land an important deal. And I also lost a very important client for the firm, losing it millions in income.*

But there's more. The deal and the client went to the company belonging to my boyfriend at the time so, while some of the people I worked for think I'm merely incompetent, the majority think I'm corrupt and unethical because I purposely let my boyfriend take the deal.

Even thinking it made her head hurt.

Before, during or after a meal didn't feel like the right time, but at the same time she couldn't really make an appointment through Jack to tell Matteo the truth.

She decided to find Alex to ask his opinion. She didn't know whether it was because she was distracted, or muscle memory from her visits to Matteo made her go to the foyer rather than take the crew stairs, but she realised her error when the guest waiting by the lift turned when he heard her approach.

She froze on the spot. She had been so careful to avoid seeing any guests and, the one time she made a mistake, she bumped into someone she knew. Not just knew—someone whose company was a client of her firm.

'Deepti, I thought I'd seen you sitting out on the deck. What a surprise!'

'Mr Partlin. How nice to bump into you. How have you been?' Deepti's mind frantically worked through the potential repercussions of this meeting and whether Mr Partlin was likely to mention it to Matteo.

'Good, good. Are you here for meetings with Mr Di Corrado too?'

She shook her head.

'Oh, do you work for him now? To be honest, I was a bit disappointed when your colleague contacted me a few months ago to let me know you were leaving the company. I would have hoped you valued me as a client to let me know personally. Then I heard you'd been let go as part of a restructuring, so I was confused.'

Deepti narrowed her eyes. 'One of my colleagues contacted you a few months ago about me leaving?'

'Yes, maybe three or four months ago. They told me you were leaving and your clients would be redistributed.'

Deepti couldn't believe what she was hearing. She'd been let go only two months ago but someone had contacted her clients well before then about her departure. Who would have done that…and why? It sounded as if what had happened with her work hadn't been a simple scenario of someone taking advantage of the situation, but that someone had perhaps engineered the situation and planned it in advance. This could be her first major breakthrough in trying to clear her name.

'Mr Partlin, can you tell me more about this, please? It's important...'

It felt like ages since Matteo had spent some time alone with Deepti, or seen her at all. She refused to join him for meals while he had guests on board, saying it didn't make sense having to give the people explanations for her presence.

He wondered whether he could spend time with her in her room later that evening, after he'd socialised with his guests for a short while after dinner—as short a time as possible. But it would still be fairly late. Matteo didn't want to turn up uninvited at night so he decided he should check with her in advance. In theory, he could send her a text, but that felt so impersonal at this stage. It wouldn't take him more than five minutes to pop down to her level and see her in person, perhaps hold her in his arms for a brief while.

If only his next meeting didn't involve a video conference with other countries—he could have asked his guests to delay their meeting. But, the quicker he got down to Deepti's deck, the more time he would have to spend with her.

He took the first couple of flights two steps at a time but slowed down when he heard his guest's voice coming up the stairwell.

'I need to prepare for my meeting, but it was a treat bumping into you here. If I can do anything to help you, let me know, Deepti.'

'No, you've already done more than you'll ever realise Mr Partlin,' Deepti said.

Matteo frowned. It didn't sound like the conversation of two people who had just met on board the yacht. How did they know each other?

'And don't worry, Deepti. I understand and I won't say anything to Mr Di Corrado about what happened.'

Hearing that, Matteo made his presence known. 'Won't say anything to me about what?'

Mr Partlin put a comforting hand on Deepti's arm. 'I'm sorry, Deepti.'

Matteo watched a slideshow of emotions cross Deepti's face. The overwhelming one was guilt. She'd been hiding something from him.

His mind immediately went to the idea the two had been having an affair but, despite his experience with his ex-fiancée, nothing Deepti had done would suggest she had another lover.

Or was he deluding himself? He would never have suspected his ex-fiancée was cheating on him but she had been. He kept his tone even when he turned to Mr Partlin and asked, 'How do you know Deepti?'

Partlin looked reluctant to answer before finally saying, 'My company is a client of her firm and Deepti was our relationship manager.'

Matteo didn't miss Deepti's sharp intake of breath.

'It was a purely business relationship,' Mr Partlin added hastily, his eyes darting from Matteo to Deepti.

'Can we please talk, Matteo?' Deepti asked.

He ignored her pleading expression and said, 'Mr Partlin, we should get back to our meeting. The others are probably waiting on video conference.' He gestured for his guest to go ahead of him.

'I'll speak to you later, Matteo,' Deepti said, putting her hand on his arm.

He pressed his lips together, not trusting himself to speak, and, shaking off her hand, he went upstairs without responding.

It was almost impossible to concentrate on the negotiations when he kept replaying the brief conversation he'd overheard.

So Deepti had had a previous career in finance. Why had she kept that hidden from him? Was it purely a coincidence that she was on the yacht?

He couldn't help recalling his initial suspicions that Deepti had engineered things to get closer to him. He'd put those doubts to the side quickly after spending time with her, even making excuses for why she was being evasive about her past. Now, it was starting to make more sense. Had he been right about her in the first place?

How much of what she'd said to him was the truth? Was she really a pastry chef with a *cordon bleu* qualification? She'd admitted she'd never crewed before and had also told him she had no restaurant experience. He couldn't see any reason why she would lie about that. So why would someone who'd had a previous career in the financial sector choose to crew on his yacht? Unless it was part of a scheme to get close to him.

He wanted to ask Mr Partlin more details but, from what he'd overheard, the man wouldn't tell him anything that Deepti didn't want him to know. He could ask her for an explanation but how much of what she said to him could he believe now? How could he ever trust anything she said to him again?

'Matteo? Matteo, do you need to take a break?' his executive assistant asked him over video, interrupting his deliberations on Deepti.

He waved a hand. 'No, let's continue,' he replied.

With a deliberate exertion of will power, he purposely put all thoughts of Deepti to the back of his mind until after dinner, when he sent her a text asking her to come to his office. He intentionally selected his office because he wanted…he needed…to keep a clear head for the conversation they needed to have. He knew himself well enough to know that was less likely to happen in a room with a bed or sofa.

Deepti had her fists clenched and her shoulders were tense when she entered the room. He pressed his lips together to resist offering her some comfort. Instead, he pointed her to the chair on the opposite side of his desk.

'Matteo, I…' she began.

He put up a hand to stop her. 'You lied to me about previous work.'

'I didn't lie. I just never told you the whole truth.'

The disappointment in her response was almost visceral.

'Don't play semantics with me. Why did you lie about your qualifications? You don't even need to have culinary qualifications to work as crew chef.'

She stiffened. 'I wasn't lying about that. I do have a *cordon bleu* certificate in pastry. That's why Alex offered me the position. But it is true he is the only reason I got it. I never crewed before.'

'You worked in the financial profession but you also have a *cordon bleu* pastry qualification. Do you know how unlikely that sounds?'

She put both palms up in a gesture of surrender.

'It's a long story,' she said with a small, weak smile.

His heart twisted at the sorrow behind her eyes. He

steeled himself not to react, not to feel sympathy. Not to feel anything. 'I don't want to hear it.' He paused. There was too much he didn't understand and he didn't like the way that made him feel. 'Why did you hide your previous job?'

'I was embarrassed.'

'Explain,' he demanded.

His worst fears were realised when Deepti told him about having failed to land a deal and losing an important client. That she would grab the opportunity to work on his boat all made sense. If she'd landed him as a client, he would have been the perfect person to help her get back into her field. She must have counted her blessings when Bella had formed an attachment to her and he'd practically begged her to be Bella's companion. Was that the real reason she'd persuaded him to spend time with Bella too—so she could get closer to him?

Or was there something more sinister behind her presence on his yacht? Had she, perhaps deliberately, joined the crew so she could find out details of his guests and exploit that information for monetary gain? She had access to the details of all the guests who came to the yacht. Coming from the financial field, she would understand exactly what kind of deals he could be working on.

He bit out the accusation, watching closely for her reaction.

'What?' She flinched, blinking rapidly. Her surprise seemed genuine, but she could be an excellent actress. She'd certainly fooled him with her feigned vulnerable openness.

'There has to be a reason you joined the crew.'

'I told you, I needed to get away for a few weeks to regroup.'

'Why should I believe anything you say?'

'You know me.'

'No, I don't. I don't know anything about you.'

Her sharp exhalation showed him his comment had hurt her. But he couldn't care about that. He didn't care about the fact she'd got fired. He didn't even care that she might have colluded with her boyfriend. He cared that she had hidden her past. He only cared about her lies.

For the first time in years, he'd opened up to someone new. He'd started to believe that he could trust someone, maybe even have a real relationship. Instead, he felt the same sense of betrayal he'd felt when Luca and Lauren had told him about their relationship. In an odd way, it felt worse.

'The helicopter will be here tomorrow morning. You need to be on it. Leave.'

CHAPTER SEVENTEEN

DEEPTI SAT ON a lounger wrapped in a blanket, watching the sun come out over the horizon. Jack had messaged to say the helicopter would be ready in a couple of hours.

She stretched. Her body wanted the rest her mind had denied her all night. She felt broken and bruised. But she refused to give into the tears pricking behind her eyelids.

Why hadn't she told Matteo the truth sooner, when he'd first asked her about job experience all those weeks ago? Nothing in her rationale made any sense, looking back at it.

Would it have made any difference if Matteo hadn't overheard her conversation with Mr Partlin? He would never believe that she had planned to tell him the truth that very day. She couldn't blame him. But he hadn't believed anything she had to say. He'd even accused her of something far worse than any reason she'd come up with for hiding the truth. Why couldn't he see that his accusation didn't even make any sense? She had gone out of her way to avoid any talk about business—why would she do that if the only reason for her to get close to him was to get information about possible deals?

Perhaps, once Matteo had calmed down, he would realise he was being unfair and there was no basis to that allegation.

She straightened her shoulders and tossed her head back.

It didn't matter. The fact he could accuse her of that demonstrated more clearly than if he had said out loud he believed she was guilty of having acted unethically. What kind of person did he believe she must be to not only come up with a plan to get close to him for her career but also to have a physical relationship with him for that reason?

Accepting the cold, stark reality that she'd developed feelings for someone who didn't know her at all hurt more than she'd thought it would. She'd slowly started to trust someone again only to find out he didn't believe in her.

She heard footsteps behind her. A glimmer of hope ignited that it could be Matteo. She swivelled her head, the hope being dashed when she saw Alex holding a plate of food.

'Morning, Dee,' Alex said. 'You didn't come to the mess for dinner yesterday and I know you didn't eat with the guests. I thought you might be hungry.'

She shook her head. 'I'm okay.'

'Jack said you're going on the helicopter.'

She nodded. 'Matteo has asked me to leave. I'm going to leave.'

'Why, though? You looked so good together, so comfortable. Everyone at the pub mentioned it. Nobody was surprised to hear he'd invited you back on the *Serendipity*.'

'It was just a fling. And now it's over.'

'Do you want to talk about it?'

'What's there to talk about? He found out I used to be a relationship manager for an investment company. That was bad enough of a deception for him. But he also knows I was fired, and now he thinks the only reason I took this job and spent time with him is because I was trying to use him to restart my career.'

Alex's jaw dropped. 'What?' he asked, with a disbelieving laugh. 'How can he even think that? Doesn't he know you at all?'

'Apparently not.' She shook her head, pressing her lips together, the pricking behind her eyes getting harder to control. 'Maybe I should have told him the truth from the start.'

Alex shrugged but his expression told her that was what he would have done.

'But was it such a bad thing to not tell him,' she said, twisting her hands. 'It didn't affect being Bella's companion. And I didn't have anything to do with his guests or business deals.'

'Of course you didn't! But Dee, you were in a relationship. Why wouldn't you tell him?'

'Oh, I don't know. Because I never make the right decisions. I do everything wrong.' She cradled her knees, resting her head on them.

'Don't you dare speak like that, Dee. If Matteo isn't listening to you and offering you support, then he doesn't deserve you.'

She straightened. She wanted to believe Alex was right.

Anger and irritation began to rise up in her, warring against the pain and hurt. What had she done that was so wrong? She hadn't told him about her past job because she didn't want him judging her like all the others had; because she'd been humiliated by her ex-boyfriend's actions; because she wanted to exist in a cocoon where the past didn't matter.

She hadn't told him because she'd been worried he wouldn't believe in her innocence. A worry that had been proved well-founded, as it turned out. How dared he doubt her innocence? Now, like then, she hadn't done anything wrong. She'd worked hard to get her *cordon bleu* qualification. He couldn't belittle that achievement. And, if he didn't believe her, he didn't believe Alex, and she wasn't going to let anyone question her friend's character. At least Alex had never doubted her.

Matteo had to realise she couldn't have conjured up Bella's attachment to her. Deepti's presence in Matteo's company had been a huge coincidence. Surely he would see that when he'd had a chance to think clearly, when he wasn't so busy with his guests? She just needed to find another chance to speak to him.

'I have to go, Alex. I need to find Matteo and speak to him.'

She couldn't find Matteo on the main deck and the offices were locked. She could go up to the owner's deck, but what would be the point? Since he'd never given her the code to open his door, she would simply be waiting out in the foyer, hoping he'd come out.

All the fight seeped out of her. What was the point of this? If she spoke to Matteo, if she managed to change his mind, what of it? Their fling was coming to an end anyway. Did it really matter if it ended while he still had a bad impression of her?

She understood that he had trust issues. He been betrayed in the worst possible way. But how could he think she was anything like his ex-fiancée? Why couldn't he trust her? She hadn't committed any crimes. She hadn't broken any laws. She had simply failed to disclose a painful situation from her past.

He should have trusted that she would never betray him. She'd gone out of her way to change the topic when he'd wanted to discuss work, and had asked Alex not to tell her who was on the guest list so there would be no way for her to get any information about what deals Matteo could be working on. She'd been very careful that she couldn't be accused of gathering inside information if she managed to get her financial career back.

And for her efforts to be scorned by Matteo...

She gritted her teeth.

It was exactly the kind of anger and outrage she needed to clear her name back home and get her life on track.

She was going to start with Matteo.

She heard the helicopter arriving above her head. She folded her arms across her chest. Matteo could try to avoid her all he wanted. She was going to speak to him. When the helicopter left with his guests, she wouldn't be on it.

She was gone.

The helicopter had left over an hour ago. Matteo swivelled his office chair to look out of the window.

Good. He didn't need people he couldn't trust around him. Deepti had proved she was just like all the others—hiding things from him and using him to achieve her own ends. If he hadn't found out the truth about Deepti's background, who knew what kind of information she could have found out and shared, affecting so many potential deals?

He'd suspected as much when he'd first met her. He should have relied on his instincts then and not let his concern for Bella affect his decision making.

Thank goodness he'd only offered her a fling. He'd almost considered asking her to prolong her stay even longer. He'd almost asked her if she would continue their relationship when he got back to England.

He buzzed Jack to let him know he could have the rest of the day off.

He was in his lounge reading a financial report when Deepti appeared at the top of the stairs.

He blinked. 'I thought you'd left.'

Deepti stuck out her jaw. 'I decided not to.'

His eyes narrowed. 'I wasn't offering you a choice.'

She shrugged carelessly. 'It wasn't convenient for me to leave today.' He stared in amazement as she sat down on the sofa next to his, leaned back and rested her head in her hands.

Who was this person? Had he ever really known her?

'Not convenient?' he repeated.

'I wasn't expecting to be in Dubai today. I don't have a hotel room booked. I chose not to spend time and effort looking for a last-minute place when I can stay on this yacht and arrive in Dubai as scheduled.'

Matteo swallowed. In his anger, he'd ordered Deepti to leave, but had taken no action to make sure she would be safe and have a place to stay. He wasn't such a cold-hearted brute that he wanted her to suffer harm for her actions.

'I'll arrange accommodation and call the helicopter to come back tomorrow.'

Deepti sat up. 'Ah, I see you're still not ready to be rational. I'll come back to talk to you tomorrow evening.'

Something intense flared in him at her determination. He steeled himself not to respond.

'You won't be here tomorrow evening,' he said.

'I'm not going anywhere. Not until we've had a chance to talk properly.'

'I have nothing to say to you.'

'That's a shame, because I have plenty to say to you.'

He'd always liked her sassiness, and the way she wasn't afraid to hold her ground against him, but there was an added anger behind her words this time.

What did she have to be angry about? That he'd discovered her secret so she couldn't use him for her career?

'More lies. I'm not interested.'

'You can call it semantics, but I never lied to you.'

'Of course, you just hid the truth.'

'Yes! I hid the truth about the most humiliating, horrible thing that ever happened to me. And you're angry that I was reluctant to share it with you.'

'Yes, because I shared the worst thing that happened to me with you.'

She flinched. He closed his eyes and took a deep breath. He hadn't wanted to admit out loud the reason her deceptive behaviour hurt him so much.

'You had every opportunity to tell me, Deepti. If it was as you're claiming, a lost deal and a lost client, why wouldn't you tell me? The truth is, you were hoping to find some information about the kinds of deals I was working on. Or maybe you were hoping to get your job back by landing me as a major client. I'm sure I'd make up for the one you lost. Just admit it; there's no need for pretence. I'm not adverse to discussing the possibility.'

And he hated how that was true despite her deceit.

'You honestly believe I'm capable of using you for that?'

Matteo pressed his lips together. A muscle spasmed in his jaw. All the fight seemed to have gone out of her. He turned his face away. He sensed Deepti scrutinising him.

Without saying a word, she left.

He half-rose from his seat, then sat back down.

It was better this way.

CHAPTER EIGHTEEN

THE FIRST TWO weeks back in London were exhausting.
Deepti threw herself into the goal of clearing her name
and finding a new job with an unearthly zeal. And, when
she wasn't trying to clear her name or search for jobs, she
was meeting up with old friends. Anything to make sure
that when it was time for bed she was so bone-weary sleep
came almost immediately.

Mr Partlin's comment that her colleague had contacted
him gave Deepti an avenue to try, since she assumed Mr
Partlin's company wouldn't be the only one they approached. While she was waiting for her contacts to get
back to her, she threw herself wholeheartedly into finding another job. The number of contacts willing to meet
her to discuss potential roles made it clear to Deepti that
she'd overestimated the effect her firing had had on her
reputation—another thing she'd got wrong.

She should have stayed in England and fought to clear
her name back when she'd first got fired instead of running away to sea with her tail between her legs. That could
have saved her a lot of heartbreak.

Deepti sighed. But she would have missed out on a lot
of fun, getting to know new people, exploring new places.

And Matteo. She couldn't regret that decision, even with

the benefit of hindsight. Not even knowing how much she missed him—every moment of every day.

She hated how much she missed him. She should be angry with him. He'd leapt to the worst conclusion about her. Not only had he disregarded her fears and feelings of shame and inadequacy at being fired from a position she'd had for over seven years, but he'd also come up with such an outlandish reason for her presence on *Serendipity*.

Her family and friends had always been behind her. It would have been good to have Matteo's support but it was never essential.

Even though she was angry, in her heart of hearts she could also understand why he doubted her. He'd been betrayed by his brother and fiancée, and in a way his parents—how could she fail to understand why trust was a such big problem for him?

He only had her word that she'd never intended to use him for her career. To him, she was probably another person who'd used her relationship with him to get what she wanted.

The reality was, after being fired, she'd lost confidence and had started second-guessing herself in a way she'd never done before. Although she had always wanted to clear her name, without her time on the yacht she might never have been prepared to fight for it the way she had been doing since coming back.

But somehow that made it harder to accept her own responsibility for the situation she was now in. Like Matteo, she'd lost her ability to trust. She hadn't been able to trust that he would be on her side when she told him the truth and she hadn't been able to trust her own judgement.

And, more importantly, she'd hadn't trusted the way she felt about Matteo. She'd been frightened of falling too fast, too soon. She'd been frightened of being able to trust her emotions after her experience with her ex-boyfriend. She'd agreed to a fling because it was safer for her than admit that she'd fallen in love in such a short space of time.

And she'd held part of herself back during their fling because she'd believed, if she didn't completely open herself up, then it wouldn't hurt so much when their affair inevitably ended—she'd been wrong about that too.

Matteo, on the other hand, had been open with her. He'd shared his past with her. Perhaps he hadn't wanted to offer her anything more than a brief fling, but he'd shown her in a hundred different ways that he cared about her.

By protecting her heart, by keeping part of her past a secret from him, wasn't she the one who'd ensured nothing real could develop between them?

She had never told him how she felt.

How she loved him.

Why had it taken her so long to admit that? Because she hadn't trusted her own feelings. She'd been scared to admit she had fallen so quickly and so deeply.

She'd accepted a brief, time-limited affair, convincing herself that if that was all on offer she would take it. But how much of her acceptance had been due to her loss of confidence and trust in herself? She hadn't believed the feelings she had for Matteo were real. They'd come on so quickly and with such intensity—she'd never experienced anything like that before.

But the point now wasn't to live in the past and wallow in the guilt of what she hadn't done. The point now was to decide what she needed to do next.

First, she was going to sort out her career. Then she was going to go to Matteo and tell him how much she loved him. If he didn't believe anything else she told him, she would make him believe that.

For the first time in a long time, she knew exactly what she was going to do, and she was absolutely certain it was the right decision.

Matteo looked out at the view of the Manhattan skyline. It had been two weeks since Deepti had left. He bit out a sharp sigh of frustration. He needed to stop measuring time in terms of Deepti.

What was she doing now? Had she managed to sort out the problems with her last job?

It hadn't taken long for him to realise his suspicion that she'd wanted to take advantage of him for business purposes was meritless. She'd gone out of her way to avoid talk about his work and had even refused to meet his guests—not the actions of someone who wanted inside information.

And it was obvious she was bright. She didn't need to use him to get her career back on track if she put her mind to it. He was confident about that.

It was easier to believe that she was untrustworthy in business than it would be to discover, one day, that she was an untrustworthy lover.

He'd grown up with his brother. He'd been with his fiancée for a few years. He hadn't suspected a thing. Which proved he couldn't trust women. He'd had a fling with a beautiful, intelligent woman. He'd enjoyed talking to Deepti as much as he'd enjoyed sleeping with her. He enjoyed her. It had ended badly a few days early, but an ending had been inevitable.

He'd had two weeks since then to put all thoughts of her

behind him. Put in context, two weeks was almost half the time they'd been together on the boat.

He gave a harsh laugh and closed his eyes. These past two weeks had dragged along, despite how many meetings he crammed in and the numerous cities he visited. In comparison, it seemed as if the time with Deepti had flown by. He'd barely spent any time with her but at the same time it felt as if he'd known her all his life.

His phone beeped, reminding him that he was due to have a video call with Bella. It took a few attempts to connect. His mother's face appeared next to Bella's.

Matteo raised his eyebrows. 'Is something wrong?' he asked.

'No, we were finishing a bedtime story from Deepti and Bella asked to read it five times. The poor dear was exhausted.'

Matteo's heart skipped, hearing Deepti's name when he'd just been thinking about her, and he damped down the impulse to ask how she was and whether she mentioned his name at all. This was his time to chat to Bella. She needed to be his focus.

Although Bella only wanted to talk about Deepti. Whenever he wasn't clear about what Bella was telling him, his mother was there to clarify. Which was how he learnt that Deepti was still looking for a job.

He thought about that after he ended the call with Bella. He didn't like thinking about Deepti struggling to find a new job. He wanted her to be happy. He ought to find a way to help her. He could put some feelers out but not have anything set in stone until Deepti said she was happy for him to go ahead.

He could introduce her to potential clients. He could even look at his personal investments. His research had highlighted that, before the incidents which had caused her to lose her job, she'd been well respected in the field and smaller companies had wanted to sign with her. His name could help open doors to some bigger companies.

He would do whatever it took to show her he had been wrong and that he trusted and believed in her completely.

He was due to stay in New York for another four days, but he didn't like the idea of Deepti suffering on her own. He contacted his executive assistant in London to discuss cancelling his meetings and returning to England. Her barely concealed surprise was understandable. He was not behaving in character at all.

'Would you like me to make an urgent appointment with your doctor? she asked, suddenly concerned.

He shook his head. 'I'm fine.' Naturally he hadn't told her about Deepti, and he had no intention of explaining himself. 'Oh, I'm also going to send you a list of people. Can you get their contact numbers and ideally line up phone calls with them over the next week?' He would get the details of people in his network who would do him a favour and help Deepti out.

'Okay, Matteo. I'll see what I can do. I'm sure I'll be able to reschedule or delegate the meetings you have set for the next few days.'

'I don't know.' Matteo paused. The Deepti he knew would not be pleased if he forged ahead, trying to sort out her career without discussing it with her first. 'In fact, get me the contact details, but put a hold on organising those meetings for now.'

'Are you sure everything is okay, Matteo?' Her concern was not unsurprising, since he'd never been this indecisive before.

He smiled to reassure her. 'I am fine. I need to sort out

something in England first. Assume I'm not available for any meetings for seventy-two hours after I get to England.'

'Seventy-two hours?' The high-pitched incredulity in her tone made Matteo's lips quirk.

'At least seventy-two. In fact, instead of rescheduling my meetings, delegate them all.' Travelling on the yacht had shown him a different pace of life. He wasn't the only person who could handle everything that came up in his business. 'If they can't be delegated, cancel them. I'm going to take a holiday. For two weeks.'

'You're taking a holiday? For two weeks?'

He was in danger of his executive assistant sending him for medical evaluation at this rate. He threw her a bone.

'I need to see someone and sort things out. I don't know how long that's going to take. But that's the priority.'

His executive assistant grinned. 'No, that's absolutely fine. I will take care of everything. I'll get you on the first flight out tomorrow morning, unless you want to charter a private jet.'

'Tomorrow will be fine.'

'Perfect. Leave everything to me. And Matteo?'

'Yes?'

'I hope everything works out with Deepti,' she said as she ended the call.

His jaw dropped, then he laughed. He shouldn't be surprised that his executive assistant knew about Deepti. She knew everything that was going on. He only hoped he could introduce them one day; they would get on like a house on fire.

He sat back and swivelled his seat towards the skyline view.

Yes, Deepti was important to him. He wanted to see her. Would she agree to see him after the way he'd behaved?

He'd overreacted to her confession because it had been easier to convince himself she was just another woman who couldn't be trusted than one day face the possibility that she would betray him, as his fiancée had.

But he knew, beyond a shadow of a doubt, Deepti would never do that. He'd been upset by her lack of faith in him; that she hadn't felt secure enough in *them* to share such an important situation with him. But the only reason she'd had the power to evoke that reaction from him was because of the way he felt about her. She was able to hurt him deeply because he had already developed a strong and deep affection for her.

It was so different from the way he had felt about Lauren. When he'd found out about Luca's and Lauren's relationship, it was his brother's betrayal that had hurt him more, and that should have told him everything. But in his anger and hurt he had made himself believe Lauren was the love of his life who his brother had stolen from him.

The reality was he had proposed to Lauren because they had been together for two years and he'd felt it was the right step to take. They had already started to grow apart soon after he'd proposed, and his loss of interest had made her become an after-thought in the busy-ness of building up his business. In all his brief flings since then, his dates had always been after-thoughts too.

Until Deepti. Deepti was always his first thought, if not his every thought. He *needed* to see to her. Not only to help her sort out her career. And not only to tell her he was sorry he'd doubted her, although he prayed she would accept his apology.

He wanted to tell her he loved her. Because he did.

He knew she had helped him open his heart to Bella and Leo, but it was only now dawning on him that he'd been able to do that because he'd started opening his heart to her too. Probably from the first day they'd met when she'd been covered in flour but still the most beautiful person he'd ever seen. Her humour and kindness had shone through.

He would give anything for a chance to be with her and hoped that one day she would learn to love him too.

And he would never give her cause to doubt whether he loved her or whether she was the most important thing in his life because he would show her every day.

But first he had to get to see her in England and hope she didn't slam the door in this face.

CHAPTER NINETEEN

IN THE END, it had been surprisingly easy to clear her name, Deepti reflected a week later. As she suspected, she could have sorted this situation out almost immediately if she'd had confidence in herself and trusted her own judgement.

Once it had been made clear that she hadn't been involved in the collapse of the deal or the loss of the client, her old employer had asked her to return, but Deepti had been firm that she needed to move forward, not take a backward step. Instead, she had accepted a new position with a smaller start-up company which would use her skills in a different, more challenging way.

But the job wouldn't start for another month so that left the last item on her list—Matteo.

If only sorting things out with him would be so easy. Matteo had made it clear to her that they would never have anything more than a short fling. It would have been over in a matter of days even if he hadn't ended it early. If she tried to contact him, would that be going backwards? This wasn't the first time one of her relationships had ended, and those ones had lasted a lot longer.

Deepti sighed, knowing it wasn't about going backwards or longevity. The intensity of her feelings and the sense of being complete when she was with Matteo wasn't something that came easily. And loving him wasn't something that would go easily, either.

When she'd first left *Serendipity*, she'd kept waiting for reason and rational thought to kick in and show her that it had only been the close proximity of being on the yacht with Matteo that had led her to develop such intense feelings for him.

But now she was ignoring those doubts and listening to her heart instead. And her heart was telling her Matteo was the love of her life. Openly admitting she loved him was liberating. But it wasn't enough, and it wouldn't be until she was able to tell Matteo how she felt.

How would he react? Putting aside the fact he didn't believe her reasons why she'd hidden the truth about her job, he'd made it very clear that he wasn't prepared to, and couldn't, offer her a real relationship.

All Matteo had wanted was a fling and, now that it was over, did she ever cross his mind? She was still scared. But she was going to gather up all her reserves and believe in herself—believe in her feelings.

The difficult part would be getting to speak to Matteo in the first place. She didn't know his home address. She didn't even know which country he was in right now. Tracey didn't have any information, even though Matteo was keeping up his video calls with Bella.

Alex had told her Matteo had never returned to the yacht from Dubai and the crew were making their way to Southampton without expecting Matteo to return. Alex promised to contact her when he had more information but all she'd received from him was a text that morning saying:

Forgiveness not permission.

She'd sent a question mark in response but hadn't heard anything since.

She pulled out her phone again. Why wasn't she taking the simplest option and phoning him, or even sending a text? Wouldn't that be better than trying to locate him and possibly force a confrontation in his office?

She scrolled to Matteo's contact details and had her thumb over the call button. Then she put the phone on her coffee table. If she was going to call him, she wanted to rehearse what she was going to say first. She went to search for some pen and paper. Words weren't her strong point and she needed to make sure she got them right. She might only have one shot at this, if she was lucky. He could reject her call. And, if she was going to have to resort to leaving a voicemail, she didn't want it to be a rambling, incoherent mess.

Half an hour later, crumpled pieces of paper with her failed attempts were everywhere. This was the reason people went digital. Why was writing from her heart so hard?

She was grateful for the ring of her doorbell—she needed a break to refocus.

When she opened the door, she blinked a few times to make sure she wasn't imagining Matteo standing in front of her.

She sighed. Had her memory downplayed how attractive he was or had he got even more gorgeous in the few weeks they'd been apart?

She stood back to allow him into her flat. Behind his back, she pinched the skin on her wrist—the pain was enough to convince her she wasn't dreaming.

'How did you know where I live?' she asked, her mind blank of anything else as she led him into her living room and gestured for him to sit down.

'Alex gave me your address.'

'Alex?' She furrowed her brow. 'Oh, that explains his text.'

'Pardon?'

She shook her head. 'Nothing. Why are you here, Matteo?'

She'd wanted to see him and been planning out what she had to say to him. But now he was here, in her home in front of her, she felt completely unprepared.

Matteo pulled a piece of paper out of his jacket. 'I have a list of people you can contact who may be able to help you with your job hunt. I can make the introductions if you need.'

A pang in her chest made it feel as if her heart was breaking. He was offering her exactly what he had suspected she had schemed to use him for. She didn't know why he was offering this now, but it didn't really matter. His offer could only mean one thing—he still didn't believe her. He still didn't trust her. The little kernel of hope that had stubbornly refused to die out over the last couple of weeks finally crumbled. And it hurt.

She took a deep breath and blinked to relieve the pressure of the tears building in her eyes.

'Thank you, Matteo. But that's not necessary. I actually have a new job starting soon. I promise you, I didn't work on the yacht to sign you as a client. I can't think of anything I can say to convince you.'

Matteo furrowed his brows. 'I don't think you were using me for your career.'

'What?' she asked, her mouth falling open.

'Okay, my immediate reaction was that you wanted to use me to help me with your career. But it didn't take long to realise I was wrong.'

'You were wrong?' Was she really hearing this?

'Very wrong. The most wrong I've ever been.' He said it with such a matter-of-fact tone, she giggled. He'd admitted he'd been wrong, so did that mean he was ready to trust her?'

'I was looking for a reason to distrust you,' he continued. 'You could have told me you were arrested for releasing the penguins at the zoo and I would have found a way to turn that into a betrayal of me.'

As Deepti crinkled her face, trying to understand his random example, Matteo reached out a finger to trace the furrows on her brow. She grabbed his hand and held it in hers. She never wanted to let go.

'I never cared about what happened with your job,' he said. 'I only cared that you hid it from me. I don't understand why you had to keep it a secret.'

'Neither do I,' Deepti replied with a grimace. 'I didn't trust myself, so nothing I was doing made any sense. I was so sure something I'd done had led to my firing. I was scared of making another mistake or trusting in the wrong people. I was so frightened of making the wrong decision, it made me incapable of making any rational decision at all. You were one of the few good things happening to me and I couldn't risk losing that.'

'I'm sorry I made you feel vulnerable. If I had shown you I trusted you, perhaps you would have been more open with me.'

'You can't blame yourself, Matteo. It was nothing you did. I love you and I just couldn't bear the idea of you thinking badly of me.'

'You love me?'

Deepti automatically covered her mouth, as if that would take back the words that had slipped out. Then she straightened her shoulders.

'This isn't the way I planned to tell you, but yes, I do. I love you. I know we've only known each other for a few weeks, and we barely know each other really, but I have absolutely no doubts about the way I feel about you. I love you.'

Silence greeted her. She could read his look of disbelief, so she continued, 'Please don't feel awkward. I'm not expecting anything—'

'I love you too.'

Deepti's breath came out in a laugh. 'What?'

'I love you, Deepti.'

She threw back her head and laughed with sheer exhilaration. Was this what complete happiness felt like? Giving a small shriek, she threw her arms around him and raised her mouth to meet his...

A long time later, Matteo leaned against the back of the couch while Deepti went to get some refreshments.

He looked around her living room. It was bright and cosy and perfectly like her. She was a little bit messier than he'd expected, judging by all the crumpled paper on the floor. He noticed a pad of the same type of paper on the coffee table in front of him and leaned forward to take a closer look.

Hi, Matteo,
It's Deepti... Deepti Roy

It read like a conversation rather than a letter. He laughed. As if he needed her surname, or even her first name! He would have known who it was the moment she spoke.

I'm sorry for not telling you the truth sooner. I have no excuses. I just wanted to let you know I love you.

The last three words were circled with an annotation:

Too soon. Move to nearer the end.

He smiled up at Deepti when she came back into the room.

'What is this?' he asked.

She squealed and almost spilled the drinks in her rush to place them on the table, before attempting to get the paper out of his hands. She landed on his chest. He dropped the paper, grabbed her closer and covered her with his kisses.

'I adore you,' he said when they finally broke apart.

'I still can't believe it,' she said with a slight shake of her head.

'I'll show you how much every day for the rest of my life, so you never have to doubt it. I never believed in love at first sight until you.'

She sighed deeply. In a quiet, uncertain voice, she asked, 'Are you sure?'

He cupped her face and, staring deep into her eyes, he answered simply, 'Yes.'

'I'm scared, Matteo. We've known each other for such a short time. Barely a month. And our actual relationship was only a few days. I know the way I feel about you is real. I know I truly love you. I want to trust this can last, but I'm scared.'

'I'm scared too. There are no guarantees in this life, but losing Luca suddenly made me realise we have to go after what we want while we still can. And I want you. I know I will always love you. I want you to believe that. I want you to trust that your love for me isn't fleeting and you will always love me too.'

'I really want to. I'm trying to. But I've never felt this way before.'

'Isn't that a reason to believe this time it's different? If we're not meant for each other, why would we feel this strongly?'

She inclined her head. 'You're right. This is the real thing.'

'Then marry me.'

'What?' Her mouth fell open. Her shocked look was so incredibly endearing, he gathered her too him and covered her in long, deep, passionate kisses until they were both out of breath.

When they broke for oxygen, she pushed him away slightly. 'Matteo, you can't just say things like that and then kiss me so I can't think straight.'

He laughed. That sounded perfect to him. He didn't want her to think straight when she was around him. When she was thinking straight, it seemed as though her brilliant, logical mind came up with every possible obstacle to their relationship.

'I'm not asking you to marry me because I want to ease your mind. I'm asking you to marry me because I love you. And I am absolutely certain I want to spend the rest of my life with you.'

Getting off the sofa, he reached into his pocket and pulled out a small jewellery box as he went down on one knee. 'This isn't a whim. You know I don't do things on a whim.' He noticed her grin and qualified his statement. 'Okay, perhaps when it comes to you it feels like I'm making and changing plans on a whim. But you have to understand, I am completely in love with you. I have been from the first moment we met.'

She tilted her head, as if she wasn't sure whether she

was hearing him properly or whether he was going to tell her he was joking. He swallowed heavily. She had to believe him. This was the most important answer he had ever waited for. He held his breath.

With a shake of her head, she said, 'I can't believe I'm doing this,' as she held out her hand for the ring.

'That sounds like a yes. Is that a yes?'

She laughed, and then nodded vigorously. 'It's a yes,' she said as she threw herself onto him, her momentum knocking him back onto the floor.

Deepti sat in Matteo's warm embrace, staring at the diamond on her finger. Her family and friends would probably think she was acting out of character but, in the end, accepting Matteo's proposal had been the easiest, most sensible decision she'd ever made.

But there were a lot of decisions still to be made. They wouldn't sort out everything that day, but they needed to make a start.

'Where do you want to live?' she asked. With Matteo's business interests, they could be facing a long-distance relationship, and she wanted to be prepared.

'Well,' Matteo said, placing a kiss on the top of her head. 'I recently proved I can work from anywhere. The middle of the ocean, if necessary. I suggest the simplest solution is for me to follow you. Where is your new job?'

'London.'

'Then we'll find a place together. Until then, I can move in here, or you can move in with me. If we're going to get married soon, there's no reason not to live together straight away.'

Deepti pulled away slightly and craned her neck to look at him. 'Soon?'

He shrugged. 'Why wait? Unless you want to organise a very big wedding?'

'Not really. To be honest, I never thought about getting married. I never met anyone I felt that strongly about.'

'Until me,' Matteo prompted.

She giggled. 'Until you.'

'Do you want to get married in England or in India?'

She thought about it for a moment. 'Actually, I think, if we're going to get married soon, I'd like to get married in Singapore.'

'Singapore? So Bella can be there?'

'She is the reason we met.'

'I think serendipity's the reason we met.'

Deepti laughed again. She didn't know if he was referring to his yacht, but he was right. It was through serendipity that she'd met Matteo and it was her destiny to love him, and be loved by him, for ever.

* * * * *

CLAIMING HIS CONVENIENT PRINCESS

SUSAN MEIER

MILLS & BOON

To everyone who posts cat pictures on Facebook.

Strawberry and Shortcake are a combination of all your fun felines!

CHAPTER ONE

PRINCE LIAM SOKOL didn't mind driving in snow. The mountains of his country, Prosperita, got snow and he skied. He'd even skied the United States Rocky Mountains, where he was driving now.

The rhythmic flip, flip, flip of the windshield wipers filled his silent Range Rover, as huge white flakes fell like rain. He was comfortable in the United States because while its citizens were interested in royals, they didn't recognize most, except England's Windsors. He could drive himself. He could go to restaurants and bars, to Broadway shows and skiing without a bodyguard.

The freedom of it was intoxicating.

Still, he wasn't adamant about having spans of freedom the way his brother Axel was. Liam liked a day or two of being anonymous, but he'd spent his life being groomed to replace his father as King of Prosperita. He knew the sacrifices that came with the job, and he'd grown to accept them.

His heart tweaked. Had someone told him three years ago that the love of his life would be one of the things he would have to give up, he wouldn't have believed it. He would abdicate the throne before he'd live without Lilibet. But in the end, she'd made the choice. She would not cost him his destiny. She'd cut him off without another word and he never saw her again.

Anger flickered through him, not just at the idea that she'd made the choice, but that fate had been so cruel as to put them in that position—

He forced his anger away. At thirty-three, he knew better than to argue with the force of purpose, the invisible hand that pushed one man in one direction and another in the opposite.

A sign came into view, indicating he should turn left. His GPS told him to make two more lefts and suddenly he was off roads that had been cleared of snow and in a winter wonderland. The heavy flakes bent the limbs of fir trees and poured to ground already covered in a foot of white. His SUV skidded and he yanked it back on the road, then the cabin came into view. Logs stacked upon logs created the small but cozy hideaway.

With everything blanketed in snow, he wasn't sure where the driveway was—or if there even was one—so he pulled onto the property, to the left of the mailbox and stopped his vehicle. Stepping out, he took a long, deep breath of the pristine air and simply listened to the sound of nothing, as snow rained down on him.

He'd never felt this peace, this *privacy*. But along with it came the sense of destiny again—this time so strong he could almost reach out and touch it. This moment, this place, meant something.

But wasn't that why he was here? To seal the deal on the second biggest part of his responsibilities as heir to the throne of Prosperita?

Not wanting to dwell on that, he raced to the cabin door. He retrieved the combination from a saved text, punched it into the keypad on the frame and heard the lock click. With a quick twist of the knob, he was inside.

An overstuffed gray sofa sat in front of a cold fireplace. To the right was a small kitchen with an old-fashioned wooden table and chairs. An open door down a hall exposed an aged bathroom. He assumed the two closed doors went to bedrooms.

He shrugged out of his black puffy jacket and headed to the fireplace. The cabin wasn't cold, but it wasn't warm either. Seeing a stack of logs and some kindling, he made a fire. Not only would that take the chill off, but it would also create some much-needed ambiance.

Twenty minutes later, a nice fire had turned the chill into comforting warmth. The door opened, and Liam automatically faced it. Blinded by the afternoon sun reflecting off the snow, he couldn't make out much about his visitor except that she was medium height and wearing a lot of winter gear.

"Liam?"

He liked her voice. Soft and melodious, it took away his worst fear that his potential bride was an angry shrew.

"Demi?"

She closed the door and his eyes quickly adjusted. As she took off her ski cap, long, dark hair tumbled out. "Yes. I'm Demi Viglianco."

He strode over, offering his hand. "It's a pleasure to meet you."

She eyed his hand. "So that's how this is going to be? All business?"

He laughed. "I couldn't exactly grab you and kiss you. I thought a handshake might be a good way to start things off."

Slipping out of her coat, she snorted. "Start things off. That's funny. It seems our fathers have already done the deal."

"Not really. If you find me repulsive, or if I find you repulsive—"

Doubtful considering that the dark hair she'd freed from

her ski cap fell to the middle of her back in big, bouncy curls and her dark eyes were wide and interesting. Her father was a prince, but he was like Axel. The second son. Not a king. Her dad had been influential in their country's parliament, but he'd begun to gamble and was in danger of not only being ousted from his job, but also losing his estate. The Viglianco family was in trouble.

Still, Demi's lineage and her family's hard times were the things that made their current deal possible. Liam needed a suitable wife. Demi's family needed a bailout. They were a match made in heaven.

"—Then either one of us can bow out. That's why I thought it was a good idea for us to meet in private, so far away that our fathers aren't any the wiser that we'd met to discuss their decision."

"You're saying I can get out of this?"

"Of course." Never in a million years would he force a woman to marry him. He was as much of a catch as she was. *Person* magazine listed him as one of the ten most eligible bachelors in the *world*. Marrying him shouldn't be a hardship.

"You're so naïve. You might have choices, but my father has seen to it that I don't."

That was when he looked at her face. Really looked at it. Her features were delicate, but there was a hardness to the set of her mouth. The eyes he'd thought interesting had filled with a defiance that matched the upward tilt of her chin.

"You most certainly have a choice!"

She gaped at him as if he were deluded.

"Why would I want to marry a woman who didn't want to marry me?"

"Why would you have your father choose a bride for you at all?"

There was that word again. Choice. The one time he genuinely could have made a choice—made a decision that would have changed the course of his life—Lilibet had snatched the opportunity from his hands.

Shoving those thoughts out of his head, he said, "When my younger brother married two years ago, it called attention to the fact that I was very single."

"Aww, did the bullies in the castle tease you?"

He frowned at the very clear insult. Pride and dignity fought to respond. He gave dignity the floor, keeping pride in his back pocket just in case he needed it. "I'm a man destined to be a king. Part of that responsibility is to produce an heir."

"Yeah. I get that." She stepped into the room, closer to the fireplace. "It's wicked out there."

Dignity seemed to have worked. Not only had she agreed with him, but her voice had lost its snark. Still, he didn't think she'd become any happier about marrying him. He had no idea what to say or why she'd even agreed to this meeting. If she was so against an arranged marriage, why hadn't she simply told her father she wouldn't have any part of it?

"Look. I meant what I said. I don't want to marry someone who doesn't want to marry me. You can back out."

"Not really."

"I understand that your family is going into this because of financial problems. But money is only money. You can figure out another way."

"Marrying you *is* the other way."

He frowned, watching as she inched closer to the fire to warm her hands. Dread and doubt filled him. Had Lilibet made him so jaded that he'd marry a woman who sniped at him?

No. He didn't have to be a genius to know this was not

the woman of his dreams. She was the woman of his night-mares. This marriage would be a battle and he'd already had his share of uphill climbs, thank you very much.

He would not be marrying her.

Demi held her hands close to the fire to warm them as she glanced at Liam Sokol out of the corner of her eye.

He. Was. Gorgeous.

Pale hair. Eyes the color of the sky on a cloudless after-noon. Tall and thin, in a sweater and jeans that displayed the body of a swimmer. If anybody took inventory of this transaction, she was the one getting the better deal.

Except she didn't like being sold to the highest bidder.

She didn't like being used as a possession that could be traded away on her father's whim.

She took a breath, then another, forcing herself to be calm when she wanted to panic.

Liam's voice came from across the room. "So, we agree? We're not going through with the deal?"

She swallowed. She had no idea how her father would handle it if she backed out. Especially when the bank was only a month away from foreclosing on their estate, but it wasn't *her* backing out. Technically, Liam had brought it up first. He'd called this meeting. He'd been the first to say they weren't going through with the deal.

Her dignity returned, but she wondered why. Her parents would still go bankrupt—

Unless she married Liam Sokol.

Her choice was one kind of prison or another.

What was the saying? Better the devil you know than the devil you don't? She would figure out how to handle her angry father. She would also find a way to make sure her mother wasn't put out on the street.

She faced Liam. "No. I don't want to get married."

And with those words she sealed her fate. But at least it was a fate she had chosen. She also felt good about making the decision face to face. Prince Liam Sokol knew there was nothing wrong with him. She hoped there were no hard feelings. But what difference did it make? With her family about to lose everything, she would have to get a job, and he was a royal. It wasn't like their paths would cross again.

She plucked her jacket from the back of the sofa. "No point in us staying here then. I should get back to Hermosa."

He nodded.

She smiled at him to take the sting out of her refusal to marry him. She hated that he'd traveled halfway around the world for nothing. But she had honestly believed she could force herself to marry him for her family's sake.

In the end, her need for autonomy was stronger than her need to take the easy way out of her family's troubles.

"I hope everything works out for you, Demi Viglianco."

He smiled wistfully and something tightened her chest. He really was good looking. And honest. He'd given her the opportunity her father hadn't. He'd let her make her own choice.

She slid into her jacket. "Goodbye, Liam Sokol."

She turned to the door but pivoted back again. "I hope you understand that this is nothing personal."

He snorted. "We don't know each other. The deal was obviously made without your consent. I understand."

One look in those pretty blue eyes and she realized he wasn't just saying that. He did understand.

Her smile warmed. "Thank you."

She opened the door and stepped out into the increasingly thick snow. A twinge of a warning bell sounded in her brain. She couldn't tell if it was from the amount of snow that covered the road or her father's potential reaction to her breaking this deal, but now that she'd made her choices, she had to keep moving. She got into her rented SUV, started the engine and pulled out, but couldn't really find the road. She suspected it was a swatch of space that split the forest into two sides, but the precise location of the road was a mystery.

She went twenty feet, her SUV's big tires not intimidated by the snow, but visibility went from bad to worse—and seriously, where the hell was the actual road?

She took a long breath, then another. She hadn't gone so far that she couldn't put her vehicle in Reverse and return to the cabin—

A weird feeling of dread climbed up her chest. She'd made a good exit. They'd agreed not to marry. The intimation that they'd never see each other again had filled the air. Now she was going back?

No. She didn't think so.

Her decision had been made.

CHAPTER TWO

LIAM DECIDED TO spend the night in the cabin. He didn't find food in any of the cupboards, but he did find a wine fridge and some marshmallows. He turned on the TV and watched a few movies, sipping wine and eating marshmallows before he fell asleep. In the morning, he woke cold and hungry, but the storm was over. Looking out the window at the thick snow, he had a moment of worry about how Demi had fared getting through the drifts, but she was an adult. Her choice had been to leave. She was stubborn enough that he probably couldn't have changed her mind, no matter how much he'd argued.

Jumping into his SUV, he reminded himself to check on her when he returned to Prosperita.

He tried not to think about her anymore, but the drive was long and boring. And their fifteen minutes together seemed to have permanently imprinted themselves in his brain. The real absurdity of the situation was that he'd liked the Demi who no longer had to marry him. The Demi who thought she had to be his bride had been angry and borderline insulting, but once they'd made the decision not to keep the bargain their fathers had made, she'd seemed nice.

He shook his head to clear it. She'd been angry for fourteen and a half minutes and happy walking out the door. That was hardly nice.

Hours later, he reached the private airstrip, where his family's smallest jet sat waiting for him. He left the rented Range Rover in the hands of an employee and climbed aboard. An attendant walked over to take his coat and offer him coffee.

He laughed. "Coffee would be great. If I could get it with a bagel that would be even better."

She bowed slightly. "Yes, Your Highness."

A feeling of normalcy settled over him. No more snow. No more driving himself. No marshmallows. He was in his jet, about to get real food and go home—

Where he had to tell his dad that his matchmaking had failed?

Damn. He'd been so intent on giving Demi the way out that she so obviously wanted that he'd forgotten that part.

He tried to watch a movie, but his attention span had deserted him. There was no point planning arguments or a clever way to break the news to his dad, the King of his country. He simply had to be straightforward and honest.

They refueled in New York, and he slept part of the second leg of the flight over the Atlantic. By the time they landed in Prosperita, he had showered and wore jeans and a T-shirt. He'd hoped to slip into the castle unnoticed, but his father happened to be walking through the elaborate front foyer with the grand stairway when he arrived.

"Liam?" His dark-haired, dark-eyed father looked at Liam's T-shirt and jeans with a frown.

Given that he was thirty-three, he knew his father wouldn't question his whereabouts for the past forty-eight hours, if he'd even noticed Liam had been gone. But the King was not a fan of anyone dressing down this close to the royal offices. Only Axel got away with it.

Still, there were more important things to discuss than

his jeans and T-shirt. Liam wasn't one to put off difficult conversations.

"I'm just getting home from a trip to the States, and as much as I'd like to crash there's something you and I need to discuss first."

"Okay."

"In private."

His father's tone changed. "Okay." He motioned for Liam to follow him down the marble floors of a silent corridor lined with portraits of their ancestors. When they reached his office, he directed Liam to take a seat in front of his desk. He hadn't said a word the entire walk, and neither had Liam. The first thing the Prince had learned from his father about being a king was discretion.

Once the door closed, he would talk.

His father nodded and one of his assistants scrambled to close the door.

Liam took a breath and jumped in with both feet. "The marriage you arranged for Demi Viglianco and me is off."

His father sat up. "What? Liam, you asked me to arrange a marriage for you! I did. Now you're saying you don't want it?"

"*She* doesn't want it."

Jozef's face scrunched in confusion. "What?"

"I needed to be sure we were doing the right thing, away from the press and away from any sort of pressure she might have felt. So, we met in the Rockies."

He gaped at him. "You met your future bride in the States?"

"No one recognizes me there and it wasn't as much of a trip for her, coming up from Central America." He took a breath. "I just wanted to be sure the marriage was what we wanted."

"Or were you trying to make sure she was as attractive as her picture?"

He laughed. "Maybe a little. But really you and mom at least knew each other before you decided to marry," Liam said, referring to his father's first marriage to one of Jozef's school friends, which had been arranged by his parents. "I didn't want to be tied to someone all wrong for me. I just needed some assurances before we committed."

His dad leaned back in his chair. "What happened?"

"She told me that she felt like she was being sold. That she hadn't been given a choice."

"Her family is about to lose everything. She's right. She didn't have a choice."

"But that's just it. Her father made *his* problem into her problem."

"She will never be able to pay off her father's debts."

He remembered her contrariness and winced. "I don't think she even intends to try."

"They will lose an estate that her father purchased with the inheritance that came with his title. He has nothing else, and he's mortgaged that property to the hilt."

"She knows her family's in trouble. She still rejected the marriage."

Leaning back in his chair, Jozef stared at the ceiling. "This is all wrong."

"Yeah, well, she was so happy when I let her off the hook that it was insulting. I'm pretty sure it's the right thing."

"Did you even talk at all? Because fifteen minutes with her should have shown you she's perfect for you. She's smart. Graduated at the top of her class at university. She has a heart for public service. Rather than get a job, she runs a homeless shelter that's connected to a food pantry. Everybody who knows her loves her. And she's beautiful. All of which mean, she would be an excellent queen."

"Yeah, well, she doesn't want to be. And I'm not the

kind of person who forces someone into something they don't want."

"I don't think you understand the whole picture. If she doesn't marry you, her dad's going to marry her off to someone. He's so far in debt he has no choice but to keep looking for a match for her until he finds one. He sees her as an asset…his only asset right now. And the next guy he chooses might not be as trustworthy as you are."

Liam frowned. "Which is it? She's perfect to be a queen or she's in trouble?"

"Both. Think of the non-royals who make arranged marriages—men who might want to have a real princess for a wife. Some of these people are looking to make themselves legitimate. Royal blood is an easy way to get in with the right people."

"You're saying her dad would marry her off to a criminal?"

"I'm saying more like cartel."

Liam's breathing stopped.

"When I didn't immediately jump on the chance to make the marriage, Demi's dad mentioned that he had other prospects," Jozef said. "One of them was with someone in a ruthless cartel. I knew he wasn't bluffing or trying to speed our negotiations along. The man is desperate. He had feelers out everywhere, doing what he believes he has to do. If you walk away, Demi's next potential suitor would be someone to whom she absolutely wouldn't want to be tied. And believe me, she could run, and she could even hide, but if her dad takes money from the cartel, her options are gone. A match with you kept her dad from even initiating a discussion. But if you two break the deal, all bets are off.

"Think again about this marriage, Liam. I chose Demi because I believe she would be a good wife, a good queen. I won't lie and say we aren't getting some important things out of the contract like trade routes and alliances that we need. As technology increases, the world grows smaller. We can't sit huddled in the Mediterranean with only our neighbors for allies. We need a strong connection to the West. But the other side of the big picture is that if we don't do this, Demi could be in real trouble. Consider who would have money enough to make the kind of deal her father needs."

Liam took a breath. Once again, his dad was right. About everything. The trade routes, the alliances and Demi's future. She might not want to be in an arranged marriage, but she could change her mind about marriage to *him* when she hears that if she doesn't, her dad fully intended to marry her off to someone.

The King rose from his seat, ending the meeting. "Get her to marry you. Not only is she a good choice for you and Prosperita, but also marrying you ends the trouble for her."

Liam nodded. "I'll go to Hermosa and talk to her."

His father headed for the door but stopped suddenly. "Use that charm you're so famous for."

"Axel's the one with the charm."

"Oh, don't be so modest. I hear the rumors. This woman is right for you. I can feel it in my bones. Don't go to Hermosa to *talk* to her. Go to *get* her. Bring her here where she belongs. Where she'll be safe. Before her father starts looking for a deal again."

The King left and Liam shook his head, as he rose from his chair and walked out of his dad's office. His father would have used the elevator to the left, so he turned right, going to the foyer and the huge circular stairway.

Given the choice of marrying him or potentially being paired off with someone in the Cartel, Demi would surely marry him.

A little voice in the back of his head did not like the idea of going to her country to convince her—especially since this deal essentially saved *her*—yet he was the one humbling himself.

Usually, he was smart enough not to let pride get in his way. He also realized his opposition to this idea might stem from being tired from the long trip. For as nice as Demi had become once he'd freed her from their deal, she'd been angry when she'd arrived at the cabin. He did not want to see her get involved in the trouble that would come her way if she didn't marry him. But he wasn't so naïve as to believe this marriage would be easy.

He stepped into his apartment, pulling his T-shirt over his head, happy at the thought of a shower. But the second the shirt was off, his phone vibrated. He pulled it out of his pocket, realizing he hadn't heard it ring because he'd sent everything to voicemail knowing he had to talk with his father.

He hit the few buttons to pull up the message and the voice he had once loved more than any other floated to him.

"Liam… It's Lilibet. I'm sorry to be calling but I wanted you to hear this from me. Not someone else." She took a long breath.

His heart stopped. She had not called him in two years. Whatever she had to say was bad.

"I'm getting married. An American businessman. He's a good man and I'm finally happy. I just…didn't want you to read about it in the papers."

She clicked off the call and he sank to a chair.

She was getting married?

His heart froze. His chest muscles tightened to the point he almost couldn't breathe. He hadn't realized he'd harbored a secret hope that she would change her mind and come back to him, but he must have. Otherwise, the news wouldn't have stopped his heart.

He poured two fingers of Scotch and downed it, then

pulled himself together. He was a prince, who would be a king one day. The news caught him off guard, but he refused to crumble.

Refused.

This was his life. He would be a king. He intended to be a good one. If he wasn't, losing Lilibet would have been for nothing.

And with the way this hurt, he couldn't let losing the woman he adored be for nothing.

The next morning, he flew to Hermosa, off to rescue the woman who didn't want to marry him. While the love of his life was about to marry someone who made her happy. Finally. As if their time together had not made her happy.

Of course, Lilibet could have been referring to the fact that their relationship had been doomed from the start. Or the fact that her inability to have children made a relationship with a man who had to produce an heir impossible.

And whoever this American was, he made her happy.

While he was off to convince a contrary woman that she needed to be his wife.

Just as he didn't want to see Lilibet unhappy anymore, he also had to accept the fact that once again his life was difficult—

No, more like a never-ending job. A long stream of duties and responsibilities. With little to no personal life. Because that's who he was. A guy who would be a king.

He had to stop thinking about love and romance and do his duty. His father believed Demi would make a good queen. *That's* where his focus needed to be.

Once again, they stopped in New York to refuel. Five hours after that, he stepped off the plane into a tropical paradise. The sun had risen on a new day, and they'd landed in a rainstorm that covered most of the midsized country nestled against the Caribbean Sea. Flying over, he'd seen the green forests and farmland soaking up the rain like a gift from heaven.

A good feeling finally filled him. Her lame duck father might be trouble, but Demi's uncle, the King, was a true leader of a strong country. This genuinely was an alliance Prosperita needed. And he would secure it. Demi might be strong willed, but so was he. He would convince her.

Black umbrella in hand, he raced to a waiting limo arranged by Russ Krajewski, head of Prosperita's Castle Admin. Russ had allowed him to go to Hermosa with only two bodyguards who would follow him in a separate vehicle and stay outside while he spoke with Demi. He would need privacy to convince her getting married was the right thing to do. He did not want anyone overhearing that her father would probably marry her off to someone in a cartel, any more than he wanted anyone knowing that Lilibet was getting married.

After a quick trip to the Viglianco estate where a member of the household staff told him Demi was in town, working at the homeless shelter, he was on the road again, heading to the small city. His two guards followed behind in their black SUV.

They cruised along streets lined with office buildings and a few banks. Those gave way to a section with restaurants and shops that led to condo buildings clumsily interspersed with houses.

Suddenly the limo stopped by a bright blue three-story building that bustled with activity. Laughing people stood along the sidewalk, as pedestrians strolled by, probably going to the farmer's market only twenty or thirty feet down the street.

Liam opened the window separating him from the driver. "This is it?"

Giorgio leaned his arm across the back of his seat and grinned at Liam. "This is it."

He noticed his two guards getting out of their vehicle but wished they hadn't. The conversation he was about to have might be difficult, but he wasn't in danger.

Unfortunately, in a black suit, white shirt and dark tie, he wasn't dressed appropriately. He shucked the jacket, whipped off the tie and unbuttoned the top three buttons of the shirt before rolling the sleeves to his elbows.

When he stepped out of the limo, he didn't feel that he fit in, but he also didn't think he'd attract a ridiculous amount of undue attention.

With a nod to his guards to stand down, he walked to the glass door, opened it and stepped inside.

Stopping the first person who crossed his path, he said, "I'm looking for Demi Viglianco."

When she gave him a blank look, he repeated himself, this time speaking Spanish.

She said, "Ah. *Si*," then told him Demi was in the back.

He walked in the direction she pointed, striding through a huge game room furnished with old sofas and worn chairs. A Ping-Pong table had a book under one of the legs to balance it.

At the door in the back of the room, he found himself looking at a huge cement block space that could have been a warehouse. Long shelves of canned goods created four rows. People standing around two tables packed boxes.

He swept the place with his gaze and saw Demi along a far wall, clipboard in hand.

He strode over. She looked up.

Her face fell. "What are you doing here?"

"You and I need to talk."

CHAPTER THREE

DEMI GAVE HIM a quick onceover then burst out laughing to cover the fact that her heart had skipped a beat when she'd seen him. He looked so good in a simple white shirt and dark trousers it was difficult not to drool.

She cobbled together enough pride to sound in control. "You'd have done better wearing your sweater and jeans from the weekend."

"It is a hundred blazing degrees in this country...even in the rain. I think a sweater would have been worse."

"Worse than a white silk shirt and trousers from a twenty-thousand-dollar suit in a homeless shelter? Hmm... I'm not sure I agree."

"Do you have an office or somewhere we could talk?"

"Yes, but no." She wasn't sure why he was here. If his dad had told him he couldn't dissolve the arranged marriage, that wasn't her problem. Her decisions were made.

"We're very busy here today and tomorrow. These are the days we pack supplies to distribute to low-income families. I don't even have five minutes to talk."

Oscar Martin shot Demi a concerned frown. Tall and broad shouldered with a head of dark curls, the man looked like a menace and frequently acted as security for the shelter. She shook her head once, but he continued advancing.

As if the rest of her staff had noticed his worry, they too began inching toward her.

Demi sighed. She could just imagine their response if she told them the future King of a country was here to talk about an arranged marriage with her. Lord only knew what they'd do.

Attempting to defuse the situation, she smiled at the crowd that was beginning to form around them. "Listen, everyone. This is my friend Liam. He's from Europe. He's vacationing here and he just came to say hello."

A sigh of understanding rippled through the small crowd. With sheepish smiles at Liam, they went back to their assigned tasks.

Full-blown annoyed now, she faced the Prince again. "You're really throwing us off schedule."

He glanced around. She could almost see wheels turning in his brain. She'd rejected their arranged marriage once. He undoubtedly knew that if he wanted her in the mood to listen to his arguments, he'd have to say something spectacular.

"What if I help?"

Okay. That was not what she'd expected. And to someone desperate for assistance it *was* fairly spectacular. Those wheels of his must have decided volunteering was the best way to stay long enough that he'd find time to talk to her.

Still, it wouldn't work. It *couldn't*. She did not want to marry him. "You? Help?"

"Hey, I can pack boxes."

Her eyebrows rose. *Actually, that might be fun.* A pampered royal packing boxes would give everyone at least fifteen minutes of entertainment before he got bored and left.

"Suit yourself." Calling to Freddie, her second in command, she told him to put Liam to work, then walked away. She wasn't changing her mind about their marriage. His arguments would be pointless. But more than that, she needed to get away from him. His accent turned her knees to rubber. His handsome face and easy smiles made her want to like him. But, worse, his amiability made her want to trust him.

Her father had taught her long ago that she couldn't trust anyone. Especially not royals. They weren't merely pampered and spoiled. They were cutthroat competitors who put on a good face for the public but would sell their mother for money or power.

Hadn't her dad attempted to sell *her*?

Liam could play volunteer all he wanted, but when he realized he wouldn't even see her, let alone get a chance to talk with her, he'd lose interest and leave.

He unbuttoned his white silk shirt and removed it, revealing a white T-shirt that clung to his muscular chest. For a guy who was thin, he certainly was built—

Not her business.

She turned to go back to the shelves where she'd been inventorying their dwindling supplies and Oscar almost ran over her with the forklift filled with boxes.

She jumped out of the way with a wince. She said, "Sorry," at the same time Oscar said, "*Lo siento.*"

Liam laughed and yelled, "Is your head in the clouds for any particular reason?"

A titter of giggles ran through her workers.

Oh, Lord. She knew what those giggles meant. They thought Liam was a suitor. She straightened her shoulders and glared at him. "No."

But he hoisted one of the boxes off Oscar's forklift. His muscles shifted and bunched beneath his flimsy T-shirt. Her heart stuttered a bit—

She walked away, going back to her work. She didn't even know this guy. Plus, he was royalty. Cutthroat. Narcissistic. Like her father. She shouldn't be—noticing. There should be no flutters or stutters or breathless feelings.

She counted canned goods until her eyes burned but she refused to look behind her where laughter and teasing seemed to be the order of the day.

She hadn't expected a future king to be so congenial—

But hadn't he been fair with her in their first meeting? He hadn't pressured her or argued with her when she'd voiced her displeasure about marrying him. He'd let her out of the deal. Like a gentleman. A nice guy.

Annoyed with herself, she sighed and told herself to stop thinking about him. But she accidentally glanced up to see him laughing as Wanda hoisted a box to her shoulder and carried it as if it were a prize.

What the hell could the joke be in that?

Who knew?

Who cared?

She had work to do. She turned away but not before Liam smiled at her. Warm and genuine, the simple lift of his lips filled her with pleasure. He clearly liked her staff of hard-working people who were down on their luck and enjoyed some joking around while they did their jobs.

Stop!

Why did she keep giving this guy the benefit of the doubt, as if he could be nice, fair, honest? He was here because he wanted something. He hadn't just come to help pack food. She had to be on guard.

Late afternoon, when most of that day's portion of boxes were packed and stacked, Liam approached her. A little dirty, a lot sweaty, he could have been a sexy model in a men's cologne ad.

"Hey."

She steadied her voice before she said, "Hey, to you too. Going home?"

"That would be a long plane ride." He glanced to the right, giving her a view of his perfect profile, then returned his gaze to hers. "I know you don't want to hear this, but you and I need to talk. In private. I learned some things from my dad that you need to know. We can't talk at your house." He looked around the warehouse space. "Seeing the kind of relationship you have with your staff, we also can't talk here. How about dinner?"

"What could you possibly have to tell me that I don't already know?"

"Lots. Things you need to know. Can I pick you up at eight?"

She hesitated, but curiosity got the better of her. He wasn't trying to talk her into marrying him? He was here to warn her of things her dad had told his dad?

That couldn't be good.

What if her father had admitted something she didn't know? Something else he'd done beyond gamble away their home and borrow money both from the bank *and* some unsavory characters?

What if it was worse than all the things she knew?

"Okay." Her fears bubbled up enough that she couldn't risk not hearing what he had to say. "Dinner. Pick me up at eight."

"Not at your estate. They've already seen me there once. I don't want your staff to start talking and alert your father than I'm in Hermosa. Can I pick you up here?"

His lack of interest in seeing her father convinced her a little bit more that this wasn't a ruse to talk about their marriage. More than that, he clearly didn't want anything to do with her dad. Her stomach soured as her fears about what her father might have done worsened.

"Sure."

He said, "Okay," and walked away.

She stared at him. The view from the back was as tempting as the view from the front. His voice could charm the angels. He was handsome, muscular—

She suddenly wondered what it would be like if they were going on a date. For real. A real date. She hadn't had a date in a year. Her heart rate jumped and her breath fluttered away into nothing. It would be nice to go to dinner, have a handsome man pay attention to her—

She shook her head, flabbergasted that her thoughts had gone there. If Liam wasn't fulfilling his father's—his *King's*—wishes by marrying her, he would never ask her out on a date.

And she shouldn't want him to!

The very thought was ridiculous.

She raced home, showered and dressed in a strapless sapphire blue dress before fixing her long hair. Focused on the upcoming conversation, she couldn't imagine what her father had told his father, but she realized her dad might not have revealed anything. A king bringing a new person into his royal family had probably done tons of research. King Jozef would have looked into her life—and her father's.

Meaning, whatever her father had done, it might already be public knowledge. Yet she didn't know.

Her heart raced as she sped up the rural road that led into the city and the homeless shelter. She only had time to park her car and walk to the front sidewalk before the limo arrived.

The big car stopped, the driver jumped out and opened the back door. She thought the door had been opened for her, but Liam emerged, dressed in a killer black suit, white shirt and blue tie that matched his eyes.

He very gentlemanly handed her into the car and she slid inside, far enough away from him that he didn't get the wrong idea.

They shared a few pleasantries as they drove to an exclusive restaurant in town, but no real conversation. After a generic discussion of the menu, they both ordered seafood.

When the server left, she waited for him to tell her the gossip he'd heard—she'd decided whatever he thought he knew, it might actually be gossip, not truth, because her father was a magnet for wagging tongues.

When he didn't say anything, she broke the silence. "So. What's this thing I need to know?"

"I was hoping we could just chat until after we ate. No sense in spoiling dinner."

"Worry has already ruined my dinner. You got me here because there was something you needed to tell me. Spill."

"Your dad's matchmaking won't stop with me."

She met the gaze of his sky-blue eyes, too stunned to speak. She'd been so focused on getting out of *this* marriage that she hadn't thought far enough ahead to realize her dad would keep trying.

"You hadn't even considered that, had you?"

Her voice wobbled a bit when she said, "No."

The waiter returned to pour their wine. Liam tasted it and approved it before the middle-aged man filled their glasses.

When he left, Liam shook his head. "What did you think was going to happen?"

She lifted her chin, annoyed with herself for underestimating her dad, but too proud to admit it. "I don't know. I thought I had until the bank took possession of the estate before I had to make any decisions."

"Well, don't look now but your father has other prospective suitors in mind."

She took a breath, then winced. "I haven't told him that you and I decided to dissolve our deal."

"That buys you some time."

Confused, and edging toward angry, she said, "Some time to what?"

"To figure out what you really want to do. Demi, my dad said your father mentioned the possibility of matching you with someone in a cartel."

Her mouth dropped open. She wanted to gasp, but nothing came out.

"Who else do you think would have enough money to buy a princess?"

Buy a princess.

She *was* being sold.

Or was she?

Why would Liam fly all the way from Prosperita to tell her something he could have put in an email? Unless he thought he'd scare her to death, then swoop in and save the day?

"You don't want your dad signing a deal with someone from a cartel. With or without your consent, there won't be any backing out. And if you run, there will be consequences."

He didn't need to tell her the consequences would be deadly. But marriage to someone in the cartel would be worse.

She sipped her wine, so angry that her voice came out harsh and sharp. "You know what I think? I think you couldn't get your dad to let you out of the deal so you're trying to frighten me into marrying you."

He dropped his forehead to his hand and ran his fingers across it before he looked over and caught her gaze. "You're so suspicious. And you're mad at the wrong people. My father did a lot of research and believes you would make a great queen. But when he hesitated in the negotiations for our marriage, your dad mentioned his backup plan. My dad did not believe your father was bluffing. Matching *us* assures you're safe and I get a good queen. We both get what we want. I'm not here to railroad you or steamroll you into something you don't want. I'm here to save you."

His voice was so neutral and logical that she couldn't argue. The thought that he believed he had to rescue her made everything he'd said very, very real.

"And for the record, I'm not any happier about marrying you than you are about marrying me."

She could tell he wanted to leave. She could see in his eyes that he wanted to stride to the maître d', handle the bill and walk away from her.

Instead, he stayed.

A virtual stranger felt he had to rescue her from her *father*.

The whole situation was surreal.

"Why don't you want to marry me?"

He didn't even hesitate. "You're contrary. You're stubborn. You can't tell the difference between someone who has your best interests at heart and someone who wants to use you."

"Everybody uses everybody."

"Now, there's a healthy attitude."

"I didn't mean it that way. I just meant that there are times when using people is inevitable." She sucked in a breath. "Even when there's a deal in which both parties benefit. Plus, all this makes me wonder why someone as good looking as you can't find your own queen."

He snorted. "That's the number one question of the media in Prosperita. Why can't Liam find a queen?"

He said it so sarcastically, she laughed. "Why can't you?"

"Do you know how hard it is to find someone willing to devote her life to *your* country? Her every move will be scrutinized. Her choices will be analyzed. She doesn't dare have a bad day or a run in her panty hose."

"No one wears panty hose anymore."

"So, imagine if my queen wears them."

She snickered. "I get it."

"I suppose you do. I just told you that you could potentially be married off to a criminal and even you don't want to marry me."

"I don't want to marry you because I don't know you. Because it's not my choice."

"Yet the alternative is to marry someone worse. Because like it or not you don't have a choice at all."

She stared at him. "You don't understand—"

"Really? You think that? I couldn't marry the love of my life because she can't have children. I posed a few possibilities to her about how I could have a child, an heir with a surrogate, and she rejected them. She didn't want me to be the King whose child was borne by another woman. When I said that I would abdicate the throne for her, she left. She changed her phone number, went to the United States and hid from me. All because she didn't want to sully my destiny. Now, tell me I have a choice."

CHAPTER FOUR

THE TABLE BECAME so quiet the click of forks and knives and restaurant conversations sounded like a roar. Liam glanced at Demi. Her strapless blue dress exposed the pale shoulders of someone who didn't get out into the sun, then it cruised along her tiny waist. Her dark hair had been caught up in a hairdo that piled her thick tresses on top of her head, showing off sparkly earrings.

She looked beautiful, perfect, and he felt like an idiot. He hadn't meant to tell her about Lilibet, but he hated the way she assumed her life was somehow worse than everyone else's. True, she had a terrible father. But Liam was offering her a way out.

Finally, Demi said, "You really think my dad would sell me to the cartel?"

He took a sip of his wine. "I don't think that. Your dad told my dad that was his next step."

Looking shellshocked and overwhelmed, she said, "Okay, then."

Their food arrived, but he didn't feel like eating. He'd told his family Lilibet couldn't have children but no one else. And in a slip of the tongue, he'd trusted a stranger with his biggest secret.

Demi picked up her fork, but only moved the food around on her plate. "This is awkward."

"Yes. It is. Maybe I should just go?"

"Or maybe I should go." She laughed. "Except I'm hungry."

That broke the tension enough that he laughed uneasily. He realized he was hungry too. Too afraid she'd leave the food pantry that day, he hadn't stopped working to get lunch.

"We are in a mess."

He couldn't have agreed more. "But you do have a few choices. You don't like some of them. Still, you have choices. But if you tell anyone what I just told you, I'll be humiliated and so will Lilibet. She's getting married soon. If this got out it would be awful for her."

She gaped at him. "I wouldn't tell!"

"Really?"

"Yes. That's personal, private! And not my information to share!"

That eased his mind enough that he picked up his fork. "What about you? What's your worst breakup story?"

"My father paid my last boyfriend to leave town."

He stared at her.

"We weren't just boyfriend and girlfriend, we lived together. We'd begun talking about getting married. I thought he loved me. Obviously, he didn't."

"When was this?"

"Last year."

Liam squeezed his eyes shut. The image of beautiful Demi stayed with him though. She was gorgeous. It was no wonder her dad thought of her as a resource. He'd known his debts were out of control. He'd known she was his only asset. So, he'd run off the one person standing in his way: her live-in boyfriend.

Opening his eyes, he said, "I'm sorry."

"Yeah."

"But you do realize this means your dad's had this plan for over a year."

She nodded.

"Once again, I'm sorry."

She waved her hand. "You're sorry. I'm sorry. Our lives are a mess."

"And our getting married would make them better."

She inclined her head, obviously thinking it through. "Maybe."

"Probably."

She reluctantly said, "Yes. Probably."

"You'd have to have at least one child with me."

Her head shot up and she caught his gaze. "You're seriously thinking about this?"

"Aren't you?"

She took a breath. He could almost see the realities of her life flashing through her brain. Marry him or marry a crime boss. Or run away and hide her entire life. Never be able to stop in one place for fear the cartel would find her. Endangering the lives of her parents.

"We have a food pantry and homeless shelters in Prosperita. I could put you to work."

She laughed.

The feeling that they were getting along filled him with an indescribable sensation. He wasn't the kind of guy who always had to win, but he was into this now. He saw what his father saw. Not just her lineage, but her poise, her beauty, her intelligence.

"And once you're married to me there's no worry that your dad will marry you off to another man."

She toyed with her wine glass. "True."

He reached for the charm his father had mentioned. The Sokol men all had it. His father and brother simply used theirs liberally. Liam was a little more discriminate.

"I think you're beautiful."

Her cheeks reddened prettily.

"And I like your voice."

She laughed. "I think you're handsome and I like your voice too."

"So are we doing this?"

"Give me a day or two to do some research."

He sat back. He liked the idea she wasn't jumping into this totally out of desperation. She was thinking it through. He had no idea what she'd be researching but it made sense.

"Okay. Let's eat."

Surprisingly, once she'd made that decision she could eat. The food was delicious and the conversation in the limo back to her car was lighthearted as Liam told her about his brother Axel marrying his bodyguard.

"He could turn off the security system for the Castle?"

"From the time he was about ten. The kid could sneak out with the best of them. But honestly, his sneaking out stopped being funny when someone shot at him, and Heather had to push him out of the way to save him."

"You're right. That's not funny." She paused a second. "Are there a lot of threats on your life?"

"We've had a few threats. Most were just people blowing off steam. Nothing serious. Even Axel's troubles ended up being the work of a man who had PTSD and needed help more than jail time."

"My father's brother, our king, might not have been so understanding."

"What you're saying is that you'd be moving into a much nicer world?"

She wouldn't go that far, but she didn't argue. Liam himself seemed very nice. But she didn't really know his country—or him.

The limo stopped. The driver opened the door. Liam got out and helped her out. When she stepped onto the sidewalk, he was so close she could smell his enticing cologne. A slight tilt of her head had her looking into his gorgeous blue eyes.

She stepped back. The last thing she wanted was hormones clouding her judgment. "I'll call you."

"No. I'll see you tomorrow at the warehouse. You said you packed goods for two days. I don't quit before I'm done."

She smiled. After the way he'd gotten her to reconsider marrying him, she believed that. "Okay. I'll see you tomorrow."

"Where's your car?"

She pointed around the side of the building. "Back there."

"I'll walk you there."

"You can't! It's an alley! I won't be responsible for you getting hurt. What if someone's waiting for me?"

"Then you'd be lucky to have me with you."

"You're saying you could handle two or three guys?"

"You're saying *you* could?"

She rolled her eyes. "People in this neighborhood know me. No one would hurt me."

He shook his head. "If someone wants your money badly enough, they'll hurt you." He motioned to a black SUV that she hadn't even realized had followed them and two tall, burly men emerged. "I have bodyguards."

Given that he had a point, she capitulated. "Okay. Sure. Fine."

They walked down the deserted alley. "See? Aren't you glad we have bodyguards?"

She laughed at his sarcasm, then caught herself. She was smarter than to let her defenses down with someone she barely knew, but more than that she had decisions to make. She would research objectively.

They reached her car, and he opened her door.

The relief of finally being able to get away fluttered through her. "Now, goodnight for real."

He said, "Yeah," then bent his head and surprised her with a kiss. His lips met hers softly, sweetly and everything inside her melted like butter.

He said, "Goodnight. Be careful going home," then turned and walked away.

The sweet surprise kiss filled her eyes with stars, and she shook her head to bring herself back to reality. She had to be objective. She couldn't make the decision to marry this man because he was good looking—

And made her laugh and kissed like nobody she'd ever met.

She snorted. After having a man leave her for money, she wouldn't crumble like a fool for a handsome man. She wouldn't crumble for any man.

Rather than use the side entrance to her upstairs apartment, she tiptoed into the downstairs of her parents' mansion. Stealthily walking by the living room where her parents sat, each with a glass of brandy, she saw her mom smiling adoringly at her father, and rolled her eyes. Her mother was hopelessly in love with her conman father and always had been. In some ways, it annoyed her.

She raced down the hall to her father's office before they realized she was home. She opened the door quietly and closed it with barely a click. Then she sat at the desk, turned on his computer and started poking around.

She looked up the Sokols first. Liam's brother Axel might have been a bit wild as a teenager and young adult, but he had begun a string of global charities that worked on everything from education to world hunger. Liam's father, the current King, had the face of a man who didn't suffer fools lightly. Pictures of him with his wife and four-year-old twins showed a softer side. Liam was clearly the guy being groomed to be the next king. He was serious in most pictures. Articles about him spoke of their country and its place in the world. There were a few pictures of him with Lilibet—the love of his life. She gazed up at him adoringly and his eyes glowed with happiness.

Awareness tightened her chest. *That* was why he was so agreeable to an arranged marriage. He'd never love like that again. He'd never love *her* like that. Their marriage would be all business for him.

But she knew that.

Plus, going into this union recognizing his position, there would be no pretense of love. Ever. And maybe that suited her? Her father had bribed the love of *her* life to leave so he could marry her off to someone who would give him a hundred times the money that had been sufficient for Barry to walk away without a backward glance. A congenial, soft-hearted dentist who'd helped her expand the homeless shelter and food pantry, he had left her for a measly few hundred thousand dollars—enough, he'd told her, to set up a dental practice back home in the States.

She'd had enough of love. It had failed her. If a sweet guy working in Hermosa for World Peace Missions could take money to leave her, then how could she trust love?

She couldn't. No one could.

In a way, she and Liam were even. He'd been hurt. She'd been hurt. The only expectations either of them would have would be spelled out in their agreement.

But the deciding issue had more to do with her father's plans, than her ability to deal with a loveless marriage.

She pressed her fingers against her lips and closed her eyes, before she hit a few keys that took her to her father's personal files. She didn't have to guess for long before she figured out his password—the date his brother was crowned king. He'd always been just a little bitter about that. It was a date he would never forget.

She pulled up his files and started poking around. After a half an hour, she found a list of names in a file called For Demi. As Liam had said, he wasn't the only potential groom her father had had in mind. She quickly scanned his emails to reassure herself that he hadn't contacted anyone yet. Then she looked at the list again. The name at the top made her blood run cold.

She squeezed her eyes shut and took a breath before she closed all her father's files, left the office and climbed the back stairs to her suite. Her cats, Strawberry and Shortcake, two shorthaired orange tabbies, waited for her in the front sitting room. They were allowed to roam the house, but a doggie door to her suite gave them access to her quarters, which they considered their home.

She stooped down to pet them. "I know. It's later than normal."

Strawberry nudged her hand with his head. Shortcake continued to glare at her condemningly.

"I had important business." She took a breath. "I think we'll be leaving tomorrow."

That got Shortcake's attention. His head tilted.

Tears began to form, but she stopped them. "We will not go into this as cowards." She picked up Strawberry as she rose. "And, yes, I've been saying we. If I'm going to be all alone in a strange country, you guys are coming with me."

Liam arrived at the food pantry in the homeless shelter early the next morning. Freddie unlocked the door from the inside, and when he saw Liam, he greeted him with a hearty handshake and directed him to the warehouse where packing had already commenced.

He knew the staff consisted mostly of residents of the

shelter, who had probably begun working after they ate breakfast. But an odd feeling flitted through him when he realized Demi had not yet arrived.

Twenty minutes later, he almost tripped over an orange cat who trotted into the warehouse. Three workers clapped. One said, "Strawberry!"

Liam frowned until Demi raced in and scooped up the unrepentant cat. "I'm going to have to get a lock for that carrier."

"Or you could let your boys play with us." That suggestion came from Oscar—the big guy who Liam assumed doubled as security.

"And have them trip one of you?" Demi shook her head. "I don't think so." After sliding the cat into the carrier that matched the one for Strawberry's twin, she picked them up and walked over to Liam.

Holding a carrier in each hand, she said, "We need to have a quick conversation in my office before we finish the packing. Distribution will be this afternoon."

He nodded and followed her to a space that looked more like a closet with a desk. Setting the cat carriers in a corner, she walked behind the desk, motioning for him to take a seat on the chair in front of it.

"My suitcases are in my car, which is parked in the back. I'm giving it to Freddie since he'll be the one to take over while I'm gone, but that also means we don't have to worry about it sitting in an alley."

Shocked, Liam said, "You're coming to Prosperita?"

"The wedding's on."

His focus had been so fixed on convincing her, that now that she'd agreed, he almost didn't know what to say. Then he glanced at the cats and remembered the way she snuggled the one that had escaped. She hadn't brought them for company while she worked today. He also didn't think she was giving them away.

"You're bringing your cats?"

"I love my cats." The significance of that wasn't lost on him. Her father had used her as an asset. Her live-in boyfriend had taken money to leave her.

The two orange felines blinked at him from behind the doors of their carriers. She loved them.

"All right then."

She forced a smile and the beauty of it could have stopped his heart, but he knew they had lots of work ahead of them. His parents had been in an arranged marriage, but they had been friends first. He and Demi didn't even really know each other.

Ten hours later, after all the packed boxes of food had been distributed, he watched her hug her staff and give them each a one-or two-line piece of advice on how to stay on track with their recovery or their life in general. When she was ready, she walked to him with tears in her eyes.

He understood the tears as much as he understood her bringing her cats. But he knew this was the best solution for her.

Now he had to hope it really was the best for him too.

CHAPTER FIVE

DEMI GAZED DOWN at Prosperita as their jet descended. The island was huge. A mountain range covered in green trees ran down the middle. Houses started at the base of the mountains and dotted the terrain to long white beaches. Small towns sprang up every few miles. As the plane rounded the island, curving to land on a clear runway, she could see a huge castle high on a hill that overlooked the ocean and the city beside it.

She nervously checked her seat belt. Strawberry and Shortcake had long ago pranced into their carriers for a nap. She was on her own—with Liam, who was across the aisle. She'd expected him to be nervous. Instead, he appeared to be ready to step into this new life they were about to create.

"Russ has arranged for a small group of people from the media to be there when we land."

She gasped. "Already?"

"Nothing official. It's going to be more like a 'Prince returns home from a trip to Central America with his new friend' kind of moment."

"Moment?"

"Yes. I'm not going to stop to speak. I'll answer a question or two, but only what fits into the time it takes us to walk to the limo. You don't have to say anything. We're supposed to look like we're two normal people returning from vacation where we met."

Relief filled her. "Oh. Okay. That's good."

"Do you want us to skip the pretense and announce that it's an arranged marriage?"

She sighed. "I don't know."

He caught her hand and kissed it, giving her a funny zig-zag feeling in her stomach. "All this happened so fast. We'll talk to my dad and Castle Admin about how we should handle it. But for now, I think it's just easier if we look like two friends or even romantic partners who found each other on vacation."

"You're going to tell them you were vacationing at a food bank?"

"Actually, I was thinking I could say Axel asked me to go check out your facility." He caught her gaze. "Then at some point, we could give the shelter and foodbank a nice-sized donation."

This time her breath did catch at his generous offer. Still, for as much as the food bank would appreciate the money, she also saw the benefit for him.

Or maybe the benefit for *them*. After all, having ready answers for the press would make her life easier.

The plane stopped. The attendant appeared at the door-way as the pilot announced that they could unfasten their seat belts.

She unbuckled hers, glad the plane had a shower and they'd been able to freshen up after the day of working at the food pantry and again after they both slept through part of the long flight. If she was making her first appearance in her new country, it would be in a clean white blouse and nice-fitting jeans.

She walked to the back of the cabin to get Strawberry and Shortcake, but Liam said, "Let the staff get them. If the press sees you carrying your cats, it's going to look like you're moving in—which you are. But it ruins our 'we met on vacation' story."

She crouched down, told each cat to chill for a few minutes then walked up to Liam, ready to meet her destiny. Or at least phase one of it.

They started down the steps of the small jet and the group of reporters raced forward.

Liam stopped them with a wave of his hand. "I know what you're thinking, but Demi is only a friend I met while on vacation."

"Demi?"

"Can we have a last name?"

"You just met and you're bringing her home with you?"

He ignored the questions. Demi did too. The driver opened the door of a black limo and Liam directed her toward it. She slid inside. He slid inside. The driver closed the door, and they were off.

"That wasn't too bad."

He laughed. "Not yet. But it will get...well, noisy. Everybody's curious. Everybody wants me married."

She nodded. She knew what was required of a monarch. She remembered being a child, making appearances with her uncle, Hermosa's king. They'd walk in his gardens or light his Christmas tree, reminding the press and his subjects that he was a nice guy who liked kids; he simply hadn't found the right woman to marry yet. Then he'd finally found a wife and had children of his own and she'd slid quietly out of the picture. In a country with a monarchy, everybody wanted a piece of their king's life. Even his private life.

As they drove along a seaside road, she took in the sights, working to stay positive. She was marrying an extremely handsome, smart guy. She might not have a normal marriage, but she refused to ruin her life over it. "Your country's beautiful."

"We're blessed. We have a halfway decent employment rate. We have strong exports. We're situated in a part of the world that commands attention, yet we manage to stay neutral."

"You say that like it's a gift but I'm guessing a lot of work goes into that."

He chuckled. "You're very observant."

"I am a princess. My uncle is a king. I might not have been raised to rule, but I heard things."

"Which is probably why my father believed you were perfect for me."

She only smiled. But hearing him say she was perfect for him tightened her chest. There was a lot of responsibility to being perfect. Especially for a king. What would he do if she made a mistake, angered him, said something he didn't like?

She tried to picture him losing his temper and couldn't. He wasn't just a nice guy. He was a very logical one. Someone who would think things through. Not jump to angry conclusions.

Which was a point in his favor. A source of relief for her. But it did remind her that she might not have to worry about a temper but there were other issues that could bedevil them. They didn't know some important things about each other.

They drove up to the stone castle with cleanly manicured grounds and gardens. "Pretty."

"Everything here is pretty."

The driver came around and opened the door for them. Liam exited and offered her his hand. She climbed out into a world of sunshine and flowers and suddenly wondered if this was what Cinderella felt like. She had never in her life seen anything so perfect.

His hand on the small of her back, Liam directed her to

the double doors that were opened by two men in dark suits who stood on either side of the entry.

They walked into a huge foyer with a circular stairway, an enormous crystal chandelier and an impressionist painting that was more like a mural. She recognized it from her studies at university and though another woman could have gasped, her uncle had similar priceless art in their country's palace.

It was no wonder Liam's father had chosen her. She might have needed rescuing, but she also knew what it was to be a monarch.

"You have a choice. Get set up in your quarters or come with me and meet my father and stepmother."

Before she could answer, a woman in a black suit and white shirt, with her dark hair in a ponytail, entered the foyer from a door in the back, carrying Strawberry and Shortcake in their crates. Seeing Liam, she came to a quick stop.

"I'm sorry, Your Highness!"

"Not a problem, Janine. In fact, I'm sure Ms. Viglianco is extremely happy to see Strawberry and Shortcake."

Janine laughed. "Cute names."

Demi reached for the carriers. "Thank you. They actually got their names because the first day we brought them to our estate, they ate my breakfast."

Janine laughed then exited out the almost invisible door through which she'd entered, indicating castle security was strong and had access to everywhere.

Liam said, "Let me carry one."

She handed Strawberry's carrier to him.

They walked up the stairs and down the hall. He pointed to the left. "Those are my quarters."

She nodded.

"And you are across from me, but down the hall thirty feet."

She smiled as he led her to the door, confused that they were in separate quarters. Except—he was a gentleman. He hadn't forced her into anything up to this point and it looked like he wouldn't. She relaxed another notch.

He opened her door without a key or having to punch in a code.

She faced him. "It doesn't lock?"

"We have extremely tight security. But you can lock it if you wish. I'll have Russ give you a key or Castle Admin install a digital lock."

She nodded and walked into the most spectacular sitting room she'd ever seen. The pale blue sofa and chair were modern, as were the metal-trimmed end tables and lamps. All of which complemented a floor-to-ceiling white marble tile fireplace.

"There's a kitchen," he said, pointing at the area beyond the sitting room with white cabinets and a shiny iridescent backsplash. A room with a television, desk, sofa and chairs sat to the right in front of a long corridor.

He motioned toward it. "The bedroom and bath are down there. With a balcony that looks out over the grounds."

"Wow."

"We want you to be comfortable."

She nodded. This castle wasn't dark and dismal like Hermosa's. It might be as old, but it was updated and homey, clearly receiving regular attention. "Thank you."

"Now, I have to spend a few hours in my office." He walked to the kitchen, opened a drawer and pulled out a cell phone. "This is your new phone. It has every number you will need already programmed into it. You can put the numbers of your friends and family into it or keep your original phone to stay in touch with them." He took a step back. "If you need me, call."

She nodded again, feeling like a bobblehead because it all felt surreal, and it seemed all she could do was nod.

He left and she immediately let Strawberry and Shortcake out of their carriers.

They pranced out and followed her to perform a real inspection. She looked in the sitting room, then investigated the kitchen, opening doors and looking at food and dinnerware on shelves. One of the cabinets was even stocked with various kinds of cat food.

She glanced down at her boys. "It looks like someone called ahead."

Shortcake meowed.

"You were fed on the plane. Just because we're living in the lap of luxury that doesn't mean I'm going to let you get fat."

Strawberry tossed out one "Meow," To voice his displeasure.

She led the boys from the kitchen to the den with the television and a computer which sat on a desk that was stocked with paper and pens and…stuff. Tons of stuff. Paperclips, Post-it notes, markers, pushpins and everything a person could need in an office.

She poked around in the bedroom and the bathroom that had every imaginable soap and shampoo for a shower or bath.

Then she came out and collapsed in a chair. The cats trotted over and sat on the floor in front of her. Both blinked.

"You're right. We are not in Hermosa anymore."

Her phone shivered. She pulled it out of her jeans pocket and saw the text from Liam.

Dinner with my parents tonight at eight.

She swallowed, and texted back.

Okay.

Your bags should be arriving shortly. But if you want to wear something other than what you packed, my stepmother has three shops she can recommend. Order anything. Castle Admin pays.

She took a breath.

Thank you but I have clothes.

Liam hoped she hadn't taken his offer of something new to wear as an insult, but he didn't have time to worry about it. Russ Krajewski, the short, balding head of Castle Admin, arrived in his office to discuss particulars.

As he sat on the chair in front of Liam's desk, he said, "So…have we got dates yet? Any idea of when her parents will arrive?"

"We're not ready with dates yet. I want Demi to meet my family and I also want her to be in on any discussions about *our* lives."

"Got it." Russ smacked his hands on his thighs and rose. "Just don't take too long to decide because we don't want anyone looking too deeply into this situation."

"No. I suppose we don't," Liam agreed. His father had used her father's need for a bailout to make sure he got a good deal in the arranged marriage, but Signor Viglianco had also gambled away double the value of his home. After the bank refused to make him any more loans, he'd gone to unsavory sources. The marriage arrangement worked, but once the press began digging there would be questions about her family's suitability. He wasn't worried about Demi passing muster or her uncle, Hermosa's king, who was a strong, fair leader. But her father was a potential embarrassment.

Still, they'd handled embarrassment before. What royal family didn't have a little something hidden in their closet?

Liam pondered that a few more seconds, then came to an executive decision. "You know, Russ, it would be a lot easier for people to accept her dad's behavior as being irrelevant if everyone believed this was a love match."

"You want to keep the arranged marriage under wraps?"

"Yes. More for our country's sake than for Demi's, though I don't think Demi will have a problem with it. After all, the circumstances could be embarrassing for her too."

Russ nodded. "Could be."

"Let's go at this from the vantage point of letting everyone assume it's a love match."

"Sounds good to me. You'll run it by the King?"

"I'll run it by the King."

Russ left and ten minutes later Axel was tapping on his doorframe. In jeans and a sloppy T-shirt with his trademark shoulder-length black hair tied with a leather string at his nape, Axel said, "Can I come in?"

Liam shook his head. "I wish you wouldn't."

"Dad just told me he arranged a marriage for you."

"Not all of us are so lucky as to be able to find a love match."

Axel fell to the chair in front of Liam's desk. "I was lucky, wasn't I?"

"The woman saved your life and helped you find a new career. You weren't just lucky... You were win-the-lottery lucky."

His brother laughed. "What's she like?"

"Skittish. Not sure if she should be happy or afraid."

Axel bounced up in his seat. "Hey! We're nice."

"We're great. But her father isn't. Her uncle, the King of Hermosa, is a strong, honorable man—but her dad? He's got problems."

"Yeah. Dad mentioned keeping this quiet until you and Demi decide how to handle it."

"I thought it through and told Russ that if we pretend it's a love match her father's behavior stays her father's behavior. It doesn't play into the situation as much."

"Makes sense. But do you really expect to keep an arranged marriage quiet?"

"I do… Once we go out in public, people will see us enough to think we're a good match."

"Are you a good match?"

"On paper, yes." He wasn't sure how to take them from looking good on paper to looking good in public to actually being partners, but his parents had done it. "We're having dinner with Dad and Rowan tonight. Why don't you and Heather join us?"

"Want Demi to get all the introductions over with at once?"

"Yes."

"All right. We're in. If nothing else, Heather should be able to put her at ease."

That's exactly what Liam was hoping.

At five till eight that night, Liam stood at the doorway to his parents' quarters with Demi. Wearing a red dress that brought out the best in her dark hair and made her dark eyes appear even darker, she looked every inch a princess.

He didn't know how he kept forgetting she was royalty. But he did. And the two other women who had married into his family weren't royals. They were also Americans. She would have nothing in common with either Rowan or Heather.

He sucked it up and opened the door, granting Demi entry first. She said nothing. He'd known she'd been taken aback by the opulence of the castle foyer and even her quarters but, apparently, she'd quickly become accustomed to it.

Or she was faking it.

He heard Axel's laugh as they walked toward the living room where his dad would be serving drinks, enjoying being host for a few minutes before dinner.

They stepped up to the doorway and Axel stopped laughing, Heather faced them. Rowan, his red-haired stepmother, rose from her chair. His dad froze. Then caught himself and strode to the door.

"Demi! It's so nice to finally meet you!"

She bowed slightly. "Thank you, Your Majesty. Your country is beautiful."

Jozef caught her elbow and guided her into the room furnished in French provincial style that complimented the oil paintings on the walls and above the fireplace.

"Everybody, this is Demi Viglianco. Demi, this is my wife, Rowan and my other son, Axel and his wife, Heather."

Axel came forward to shake her hand, then shifted away so Heather could also shake her hand. "It's a pleasure to meet you."

"The pleasure is mine," Demi said, and Liam relaxed a little.

Rowan walked over from her seat by the fireplace. She gave Demi a quick onceover before she smiled and hugged her. "It is such a pleasure to meet you. You're even prettier than my husband said you were."

Liam snickered. "No smart man goes overboard about another woman's beauty to his wife."

Rowan laughed. "True."

But Liam had to admit Demi was the kind of beautiful that stole a man's breath and forced him to struggle to get it back. Unexpected feelings shot through him like a bolt of lightning. He could picture them on the balcony of his quarters, looking at the stars. Laughing. Happy—

But no sooner had the picture formed than it blinked

into nothing. This marriage wasn't about happiness. It was about partnership. Though he wanted them to get along and be content with each other and their deal, he did not expect giddy joy or runaway romance. He'd had that. It hadn't worked out. This time, he'd planned a relationship that wouldn't be dependent on something as insubstantial as emotion.

The King strode to the bar. "What would you like? Wine? A mixed drink? I can make anything you want."

"Because he took up mixology as a hobby," Axel said.

"A king has to have a release valve."

Rowan rolled her eyes. "You'd think the Jet Ski would be enough."

"You would, wouldn't you?" Jozef agreed with a chuckle. "Now, Demi…wine? Mixed drink? Good old-fashioned beer?"

Demi could only stare at the King. He'd looked so damned formidable in the official photos she'd seen. Yet, he seemed nice—comfortable. Like just a guy.

"I…"

She suddenly remembered the words of her mother. *"When in doubt, choose wine."*

"Wine, please."

Jozef snapped his fingers. "I know. This calls for champagne."

He brought six glasses from below the bar and two bottles of champagne. Rowan helped him distribute the glasses after he poured and then he made a toast. "Demi, here's to a pleasant stay and hopefully a good final decision."

She liked the way he hadn't pressed her into a corner. She also liked his eyes. And his sons. She could see where they got their good natures. But she could also see that they weren't men you messed with.

Dinner was served immediately after they'd finished their champagne. Demi knew servants probably watched the room and kept everything flowing smoothly. She'd lived this model years ago, before her uncle married, when she and her parents resided in Hermosa's palace with him. But now living with constant servants was her reality.

Yet another thing to get accustomed to.

Dinner was a simple orange pork with baked potatoes and broccoli. Dessert was the King's favorite: chocolate cake with peanut butter icing.

The Queen told stories of their four-year-old twins who were already in bed.

"Arnie is such a ham," she said, shaking her head. "Georgie spends a lot of her time rolling her eyes."

"At four?" Demi asked, her curiosity piqued.

"Oh, you should see those two," the King said. The sheen of pride in his eyes could have lit the room. "Arnie might be the outgoing one... But I see bits of Axel in Georgie."

Everybody groaned.

Demi looked around. "What?"

"Remember how I told you he snuck out at nights?" Liam said, laughing.

Demi sighed with understanding. "You think Georgie's going to be a scamp?"

Affronted, Axel said, "Scamp? Don't downgrade my world class mischief to scamp!"

Jozef said, "It was world class."

With dinner eaten and dessert a memory, Jozef rose. He picked up his wine glass and said, "One final toast to Demi before we say goodnight—"

Axel stopped him by rising. "Actually, Heather and I have a sort of announcement of our own. Not to throw shade on you guys—" He glanced at Demi and Liam. "But Heather and I are—"

"Pregnant!" Heather said, bouncing out of her seat. "You would have guessed if one of you had noticed that I didn't drink any of the champagne for the toast or have wine with dinner!"

Liam laughed and rose to walk over and hug his brother. "That's great!" He hugged Heather. "And I did notice you didn't drink any champagne. I just thought you were dieting."

She squeezed him once, then swatted his arm as she pulled away. "You know I don't diet."

"Lucky woman!" Rowan said as she too hugged Heather as Jozef hugged Axel.

Then the King and Queen switched, and she hugged Axel while Josef hugged Heather, saying, "My first grandchild."

Tears came to his eyes and Demi got misty herself. For such a formidable king, he was something of a softie.

The thought stayed with her as Liam walked her to her quarters a few minutes later. It seemed like such a nice family she was marrying into.

But every family had skeletons. This was her first day in the castle. Her first impressions were good, but she nonetheless had to be on guard, watch her step, study how they behaved before she finalized her assessment of any of them.

They approached her door, and she used the combination Castle Admin had given her to unlock it.

"I see you got a code."

Her breath shivered in her chest. Technically, the lock meant she was keeping him out of her quarters, more or less demanding privacy. "I hope you don't mind."

"Not at all. We're both getting used to each other."

That simple acceptance mixed with his father getting misty over the thought of his first grandchild and the overall niceness of his family. Her conscience rose. Was she wrong to be so suspicious? Maybe she should trust these people?

Blindly?

After knowing them only a few hours?

A wise person wouldn't jump to conclusions.

Liam scuffed his shoe across the floor, as if nervous. He took a step back, then he changed his mind, stepped forward, caught her shoulders and brushed his lips across hers once. Chills tumbled down her spine. She told herself it was because he was forbidden fruit. While one part of her wanted to like him, the other part knew the truth. He'd had the love of his life, and this was an arranged marriage. She would always have to hold back a little of herself. Even after they married. Otherwise, she'd find herself in love with a man who didn't love her back, staring at him adoringly the way her mother always did with her dad.

That wasn't her. She was a take-charge, smart woman who would not lose her self-respect by mooning over a man who'd married her out of convenience.

His mouth hovered over hers for a second as if he was contemplating kissing her again. But he pulled back and smiled.

"Goodnight."

She stared at him. His pretty eyes. His serious face. It was really too bad they'd never be a love match—

She stopped that thought, reminding herself neither one of them wanted that. She would be a good queen. He would be a good husband. That's what arranged marriages were all about. She would not make a fool of herself by falling for a man who didn't want to love her. He wanted a queen and kids. Not hearts and flowers and a woman who sighed with happiness when he spoke.

"Goodnight."

After stepping inside her room, she leaned against the door. The warmth and intimacy that had rippled through her when he'd kissed her still rode her blood. They might not be a love match, but she loved the feeling of his lips on hers.

Which was good. They would be intimate. Sex could be fun, passionate. She simply had to keep her heart to herself.

But maybe that's what her confusion was about? It might actually be more difficult to *not* fall for a nice guy who was also extremely good looking.

That made her laugh. She'd learned some hard lessons with Barry. If that wasn't enough, she'd seen what happened to women who fell for men who didn't love them. They got used. The way her mother did.

Her dad had brought her mom to his country, married her and showed her off as something of a trophy. But her mom didn't see any of it. She loved him as deeply as she had when he'd whisked her away. In a way, she was a prisoner of that love. Otherwise, she'd have left Neil Viglianco one of the many times he'd brought them to the brink of disaster with his gambling—

Or now…when he'd basically sold their only child to pay off his debts.

She shook her head. Yeah. She didn't have to worry about falling in love with a man who didn't love her. She could handle this marriage. All she had to do was think of her mother, and her strength and common sense would return.

CHAPTER SIX

THE NEXT MORNING, Liam texted Demi to tell her he was having breakfast in the main dining room with his parents and the twins. If she wanted to join them, he would stop by her quarters to walk her there. If she didn't, her kitchen held things like bread, eggs and pancake mix to make her own breakfast. Or she could call Housekeeping to have a cook sent up to prepare whatever she wanted.

It took ten minutes before she answered that she had found bagels and cream cheese and would be eating in her quarters.

He frowned at his phone, picturing her arguing with herself about joining him for breakfast. Disappointed that she was staying in her room, he ambled to the main dining room where he found Rowan and the twins.

"Your father got a call," Rowan said, explaining the King's absence.

"That's his life. Always busy." He scooped up dark-haired Georgie, swung her around, then set her on his arm so he could tickle her belly. As she giggled with delight, the strangest thought caught him off guard. With his marriage in the works, in a matter of a few years, he could have a child. Or two. He looked at Georgie's big brown eyes and impish smile and his heart stuttered. He would become a father. Certainly not tomorrow or even next year, but not some day off in the far distance. His parenthood was no longer a wishful idea for some time in the future. It would be reality.

"My turn!" red-haired Arnie whined.

After depositing Georgie in her booster chair, he lifted his four-year-old half-brother, swung him around and tickled his belly. But as he set him in his booster chair, he gazed at the little boy's face, totally amazed at the idea that someday he would have one of these.

He would be a father.

Not if his bride wouldn't even have breakfast with him.

"They're in a mood this morning," Rowan said, urging Georgie to eat her toast and drink her juice.

"They're not alone. I am too."

"Oh, so all my kids need me."

He laughed, took some pancakes from the existing stack and slathered them with maple syrup. "It bothers me that Demi didn't come down for breakfast with me."

"You just spent the past few days showing her she had no choice but to marry you. Then you yanked her out of her homeland, took her away from her life's work. Did you ever stop to think she might be confused? Or at least shellshocked?"

"I like to think I rescued her."

"Oh, so you're Prince Charming?"

He laughed. "No. Well, yes...to a degree."

Rowan shook her head as she chuckled. "The Sokol men have charm coming out of their ears. But maybe this is a circumstance that calls for less rather than more charm."

He set down his fork. "I'm not sure I follow."

"You didn't win her over with charm. You won her over with facts. She's a smart, successful woman who's literally been forced into marriage. She knows it's for the best, but it's still new to her."

"It's new to me too."

"Yes, but you're at least in your home, your world. When I fell for your father—a widower, whose subjects adored your mom—I went through a harsh indoctrination about life as a royal. And let me tell you, getting the facts about life here helped."

She rose from her seat, lifted Arnie from his chair and then Georgie. "Actually, I'm the person who needs to talk to her right now." She took the twins' hands. "Jozef said she brought cats?"

"Two bright orange sassy pants cats."

"That's my in to talk to her." She glanced down at the twins. "Wanna see some cats?"

Georgie said, "Yes!"

Arnie fist pumped.

She shook her head. "Who teaches him these things?"

"My money's on Axel."

He watched them leave with a funny feeling in the pit of his stomach. For the first time in this arranged marriage, he wasn't calling the shots. Even as he thought that, he realized that was probably how Demi felt. Out of control. If he didn't like the feeling, he imagined she wouldn't either.

Maybe the right thing to do would be step back. Not push. Let her come to him on her own terms—

What did he know? Given that they had no intention of falling in love, they might have to create a whole new paradigm for how their relationship would work.

Demi opened her apartment door to find Queen Rowan and two gorgeous kids. A dark-haired little girl and red-haired little boy. "Your twins!"

"We're told you have cats."

Shortcake poked his head from behind Demi's calf. Strawberry trotted up beside him.

"I wub them!" Georgie cried as she stooped down to pet Strawberry.

Rowan encouraged her to stand again. "Let's get inside the apartment. Then you can play with them all you want."

Strawberry and Shortcake looked at Rowan as if wondering who she was to be giving orders. But within seconds, everyone was inside, the twins were playing with the cats and Rowan and Demi stood over them, watching.

"They're gorgeous children."

Rowan laughed. "They are, but they are also a handful."

"I can imagine."

"I was a public relations executive on the verge of leaving my employer to start my own company." She sighed. "Then I met Jozef and my whole world turned upside down."

"Love at first sight?"

"For him, yes. For me it was more like why the heck am I finding a client attractive? A widower no less...who's significantly older than I am." She caught Demi's gaze. "I was an ambitious workaholic. But that's not a bad bunch of traits for a queen to have."

"Okay. Now you're telling me something I need to know. This is all so confusing."

"I'd be happy to answer any questions."

"I'm not even sure what my questions should be."

Rowan laughed. "I can help you." She glanced down to see the kids happily engrossed with the cats. "You wouldn't happen to have coffee, would you? I barely got to eat a half a pancake before we decided to come up and meet your cats."

"Yes. There's coffee...and some pastries if you'd like."

"Just coffee would be great."

Arnie's giggle floated to them in the small kitchenette. "I'm hoping your cats will help burn off some of their energy."

Demi offered Rowan the choice of one-cup coffee pods. "It will. Strawberry and Shortcake love to play."

"Good." Rowan found a coffee mug, put the pod in the coffee maker and set it to brewing. "And if you're ever going to be out all day for royal duties, let us know and I can bring the twins down for a while to check on things and amuse the cats while you're gone."

Demi bit her lower lip. "Is that how this goes? You have to do what your royal demands?"

"Oh, there are no demands here in Prosperita. The Sokols are polite to a fault. But you'll soon figure out that you have duties, and you'll want to do what needs to be done to please your subjects."

Demi grimaced. "Really? That seems a little fairytale-ish."

"Everything's happy here, positive." Rowan laughed. "You'll see. I won't lie and say life is simple. Prosperita has a unique place in the world, both geographically and politically. The King isn't just a figurehead. He works. But it's a beautiful country and the Sokols are good men."

"I don't even know Liam. I can't say if he's a good man."

"The way I heard the story about Jozef's arranged marriage, he and his bride started out as friends and everything turned out very well for them," Rowan said with a smile. "So maybe your next step should be to become friends?"

"Maybe." It sounded like a good idea. If they became friends, she'd understand better what he expected of her, and she'd stop worrying about things that might not happen.

Rowan winced. "I didn't come up here to add to your stress. I wanted to introduce you to the twins and to offer our services about cat sitting."

Demi smiled. "That's wonderful. Strawberry and Shortcake do hate being alone. Your twins would be a welcome diversion for them if I have to be out of the castle for long stretches. Thank you."

"I also wanted to let you know that I'm here to give you any help you need. You'll be meeting with Castle Admin today to set some dates like when to announce your engagement and your wedding." The Queen opened the refrigerator, found cream and fixed her coffee. "Jozef told me last night that Liam suggested we not announce this is an arranged marriage. Honestly, he thinks a love match minimizes your father's troubles in the press."

She frowned. "It does?"

Rowan nodded. "Sure. The whole thing will play out like the Sokols know your dad is a gambler but overlook it because Liam loves you."

The idea grew on Demi. "That's kind of brilliant."

"Trust me. The Sokols are very good at diplomacy."

"You don't call it a lie?"

Rowan shook her head. "I call it protection. Jozef, Liam and Axel have this royal thing down to a science. It's their duty to keep their country safe. Part of that is keeping confidence high in the royals. Usually, they are transparent. But there are some things they keep to themselves if they believe it to be better for national security." She took a sip of coffee then said, "But that's not the only reason to make your situation look like a love match. Liam also worries that because you're successful and smart, the fact that your father arranged a marriage for you might be an embarrassment to you."

She swallowed. "It is."

"Then this works for everybody."

The idea that Liam had thought of it—thought of *her*—gave her a quick jolt of relief that led to the feeling that this was not going to be as difficult as she'd worried. "Yes. It does work for everybody."

"Okay. Back to your meeting this afternoon. Russ Krajewski looks like a grump but he's actually a big teddy bear. Don't be afraid to say what you want. Including bringing your parents here to meet the Sokols."

Demi balked. "Let's get me accustomed to being here before we add my parents to the mix."

"Okay, sounds like a plan."

"Is there anything else I should know? I mean, what's expected of me after Liam and I are married?"

Rowan inclined her head. "Well, as a member of the royal family, you'll be encouraged to support the charities of your choice. Publicly. It's our way of saying, royals are people too, with causes and fears and hopes for the future. I hold fundraisers. Jozef and I, of course, make large donations. And most of my public appearances are geared toward raising awareness. You can do a lot of good here. You don't have to sit around and bat your eyelashes at Liam."

Demi couldn't help it. She laughed. She'd figured out the night before that was something she definitely wasn't going to do. "I certainly hope not. And, honestly, supporting charities was how I found my sanity in my own country." Realizing she'd come close to admitting things she didn't wish to discuss with someone she barely knew, she quickly added, "I've heard Axel has a huge global initiative. I'd like to do something smaller, something more personal."

Taking a sip of her coffee, Rowan nodded. "You can start looking into that now. But before you get too involved, remember planning the engagement ball and the wedding itself will require most of your attention. I'm happy to help. I have contacts here in Prosperita and in Paris when you're ready to choose gowns. Flowers are handled here. Dinner of course is handled here. Your wedding reception will be held in the gardens and move to the ballroom in the evening."

"That doesn't sound godawful."

Rowan laughed. "It isn't. You have tons of help for planning, including me. For right now, your main job is to focus on getting to know Liam. He's a good guy and he's smart. He's going to make a wonderful king." Rowan caught

Demi's hand and squeezed. "And you're going to make a strong, important queen. Take all the time you want to adjust."

Demi agreed. She knew she could make a good queen, but step one was getting to know Liam. Here in his country, in his castle, she'd get a much better image of who he really was than she had either in the cabin in the Rocky Mountains or in her country when he was working to persuade her to marry him—where he'd also been handsome, charming, good with her staff.

But that was her country. This was *his* country. A country he'd someday rule. *This* was where she'd see the real Liam.

Rowan led Demi into the sitting room and all discussion of her new life ceased. They spent an hour laughing at the twins and the cats. Then the Queen and her toddlers left with promises that they would come back.

When she closed the door, her quarters rang with silence, and she literally had nothing to do until her meeting with Castle Admin. She could investigate local charities, start finding her place in her new country. But this wasn't her country yet. And she might look foolish calling charities.

It suddenly seemed that the sooner they got this wedding over with, the sooner she could get on with her life, figure out her place here, decide what she could and couldn't do married to a prince who was to become a king.

She knew there'd be restrictions. She knew there would be limits. But she refused to spend her time locked in a castle. She might be in a marriage that wouldn't include love, but that was only part of life. She needed to use her brain and she would.

A few hours later, she was in the King's office, with Jozef, Rowan, Liam and the head of Castle Admin.

Russ Krajewski's first question had been about arranging for her parents to come to Prosperita.

She didn't hesitate. There was no way she wanted her father pushing her or pestering her to angle for more money. She needed to find her place in her new home on her own.

"I don't want my parents here until the press and your country are accustomed to *me*."

Russ scribbled the note. Jozef said, "Are you thinking that they shouldn't arrive until the engagement ball?"

"Yes." She glanced at Liam. "Bringing them here sooner would confirm that we're getting married."

Liam's voice was soft, careful. "We *are* getting married."

"Eventually, but wouldn't it be fun to let your country guess for a while? We want this to be seen as a love match," she said referring to what Rowan had told her that morning. "Love matches aren't guaranteed. Maybe it doesn't hurt for people to look at us and wonder a bit."

Rowan laughed. "I like that! You know? Put some mystery into the scenario. Spice it up. Make it interesting for people."

Jozef rolled his eyes. "It seems counterintuitive to me, but Rowan was in PR. If anyone knows how to handle a situation like this, it's Rowan."

Rowan winked at Demi who said, "I like the idea of a little mystery. Something of a guessing game."

Russ spread his hands. "I don't see any harm in it. If it keeps people happily amused, I'm all for it."

Demi took a breath and jumped in with both feet. "Well, they won't be guessing too long. It's almost the end of October. If we wait to make our announcements, they will bump into the holidays or have to be put off until after Christmas."

Jozef sat back. Dressed in a dark suit, white shirt, and pale tie, he looked every inch the King that he was. "What are you saying?"

"I'm saying we should have the engagement ball in late November and get married in January."

Liam balked. "What?"

"You're opposed to getting this over with?" Demi asked.

"I really don't want to think of my wedding as getting it over with."

She raised her chin. "I don't see any reason to wait."

Jozef agreed. "Neither do I." He rose from his seat, an indication the meeting was over. Maybe because he was getting what he wanted with the quick wedding? "Demi, the entire castle is at your disposal."

Rowan stood too. "Including me." She hugged Demi fiercely. "Welcome to the family."

"Thank you."

Russ reached out to shake her hand. "Rowan can help you with the fancy stuff. I'll have the castle and gardens in shape for the biggest event since Jozef married Rowan. I'll also guarantee the tightest security known to mankind."

She laughed, but she also noticed that while everybody seemed to be celebrating, Liam hung back.

Dismissed, the group dispersed. She walked out into the corridor and Liam caught her arm. "A word?"

"Sure."

They went to his office. Though the floors were the same marble that ran through all the corridors and most of the offices, his furniture was light wood. The drapes on his windows were sheer enough that light seeped in.

Closing the door, he said, "Have a seat."

She sat.

He walked to the chair behind the desk. "You want to explain what happened in my dad's office?"

"You mean the wedding date?"

"Yes."

She shrugged. "Why put it off?"

"Why speed it up?"

For thirty seconds, she studied his handsome face and the confusion in his blue eyes. Part of her wanted to tease him and make light of their situation, which would have baffled her except he was extremely good looking and when they were together she felt…something. She tried to analyze the pleasant sensation tingling in her chest but couldn't name it. She'd call it attraction because it was part attraction, but the other part was baffling. It was sort of like trust, but it wasn't that pragmatic.

This was warmer, kinder, better than trust.

But that was foolish. Nothing was better than trust. Except love and Liam was never going to love her, and she had no intention of loving him.

Maybe they needed to talk about that?

"No matter what we're about to try to make people believe, we're not a love match. Why wait?" she said.

"I think it helps us create the *appearance* that we're in love?"

"That's why we're not telling them this is an arranged marriage. We're giving them a chance to see us and draw their own conclusions. We'll be happy and fun the next few weeks as we're seen around town. Our engagement ball will be fabulous. Our wedding will rival the Windsors'."

"But it will all be fake."

She gaped at him. "You want real? You want to come right out and say my dad needed a bailout because he's involved with some seriously bad people? You want your subjects to know Lilibet, the real love of your life, dumped you, and the love of my life took money to leave?"

He winced.

She snorted. "That's our reality. Since we don't like it, we're creating one that works better for everybody. If we pretend otherwise, we're fooling ourselves. And that's the one thing I refuse to do. I might cater to the need of your people for romance and kisses to believe we're a love match. But I won't fool myself."

Liam picked up a pen and twirled it. "Yeah," he agreed. He sighed heavily as if seeing her point. "If there's one thing I won't do either, it's fool myself. You're right about our situation. We've each had experiences that make us wise to the pitfalls of believing in happily ever after. We can have a perfectly healthy relationship without risking things we don't want to risk."

Relief trickled through her but so did a bit of sadness, and she finally realized that *thing* that tingled in her chest was anticipation. As if part of her really did want to be Cinderella. But her mom was a Cinderella of a sort. A handsome prince had whisked her away. He'd promised her heaven and had given her a life of chaos. Still, she stared at him as if he were the king of the world. Demi did not want to end up like that.

Liam tossed his pen to his desk. "Our subjects will love the idea of a royal romance, but *we* need to keep our feet on the ground."

That's exactly what she planned to do. No matter how good looking he was, no matter that they'd be sleeping together, she had to be painfully honest with herself about what he wanted out of this relationship. A queen and children.

What did she want? Stability. And it appeared that was Liam in a nutshell. Stable. Kind. Honest.

All of which were better than love.

"Rowan reminded me this morning that I don't have to stop my charity work. In fact, in my position, I will be able to do even more good than I'd been doing in Hermosa. I'd like to get that part of my life started."

"Okay."

This time instead of tingles of anticipation, a sense of connection arched between them. He always seemed to understand her.

Her tension dropped another notch, softening her muscles. She took a breath. "Thank you."

He caught her gaze. "The quick wedding date means we'll have to be seen out in public a lot over the next few weeks."

"Yes. I realize that."

He rose and said, "We have a week or two before we need to pick the actual dates for the engagement announcement and wedding. But start thinking it through. Maybe talk to Rowan about how long it takes to plan a ball and a wedding, and when you should be talking to the chefs about meals and Russ about support staff, that kind of thing."

She rose too. "Okay."

As she walked to the door, she commended them both for being so smart, but she felt a twinge of sadness that expanded into emptiness at the realization that she'd never be in love again. But she reminded herself that the more pragmatic this deal, the better the chance she wouldn't be hurt.

Liam sat down again, watching Demi leave. Now that he understood her thinking, he respected her request to speed up their wedding. She didn't need time to know their arranged marriage wouldn't magically morph into a happily ever after. From the way she'd mentioned Lilibet, it was clear she understood his position. He'd had the love of his life and she'd hurt him. Demi herself had been hurt. They weren't school kids or starry-eyed idealists. She would approach this marriage wisely, objectively.

Once again, his father had been correct. Demi was the perfect choice for him. Not just because she saw the reality of their situation. But because she had a good head on her shoulders. She stepped up. She'd realized getting married sooner rather than later put them on the right path. A path where she could get something done. She was a worker. She would be out and about, doing whatever good she could do because of her position.

This marriage would fulfill both of their expectations.

Around three o'clock he pulled out his phone to text Demi, then changed his mind and hit Speed Dial for her number.

She didn't answer until the fifth ring.

"Did I interrupt you?"

"No. The cats and I were on the balcony. They made clicking noises and did some screeching when they saw birds—as if they were annoyed that they couldn't chase them. At home they had the run of the grounds. I'm not going to be able to keep them inside forever."

"If you let them outside, how did you prevent them from running away?"

"Fence."

"Fence?"

"There are fences made to keep cats inside."

"A cat fence around the entire property?"?"

"I'm sure you already have a fence around the entire property for security. But the cats might be able to jump it. We'd use the cat fence to cordon off a big area for them to run around in, so they have at least a little freedom."

"Okay…"

"You asked. I explained."

He liked that she was sensible, but a funny feeling flitted through him. The part of him that had loved Lilibet and had loved having someone he could talk to and laugh with rose, creating a weird longing in his chest. He didn't miss Lilibet anymore. But he missed that closeness, the connection. Especially with the woman he'd be spending the rest of his life with.

That was all frivolous nonsense. Demi was the right queen for him. Eventually, they'd warm up to each other and their partnership would be more friendly than practical.

"Where would you like to go tonight? You've given us about a four-week window to be seen, then we'll announce our engagement, and the ball will take place almost immediately after. The smart play here would be to be seen at a few of my official events and out for entertainment two or three times every week."

"Why don't we start with dinner tonight?"

"Do you have a preference for where we eat?"

"I like just about anything. But I don't suppose there's a good Italian restaurant here?"

"We're close enough to Italy that we have more than our share of Italian restaurants. The question is do you want to dine by the lake? Do you want to dine on the yacht—"

"On a yacht?"

"Yes, it's free for the rest of the week."

"Let's save that."

"Okay." Liam smiled. He didn't know what he was worried about. So she was crisp with her answers? They actually seemed to agree about a lot of things. "We're choosing Italian?"

"Yes."

"I'll get reservations. Dinner at eight?"

"Yes."

"I'll come by for you at seven thirty?"

"Yes."

"All right. See you then."

He disconnected the phone shaking his head. Not a wasted word. That was weird but good. There was no reason for chitchat. They were both smart and committed. That's what really mattered.

He finished the afternoon's work and went to his quarters to shower and change into gray trousers, a white shirt and navy-blue jacket. Dinner by the lake wasn't formal, but it wasn't "come as you are" either.

He realized he hadn't told Demi that, then decided those kinds of things were Rowan's purview. He knew from the looks that passed between them that they had become friends or even allies. So, questions about what to wear now belonged to her.

He took a breath then knocked on Demi's door. In less than a minute, she opened it to him and the breath he'd taken fluttered away. Wearing a shimmering pink dress, with her dark hair cascading all around her, she all but stopped his heart. The attraction he felt for her went through him in a whoosh. And all thoughts about her being overly practical disappeared into nothing. She was stunning, physically perfect. She already looked like a queen. Looked like a woman a man went to war over.

He stopped those thoughts. *Like a woman a man went to war over?* That was ridiculous. Being outrageously attracted to someone was the kind of thing that caused a man—a *king*—to lose control. He wanted to be attracted to Demi. He liked that they had a spark of something physical between them. But he would not let himself tumble over the edge into dangerous ground. In fact, it was her reminder about Lilibet that afternoon that had stopped him.

He would have abdicated his throne for Lilibet.

Abdicated.

He'd have given up his destiny for her, the life he'd been training for since he was born. And she'd dumped him.

He'd slipped once with love, but he would never allow himself those feelings again.

Still, he was with a beautiful woman who would soon be his wife. There was a balance to be struck here and he would find it. "You're gorgeous tonight."

She smiled. "Thank you."

Strawberry and Shortcake peered at him from behind her legs. She gave him a slight nudge and jumped into the hall so she could hurriedly close the door.

"Didn't want them escaping."

He barely heard her. A million tingles had formed on his skin when she'd touched him.

He stared at her, totally confused. After such a short time of knowing each other all those tingles weren't love. They were purely physical. She was beautiful. He was attracted to her. There was nothing wrong with the desire tumbling through him. If he wasn't so concerned about not rushing things, he'd be more than happy to start their physical relationship that night.

Was there any chance she wanted that too?

CHAPTER SEVEN

DEMI SMILED AT HIM, then turned to the stairway, walking down the hall. He stared after her. Her eyes sparkled. Her dress sparkled. And, technically, sleeping together was part of their deal. But it was only the beginning of their relationship, and while he would like to think she'd worn that dress just for him, he couldn't assume that.

Women wore pretty, sexy things all the time. She probably just intended to look great on their first night out.

Because she did look great.

And tonight was her introduction to the world as the woman he was interested in. So, yeah, she wasn't sending any signals—except to his kingdom that she was a spectacular choice for a companion.

Realizing he was standing there like an idiot, he raced to catch up with her at the stairway and placed his hand on the small of her back, guiding her down the steps. But the feeling of the sparkly dress against his fingers made him swallow hard.

"The restaurant I chose is on the lake but also it was opened by two Italian brothers who moved here after their family matriarch died. They wanted a fresh start but more than that, they wanted to bring their mamma's food to a new group of people."

They finished the walk down the stairs and to the door. A guard opened it ahead of them.

Ten steps took them to a waiting limo. The driver caught the door handle and pulled it open. "Evening, Your Highness."

"Good evening, Leo."

Leo turned to Demi and smiled before tipping his hat. "Ma'am."

She smiled. "Good evening… Leo."

The driver's cheeks pinkened at the way she'd said his name. Liam totally understood. If there was anything sexier about her than her physical appearance, it was her soft, velvety voice.

She slid inside the limo. Liam entered after her. Leo closed the door and within seconds, they were headed toward the restaurant. He considered taking her hand or sliding closer to her on the seat. But would that make him look needy?

He didn't know. Though he did realize they should hold hands. Especially if they were intending to make people believe they were dating—and eventually a love match.

Still, unsure of what they should be doing in private, he stayed on his side of the seat and kept his hands to himself, then wondered how the hell his subjects would recognize they were dating if they kept acting like strangers. Or, worse, nothing more than friends.

He had to snap out of this. He'd dated beautiful women before—

Yeah, but none that he'd talked into marrying him with tons of benefits to her father and very little benefit to her—except that she got him.

But he was a prince. Eventually, she'd be a queen. Would she see that as a good deal? How could he make sure she did?

Mamma's Heart Restaurant was housed in a large white villa with brown shutters. Surrounded by a dock, the two wings that curved from the sides of the building made it appear the house was embracing the lake.

"That's beautiful," Demi whispered, taking in the view and the quaint restaurant as Liam helped her out of the limo.

When she was beside him, he almost dropped her hand, but decided to keep it tucked in his. "I'm glad you like it. The food's even better than the ambiance."

Walking inside, they were greeted by Enzo, one of the two short bald owners. "Prince Liam!" he exclaimed, then probably broke a thousand rules by hugging him.

Surprise caused him to drop Demi's hand, but he laughed. Enzo's enthusiasm wasn't to be denied. "Good evening, Enzo." He introduced Demi. "This is my guest, Demi Viglianco. She's from Hermosa."

Enzo kissed her hand. "I saw your reservation." Pride puffed out his chest and filled his eyes as he turned to Liam. "You, my friend, are at the best table."

"You always give me the best table."

"Because you are special!" He grabbed two menus and motioned for them to follow him to a four-person table in the back of the room. Two servers' helpers raced over to remove two of the chairs.

Accustomed to dining here, Liam barely noticed the empty space surrounding their table. All nearby accommodations had been moved a foot or two away to put some distance between him and the other diners. He also paid no attention to the four guards in black suits who materialized after they got out of the limo.

But Demi saw. He watched her eyes scan the room, pick out the guards and widen.

Liam seated her before he sat beside her.

Enzo distributed the menus. "I'm excited for your order."

Falling back into her role, Demi said, "I'm excited for your food. I love Italian."

Enzo's face all but glowed with happiness. Liam suggested a wine and Enzo puffed up with pride again. "I leave you to get it."

When he was gone, Demi said, "So the owner of the restaurant is our waiter?"

Liam hid a smile. "I get a few perks like that."

Her composure wavered a little, the way it had when she saw his bodyguards. She quickly got her reaction under control though. He realized again that all this was new for her and he shouldn't expect too much, too soon. At the same time, they were getting married in less than three months. This outing was his subjects' first sighting of them as a couple. They had to look like a couple.

Enzo brought the wine, sang the praises of Liam's choice and poured a sample.

Liam tasted it, then grinned. "It's wonderful."

Enzo said, "I know! And it will pair well with pasta." He waited, as if he thought they'd be ready to order. When they continued looking at the menu, he bowed slightly. "I give you some time."

When he left, Demi said, "I don't want to disappoint him, but I wasn't thinking of a seven-course meal. I just want some spaghetti."

"He said the wine pairs well with pasta. Let's at least go fancy and order the Bolognese."

She closed her menu. "Okay."

Obviously watching, Enzo raced over.

Liam ordered the spaghetti and Enzo scurried away to get bread and salad.

She shifted on her chair, back to being uneasy again. But

he finally recognized that if they got their ruse of being in love started, she might slip into that role and stop being nervous.

He caught her hand and brought it to his lips. "You really do look stunning tonight."

She cleared her throat. "Thank you. This restaurant is lovely."

She'd missed the cue he'd given her. He couldn't come right out and tell her they needed to get into character. He'd have to nudge her otherwise. He held her gaze. "You're lovely too."

"It's the dress."

He smiled slightly. She might have missed another cue, but he could answer this one like a man in love. "Really? You think it's the dress?"

"I know that. Every time I wear it, I get all kinds of compliments and attention."

"So, you know you're beautiful?"

Her breath stuttered. The compliments were one thing. But his hand holding hers was quite another. She knew they were supposed to be pretending to be smitten with each other, but just as she'd liked his kisses, she liked the feeling of his hand holding hers. She liked having his undivided attention. But that response was crossing the line. Not for their charade, but for their intentions.

"You make me sound vain."

"Or honest. I always find it refreshing when a person knows their strengths and doesn't have false humility."

"Oh, believe me. There's no false humility here."

"Good." He gave her knuckles another quick kiss, then released her. "Because you look spectacular in that dress."

Enzo arrived with their salads, stopping her from responding, but his compliment warmed her a little too much. She smiled at Enzo, using the diversion to get her inappropriate feelings under control.

Liam thanked Enzo, then dug in. "Delicious as always." Enzo puffed up like a peacock and scurried away.

Demi took a bite of her salad. She saw Enzo hovering by the kitchen door and the way he kept glancing at Liam. Not in fear. In anticipation. He wanted everything to be perfect.

"He likes you."

"A lot of people like me."

She snorted. "Who's vain now?"

"No one. We're back to talking about respecting our strengths."

She couldn't argue with that. He was good looking, had impeccable manners and was easygoing. Of course, lots of people liked him. Including her.

That was the problem. She was starting to *like* him. It might have begun as a feeling of anticipation and morphed into a sense of connection, but the more she was with him, the more she liked him.

"Eat your salad. I wasn't lying when I said this food is wonderful." He leaned in as if sharing a secret, but he whispered, "You're doing great, but you need to relax and flirt a bit."

She nodded, knowing she had to get her head in the game and reminding herself that it was okay to like him as long as she didn't take it too far. Her genuinely liking him might even help their charade.

Before their forks had been rested on their salad plates, Enzo arrived with two heaping plates of spaghetti.

Demi looked at the plate of pasta, filled to the rim. "If I eat this after that salad, I won't fit into this dress tomorrow."

"If I were you, I'd be more worried about staying in the dress tonight." Liam took her hand, kissed the knuckles.

She fought the heat that scurried through her. Liking him was one thing. It was quite another to react to things that were part of a plan to get people to see them as a couple. Obviously waiting for them to taste the spaghetti, the restaurant owner still hovered over them, and his ears had reddened at Liam's comment.

But her insides had shivered. Liam's deep masculine voice wrapped around the comment and made it even sexier than he'd probably intended. But this was a good warning for her. It might take more fortitude than she'd expected to keep her wits about her.

Liam took a bite of spaghetti and groaned. "Enzo, if our country had an award for the best food, you would get it tonight."

Enzo's ears reddened again. He bowed, thanked Liam and hastened off to the kitchen.

After a bite or two of spaghetti punctuated by sighs of appreciation, Liam said, "So? What do you think?"

She took a breath. "I think the restaurant is wonderful, the food is amazing and Enzo is darling."

"He'll be thrilled to hear that."

The normal conversation and Liam's very normal tone of voice stilled the attraction bubbling inside her. But she knew the truth. Keeping herself neutral with him was going to take some doing. She hoped he hadn't meant his comment about staying in her dress because she couldn't sleep with him that night. She wanted time to get to know him, time to get oriented, time to remind herself that sex didn't have to mean love before they crossed that line.

She picked up her fork again. The best way to regain her equilibrium was to talk about something real, something that would remind her of what this marriage could accomplish for her causes.

"Now that I sped up our timetable," she said carefully, just in case anyone was listening, "so that I can continue my community work, I'm sure I'll find plenty of worthy causes in Prosperita. But my heart is with my homeless shelter and food bank in Hermosa."

His face softened with understanding. "I get that. We'll find ways you can support them." He took a drink of wine. "Do you still think Freddie is the right person to take over for you? Or should we set something up for you to begin looking for your replacement?"

Relieved that he'd picked up the conversation, she almost sighed. "No. Freddie's perfect." She paused, took a second to think this through then decided to be honest. They might not fall in love, but they would be life partners. They needed to know things about each other if they were going to be in each other's lives for real. "He was an executive in a tech company before addiction ruined his life. He needs something like this."

"That's generous of you, but I also agree. Everybody needs a second chance."

The kind way he said that filled her heart. If she had to be paired with someone, it was nice to know he truly was understanding and compassionate. Those were the important qualities. Not his sexy voice or the way he'd made getting out of her dress sound delicious, sensual—

She quickly turned her attention to her food. "Everyone at that shelter deserves a second chance." She paused, considering the truth of that. "Maybe my leaving was good for them."

He smiled at her. "And lucky for me."

Her chest warmed. She told herself he was probably taking the conversation back to flirting to further the perception that they were falling in love. But what he'd said sounded so real.

She studied his face. She knew their partnership was lucky for her, and she supposed it was lucky for him too. So, he could really feel that way. Not for romantic reasons. For logical reasons.

She returned his smile, fighting the force of the connection she kept sensing growing between them. They needed to be friends. Some of what they were experiencing would be real and some only for show. The trick would be separating the two.

Liam ate more of his spaghetti than she ate of hers. Enzo returned a time or two to refill their wine glasses and accept their compliments on the food, and Demi allowed herself a few smiles at Liam, especially if he said something funny to Enzo or caught her hand to squeeze it like someone falling in love would.

But now that she knew some bonding would naturally occur between them—something more than friendship, not quite love—she understood what was happening. They would sleep together, have children together and she had to be ready to do that as his partner.

They would be partners.

Defining the relationship that way, she could envision it and envisioning it, she could do it.

But reminding herself of the consequences would also keep her grounded. Liam had no trouble with this ruse. He wouldn't cross any lines or indulge any emotions. He'd had the love of his life and this marriage was all business for him. If she forgot that, she'd end up like her mom, loving a man who would never love her.

That's what she needed to remember. There was no chance of love with Liam.

When they were ready to leave, they had a short tussle with Enzo who begged them to take dessert home for later.

Liam laughed. "Thank you but I don't think I could eat another bite."

"Me neither," Demi agreed.

Enzo chortled with delight before he grinned at Demi. "You will come see me again?"

"I could eat here once a week!" she told the happy restaurant owner.

Enzo laughed then squeezed Liam's arm. "I love her... and I love you two together!"

"I like us together too," Liam said as he took Demi's hand, sealing the notion that they were romantically involved. Demi took a breath. She was growing accustomed to him holding her hand, kissing her knuckles, paying her compliments. She just had to find that sweet spot where they could be friends and partners, people who wanted to have a family together—without making it into something it wasn't.

Liam said, "We'll see you soon, I'm sure," and they walked out into the comfortable October night.

Leo opened the limo door, and they eased inside. Within seconds the driver had them on the road to the castle.

"You know, we don't have to go home. If there's somewhere else you'd like to go, we can stay out as long as you wish."

She'd spent enough time interpreting her feelings, trying to figure out what was acceptable, what wasn't. Right now, a few hours with a book felt like a much-needed break. Or maybe a reward for recognizing how to be a good girlfriend without succumbing to the charm Liam was pouring on.

"I'm very tired. After meeting with Castle Admin, the cats about drove me crazy."

"Really?"

"I told you. They aren't accustomed to not being allowed

outside. They don't understand why they're stuck in the same six rooms."

"I'll talk with Russ about the fence tomorrow."

"Thank you."

The back of the limo became quiet. She leaned against the comfortable seat and closed her eyes. It had been a long busy day. But a lot of good had come of it. She'd found a friend in Rowan. She'd stated her wishes in the meeting with Castle Admin and they'd accommodated her. She and Liam had had an honest discussion about who they were and what they wanted. Interacting with Liam at dinner had shown her how difficult this charade would be because he was a handsome, sexy guy who was also smart and considerate. If she didn't remember he didn't want a love match, she might find herself falling for him. But awareness was ninety percent of the battle. Now that she knew she had to be on her toes, she would be.

Better, though, Enzo hadn't questioned her being with Liam. He'd said he liked them together. Easily accepting their relationship. He didn't think they were in an arranged marriage. Technically, they'd had a very good first outing.

Liam caught her hand and squeezed. "Demi?"

Her eyes shot open, and she sat up. "I'm sorry. Did you say something?"

"The limo's stopped."

"Oh!"

He glanced at the door beside him which had been opened. Leo stood on the castle threshold grinning at them.

She winced. She'd spent the entire drive sorting out her thoughts. Ignoring Liam.

Liam peeked at Leo. "Sorry."

"No problem, Your Highness."

Liam slid out and offered his hand to her. When she took

it, his hand felt warm and familiar. All her thoughts co-alesced. She was marrying this man. He would never love her. But they could have something important. That was reason enough to be happy.

They walked into the castle, up the circular stairway and to her quarters.

She input the combination on the keypad to unlock her door. The lock clicked open and she turned to Liam.

"I'll see you tomorrow?"

He laughed slightly. "Yes, with our new timetable we're going to have to make sure we're seen out a lot more than I'd originally planned—"

"You don't like it?"

"Actually—" He moved closer to her. "I like it a lot."

Oh. She did too. But as good as it was to be attracted to the man she was to marry, she had to shore up her de-fenses, get her new life into perspective, before they be-came intimate.

He stepped closer. Their eyes met and held. She knew he was going to kiss her. Her nerve endings shivered with anticipation. But he didn't give her time to think about it. His hands went to her waist as his mouth opened over hers.

The boldness of it left her paralyzed for a good thirty seconds. Arousal swooshed through her with a swipe of his tongue over hers and his hands tightened on her waist. He pulled her close enough that her breasts smashed against his chest, and he deepened the kiss.

Her blood warmed like rays of the sun, peeking into the empty corners of her lonely heart. The kiss shifted to the next level and the sensations filling her sharpened. Warn-ing bells went off. She hadn't yet figured out how to sepa-rate normal emotions of making love from actually falling in love.

He was too good looking, too charming, too nice of a guy. She could handle this. She was sure. But not tonight. She needed a little more time to get accustomed to him and to the reality of their situation, so she could keep her guard up.

She stepped away. "Goodnight." She turned and opened the door she'd unlocked.

CHAPTER EIGHT

LIAM WATCHED HER push open the door.

He took a quick breath to get his bearings. He'd meant for their kiss to be erotic, to take them closer to where he wanted to be with her—not quite falling into bed, but not kissing a woman who was just a friend.

But when he'd made his plan, he'd forgotten that a kiss like that would affect him too and he knew the smart play would be to leave before he said or did something out of line.

Something bumped against his shin. Something else slithered against his other leg.

He bounced back. "What the—"

"Strawberry! Shortcake!" She groaned, as her cats darted out the open door into the massive hallway. "Damn it!"

She raced after the two orange cats who were crafty enough to go off in different directions when they reached the center of the hall. The one with the slightly fluffier tail headed down the circular stairway. The other one galloped down the hall where he would find another stairway. That one was marked private, and one with which Demi wasn't familiar.

"You go after the one headed to the entryway. I'll go after the one who could end up in the kitchen."

She didn't even reply. She darted off in the direction

he'd told her and down the stairs. "Strawberry! You evil cat! Get back here!"

He would have laughed at the picture she made hopping out of her spike heels as she ran, but he had to find Short-cake. He barreled down the hall, pausing when it split in two directions. One went to Axel and Heather's quarters. The other to the stairway.

Considering this hadn't been the luckiest night of his life, he reached for the worst possible scenario: the cat had gone down the stairs.

He headed that way. But confusion suddenly slowed his pace.

He'd kissed her. Not a quick brush, but a real kiss. And she'd responded. How could he think this night hadn't been lucky?

Because she'd pulled away.

Yeah, but he'd made his point. She was as attracted to him as he was to her. They might not be a love match, but they were a match. Two people who liked each other enough they could be intimate. And maybe if they did this now, before there were any messy emotions between them, they could get a feel for how their relationship might be after they were married.

Reaching the stairway, he stopped. The wayward cat sat at the bottom of the steps, blinking up at him. The stairs led to a door that opened onto the kitchen. It wasn't locked, but the cat couldn't open it. The only way he'd have gotten through was if someone from the kitchen came out.

Taking his time, Liam ambled down the steps and scooped the furball up off the floor. "I think you're in big trouble... *Shortcake*." He said the cat's name as if his knowing it somehow gave him power.

The cat stared at him, his expression challenging. Almost

as if to say that Liam was new, and the cat was a beloved buddy. He knew who Demi would pick if push came to shove.

"Yeah, well, you should have seen the way she kissed me tonight," he told the miscreant feline as he climbed the stairs that he'd just gone down.

But even as he realized the stupidity of getting into a popularity contest with a cat, he remembered what he'd been thinking about before he'd found Shortcake. Demi had pulled away from him. Almost as if she was resisting their attraction.

Why would she not want an attraction?

Attraction was what would make their partnership fun.

Maybe that was the problem? Maybe she liked the attraction enough that she was afraid it would turn into something more.

Well, she didn't have to worry about that. He wouldn't let their relationship become messy and foolish. He wouldn't let them cross that line.

They'd talked about that this morning. They both knew this marriage wasn't about love.

The next morning, Demi had just finished feeding Strawberry and Shortcake when her phone buzzed with a text.

I have an appearance at ten. We're breaking ground for a new children's hospital. Afterward there's a lunch where I'll say a few words. This feels like the perfect opportunity to ease you into my public life.

Demi took a breath then expelled it slowly. This event did sound like the perfect time and way to ease her into his public life. Step two of introducing her to his subjects, his world.

After their kiss the night before, the feelings he'd ignited in her had shocked her, but memories of her mother's complete devotion to a man too narcissistic to love anyone helped her to remember the reasons she couldn't fall in love with Liam. The men might be total opposites. But the situation was the same. Her dad didn't love her mom and now Liam wouldn't love her. If she forgot that, she'd be miserable. And really that was her defense. All she had to do was think of her mom and she wouldn't have to worry about falling in love.

For today, though, she would be a smitten girlfriend, furthering the notion that she and Liam were in a love match, so she didn't have to face the humiliation that her father had used her to get himself out of trouble.

That was the deal.

She texted Liam. I think you're right. It sounds like the perfect opportunity.

She dressed and was ready when Liam arrived at her door. Preparing to be his girlfriend in public, she smiled.

He smiled back. "Once again, you look perfect."

She glanced down at her simple navy-blue sheath. "I googled Jacqueline Kennedy Onassis."

He looked at her. "You...what?"

"I googled one of the most celebrated first ladies of the US turned wife of one of the world's first billionaires. She knew how to dress."

He laughed. "You know how to dress. Just relax and be yourself."

"This is too important to me. I don't want to get it wrong."

"You can't get *being yourself* wrong."

His answer surprised her, except all along he'd been saying his father believed she'd be the perfect queen. She hadn't really analyzed that sentiment before this, but today she saw it as a commentary on her public duties. If Jozef had investigated her, and she was sure he had, he would know she'd attended events and been part of PR campaigns for her uncle before he'd had his own children. He would know she was educated and a hard worker. He probably *did* want her to be herself.

She closed the door, and they walked down the hall and the circular stairway to the front entrance, which guards opened as they approached.

The morning was beautiful. Warm from the sun, but not scorching hot. The air smelled damp and earthy.

As they walked to the limo, she said, "It's a beautiful day."

He glanced around as if confirming what she'd said. "It is. I love this time of year." Leo silently opened the limo door. "Though the summer months have their good points too. I love to swim in the ocean."

"And don't forget your father has a Jet Ski."

His laughter followed her into the limo.

As he entered, she took two quick, life-sustaining breaths. Her future father-in-law believed she could easily fill the role as a future queen. Now, a little pleasant conversation in the limo would assure they'd look happy, cozy in public.

Liam was right. She did know how to manage this. She should just be herself.

It wasn't unexpected to be photographed as they exited the limo and walked to the center of a grassy field. A portion had been roped off. A big sign indicating this was the site of the new children's hospital sat on the right. Several of the men and women held shovels. A shovel with the spade end painted gold was given to Liam.

Only a few of the attendees bowed, but everyone said, "Good morning, Your Highness."

He said, "Good morning." Taking Demi's hand, he pulled her closer to him. "This is my friend, Demi Viglianco."

Everyone said, "Good morning."

She smiled and said good morning too.

Again, the ease with which she fit filled her. It had been weird to be the stand-in child when her uncle needed to look like a family man. But the experience certainly helped her now.

And who couldn't love that Liam had introduced her? He hadn't ignored her or assumed the men and women would eventually figure out who she was. He'd brought her to everyone's attention. Exactly what they needed.

Photographers snapped photos. Several zeroed in on her. She kept her smile in place, as she paid attention to the ceremony. Liam said a few things about the necessity for this new hospital. Then everyone forced their shovel into the ground and pulled out a clump of dirt. Most simply let the dirt fall where they stood. But it was the symbolism of the gesture that mattered.

Liam took her hand and after a few quick conversations with the other shovelers, they walked back to his limo. Within minutes they were on their way to a hotel for the luncheon.

What Liam hadn't told her was that the first half of the luncheon was something of a meet and greet. She supposed it could have slipped his mind, or maybe he assumed she would realize that he'd be introducing her to hundreds of people, most of them members of their parliament and high ups in the local medical profession.

She accepted the introductions cordially and worked to remember as many of the names as possible. Then she accompanied Liam to the main table where they ate lunch, and he gave a lovely speech.

About kids.

The man clearly wanted children.

She tried not to let it trouble her that kids would probably be the first thing on their marriage agenda. But it would have been impossible to miss how he wanted to be a father.

She'd always wanted kids. Always wanted to be a parent. She'd thought that opportunity had been lost when she'd lost all faith in men after Barry left her. Now, she saw another upside to marrying Liam. She would have children.

True, she'd be parenting with a man she barely knew, but by the time they had kids she would know him. Probably well. And they'd be good to each other because if nothing else, Liam was a gentleman.

Happiness swelled in her. But she reminded herself that though this marriage would have blessings, one of them would not be love. She couldn't be too happy. Couldn't be blind to reality the way her mother was. She had to be smart about this.

After the luncheon, Liam and Demi headed home. Demi had been spectacular through the groundbreaking and the luncheon. As a royal who'd preformed duties with her uncle, she'd been comfortable and on point. But Liam had noticed her shrink back into her shell as he gave his short talk.

Now she was quiet. He thought back to what he'd said. Basically, he'd spoken of the country's need for a dedicated children's hospital on both sides of the island. She might have been critical of their government taking this long to figure that out, but her silence wasn't critical. It was—

Sad?

The expression on her face as she stared out the window made *him* sad. She looked like a wounded bird. Delicate. Fragile. He knew she wasn't. He also couldn't fathom that anything he'd said in that short speech would bring her down. His talk was about children. A happy, wonderful thing in a couple's life.

Yet she was sad.

He thought again about what Rowan had said the day before about the way he'd first persuaded Demi to marry him—basically pointing out that she'd had no choice. Then he'd taken her from her country to his. Now, she'd been shoved into the limelight.

Rowan had mentioned facts being more important than romance, but in this case, he wondered if too much reality wasn't exhausting her.

Maybe she simply needed a break?

Or a little romance— Not seduction. Not sex. But romance.

Actually, he knew how to give her both a break and a little romance.

About an hour after Demi had been returned to her quarters by Liam, there was a crisp knock at her door. She frowned and walked over to answer it.

A tall man in a butler's tux presented a silver tray to her. An envelope sat on the tray.

She took it with a smile. "Thank you."

He bowed. "You're welcome, miss. For the future, I'm Perry."

Expecting to see an invitation from the King or Queen, she froze when she saw it was from Liam. Written in beautiful script, the missive invited her to an evening on the yacht. A driver would take her to their private pier, and Liam would meet her there.

PS Dress casually.

She gulped. A private, romantic dinner on a yacht meant one thing. If she'd thought he'd been flirty and seductive the night before, tonight would surely be all about good wine and moonlight kisses.

She still wasn't entirely sure she was ready to sleep with him, but she also didn't want to say no to his invitation. Plus, she could be jumping to a wrong conclusion. She should simply accept his invitation and see what happened. He'd never try to seduce her. He might romance her, but he would be fair. She could make her decision about whether this was the night based on what happened between them.

With a few hours to kill, she changed out of her navy-blue dress and into jeans and a T-shirt. Prepared to carry her cats outside for a break, she realized the only door she knew was the front entry. She didn't really consider it appropriate to use the main entrance of a castle to take her cats outside for exercise.

Picking up the phone Liam had given her, she called Rowan. "Are the twins busy right now?"

"No. Are your cats looking for someone to play with?"

"Yes. Outside if possible."

"Very possible. I'll be at your door in ten minutes, and we'll go to the back garden."

"Sounds like a plan."

Dressed in jeans and little T-shirts, the twins looked ready to play. Georgie wanted to carry Shortcake, but Demi insisted on taking them in their carriers. She had no idea of the protocol, but having a cat get away from Georgie and run through the first floor of the castle was not the way to introduce her two pets to the staff.

Rowan guided the group down a back staircase through a short hall and to a huge, comfortable room.

"Our den," she said, leading Demi to the French doors that opened out on a patio.

Demi sucked in the fresh air. "I'm not accustomed to being inside for so long either."

"What have you been doing these past couple of days?"

"I've read and I video-conferenced with my staff from the homeless shelter, but today Liam had an event."

"The hospital ground-breaking!"

"Yes. It was very nice. Liam's a convincing speaker."

"Liam's a great guy," Rowan said.

Demi opened Strawberry's crate, and he eased out, blinking as if he'd been deprived of sun for so long the light would blind him.

She shook her head. "Such a diva."

Rowan laughed.

Shortcake got his freedom next. The twins clapped and the four-year-olds and the two cats bounded out into the green grass.

Rowan offered Demi a chair beside a glass patio table. "You know they could play for hours."

She had three until she had to be at the limo. Plenty of time. "That's okay. The cats need to be outside for a while. I talked with Liam about providing some sort of fencing so they'd have a space to be outside. I probably can't let them come and go as they please. But they need space outside."

"Well, that's going to mix things up here at the castle."

Demi worried her lower lip. "Really? You think I should take back my request?"

"Oh, absolutely not. There are so many things you have to get accustomed to that you need some personal freedoms. When I arrived, there were no women here. I was like a bull in a China shop. And Jozef accommodated me. Heather changed Axel."

A maid arrived with a tray holding a pot of coffee and mugs. Rowan nodded and said, "Thank you."

Pouring a cup for Demi, she said, "Not that Axel wasn't ready to change. He definitely was. And the changes had already started. But she was like a happy nudge for him to step into his real role on the world stage."

She handed Demi her mug of coffee. "So now we're all wondering how Liam's going to change."

Demi frowned. "You think practical Liam is going to change?"

Rowan laughed. "You don't put two people together—any two people—without some sort of friction and change."

"Liam seems like the kind of guy who likes himself exactly as he is and I sure as hell don't want to change."

Rowan laughed again, but Demi suddenly realized the obvious. When she and Liam married, there'd be an entire castle full of people watching to see how they behaved, if they changed—

Not to mention an entire country and a media that loved a good story.

Everything she did would be monitored and she'd have to be careful not to embarrass him or hurt him politically.

All this time she'd thought her biggest problem was marrying him without falling in love with him, but what would happen when they got married? Would people notice they didn't love each other? Would people care? Would it change how they saw him as a ruler?

* * *

Those thoughts followed her that evening as Leo drove her to the pier. She'd worn white pants and a simple white T-shirt with a navy-blue blazer in case it got cold. The captain stood at the bottom of the steps and took her hand to assist her onto the stairs that led to the deck.

Wearing jeans and a football jersey, Liam waited at the top. He handed her a pink drink in a martini glass. "Welcome aboard."

She smiled, curious about the jersey, confused that he'd gone overboard with the casual attire and wasn't wearing shoes, but mostly on her guard. She had no idea what he expected from this night, but that wasn't as important as her worry that from here on out her every action could reflect on him.

She took the drink. "Thanks."

He motioned to her feet. "No shoes on the deck. It's policy."

She laughed. That explained one thing. "Really?"

"Floors are teak."

"Why are you wearing a football jersey?"

"I said dress casual."

That answered question number two.

The sun had set. The scent of the sea filled the air. He motioned for her to follow him. "We'll have dinner in about an hour. For now, I thought you'd enjoy some time to relax."

Relaxing sounded so good. She hadn't fully considered the repercussions of their relationship when they'd made their deal, because he was a stranger. Now that they were getting to know each other, she saw he was a committed person, a nice guy, a *good* guy and not ruining his reputation mattered to her.

Grateful, she said, "I would like to relax."

He led her to a part of the deck with two chaise lounges. Though she hadn't felt the big boat move, they were away from the pier. Lights dimmed as they drifted into the dark waters.

She sat back, took a sip of her drink. "Cosmopolitan!"

"You like those?"

"Love them."

"I'll remember that."

The weird feeling of being wooed filled her. Though she knew she should be cautious, it was difficult not to enjoy being pampered.

She settled a little deeper into the chaise. "The cats are in your father's quarters with the twins." She laughed. "They're having a sleepover."

Liam chuckled. "Now, *that's* funny."

"I think Rowan is trying to determine if she should get the twins a pet. They played with the cats this afternoon. Now the sleepover. It's like she's checking things out."

"Or getting my father adjusted to the idea of a pet."

"Oh." She smiled. "I hadn't thought of that. But she did say that she'd changed castle life a lot since she'd become queen."

"Absolutely."

She risked a peek at him. The night and the yacht were comfortable, wonderful. She didn't want to disturb this peace, but she did need to understand this life as much as she could. Especially from his perspective, not Rowan's.

"Were the changes for the better?"

"Yes. Mostly for my father's betterment. He was so alone when he met her. My mom had died five years before that, and he'd sunk himself into the job. Though Axel and I were young—our early twenties—we had started to worry about him. It's not good for a person to be so devoted to their country that they have no life."

She whispered an "Oh" that she was fairly certain he hadn't heard. Then she said, "You're not worried that I'm going to make you look bad in the press or embarrass you or say something really out of line?"

He laughed. "My dad chose you because he believed you would be a great queen. The more I get to know you, the more I agree. The fact that you realize things you say and do could affect my reign proves you understand what it means to be a queen and you'll be careful."

"I don't want to hurt you."

"I'm a pretty strong guy. I don't bruise easily, and I can hold my own with the press." He motioned to the sky. "Look at the stars."

They'd gone out far enough now that the only lights in the area were the lights of their yacht. With no ambient glow to impede them, the stars sparkled overhead like a network of diamonds.

"That's amazing."

"When I look at the sky like this, I realize this is what people used to see all the time before civilization's lighting dulled the stars' brilliance. I feel like it puts me in touch with the past and the people who started our country, what they fought for and why."

"That's a lovely sentiment."

He smiled. "Don't let that get around. Everybody knows a king has to be a deep thinker, but when push comes to shove, they want him to be strong more than kind."

"I get that."

"You should. Your uncle's a real hard ass."

She laughed. "But like your dad, he's fair. He also has

his kind points and compassion. It's how I got the start-up capital for my homeless shelter."

"I read how they trotted you out when you were a kid like a prize pony. To me, it appeared that anytime they needed to remind your subjects your uncle wasn't merely a good king, he was a nice guy, they dressed you up and took pictures of him showing you the gardens or playing in his office."

"That was it exactly. But you should be glad he did. I've already been on the stage so to speak. I know how to be the pretty girl in the picture."

He said, "Hmmm," then shifted on his chaise until he was sitting sideways, facing her. "I don't want you to be just the pretty girl in the picture. Rowan certainly isn't. She's my father's trusted advisor. You're smart. At the home-less shelter you got experience with people who are living through the worst time of their life. Wouldn't it be a shame for all your knowledge to go to waste?"

"I'm expecting to support charities, remember?"

He nodded, then took the empty glass from her hand and held it out. A servant quickly scooped it up and disappeared into the darkness again.

"Those are your outside duties. But the more I get to know you, the more I realize you could be as trusted an advisor to me as Rowan is to my father."

The worry that she could screw something up caused her heart to freeze, but she knew his idea of advisor could be totally different from hers.

"Your stepmother makes policy?"

He rose and held out his hand to her. "No. She has the ear of a king though. And she knows how to get things done." He helped her stand. "Let's take a walk around the deck. Enjoy the night."

She smiled and took his hand. He hadn't hedged her

question, even if he was ending the discussion with a walk on the deck.

They ate dinner on the highest level of the yacht. From that vantage point, she could see the twinkling of lights on the island. The world was dark. Private. And the dinner was like nothing she'd ever eaten.

Given that she suspected this whole yacht experience was part of a planned seduction, she expected him to ply her with wine. But he offered only when her glass emptied.

When she said no, he casually nestled the bottle back in the ice bucket.

He talked a bit more about Axel and Heather before he told her a few things about his mom. Then he said, "How about you? What was it like growing up without siblings?"

"Hard." He'd told her so much about himself that she felt it only fair to even the score. "There's no one else to blame anything on."

He laughed. "I tell Axel that all the time. He made an excellent scapegoat."

"I also had to figure everything out for myself."

"Yes. I was older and I showed Axel a thing or two, but he was the one who worked out how to sneak out of the castle and hide it from our parents. I owed him for that. Our experimentation was fifty-fifty. I learned some things I could explain to him, and he learned a few that he taught me."

"Luckily, I had some good friends."

"Friends who will come to the wedding?"

"I'm hoping. I'll need bridesmaids, right?"

He nodded. "Yes. And they should be your friends. Just as mine will be Axel and however many friends I need to round out a wedding party."

"How does a future king make friends?"

"The same way any kid does. In school or sports."

"You played sports?"

"Soccer." He paused for a second then caught her gaze. "You?"

"I've been known to slap a volleyball around."

He laughed, leaned back, and she could see he was enjoying the peace and quiet, the space of time to just talk and get to know each other.

It hit her then that if she'd felt a bit trotted out in the appearances she'd made with her uncle before he had his own child, Liam had lived his entire life this way. With no reprieve. Because he was being trained to live this life forever.

"How about one more walk around the deck, then we'll call Leo."

The question surprised her so much she almost couldn't answer. She'd been so sure he'd brought her here to seduce her—

"Or maybe you'd like another glass of wine before you go?"

She worked not to gape at him. The night before, she'd thought he'd started a path to beginning their sex life. Tonight, he'd talked with her, eaten with her, walked with her.

The romance of it flitted through her.

He poured two glasses of wine. "We'll sip this while we walk."

The entire mood changed in the second walk around the deck. With the pressure off, the sea air seeped into her soul. The stars filled the night with whimsy. She could tell from the way the lights of the city grew closer that the yacht was headed back to the island.

Suddenly, they were at the stairs to the dock.

A servant appeared to take their wine glasses, then disappeared into the darkness.

"Thank you for a lovely evening."

She blinked in surprise. "Thank *you* for a lovely evening."

"This afternoon, you looked like a woman who needed a break." He glanced around. "Dinner on this yacht is my favorite way to decompress."

"It could absolutely become mine too."

He laughed. "Then you're lucky you're marrying me."

Right at that moment, she believed him. She simply didn't know how a woman arranged things so that she wasn't so starstruck with the Prince she'd married that she lost herself in him, in his life. She wanted so much for all of this—the moonlight, the honest conversation, the *connection*—to be real, to mean something. But he'd had the love of his life, the perfect high of being with the mate of his dreams. An arranged marriage could never compete with that. Even if he wanted to, he'd never fall in love with a woman who'd been chosen for him.

She slipped into her shoes and faced him again. "Goodnight."

"Goodnight." He put his hands on her shoulders and pressed his mouth to hers. She thought about how she needed to keep control, about how awful her life would be if she fell in love with a man who could never love her—

But she kissed him back anyway. He lured her in with his clever mouth and the perfect night.

He might never love her, but she was sure their marriage would have its moments, its high points. If they wanted to get along, to have a real partnership, she had to find those high points, maybe even cherish them.

Her mouth opened beneath his. He took the invitation, not merely sweeping his tongue over hers but also sliding his hands down her arms, to her hips, pulling her close to him, aligning their bodies intimately.

Need swam through her blood. Her heart and soul yearned to melt. She followed their urgings, ignoring the constant chants of reminder that she wasn't his first choice. Technically, she wasn't his choice at all.

And the thought that she was capitulating stopped her again. She pulled away from the kiss and he smiled at her. "I'll see you tomorrow."

She stared at him. He never argued when she stopped things. It was a point in his gentlemanly favor, but it also reminded her that he hadn't been swept away by her. "See you tomorrow."

Then she was being walked down the steps to Leo who leaned against the waiting limo.

The confusion of knowing Liam was a great guy, someone she was drawn to and yet realizing he didn't share those feelings tightened the muscles of her chest, made her want to run away and protect herself from the heartache she knew was coming.

But she couldn't. They had a deal.

And she would do everything in her power not to let herself get hurt.

CHAPTER NINE

LIAM WOKE THE next morning to the ping of a text message from Demi saying she would like to join the family for breakfast. He took a long breath of relief. She had needed a break. And he'd given her one. He could have been proud, but it struck him that that was something a husband should do.

When he arrived at her door to walk with her to the dining room, he almost groaned. She wore typical jeans and a lightweight sweater, but her hair had been curled and fell around her like a sexy temptation and she looked like a woman made to be loved.

"Good morning. How are the cats?"

Even as he said that they trotted to the open door and eyed him suspiciously. Obviously, they'd been returned from their sleepover with the twins and could be thinking themselves pretty important because they'd stayed in the quarters of a king and queen the night before.

Shortcake stared at him as if he'd finally figured out Liam was in Demi's life to stay. Strawberry gave him a head nudge, almost in challenge. Shortcake stared at him a few more seconds, then sat and began grooming himself as if to say he didn't see Liam as a threat.

He supposed it was easier for cats to feel secure with their place in Demi's life. All they had to do was purr and provide comfort. He had to set up a real relationship with her with give and take and agreeing to disagree about some things. Eventually, they'd have to raise a family together.

While the cats stared at him, she said, "Ready?"

"Yes." Remembering his manners, he held the door for her, but he also kept one eye on the cats. Not merely to make sure they didn't dart out, but to get the final word with them. They might not like him, but he was in the mix. He wasn't sure if asserting male dominance worked with cats, but it did with dogs. So, he held their gazes.

They stared back.

Yeah. They knew he was here to stay, and they were telling him they weren't pushovers. He'd have to win them over too.

He closed the door on them, then directed Demi down the stairs. "Russ will be at breakfast this morning to discuss the fence."

"Really? You broke up his morning to talk about a cat fence?"

She sounded so distressed that he laughed. "It's not a hardship. He loves the pancakes the morning chef makes."

She paused at the bottom of the steps. "I'm sure he has more important things to do than create a way for my cats to be able to roam outside a bit."

"Pancakes, remember?" Seeing his opportunity to explain some things, he motioned for her to walk to the left. "Plus, you're not small potatoes here. You'll be queen someday. You won't get every little thing you want, but your cats are clearly your beloved pets. We want to take care of them."

He watched her expression as she sorted that out. It would take some planning to create an outside space for Strawberry and Shortcake. But a place for the fence would be found. He wasn't lying when he told her what she wanted counted.

Her expression changed from confusion to acceptance. As he'd expected, the reality of getting the fence made her relax. Still, though the wariness had disappeared from her eyes, happiness hadn't filled them.

Disappointment rattled through him. He'd thought they'd made real progress on the yacht the night before. He didn't want his wife to feel pressured or unhappy. They might not love each other, but they could become friends and they could be good to each other. He'd thought they'd made great strides toward that.

But she was back to being careful again.

They entered the dining room. The King sat at the head of the table. Rowan sat beside him. The twins were on booster seats. One beside Jozef. One beside Rowan.

"Good morning!" Jozef rose as Liam pulled out Demi's chair. "How are the cats?"

The twins' heads swiveled toward her, as if anything to do with Demi's cats was the most important thing in the world. And who knew? Maybe to four-year-olds it was.

Demi laughed. "Feisty as ever. I was hoping that the twins could run in the yard with them again this morning and burn off a little of their energy."

Rowan winced. "Can't. Piano lessons."

"Oh, well. They'll probably nap all morning anyway."

Liam saw her disappointment and realized she could have been looking for something to do herself. The cats were just a good excuse to have company for a few hours.

"I have an idea. Why don't you spend the morning with me in my office? That won't just give you something to do. It will give you a perspective of my job—that part of my life."

"Excellent idea," Jozef said as Russ arrived.

"I hear there are pancakes."

Rowan laughed. "There are always pancakes."

Russ took a seat across from Liam and Demi. For the next few minutes everyone filled their plates.

Liam reminded Demi that if she wanted something other than pancakes, scrambled eggs, bacon and toast, the staff would happily accommodate her.

She smiled at him and said, "This is fine. Great really. I love scrambled eggs and bacon."

"The menu changes daily," Liam told her. "So, if you ever don't like what's available, just ask. Whatever you want is yours."

Demi stared at him for a few seconds, and he saw that shadow in her eyes again. Not quite wariness, more like a struggle as if she didn't know what to make of being pampered. Or as if she didn't quite know what to make of *him*.

That made the most sense. They might have spent the past few days doing things. But they'd been together days, not years or months or even weeks. She had a right to be feeling her way around her new life.

Still, he *had* pleased her with the outdoor space for the cats and the time on the yacht. They'd also shared some heated kisses the past two nights. There was hope that they could become friends, confidantes, and form a strong partnership.

The night before he'd pulled out the Sokol charm. Tonight, he'd have to plan something better than a moonlight stroll on a yacht—

That would take some thinking.

Getting his head out of the clouds and back in the real world, Liam asked Russ about the fence.

Russ told him that he'd been researching. "I'd like another day or two to pick the best spot. We want something with access to the castle and a place big enough they won't feel hemmed in. That'll take some planning. Especially since it's two cats. Not just one."

"Two rambunctious cats," Liam said.

Demi shook her head. "They aren't rambunctious. They're spirited."

Russ laughed. "Spirited or rambunctious. Either way, II need a spot with no trees. Otherwise, the fence might be pointless."

Demi shook her head. "No. Going outside is more about laying in the sun for them. Though they do like to trot and play a bit, they don't climb trees."

Russ nodded. "Okay. I'll keep that in mind."

When breakfast was over, everyone went their separate ways. Rowan took the kids upstairs. Russ went to his section of the castle and Liam led Demi down the hall to his office. Maybe watching him at his job was what they needed for her to get to know him.

"Am I going to look silly in jeans and a sweater when you're wearing a suit?"

His gaze involuntarily ran from her sweater-covered shoulders to the perfect butt displayed in straight-leg jeans.

His first reaction was to say, "You look anything but silly in those jeans. You're sexy as hell." But remembering he was trying to win her trust, he toned that down.

"No. You're fine. I only have one meeting and three or four phone calls...which might bore you. I hope you brought your phone so you can check messages or play a game on an app."

She peeked up at him. "No. I don't like being attached to a phone. If you ever text and I don't answer that's why."

"Good to know."

"Plus, I'm interested in what you do. I'd like to see how your life works." She shrugged. "Hear your conversations."

The fact that she was curious about him pleased him way too much. He might not have been able to get a woman to marry him, but he never had trouble attracting them. He considered that he should enjoy the challenge of getting Demi to like him, but his hormones disagreed. In three months, they'd be married, and he'd barely touched her—

He took a slow breath to stop that train of thought. "Okay. Right this way."

Her appearance in his office that morning gave him another chance to show her off, but also she genuinely was curious. In a good way. A way that spoke of partnership. She really was smart enough that she could be a confidante, the way Rowan was to his father. That in and of itself bolstered his faith, gave him some more hope. A few hours later, they ate lunch in the big dining room, then he walked her back to her quarters.

She smiled up at him. "What are our plans for tonight?"

He desperately wanted to do something spectacular with her, something private so he could woo her until they fell into bed naturally. But the whole goal of the next few weeks was to be seen in public. He'd also forgotten his family had plans that night. He didn't believe the outing would take them to the next level romantically, but duty was duty.

"There's a gallery having a special exhibit for the next few weeks. Tonight is opening night. Our family used to always go to this gallery's opening nights as a show of support—and because Rowan loves art."

"Used to?"

"It's under new management. Only reopening now."

"Oh." She casually lifted her hand to his lapel, running her fingers along the rim as if curious about the fabric. "And your family will be there?"

The touch of her fingers leached through the material of his jacket and grazed his chest. He pictured them on the yacht drinking champagne, kissing and losing clothes as their desire to touch flesh consumed them.

He had to clear his throat before he could say yes.

"Sounds like fun."

Anticipation sparkled in her eyes and even though he knew he should be thrilled she was happy about the trip to the gallery with his family, disappointment fluttered through him. He suddenly wanted more of *this*. More privacy. More touching. Some intimacy to build a relationship.

Instead, they were going out with his parents and brother.

She stepped back. Her hand slid off his jacket. She smiled before opening her door and almost jumping inside—probably having seen the cats trotting toward her.

The door closed quickly.

He sighed.

It did not help that the gallery opening that night was at the gallery that had formerly been named Lilibet.

Rowan called Demi that afternoon with information about the evening out. The King and Queen would be dining at home with the twins. Axel and Heather were just returning from a trip so they would meet them at the gallery. She and Liam would be dining alone.

"Dress is fairly fancy. Not gowns but your best cocktail dress."

"I have something."

"Color?"

"Emerald-green."

"Oh, nice! I have a purple sparkly thing. It's a deep, dark purple, so even though our colors won't match, we won't burn out people's retinas."

Demi laughed. "So, we'll see you around nine?"

"Yes…but one more thing, Demi." Rowan took a breath. "I think it's fair to warn you that the gallery we're going to was owned by Liam's former girlfriend."

"Lilibet?"

"Oh, so you know about her?"

"I know of her."

"Liam was extremely upset when he and Lilibet broke up. She left abruptly and went to the States, selling the gallery through an agency. She hasn't set foot in Prosperita since."

"He told me some of that."

"None of us is entirely sure how he'll behave tonight. After a couple of weeks of being angry after she left, he suddenly became resigned to her leaving. He rarely even mentioned her again. And years have passed. He could be perfectly fine being at her gallery."

She didn't think so. He'd told her Lilibet had been the love of his life. She'd seen the pictures of them together. A man didn't get over a love like that after a few weeks of being angry. He might have fooled his family into thinking he was over Lilibet, but Demi suspected otherwise.

She also knew him well enough now to realize that he could be overwhelmed with pain, but he'd never show it.

"He is extremely pragmatic, isn't he?"

"Yes. But so is Jozef. It was difficult for him to feel so out of control when we fell in love. I imagine Liam will be like that too."

She tried to picture Liam out of control and couldn't.

"We planned secret meetings. And met at my apartment rather than the castle. It was passionate and dreamy."

She could hear the romance of it in Rowan's voice. But Liam didn't have to sneak around or lose control to be a romantic. The night on the yacht proved that. He'd nearly swept her off her feet. His kisses had made her breathless.

Remembering that almost made her dizzy.

Still, romance was one thing and love was another. She had to learn to enjoy the romance without falling in love.

Rowan's voice brought her back to reality. "We'll see you tonight, then."

"Yes. Tonight."

She played with her cats then read a big chunk of a best-seller before it was time to get ready for the evening out. She dressed carefully and completely. After a long soak in a tub of scented water—while listening to meditation music—she spent an hour on her hair and makeup. When she was done, she looked good, she smelled good and she felt good.

The country would be examining her as much as they would be watching Liam. They'd be judging them as a couple. Judging her as a future queen. She couldn't be found wanting. She might not be able to give her whole self to Liam, but she would make damn sure she would be a good queen. Especially on an evening when too many people would be remembering him and Lilibet.

She tried not to think about that. The woman had left Liam, hurt him. She refused to be jealous. He was ready for a marriage and children with Demi. But she couldn't be so naïve as to think going to Lilibet's gallery wouldn't unearth some ghosts. Worse, she couldn't let him spend even one minute brooding or the press would catch it.

Liam came to her apartment door at seven thirty. They drove to the restaurant and ate a sumptuous dinner. Then a happy Leo drove them to the gallery.

But the chauffeur's over-the-top cheerfulness made it clear to Demi that everybody was a bit worried about Liam going to the gallery that had been owned by the love of his life.

In the alley behind the building, Liam stepped out of the limo and extended his hand to help Demi out. He took a weird breath. "This is actually where the sniper shot at Axel."

Oh, great. This gallery is just chock-full of happy memories for the royals!

"But it all ended well," Demi pointed out, sliding her hand around Liam's elbow possessively. She refused to let the ghost of bad memories ruin their night. He was with *her*, not Lilibet. If it took every ounce of her energy, she would capture and keep his attention. "Axel didn't get shot. He married his bodyguard, and the shooter got the help he needed."

Liam's eyes shifted as he thought that through. He relaxed and smiled at her. "Yes. You're right."

With his attention off everything but her, Demi smiled back. "So let's go see this art."

"Yes."

Arm in arm, they turned toward the rear door. They entered the gallery. In a few steps, they were in the back of the main room. Liam looked around pensively.

"We never arrive in front," he explained. "Not just because of paparazzi but also so we don't make a big deal out of our appearance. It's one of the few times when we are simply ourselves."

"That's a great idea." Determined not to let his mind roam to Lilibet, Demi redirected his attention again. "Now, show me something pretty."

"I haven't been to this exhibit before, but I see the name of an artist I love." He pointed to the right. "Let's start there."

They walked to the painting. Liam discussed the animated imagery of the work. While Demi recognized the talent of the painter, the picture wasn't a favorite.

They strolled to the next painting and were joined by Jozef and Rowan. Rowan hugged her. "See. We don't clash."

"Your dress is beautiful!"

"So is yours."

A waiter came by with champagne and Liam snagged two glasses for them. Jozef enjoyed the same artist Liam did and Rowan rolled her eyes.

"I'm not a fan either," she whispered to Demi.

Axel and Heather arrived, walking over to the painting where Liam and Demi, Rowan and Jozef stood. After a few general hellos, they talked about her pregnancy, then the group began strolling through a gallery filled with Prosperita's aristocracy who said hello to the royals, sometimes engaged them in conversation, but basically treated them like any other art lovers.

"It is weird the first time you see the royals out in public behaving like normal people," Heather said to Demi. "But it's another one of those things that makes Prosperita different."

The three Sokol men shook their heads at Heather's observation, but Demi could see what she meant.

But while Jozef and Axel were light and amusing, Liam held back. Demi saw him glance around occasionally and her heart sank.

Heather tired quickly, so they were the first to leave. Rowan worried about the twins so they left next.

A half hour before the gallery would have closed, Liam suggested they also leave. They walked out into the alley. Leo jumped to attention to open the limo door. They slid inside and headed back to the castle.

Liam settled into the comfortable seat. "Well, that went okay."

Just okay. It wasn't fun. He wasn't happy. He was resigned. Just as Rowan said he had been two weeks after Lilibet left him.

She wondered if this was the rest of her life. Competing with a woman she'd never met. A woman who'd loved Liam first.

A woman who had *loved* Liam.

Not the woman he'd been assigned to marry.

Trying not to let it bother her, Demi said, "I thought it was a lovely evening."

"I like art—not like Rowan does—I don't sigh with love over a painting. But I do like champagne and mingling."

And he'd probably been avoiding the gallery formerly owned by Lilibet.

The limo grew quiet. The ghost of Lilibet hung in the air.

She wondered why she cared. They weren't a love match. Their marriage had been arranged. There would be things like this happening all the time. Vacuums. Spaces where he might remember Lilibet and where Demi herself would long for deeper feelings that would never be. That was the truth of their relationship.

Still, she *would* be a good queen. But for the first time she wondered if he could be a good husband.

Leo pulled the limo up to the castle, came around and opened their door. Liam exited and reached in to help her out. They walked into the castle, up the stairs and to the door to her quarters.

He smiled down at her.

The warm, fuzzy sensation that filled her made her wish their romance was real. What would it be like to have the love of this strong, handsome man, who came from a happy family? She wondered how Lilibet could have ever given him up. But she *had* given him up. There had been no fairytale ending to the Lilibet romance. No happy ending to her romance with Barry, either, who'd wanted money more than he wanted her. Then there was her mother, a woman who pandered to a husband who barely paid attention to her. No happy ending there either. Her mother loved her father and had lost herself, her self-respect.

Though all that should have gotten her on point again, that cautionary fear didn't work as well tonight as it usually did. Liam hadn't been the bad guy in his relationship. His father and stepmother were extremely happily married. So were his brother and Heather.

Because this royal family was filled with nice people. And she would be one of them soon, but she wouldn't have the happily ever after she yearned for.

And unless she got this longing under control she would be in trouble. Falling in love with a man who couldn't love her.

She impulsively rose to her tiptoes and kissed him. Quickly. Hoping to pretend that was their goodnight kiss, then spin away from him to race into her apartment. But he caught her elbows and kept her right where she was and she melted. At first, he kissed her normally. Then as he realized she was enjoying this as much as he was his mouth and his kisses grew hungry.

Arousal sprinted through her, reminding her of needs she'd forgotten. Especially the need to let go. To enjoy. To be herself. To trust. But he loved Lilibet. Even if she could dismiss her own dismal experience with loving Barry, she could not forget Liam had had the love of his life.

She pulled away from their kiss the way she always did, but this time she didn't just see the confusion in Liam's eyes. Her heart hurt. The rest of her life lay before her as good, solid, but loveless.

Still—wasn't that preferable to being humiliated because of being vulnerable?

Yes. It was.

When a woman married a man who'd admitted he would never love her, that he didn't want love, she had choices to make and Demi had made hers. Being with Liam was preferable to being alone, never having children…or worse, trusting another man.

She stepped back, away from Liam, and opened the door. "Goodnight."

Not giving him a chance to say goodnight to her, she slipped inside her quarters without another word.

CHAPTER TEN

LIAM QUIETLY GROANED when she closed the door on him. He squeezed his eyes shut then headed for his rooms. He'd promised himself he would give her all the time she needed to get adjusted to him and this marriage. He could not let one closed door upset him.

The next two weeks, they were seen in public enough that the media began to speculate—just as the royal family wanted them to. Liam could see that being patient with Demi and their relationship was the right thing to do. She was perfect. Beautiful, articulate and committed to causes. She would make a wonderful queen.

If it took a while for those qualities to translate into them having a wonderful marriage, then he shouldn't interfere with the process. He should let their relationship happen naturally.

The national news exploded when they discovered that Demi hadrun a homeless shelter in her country, but they'd gone wild when they learned that Liam had also packed boxes to distribute food to the poor.

Reporters even flew to Hermosa to get the scoop on her and her life there. Oscar and Wanda talked on camera about how much they liked Liam and what a good worker he was. "And funny," Wanda had told them.

The story became almost a fairytale of him being smitten the way Jozef had been with Rowan and doing whatever he needed to do to get Demi to fall for him.

It was a great story. Especially when they announced their engagement. She looked like a woman who could be a formidable queen and they appeared to be the happiest, most perfect couple.

While he made an emergency diplomatic trip to the country of a struggling ally, the date was announced for the engagement ball. Silk paper invitations, printed in script, were to be sent to friends and family, including the King of Hermosa.

But before they could be delivered, mere minutes after Liam returned from his trip, his grandparents showed up on the doorstep of the castle.

Angry.

Stopping only to tell Russ the entire family should report to Jozef's office, they stormed down the marble corridor.

In less than five minutes, everyone had gathered, and the reprimand had begun.

"And no one thought to tell us Liam was getting married?" his grandfather the former king, Alistair, asked, as he paced in front of Jozef's desk.

His grandmother, Monique, sat in a chair, her face pinched to the point that she looked like she'd eaten a lemon.

Liam and Demi sat on a sofa near the window. Axel and Heather stood by the door—Axel looking like he was plotting one of his great escapes. Jozef sat at his desk, with Rowan standing behind him off to his right.

Jozef leaned back in his chair. "Things happened very quickly."

Monique glanced sideways at Liam. "So, we heard. *From the papers.*"

"I should have called," Rowan said.

"*Liam* should have called," Alistair said.

"I'm sorry," Liam quickly apologized. "In all the hub-bub of introducing Demi, getting out in public, throwing together a ball—"

"And falling in love," Monique said shrewdly.

"And falling in love," Liam agreed, because his family had decided not to announce that this was an arranged marriage to anyone outside their immediate circle of six. Unless his father chose to bring his parents into his confidence, Liam would hold up his end of the deal. "Things just got away from us."

"And such a quick wedding!" Alistair railed.

Monique glanced at Demi's middle, as if checking for a pregnancy.

His grandparents thinking his bride was pregnant would have made Liam laugh from the irony, except all of a sudden he was tired. They really had had an accelerated relationship. He'd been wooing his future bride as he'd introduced her to his country and performed all the duties of a prince—including a trip where he'd barely slept.

It was like being the lead in a play. An actor who never actually got to fall for or sleep with his leading lady. Just pretend he did.

He knew it was the right thing to do, for both their sakes, but at this moment he was tired.

Weirdly tired.

He'd endured a million things, and now he was getting yelled at by his grandparents.

He rose from the sofa. "You know what? I'm tired."

Everybody stopped talking.

"I'm *tired*." He said it again in case somebody hadn't heard. "I'll see you all at dinner."

He rose and left the office. Only when Demi came scurrying out behind him did he realize he'd left her there as well.

He headed for his quarters. She kept up with his long strides.

"Are you okay?"

"I said I was tired."

"Yeah. We all got that."

"So?"

"So... I take it your grandparents might not rule the country, but they still rule the family, and they were angry that they weren't told."

"Then maybe they shouldn't live in *Paris*? Maybe they should live in Prosperita where they'd actually see things for themselves."

Demi couldn't help it. She laughed.

He stopped walking. "Why are you laughing?"

"Because I've never seen you like this. There's clearly something wrong."

He took a breath. Started walking to his quarters again. "I'm tired."

"Okay."

She followed him to his quarters. When he reached the door, he paused. "You're coming inside? Into *my* quarters... where God only knows what horrors lurk."

This time, she took a good look at his face. This wasn't like him at all. She looked in his eyes. They were a tad glassy.

She raised her hand to his forehead. "You're burning up."

He sighed, shoved open his door. "Whatever."

She scrambled inside after him. "Come on. Let me call the kitchen. I'll get you some chicken soup."

Heading down the hall, he said "Okay," dropping clothes as he went. First his tie hit the floor, then his jacket. He kicked off his shoes. Then tossed his shirt. She found his trousers right outside the door she assumed led to his bedroom.

She knocked once. "Are you okay?"

Nothing.

She knocked again. "Are you okay?"

Nothing.

Concerned, she sucked in a long breath and called, "I'm coming in," then pushed on the door.

There was a sitting room, of course, then some sort of anteroom, then a slight nudge on another door took her into his bedroom.

He lay sideways across the bed, facedown, in his underwear.

Oh, Lord, he had a perfect behind.

She raced over and gave his thighs a light shove trying to move him more securely onto the bed. "Come on, let's get you straightened out, maybe under the covers."

"No."

"Really. This can be easy. We'll get you under the covers and I'll grab some ibuprofen—" She glanced around. "Do you have a medicine cabinet?"

"Of course, I have a medicine cabinet!"

"Good, then you get yourself under the covers. I'll get the ibuprofen and call the kitchen for chicken soup."

He didn't move. "Great."

She went into his bathroom and gaped. The walls were marble, and she swore the fixtures were real gold. Lots of bathrooms could pull off a spa-like look, but this bathroom was—regal. There was no other word for it.

It took a minute to find ibuprofen then fill a glass with water. When she returned to his room, he was still facedown on the bed.

"You have to get up to take the meds."

He said nothing but rolled over and hoisted himself into a sitting position. Demi blinked, keeping her eyes upward, not even peeking at things that weren't her business, as they weren't at that point yet.

He took the pills and downed them before he took a long drink of water. As he did that, she pulled back the covers, more than a hint that he needed to get into bed properly. He rose and rebelliously yanked down the covers on the other side then slid into bed.

"I'm going to call your parents and cancel dinner tonight."

He nestled under the covers. "My grammy's going to be mad."

She pressed her mouth together to keep from laughing. "Your grammy will get over it. You need some rest."

She called Rowan's cell and told her that Liam appeared to be ill. "I didn't check his temperature, but when I put my palm on his forehead he was burning up."

"Did he take something?"

"I made him take some ibuprofen and I'll call the kitchen for soup. Go ahead with dinner without us. I want to stay here to make sure he's okay."

"Want the twins to feed the cats?"

"Yes! Thank you. I didn't even think of that."

"We'll also be sending up a doctor. It's protocol."

"Oh."

"He might only have a cold, but he has to be checked out."

Now that Rowan mentioned it, Demi was glad it was protocol. "Seriously, it looks like a mild virus but I'd be very happy to have that confirmed."

"Good. The doctor will be up in a few minutes."

The doctor turned out to be a middle-aged woman, who arrived with a physician's assistant and a nurse.

They took his temperature, took blood and inserted an IV.

"Fluids," the doctor said as she scribbled something on a chart.

"And vitamins," the male PA added with a smile.

"Once we get the results of his blood work, we'll know what's going on. Then treatment might be more specific."

"It looks like a simple virus."

The doctor snorted. "I think we've learned in the past few years that not all viruses are simple." She headed for the door. The nurse and PA scrambled to gather up everything.

"I'll report to the King."

Demi shook her head. "I can call him."

The doctor, PA and nurse looked appalled. "There'll be an official report."

"Really? For a cold?"

The doctor sighed and walked through the anteroom saying, "Even if it's a common cold there's an official report."

Within seconds, the team was gone, and Demi was alone in Liam's quarters. She ambled into the bedroom to confirm that he was sleeping peacefully—despite the IV in his arm.

He still lay under the covers in only his underwear, but the doctor hadn't said anything about dressing him in royal pajamas, and he didn't appear to be uncomfortable, so Demi left him as he was.

She turned to the doorway but found it difficult to leave the room. An odd emotion filled her. Not tenderness. More like responsibility. But not cold, hard facts responsibility. More of a need to care for someone she liked.

She strolled to a chair a few feet away from the foot of the huge king-sized bed. As she sat, she noticed a book on the lamp table beside the chair. She picked it up and smiled. He was reading the same bestseller she was.

Careful not to lose his place, she scrolled through the pages to the spot where she'd left off and began reading. But after a few minutes she stopped.

The dichotomy of something as simple as a book amid the majesty of the bedroom suite shifted through her. She'd seen it a million times in his life. One minute, Liam was a normal guy. The next he was a future king. Some people treated him like a friend. Others bowed and scraped.

It must be weird to live like that.

But he never complained. He never behaved as if he himself saw it.

After about an hour, he woke up to go to the bathroom. When he swung his legs off the bed the IV pole shifted and swayed.

"It's only some fluid, spiked with vitamins," she said, rushing over to help him.

He brushed her aside and rolled the IV pole to the bathroom on his own.

More weirdness fluttered through her. This man would be her husband in a few weeks, and he didn't want her helping him.

But why would he? She might act like a queen, but she never behaved like a future wife.

And he'd clearly stopped wanting her to.

He'd lowered his expectations.

Sadness rippled through her.

Still, maintaining some distance between them was for the best.

Wasn't it?

It was. They could be happily married without either one of them being vulnerable. There was no need for love when there was respect and courtesy.

She would see to it.

CHAPTER ELEVEN

TWO DAYS BEFORE the engagement ball, Demi's parents flew into the private airstrip of Prosperita's royals. She'd tried to dissuade Liam from meeting them at the airport with her, but he was insistent.

Here was where the reality of their arranged marriage would begin. Where he would finally understand why it was better for them to maintain some distance between them. Once he met her parents, he would see what he was really getting himself into.

She might be protecting herself from a broken heart, but she was also protecting him, distancing him, from her corrupt father.

Her short, chubby, dark-haired dad—Neil Viglianco—emerged from the small jet first. Wearing lightweight trousers and a short-sleeved linen shirt, he grinned as he glanced around. He saw Demi and Liam standing at the bottom of the steps and his grin grew.

"Your Highness!"

The men shook hands. Her father bussed a kiss on her cheek.

She worked not to stiffen in revulsion. In the real world, her father didn't kiss her cheek. He barely acknowledged her. Except to use her to get himself out of his debt. Now that she was about to marry royalty, he wanted to pretend they were close? The whole thing felt so much like an admission of defeat she had to fight herself not to run.

Her mom scampered down the steps a few seconds later. She wore beige linen trousers and a white blouse. Her dark hair was caught up in a knot at the top of her head. Not yet fifty, she had the glow and beauty of a much younger woman.

Completely ignoring protocol, she hugged Demi. "Sweetheart!"

Demi returned her hug. "Mom." For as much as she wanted to be angry that her mother had never protected her, she realized her mother had met and married a conman before she was twenty. In her heart of hearts, Demi knew her mom was clueless and sometimes overwhelmed.

Juliette Viglianco faced Liam. "Your Highness."

Liam accepted her hug. "You may call me Liam."

Juliette smiled. "Such a lovely name!"

"My mom told me it means warrior and protector." He smiled back at her mother and Demi's heart twisted. He was such a great guy. He really didn't deserve the awfulness that was her family. "Knowing I was the heir to the throne, she thought it appropriate."

"Very appropriate, Liam," Demi's dad said, overenthusiastically assuming the right to call a future king by his first name. "As I was not our family's heir, my mother could have given me a less commanding name." He snickered. "But paying homage to her Irish ancestry, she called me Neil... Not warrior but champion." He glanced at Demi. "I always win."

Demi's breath caught in her throat. Was that a warning? Or did he truly believe that? Did he truly believe that marrying her off to pay his debts and losing her respect was a win? She could barely wrap her head around it. But, then again, she rarely understood anything her father did.

The ride to the castle was lively as Liam pointed out the island country's elements of interest to her parents. They ambled into the foyer, where her father commented on both the chandelier and the impressionist painting on the wall.

Liam smiled and explained how the Sokol family had acquired the painting and her father nodded approvingly.

As her dad calculated the value of the items in the foyer, Liam caught her arm and pulled her to the side. "Russ will be showing your parents to their quarters in about a half an hour. He's in a meeting right now. And, honestly, I have two meetings this afternoon as well." He glanced at her parents. "Are you okay?"

"With my parents? By myself?" She laughed lightly. "I've lived with them on and off forever. I can handle them."

He kissed her forehead. "I'll try to find time this afternoon to stop by with my parents so everyone can meet. Our fathers, of course, already know each other. But there should be an official meeting."

"No. Get done the things you need to get done." Now that she had her head around her duties as wife, it was easy to support Liam. Especially after having seen him so sick, so vulnerable. So real. In the past weeks, the idea of their marriage had begun to gel in her head. It didn't hurt that Liam was a very nice man with so much responsibility it was clear why a good queen was important. Why it was better to choose someone with strength than to want a love match.

"Our parents can meet at dinner tonight," she said, referring to the fact that a dinner with the King and Queen had already been planned.

He said, "Okay," and raced away.

She pulled in a breath and faced her parents. "The head of Castle Admin is in a meeting right now. We can go to my quarters and rest for a bit or have something to eat if you haven't had lunch."

"Look at my girl," her father said, his chest puffing with pride. "Already sounding like a queen."

Ignoring that, she motioned up the stairs. "We're on the second floor."

They walked the curving stairway with her father's head swiveling from left to right and back again, as he took in the opulence of the Sokol castle.

When they reached her room, she punched in the code that opened the door and invited them to enter first with a wave of her hand.

Her dad's look of approval became a frown. "These are the quarters of the heir apparent?"

She sighed as she walked into the kitchen. "I have pastries from this morning if you wish. If you're really hungry, I can have a cook come up and make you something."

"We had lunch on the plane," her mom said, smiling as she looked around. "Such a fancy jet your prince sent for us."

Her dad sighed heavily. "I like that your prince can have a cook sent up at his command, but I still think these are shabby quarters for a future king."

"These aren't his quarters, Dad. These are mine."

Her father stopped pacing. "You aren't sleeping with him?"

Her face reddened, but not with embarrassment, with anger that her father assumed he had the right to pry. "We aren't married yet."

Her father clucked his tongue. "*Chica.* Since when did you become so modest?"

"I'm not modest. Things are done differently here."

Neil considered that. "Are you unhappy with the match?"

A familiar wave of nausea rose from her stomach to her

throat. Her father wasn't concerned about her, but his deal. "I'm fine."

"Or not," her dad said, walking to her. "It's interesting that you're here and he's elsewhere. Almost like an item for negotiation."

She wanted to say, "Don't you dare!" But knowing her father wouldn't hear her protests when he was seeing a potential opportunity, she had to calmly dissuade him.

"Don't worry about me and Liam. We're very happy and you'll get nothing more from the Sokols."

Her dad said "Humph," and walked around the apartment some more. "Call the cook. I would like a sandwich."

Relief fluttered through her. She couldn't believe she'd forgotten that with her father nothing was ever settled. Including this deal. Until she and Liam walked down the aisle, her father would be looking for an angle to get more.

Liam arrived at Demi's door at seven thirty to walk her to his parents' quarters. When she opened it, she looked even more skittish than she normally did.

"Everything okay?"

"Yes. Fine."

"Your parents get settled in?"

"Yes. Russ came by right after my father had a sandwich and I went with them to their quarters."

"Were they okay with where he put them?"

"Are you kidding? They have a view of the pool and the big gardens to the left. My father was very happy."

"Good."

They walked down the hall to the elevator that took them to the King's level. She didn't say another word in the little car as it rose, and neither did Liam. He had no idea what to expect from an evening with her parents, but her father wasn't an easy man.

When they arrived at the castle's main quarters, he heard Demi's dad even though he was in the living room.

He saw Demi wince.

"It's fine. Your dad's a gregarious guy. Our family's not made of glass. We can handle some enthusiasm."

She caught his gaze. He saw something pass through her eyes, but he also saw her bank it, as if she was well accustomed to her father's need to be the center of attention.

They walked into the living room. Rowan immediately came over to greet them, as his father called out for drink orders.

"Bartending is an interesting hobby for a king."

At Neil's comment, Jozef laughed. "It's mixology. And it *is* an interesting hobby. It combines my love for my guests with chemistry." He handed Neil the martini he'd requested. "Try this and tell me mixology is a hobby."

Neil took a sip. He paused to savor, then laughed. "You are correct. I do you a disservice by calling your talent a hobby."

Axel and Heather laughed. Jozef slapped Neil's back. Demi tensed.

As they entered the room, Jozef called out, "Demi? What can I get you?"

She glanced at Liam. "How about a cosmopolitan?"

Liam smiled. Had she just reminded him of a happy memory? Like someone in a real couple would?

Jozef said, "Good. A challenge. I haven't made a cosmopolitan in a while."

He fussed behind the bar with various bottles and juices, then began mixing her drink. Liam glanced at her father who'd taken a seat and was enjoying his martini. The guy was more than rough around the edges but as he'd told Demi, the Sokols weren't made of glass.

When the initial round of drinks had been consumed,

the butler arrived to announce dinner. Liam's dad had positioned the Vigliancos beside him at the long dining table, with Rowan on his other side. Demi sat beside her mom. Liam sat beside Demi. Axel and Heather sat beside Rowan.

Demi was nervous all through the meal and the hour of conversation in the den afterward.

Neil had suggested a game of pool with the King—asking for a bet to make it interesting, but while Jozef loved pool, he didn't bet.

Neil took a step back. "Well, of course," he said, conceding the issue. "I forget rules are different for kings."

Jozef laughed and while Neil tried to keep up his jovial demeanor, he'd lost some of his pizzazz for the rest of the evening. Liam couldn't tell if he'd been trying to make some money, or if he was angling for a place in the King's life—maybe his inner circle. Either way, Jozef won the game, something his father wouldn't normally do with a guest. Typically, he lost as a way of making a guest feel comfortable.

Liam almost smiled. His father always knew exactly how to handle people. Liam admired that and hoped to someday emulate it.

Blaming being tired from the flight, Neil and his wife retired. Shortly after, Demi asked to go back to her quarters too.

As they walked to the elevator Liam said, "See? That didn't go so badly."

She smiled. The first real smile he'd seen since she'd asked for a cosmopolitan. "No. Thank you for being so kind to my parents. I'll thank your father tomorrow."

"He'll be insulted that you assume he should be thanked for simple kindness."

She laughed, the relief in her voice evident. He knew she'd feared her parents' arrival. But everything had worked out.

"I planned a private evening for us tomorrow night."

She glanced up. "You did?"

"Just dinner. But dinner by ourselves, given that you'll probably spend the afternoon with your parents tomorrow."

Relief filled her pretty brown eyes again. "Thank you."

"You're welcome."

They were silent in the elevator and equally quiet on the walk to her quarters. She punched the lock code into the keypad, then faced him. "Things really did go a lot better than I'd worried they would."

He grinned. "I told you. We're not made of glass."

"Plus, your father is even more gifted with handling people than he is with making drinks."

"I know. I watch him all the time. He rarely insults. Rarely shouts. Rarely reprimands. But he controls the room. It's a skill I hope to develop myself."

She shook her head. "Oh, you already have it."

The smile she gave him was half-warm, half-confused. He tried to imagine what it would be like to go from her world into his and his head spun. Yet she was excelling in Prosperita and he admired her so much for rising to the challenge.

Their gazes met and held. Then she rose to her tiptoes, took his chin in her hand and kissed him. Soft and sweet, he could have thought it a thank you, but the touch of her lips on his had more of an experimental feel to it. This time passion or lust didn't control her. This time, she was really kissing him.

And suddenly, he got protective. The emotion that rolled through him was different than anything he'd ever felt. It wasn't warm. It wasn't fuzzy. It felt more like an infusion of anger-based strength. He'd die before he let anyone hurt her again.

Especially her father.

* * *

The following afternoon, when Liam glanced out his office window and saw the Viglianco family at the pool, he rose and went to his quarters. Wearing swim trunks and a T-shirt, he joined them, relaxing on a long chaise. It didn't take a genius to see that her father was the source of her anxiety. But it had taken him a while to realize how strong Demi was to have dealt with this man for over two decades.

And won most of the time.

In fact, being forced into an arranged marriage with him seemed to be the first time she hadn't been able to hold her own.

"Your Highness!" her father boomed. "What a pleasure to have you join us."

"The pleasure is mine."

Demi gave him a confused look, but he only waggled his eyebrows. The weeks she'd been living in the castle he'd left her to her own devices most of the time. That had resulted in her forming good friendships with Heather and Rowan. She'd needed time for that. But their public appearances and dinner dates had forged a relationship for them too.

He wanted to protect her from her father. She'd been nothing but accommodating with his family. And though she still wasn't ready to sleep with him, she kissed him like no one ever had before—

The thought rumbled through him until he realized his feelings for her had gone beyond their deal. He wasn't settling for her. He liked her. Their marriage might not be fueled by love. But they liked each other. In some ways that was better than love.

"Can I get anyone anything?"

Demi's mother smiled. "A pitcher of iced coffee would be great."

He pressed a few numbers on his cell phone, then set it on the table beside his chaise. "So how is everyone today?"

"How can a man not be happy in this paradise! Our suffocating weather wrings the life out of a man. Yours is always pleasant."

"In the summer, our temperatures could probably rival yours," Liam said, as a server arrived with a pitcher of iced coffee and one of iced tea. He motioned to the table near his chaise, then sat up, so he could pour the drinks.

"And look at these grounds! So perfect."

"Our palace is equally beautiful," Demi said congenially.

Her dad snorted. "My brother likes garish things, as if he's trying to prove his worth." He looked at Liam. "Your family has nothing to prove."

"Oh, don't be so sure. Every royal family gets its tests."

"But you win."

"Let's just say we prefer diplomacy. But if that doesn't work, we know how to fight."

Neil's chest puffed out. "Yes, you do."

Happy with himself, Neil didn't seem to get the message. Taking another tack, Liam said, "Have you made your plans for dinner?"

"Why no! We haven't."

"If you're interested in seeing the island, there are plenty of wonderful restaurants. Or you can eat here at the castle. Our chefs are amazing."

Neil looked affronted. "We were hoping to have dinner with you."

"Demi and I have reservations for a private evening." He held out his hand to her and though she appeared to be confused, she walked over to his chaise and took it. With a nudge, he suggested she sit on the chaise beside his. Finally seeing what he was doing, she smiled and sat.

And that was it. That was the moment he freed her from

her father. Not with an argument or a threat. With a gesture. If Neil messed with Demi again, the entire weight of the Sokol family would come down on him.

He didn't have to say the words. He could see from the expression in Neil's eyes that he got it.

CHAPTER TWELVE

THE DAY OF the engagement ball, Demi dressed for the official pictures which would be taken that day for the royal archives. Rowan had suggested a light-colored dress, as she had for Demi's ballgown.

"You look amazing in pink, yellow, pale blue. You should wear one of those colors."

She chose a collarless yellow dress with cap sleeves and a white belt. Liam wore his military uniform. He seamlessly obeyed every suggestion of the photographer. Stand here. Put your hand there.

Not for the first time, Demi realized how dedicated he was to his country, his duty. But she couldn't stop thinking about how he'd handled her father. She'd been so worried her dad would either steamroll the Sokols or sneakily try to get one over on them. But she needn't have even been concerned. Liam had handled him so smoothly her father couldn't even get angry.

The first three pictures had her sitting on a Queen Anne chair with Liam standing behind her, then standing on her right and then on her left. Another set of pictures were taken with them sitting on a bench. One shot had her standing behind him with her hands on his shoulders.

With every picture she relaxed a little more—until the end of the shoot, when somehow or another her father not only found them but barged in.

"I'd like copies of these."

"Of course," the photographer said.

"You are beautiful," Demi's dad said.

She smiled, but she'd lived with her father too long to believe this was a coincidence. He might not be plotting something, but he had to have realized he'd fallen out of favor with Liam and might be working to close that gap.

Oblivious, Liam rose and held out his hand to her. "Yes," he said, looking at her, though he spoke to her father. "She is beautiful."

"And you are quite lucky."

Liam smiled. "I know that."

Gazing into his sincere eyes, Demi could see he believed that. She'd shown him all along that she could make a good queen. She'd even melted for his kisses. But she'd held him at bay for so long, another man might be put out. Liam seemed to have grown to like her more.

Something inside her fluttered to life. If she was ever going to trust a man, Liam would be that man. She didn't care that he'd had the love of his life. He was extremely kind to her, and he intended to do his duty—which included being a good husband.

There'd be no love. But to a woman who'd known so many lies, trust somehow seemed like a much better bet.

She took a breath, then another and said the one thing she knew Liam needed to hear. "I'm lucky too."

Their gazes held. The air in the room filled with something she could neither define nor describe.

He was giving her a shot at a life thousands of miles away from a father she'd had to fight nearly every day.

It was up to her what she did with that life.

The truth was so staggering she nearly swayed.

Oddly, this arranged marriage really was her chance to be herself, live her own life.

* * *

Liam walked her from the photo studio to her quarters. The feelings that rumbled through him were almost sacred. Though she wore a ring that had been in his family for generations, tangling with her father had been the real sealing of their commitment for him. The pictures that afternoon had made it official.

Now, every step they took seemed more weighty.

Maybe because he knew he could not back out. His feelings for Demi might not be love but they were strong, and they bound him to her.

He could have kissed her goodbye at her door, but something stopped him. Though she and Rowan wanted hours to get her ready for the ball, he spent those hours in his office, staring out the window. He was marrying a woman he genuinely liked. Someone he'd protect to the bitter end. It all felt very husbandly, but she didn't seem to have the same feelings for him.

He wondered if she ever could. Growing up with a domineering, dangerous father had probably made her cautious, but having the man she loved leave her because her father had paid him had probably doubled her doubts about men and commitments.

Part of him couldn't blame her. If life hurts someone enough, they will build walls high enough that no one could hurt them again. He knew that all too well from how Lilibet had hurt him.

Truth be told, he wasn't any more willing to trust again than she was. They might not have secrets and they might not have told each other lies, but they would always hold something back from each other.

They were even. Except, given the chance he'd sleep with her.

The observation made him laugh and shake his head.

Then he returned to his quarters and dressed for the ball. Most grooms had hopes and expectations. He was absolutely clueless what his marriage would hold.

At the appropriate time, he walked to her apartment to escort her to their engagement ball. When she opened the door to him, his breath stuttered the way it always did.

He'd never met a more beautiful woman and for a second he wished they could be in love. He wished he was smitten with this beautiful woman, and she had tumbled head over heels in love with him.

"You're..." Words failed him. Her peach-colored gown complemented both her complexion and her hair and shimmered with sparkly things that seemed to have been sewn into the fabric arbitrarily to make it look like the dress had a life of its own. The bodice dipped low. The full skirt flowed with energy and light. "Stunning."

She ducked her head as she slid a bracelet on her wrist. "Thank you." She picked up the skirt of the dress. "It's embroidered tulle. Rowan suggested the color. Once I saw it on me, I knew she'd chosen well."

Something was different tonight. Demi always accepted compliments gracefully. Today she was subdued. He knew she'd appreciated his kindnesses to her parents, and the show of strength and independence he'd made with her father. Maybe her acquiescence was her thank you?

His chest pinched. He might not be smitten but he did like her. Deep down, she was a good person who had had a terrible life—

The urge to talk to her about all this tiptoed through him. To ask her how she felt, ask about her dreams, ask what she wanted from their marriage.

Instead, half afraid of her answers, more afraid of revealing himself to her, he held out his hand. "Ready?"

She smiled. "As ready as I'll ever be."

The smile hit him in the chest again, filling him with a longing for closeness that he couldn't deny he felt. But once again, he ignored it.

She gave her hand to him, and they walked out into the wide corridor and to the elevator that would take them to the waiting area for the ballroom.

As the little car descended, she quietly said, "You look very handsome."

He laughed and squeezed her hand. "Thank you."

"Are you required to wear a military uniform for everything formal?"

"Mostly. I did serve in the military. And as heir to the throne, I hold the title of general until I assume the role of king. Then I will be the official head of the military."

She peeked up at him. "You do a lot of things."

"My father does more."

"Yes. But you do your share."

"That's only fair, isn't it?"

She laughed again. Something warm passed between them. He realized how casually they held hands now. Almost without even realizing they were doing it. Like two people who really cared about each other.

Then the elevator doors opened, and they were all but accosted by Axel and Heather.

"Where have you been? The media's chomping at the bit."

Heather fluffed Demi's hair. "You look spectacular. Good God! That's the most beautiful gown I've ever seen."

Only a few weeks pregnant, blonde-haired, green-eyed Heather didn't look like she was carrying a child and could still wear a form-fitting red dress that made her look like a siren. Her eyes sparkled and so did Axel's. Liam had never seen two people more spontaneously, more perfectly in love than his younger brother and his wife.

He felt a moment of envy, a few seconds of longing to

be able to love Demi, to trust her with his heart, but he banked it.

This was his life. Doing what needed to be done.

Axel said, "Dad and Rowan have been amusing guests in the reception line. Now that you're here, we can move along."

Liam laughed. "We're not cattle. Give us a minute to adjust."

He faced Demi. "You good?"

"Yes. I'm good."

Axel groaned. "I hope that means you're ready." He gave a signal to one of the guards, then he and Heather left the anteroom.

"They'll get my parents from the reception line, then join them at the main table. Your parents should already be there." He wasn't sure why, but he felt he had to explain things to this quiet Demi. "Then we'll walk out to a spotlight. The media will be there, taking what they consider to be first pictures of us as an engaged couple, even though Castle Admin really had the first pictures taken."

She laughed.

He nodded to a guard who reached to open the door. "Let's go."

They walked into the ballroom. When the spotlight hit them, Liam squeezed Demi's hand and something warm and happy floated through her. It stayed with her through the announcements, the toasts, the first dance and meeting the hundreds of people who wished them good luck.

Close to the end of the evening, a waltz began to play, and Liam escorted her onto the crowded dance floor. A million jumbled thoughts and feelings had hounded her all night, but mostly the idea that Liam was giving her a chance— not at a better life—at a real life.

He was strong. He was smart. He was confident. And he liked her. She could tell he liked her. He wasn't stuck with her because of a deal. He wasn't seeking a good queen. *He liked her.*

As they glided along the dance floor, their gazes caught. He was the most honorable man she'd ever met, and the sense that they were meant to be together rose up in her. Instead of tightening her chest, something deep inside her shook loose.

They'd never have the wild, stupid love of people who fell for each other normally, but they could—they did—have a certain level of trust.

Something in his eyes shifted, sharpened.

Their gazes held.

Her thoughts solidified. This man was hers.

When the music stopped, he kept ahold of her hand, leading her to a secret exit.

"Where are we going?"

He stopped, kissed her.

She melted. She knew exactly where he was leading her. "Won't someone miss us?"

"Who? Everybody will just think we're with somebody else."

She laughed. "Don't we have to say goodbye?"

His blue eyes held hers. "Do you want to say goodbye? Break this mood?"

"No." The sheen in his eyes made her heart hammer in her chest. He wanted her as much as she wanted him. They wouldn't have love, but they would have trust.

And this.

CHAPTER THIRTEEN

HE KISSED HER in the elevator, kissed her on the way to the door to his suite and kissed her through the sitting room and anteroom until they got to his bed.

A slight bump on her shoulder had her tumbling backward and she skittered to a seating position. Laughing at him, she said, "Stop being silly. Don't you think we should take our time?"

He undid his tie. "No."

He shucked his jacket and shirt. Kicked off his shoes. Crawled to her on the big bed.

All night long he'd been touching her gown, feeling it slide against his palm, now he wanted her naked.

His hands went to the back of her dress. Finding the zipper, he lowered it to her waist, watching as it fell off her shoulders, down her breasts.

"You are beautiful. Perfect."

She smiled. "You're only saying that because it's true."

He laughed. "Are we going to go back to that discussion on vanity?"

"You said a person should know her strengths. I know mine."

She gave him a light tap and he fell to the bed. Not from the force of her tap, but from his own need to see what she intended.

The top of her gown clinging to her waist, exposing her perfect breasts, she straddled him. When she bent to kiss him, her breasts grazed his chest. Liquid heat roared through him. His hands caught her breasts. The softness, the suppleness nearly did him in.

He wanted to savor, to enjoy her, but after waiting so long, his patience deserted him. He found the zipper of her dress again, yanking it the entire way down. But that still left her in hundreds of yards of tulle. She shifted to the side, freeing her dress which he literally threw across the room. Though he liked her pretty peach panties, he yanked them off and tossed them too.

He rolled her to her back and kissed her again as she undid his belt. He managed to get rid of his clothes while still kissing her. With them both naked, he finally touched her and found her ready.

Without need of further invitation he entered her, then stopped to groan. "You are so perfect."

She ran her fingers through his hair. "So you have said."

He caught her gaze. "Well, that makes me very lucky."

She slid her fingers through his hair again. "I think we are both very lucky."

He moved slowly at first then brought them to a fevered pitch that provided a release for both. In the same way that his simple gesture at the pool had shifted her from her father to him, making love seemed to create another connection between them. There was no denying they were together now.

The second time they made love their movements were slow, deliberate. His fingers grazing her skin, Liam caught her gaze. The intimacy of it sent a shaft of lightning through her that softened her heart, making her remember how easily she'd told him she believed they were both lucky. She might want to be a good queen and have a good relationship and even trust him to a point. He'd proven himself to her over and over again the past few weeks. But she hadn't changed her position on holding part of herself back. Slips like telling him they were both lucky could build over time, shift her viewpoint, soften her heart. And if she wasn't very careful, she'd be in love.

She couldn't love him. Not if she wanted to protect herself from being hurt.

But she also didn't want to hurt him. They had duties to each other, unspoken promises. She would keep those to the best of her ability. She would give him what he needed through being a good wife.

She threw herself into the physical aspects of what they were doing, touching him, kissing him, retaining their intimacy but in a way that gave them closeness but wasn't love.

She was glad that they both fell asleep, but she was even happier when she woke in the middle of the night and could slide out of his bed. Leaving was the best way to keep herself grounded in the truth of their relationship.

She gathered her clothes, silently slipping into her gown again so she could sneak down the hall and go to her room. Her own quarters.

Her gown swishing as she moved, she felt her perspective and her resolve returning. She truly liked Liam. She trusted him on some very important matters. But not all. She would never completely give herself to him.

Her cats met her at the door, and she stooped down to pet them, refusing to let herself acknowledge the dangerous ground she was on. She could have slipped tonight and fallen in love with her soon to be husband.

But once again, she'd hit a new level of awareness. Recognizing how easy it would be to slip, she'd raised her guard a little more.

* * *

Liam showed up at her door the next morning with flowers. While he was a bit confused about her leaving his quarters in the middle of the night, he was so blissfully happy that they'd finally found their footing as a couple that he could forgive her anything.

"We can do whatever you want." He walked up behind her in her small kitchen, wrapped his arms around her waist and kissed the back of her neck. Wearing the jeans he liked and a light blue sweater, she looked to be ready for the day. Though he wanted to entice her back into bed, he'd decided to save that for tonight. He'd have champagne chilling, strawberries and romantic music waiting for them when they returned. "Including go out on the yacht."

She peeked over her shoulder at him. "Private time?"

"Rest time. We've both had a very difficult week. There are plenty of swimsuits available if you want to swim, or we could just watch the water and the skyline."

"For hours?"

With a chuckle, he turned her in his arms. "I'm going to have to teach you how to rest."

"It sounds lovely." She bit her lower lip. "But I haven't spent very much time with my parents. I should probably at least have lunch with them."

"Let's make it breakfast. Then we can change into something comfortable and just enjoy the day."

She clearly tried to hold back a smile, but the lift of her lips wouldn't be denied. "That might work."

"That *will* work."

And so would his plan to keep her to himself that day.

On the yacht, they swam, then slept on chaise lounges on the top deck, like two cats in the sun. A chef prepared a seven-course meal for dinner, which Liam deemed appropriate given that they'd skipped lunch.

She'd seemed surprised when Leo appeared, ready to take them back to the castle, until Liam opened the doors on his quarters and she'd seen the front room full of flowers, and the strawberries and champagne in his bedroom.

He'd expected to have to seduce her, but she walked willingly into his arms and kissed him in a way that left nothing to the imagination of what she had planned for that night.

Though she didn't appear to need to be wooed, he courted her anyway with soft touches and kisses that lured her into relaxing so much she all but melted under his eager hands.

This time, though, he didn't fall asleep. He wanted to wake up with her in the morning. He wanted to reach out and know she had been with him all night.

He knew better than to talk of love. Technically, they'd only known each other a few weeks. She was still skittish and he wasn't in love.

He liked her. He liked so much about her. But they were also very, very different people. With different upbringings. Different internal rules. Different responsibilities. His first was to his country. He had no idea where her loyalties lay. But at some point, they had to be with him.

That was their next step. Even without loving him, she could be loyal to him first, his country second. After that, she could make her own choices—

And if he had his way, her over-the-top parents wouldn't even make the list.

When he rolled over and rested his head on his pillow, he took her with him, nestling her against his side.

"So…you had a nice day?"

"A wonderful day."

"That's good because tomorrow we have two public appearances. One in the morning and one in the evening. The visit to our veterans' hospital will be our first appearance after our engagement ball. Reporters will ask you a million questions. Some of them will be stupid, like did you enjoy the engagement ball."

She laughed. "You're right. That's pretty stupid."

"Yes, but the people want to know. It's like they want a peek into your private life—or who you are. Remember... you're still new to them."

She nodded. "But you keep forgetting I'm not new to royal life. I'm pretty sure I can handle a few questions."

He kissed her forehead. "Good."

She tried to roll away. He held her fast. The dilemma of his growing feelings tiptoed into his brain and reminded him to be careful. She'd been hurt and he'd been hurt by the woman he adored. He was smarter now, careful. Kings could not be vulnerable.

But he was also ready to take the next steps in their relationship. They would be married in six weeks. It was not out of line to want to live with her.

In fact, he saw it as the clearest path to getting her even more accustomed to him and the new life they would be creating together.

Given their situation and her past, he knew blunt honesty was the only way to go. "Move in with me."

She propped herself up on her elbows and gaped down at him. "What?"

"I love having you here. And, admit it, you're starting to like me too."

"I liked you all along."

"You had a funny way of showing it."

She laughed. "I wasn't exactly testing the limits, but it was nice to know you weren't going to steamroll me."

A sigh of relief whispered through him. He'd done the right thing by being patient. "I want a partner. There will always be things we have to do, but our personal lives should be about give and take. Compromise. As all good relationships are."

She studied his face. "I'd like that."

"Everybody likes that in a relationship." He sat up too, caught her arms and gazed into her eyes. "So, live with me."

He watched the debate going on in her brain. Finally, she sighed. "No."

He felt as out of control as he had every time he'd kissed her goodnight and she'd jumped into her quarters. He knew she'd done that to stop her cats escaping. But she'd still gone in without him.

Now she wouldn't move in with him.

"I don't want to cite religious rules or the question of appearances. Because that's not it. Really, I want our wedding day to be special." She held his gaze. "I want it to mean something. I want it to mark the beginning. Not be an extension of something we started almost without thought."

"Trust me. I've given this lots of thought." And so had his hormones and a few body parts.

"We have weeks. Not years or even months before we will make our commitment. I'd like to save living together to make it special."

He heard what she was saying and, if he were honest with himself and ignored his hormones, he totally understood. He also saw the romance of it. Being in an arranged marriage, they needed all the romance they could get.

He sighed. "I understand."

She leaned forward and kissed him. "Thank you."

The two simple words fought their way into his heart and made him glad he'd agreed.

Though they made love a second time and he'd been awake when she'd fallen asleep, he woke once again to find her gone the next morning.

He understood her not wanting to live together. He did

see the romance of starting their new life the day they actually made their commitment to create that life. But seriously, she couldn't even sleep over?

He kept that thought as he showered and dressed for the visit to the veterans' hospital. Ten minutes before their scheduled time to leave, he arrived at the door of her quarters and knocked.

The door immediately opened. Her father grinned at him. "We are joining you for your visit to the veterans' hospital!"

The door opened wider, and he walked inside. Demi wore a tight smile.

Neil slapped him on the back. "Rowan believes this will be good PR. A way for us to be seen in your country."

Demi said, "Dad, Rowan was being polite when she agreed with you about that."

"Nonsense! I know a bit about public relations myself," Neil replied, walking over to a chair to get the navy-blue jacket that matched his trousers. "And we've barely been present in the newspaper articles about you and your marriage." He clucked his tongue. "Somebody fell down on the job. We should be front and center."

Liam said nothing, wanting to hear her dad's entire reasoning before he tried to figure out a way to combat it.

Unfortunately, there was none. He couldn't even think of a good reason to take separate limos. Everybody piled into Liam's limo with Leo graciously greeting everyone as he held the door.

But Liam watched Demi. Despite her desire to keep her distance from them, she was a good daughter. It was also clear that she loved her mother.

In the interest of honesty, he asked her about it that night.

"My parents met when my mom was very young, not even out of her teens. I'm sure my father painted a very pretty picture for her about life in *his* kingdom, and she fell for it because she didn't want to see the truth—I think she's afraid to see the truth. I'm not even a hundred percent sure she knew how bad their financial situation was when he arranged our marriage to bail him out."

Pulling himself off his pillow and leaning against the headboard, Liam said, "That would make sense."

"She's a nice person," Demi said urgently. "And I genuinely believe she loves him."

Liam conceded that with a, "Hmmm. Maybe. How do you feel about him?"

"He's my father," she said carefully. "But let's just say I'll be very happy to have a few thousand miles between us."

Liam laughed, pulled her to him and kissed her.

But when her father suggested that it was so close to Christmas that it might be better for him and Demi's mom to stay until after the holiday, Liam politely suggested they go home and return on Christmas Eve. He realized that after the holiday, her dad could say it was so close to the wedding they might as well stay, and he didn't want Demi to have to deal with them while planning their wedding.

He played the bad guy, suggested they go home for some recoup time and return on Christmas Eve—or even the week before the wedding.

CHAPTER FOURTEEN

THE PLANS FOR the wedding got set aside the week before Christmas and the week after. Christmas morning included breakfast with the King and Queen and opening gifts with the twins. But Liam came to her quarters early, suggesting they open their gifts alone.

Glad to have some private time, she reached under the small tree Castle Admin had assembled in her room and handed his gift to him.

He opened it and chuckled. "A leather-bound edition of the first Sherlock Holmes novel."

"Russ suggested it. I knew you read," she said hastily. "Actually, we were reading the same book when I stayed in your room the night you were sick. It didn't cost a fortune, but Russ said you loved Sherlock Holmes."

He leaned forward and kissed her. "I do. And I love the gift. It's perfect. You know there's an Enola Holmes now?"

She shook her head.

"Written by an American, Nancy Springer. Enola is Sherlock's little sister. I'd like to reread all the originals before I jump into those."

"I did good?"

He laughed. "You did good."

He reached into his trouser pocket and produced a jewelry box. Half afraid to open it, she took a deep breath, undid the ribbon and lifted the lid.

She gasped when she saw a ruby necklace. Not a chain with one ruby or a ruby pendant. But a string of perfect rubies. She stared at it in wonder, finally understanding what it was to be a princess. The necklace meant more to her than her engagement ring. The ring might be a symbol, but the necklace was a gift. A statement of how he felt about her.

She freed it from the box, held it like the precious jewelry that it was.

He took it from her. "The color is for passion," he said as he slipped it on her neck. "Which we have in abundance."

She looked at it in a mirror on the wall behind the sofa, and a million points of light winked back at her.

"The extravagance of it," he said, as he turned her away from the mirror and to him. "Is to help you understand your place here. You are a princess," he said, holding her gaze. "You will be a queen. But you are also mine and I am yours. We were lucky to be matched. That's worth more than gems. More than gold. The necklace represents that."

She touched it reverently, working to hold back tears. He had to be the most wonderful person in the world. Not merely kind, but with the soul of a poet.

She wore the necklace to breakfast, even though dress was casual, and she'd dressed in jeans and a sweater. Even her father had chosen a sweater and jeans over trousers and a jacket. Her mom looked amazing in white pants and a white cashmere sweater.

Oddly, they'd begun to fit in with the Sokols. Her father was more subdued. Her mother ebullient. As if their personalities had flipped. For the first time in Demi's life, she truly believed her mother was relaxed and happy.

Christmas moved into New Year's Eve which Liam and

Demi spent alone. New Year's Day seemed to be dedicated to the twins.

They woke the day after the holidays to the realization that they'd be married in two weeks. Their phones blew up with texts. Hers from the castle chefs, florist, decorators and Russ who wanted a few minutes to coordinate a few things with her. Liam's texts were from reporters. Everybody wanted an interview. Everybody wanted the scoop on the happy couple.

From them both.

Everybody could see she was happy. Everybody could see he was happy. His subjects wanted to be part of that.

She started to climb out of bed to get busy, but he caught her hand and pulled her back for a long, lingering kiss.

"Good morning."

She laughed. "We shouldn't ever pick up our phones before we say good morning."

"That's an excellent rule. I think we should keep it."

Staring into his pretty blue eyes, she agreed. Looking at him, talking to him was the most wonderful way to start the day.

"I'd suggest a little time in the shower together, but I have to handle some of this now."

She glanced at her phone, saw the time and winced. "I can't remember the last time I slept this late!"

He slid himself up into a seated position. "Sleeping late is one of the perks of being royalty."

She gaped at him. "You lie! You're worse than I am about being up and ready to go before everybody else."

He leaned across the bed to kiss her again. "It's the job of a king."

She laughed and would have hauled herself out of bed and into her clothes, but he held her where she was.

"You do realize you slept with me last night."

The realization sort of shocked her. They'd become so comfortable with each other she'd awoken that morning as if she was meant to be there.

"I liked it."

"I liked it too." She smiled and ran her fingers along his jaw, enjoying the feel of him. "But don't get used to it. I'm still holding us to the no living together deal."

He laughed and let her scoot away. She all but jumped into her clothes, then leaned across the bed to kiss him goodbye.

In her apartment, she said hello to the cats as she raced down the hall, shucking clothes for her shower. Even though she had a day packed with meetings, she felt light and airy. She almost asked Rowan to attend her meetings with her but in the end decided she wanted the final decisions to be hers.

The realization that she was comfortable in her role climbed through her. All along her goal was to be a good queen for Liam and now she knew she would be.

Everything was falling into place exactly as it should.

Except her meetings took longer than expected and what she'd thought would be a morning of conversations and decisions became a week of conversations and choices.

It seemed the only times she saw Liam were crawling into bed or crawling out of bed.

"I think you're kidding yourself if you believe sleeping together every night doesn't count as living together."

She groaned. "My days are so packed that I don't have time to think straight. And since I'm planning my wedding to *you*, you should leave me to my illusions."

He rolled her over on the bed and landed on top of her. "Okay." He kissed her. Even as every cell in her body relaxed with the comfort of being with him, they sprang to life in a different way. Lately, he couldn't look at her without her heart skipping a beat or her breath stuttering. She hadn't had the horrible feeling of being trapped in weeks. She knew she was home.

She brushed her fingers through his hair. "Have I told you—"

She stopped herself as her mouth fell open in disbelief. She'd almost said she loved him.

His lips slid down to kiss her neck. "Told me what?"

"That this wedding is complicated?"

"Which is why you're so busy."

The conversation took such an easy turn that it was clear he had no clue what she'd almost said, but the feeling of it shook her to her core. All these wonderful emotions pouring through her, all the security of being with him, being part of his life, all the happiness meant love.

This was love.

The ease of it. The silliness they could share without fear. The happiness that bubbled up. The warmth of joy of just being with him—

This was *love*.

She loved him.

The ecstasy of it made her blood sing, even as it made her bold. She wanted to say it. But he had to say it back. She could not be in love with a man who didn't love her. She could not be like her mom. So happy, so starry-eyed she didn't see the truth.

If he said it, they would be even. Because if he said it, she would know he meant it. Meant every aspect of it.

Meant she could trust him.

Completely.

Then they could let the chips fall where they may.

She took a breath. "It's interesting the way everything turned out for us."

"You call it interesting. I call it lucky."

"You keep calling us lucky—"

His lips trailed down to her chest. "Very lucky. I mean look at us."

He didn't seem to be getting her hints, so she pushed him again. "Look at what?"

"The fact that we get along. That's because we genuinely like each other."

Like…not love.

But she knew this was love. Real love. Not infatuation or romance. Real love. She didn't merely trust him. She *loved* him.

It felt like the time to get him to admit it, but doubts stopped her.

He might not feel as she did. He'd had the love of his life. He'd always spoken as if that meant he couldn't have a second love. But Lilibet wasn't anywhere around. She was getting married too.

And Liam was a powerful man with lots on his mind. Demi had every inch of his attention when they were alone. And when they made love, they were perfect together.

He was right. They were lucky. And maybe she shouldn't push it? Maybe she shouldn't push *him* when he had so many other things on his mind, including marrying her.

But the next morning, watching the way he played with the twins at breakfast and then greeted her parents when she and Liam picked them up at the airport, as they arrived for the wedding, she *did* question their luck.

Not that she believed they somehow didn't deserve the good things that seemed to be coming their way. But she suddenly saw that Liam deserved more than to "like" the woman he was committing to for the rest of his life. He was kind, generous, diplomatic and self-sacrificing. Life, fate, destiny, whatever, should be giving him someone he *loved*. Not someone he liked.

He's had the love of his life. But maybe not getting Lilibet means there isn't another love out there for him? Maybe she was exactly what he needed?

That sounded right. But what did she know? The man she'd loved had left her for money. And she had been gobsmacked. She hadn't had an inkling he could be bought.

Maybe it was smarter for her to accept what she could get from a man she knew wouldn't hurt her?

The last thought bolstered her. Liam was busy. He probably didn't have time to think through the differences between like and love. And why would he? It was a nitpicky distinction. A word choice.

His kindnesses to her parents that night at a private dinner with them flooded her with honesty. He'd rescued her, changed her father, made her mother happy. He'd taken care of her cats. Eased her into castle life. Courted her.

While she'd accepted all these good things, what had he gotten?

Her. A princess from a disgraced father.

How could he love her? Dear God, it was a miracle he trusted her.

That afternoon she found herself on the internet, scrolling to find the pictures of him with Lilibet, the woman Demi knew he had loved. She only had to look at the pictures she'd found when she'd first investigated him to remind herself he didn't love her the same way. He'd never looked at Demi like that. Never seemed so giddy and young.

Liam liked her. He liked sex with her. He took care of her. But he didn't love her.

She told herself to forget it, to not worry about it. Not only was Lilibet marrying someone else, but Liam had made this choice. He seemed happy with her.

But he didn't love her.

He didn't have the bubbly joy inside when he looked at her the way she did when she looked at him. He didn't have the breathless anticipation of sharing their lives the way she did with him.

He had friendship, duty and responsibility.

Dry. Dull. Lifeless obligation.

Demi had been so quiet at dinner that Liam got worried. Knowing how much she loved Enzo and his restaurant, he'd taken her there for dinner, expecting that would cheer her up.

A million possibilities roamed through his brain about what could be wrong. Not the least of which was her dad. Only he had seemed subdued too. But who knew? He could be subdued in public and a holy terror in private with his daughter and wife.

"So, how's your dad?"

Her head snapped up. "Fine. Better than fine. He seems to have found his place and he's staying there."

"That's good," he said. Unfortunately, that took away his best guess about what could be troubling her. Unless he counted prewedding jitters. But they were so coordinated, so much on the same page, he couldn't believe she'd be afraid of their upcoming marriage.

He broached the subject after they drove to the castle and were entering his apartment.

"You're not having prewedding jitters, are you?"

She laughed. "No."

"I mean, I wouldn't be surprised. Lots of people have them. I could talk you through it."

"Really?"

"Yes."

"You know how to talk someone through prewedding jitters?"

"I would know how to talk *you* through prewedding jitters. I'd remind you of how much we have going for us."

She seemed to consider that, her teeth nibbling the rim of her bottom lip. "How much we have going for us?"

"Yes."

She paused again, then said, "You'd remind me of everything we have like a guy who loves me?"

He laughed. "Okay. *Like* a guy who loves you."

"Just *like* a guy who loves me?"

"You and I didn't form this relationship on something so untrustworthy as love." He walked over, took her hands. "We've both had love or someone's version of love before this and it failed us. What we have is better."

She caught his gaze. Her eyes examining his as if she were looking for the secrets to the universe. "Do you think?"

"Honestly, Demi... I *know*. Remember? I lost at love."

"You're still upset about losing Lilibet?"

He laughed. "No! That's my point. Love is insubstantial. Risky. I'm glad to be out of that relationship with Lilibet. Friendship, obligation, duty, passion...those are better. We don't need love."

He kissed her then and though she seemed to hold back for a second, she suddenly threw her whole self into the kiss, and he took everything she gave. Because this was what they had. Something better than love.

They made love with all the passion he'd spoken about. The thing he thought was better than love. In her eyes that proved their love. But the things he said, the way he dismissed love gave her a strange feeling of doom.

The consequences of him not loving her loomed over her. The emptiness she'd felt when she'd first realized she would have to marry him returned. A loss so deep and profound it stole her breath.

Plus, she couldn't stop thinking of her mother. Loving a man who didn't love her. Always seeking his approval and attention—

Would that be her someday?

Would loving Liam when he didn't love her turn her into that?

Would she follow him around, hang on his every word, wish for things that couldn't be?

The thought squeezed her chest. She saw herself losing herself. Losing her dignity, her self-respect.

And weren't those the things she'd sworn she'd never risk?

They were. She could not live like that.

They were quiet for several minutes. Long enough that she wondered if Liam had fallen asleep. But his hands began to roam, and soon he was kissing her neck. Wonderful warmth filled her. The love she felt for him rose like the morning sun—

No. She couldn't believe he didn't love her.

All this was too perfect to believe he didn't love her.

He did love her. She might not have known him long, but she understood this feeling. She took a life-sustaining breath and jumped off the deep end.

"I love you."

He stopped kissing her then started again. But he said nothing. He didn't even take the time to think it through or to argue with her, to remind her of what he'd said before. What they had was better.

The awful truth of that filled her with pain. He hadn't changed his mind. Nothing she said would change his mind. He did not love her.

He wasn't filled with anticipation of what their future could hold the way she was. She didn't make him breathless with wonder.

The most wonderful person she'd ever met didn't love her.

More horrible truth tightened her chest. He deserved to feel love—but she also deserved to be loved. She deserved to know the man she loved felt the same giddy, wonderful feeling for her that she felt for him.

This wedding was all wrong. Good enough. But not *right* for either of them. And at that moment, she knew what she had to do.

When he fell asleep, she slid out of bed and dressed in the clothes that were strewn around his bedroom. Tears filled her eyes when she leaned down and kissed his cheek.

How could she fall in love, so deeply, passionately in love, with a man who didn't love her in return?

She didn't know. But it had happened. She believed it had to do with expectations and fears. But, seriously, loving him had killed her fears. His feelings for her had not killed his. And considering how strong their feelings were, his not falling in love with her only proved she wasn't the right woman for him.

She returned to her quarters, packed only necessities and called Leo. She also called Russ to arrange a plane and made him take a vow of silence. He couldn't wake up Liam to tell him Demi had gone. He had to wait until morning, until Liam had time to listen to the voicemail that she would leave for him.

Then she put Strawberry and Shortcake in their carriers and walked out of the apartment she'd begun to think of as home. Because maybe it had been her home. Certainly, it had been the first place she'd felt respected and appreciated.

Leo frowned at her when she came out of the castle, but he didn't ask questions. For all he knew, she could have been returning to Hermosa to handle something urgent at the homeless shelter.

Except she had her cats. Normally, the twins watched them while she was spending time away from the castle or with Liam.

Leo knew that. Information traveled fast in the castle. The staff liked to be prepared.

He knew her taking the cats meant something.

She said nothing as she got into the limo and let herself be driven away. If she could have kept herself from loving Liam, they would have lived a very happy life. But loving him made her vulnerable. She'd be hurt again. Or, worse, she'd become like her mom. The dedicated wife of a man who all but ignored her.

Liam woke the next morning to an empty bed and rolled his eyes. The woman had the strangest fixation about making their living together special.

He almost picked up his phone but decided to shower before he began the daily grind. In six days, he and Demi would be married. They were going on an extended honeymoon. He had to have everything done before the wedding. Everyone in the castle knew that and they were flooding his inbox.

After showering and dressing, he picked up his phone to

text Demi about breakfast. Before he could, he saw a voice-mail message from her and clicked on it.

"Liam... I'm sorry."

He frowned. Her beautiful voice trembled. Those two simple words had seemed difficult for her to say.

"I'm on my way home. To Hermosa."

His frown deepened. There were wedding plans she was supposed to be attending to. If her father had done some-thing—

"You are the most wonderful person in the world. I am so in love with you that some days I almost can't breathe."

His brain stumbled as he heard that. Love wasn't a for-eign concept to him. But this wasn't a love match. This was a strong match. The perfect match. Love failed people. That's why they'd kept love out of it. They'd talked this out the night before. It had always been their plan.

"I'm leaving because I love you too much. You deserve to find someone you can love, someone who takes your breath away. And I deserve that love too."

He heard the rumble of noise around her and recognized it as the sound of a small jet beginning to taxi.

She quietly said, "I'm sorry," again and the voicemail stopped.

His entire body froze. They were so perfect for each other. It seemed inconceivable that she'd leave—until he remembered she'd said she loved him.

Oh, God. He'd ignored what she'd said, assuming it was a weird force of passion exclamation, because they both knew love was the most untrustworthy emotion of all.

They'd both had it; they'd both been hurt by it.

He'd thought they both recognized that love made people do irrational things and it was important to keep love out of what was such a perfect arrangement.

But she'd said she loved him. She'd said it. And meant it.

Anger exploded through him. Not just because she'd broken their deal, a deal that worked for them both. But because she'd broken the most basic promise of their relationship. Keep love out of it.

She hadn't and now she was gone.

He took a minute to breathe. He hated love so much. *Hated* it. All it ever did in his life was cause trouble. This time because the woman he wanted, the woman who seemed perfect for him, loved him.

The irony of that made him want to punch something.

Not ready to face Castle Admin or the media, he walked into the dining room for breakfast.

His father grinned when he walked in. "Where's Demi?"

He took a quiet breath, calling on his ability to absolutely control his emotions and said, "She's gone."

Rowan's face scrunched. "Gone? All her meetings are here. Where could she possibly have to go?"

"Back to Hermosa. She doesn't want to marry me. She left me a voicemail."

Jozef's face fell. Rowan's facial expression shifted several times before she said, "I can't believe it."

"I'm sure if we call Russ, he'll admit that he made her flight arrangements last night."

Rowan looked like she still couldn't believe it.

As much as he hated that he had to control this narrative, he did. Understanding the pressures of royal life the way he did, he wasn't about to jump off the deep end and admit how angry he was, how hurt he was.

He very calmly said, "I want to keep it under wraps, in case she changes her mind. She could go home and discover that it was just prewedding jitters and come back and go through with the wedding."

Jozef put his napkin on his plate, focused now on the problem at hand. "What exactly did she say in her voicemail?"

Liam shook his head. "It's kind of private."

Rowan reached across the table to smooth her hand across his consolingly. "If we're going to make decisions, we need to know."

He snorted. "Fine. She said she loves me. She believes she deserves to be loved too."

Jozef said carefully, "You don't love her?"

He snorted again. "Given my history with love, don't you think it would be stupid for me to trust in that again?"

"But Demi's so beautiful and fun and personable," Rowan protested. "How could you not love her?"

"I'm protecting myself," Liam said, getting annoyed that he was the one who had to explain himself when *she* was the one who left. Just thinking that sent an arrow of pain through his heart which he quickly relabeled anger. "We've not known each other long." A thought occurred to him, and he addressed his father. "You've told me and Axel about your arranged marriage to our mother. You said you went into it as friends and fell in love eventually. You'd known mom since grade school but didn't fall in love until I was born. Now, you think I should love a woman I've known three months?"

Rowan reached out and caught his hand again. "No. Liam. You're right. I was out of line. But we do need to discuss the possibility that this is cold feet and she'll be back."

"She might be. We had a weird conversation last night about getting prewedding jitters. I told her I could talk her out of it. She seemed skeptical that I could," he said honestly, ignoring the hope that blossomed at the thought she'd come back to him by reminding himself that if he hoped she would return it was only because they were a good match.

"Okay," Jozef said. "Let's go with that. All the preparations are being done here. It's not like we have to call outside contractors and cancel things. Let's keep a positive thought. Let's assume she really does have prewedding jitters and she'll be back in a day or two."

Rowan said, "You should call her."

He said, "I will," but knew he wouldn't. She had to come back on her own.

Demi spent her first night in Hermosa in the homeless shelter. She could have gone to the estate. Her parents weren't home. They were in Prosperita, waiting for her wedding. Plus, all her father's debts had been paid by the Sokols, so there was no more cloud hanging over the house. No fear that the bank would call in the mortgage and kick her out, or, worse, that her father's more unsavory lenders would come looking for their money.

She winced. Not having seen the actual agreement that married her off to the Sokols, she didn't know what happened if she didn't go through with the marriage. They might not owe money to her dad's former lenders, but now they would owe it to the Sokols.

Sick though it made her feel, she called her father. She had no idea what had happened when she left, but if they'd put her dad and mom on a plane home, she needed to know.

He answered on the first ring.

She took a breath. "Hey, Dad. I just wanted to let you know I'm back home."

"You're what?"

Well, that answered one question. The Sokols hadn't yet announced that she'd backed out of the wedding. They hadn't even told her parents.

"I'm in Hermosa. I decided not to marry Liam. I need

to know what happens now. Do we owe them the money they paid you?"

"Yes!" Her father's incredulous voice roared to her through the phone. "What kind of person would sign an agreement that lets me keep the money if you don't uphold our end of the deal?"

"I don't know. The Sokols are very kind."

He said nothing for a few seconds then said, "They haven't retracted their money or even asked for a meeting."

"Since you didn't know, I'm guessing they also haven't announced that the wedding is off."

"No." He paused again. His voice brightened as he said, "This gives you time to change your mind."

She wished she could. She loved the life she and Liam were building but he didn't love her. As much as she wanted what they had, she also wanted him to love *her*.

Her father's voice came through the line again. "I need to think this through."

"Maybe you and Mom should come home."

He sighed. "You're really breaking this deal?"

"I have to."

His voice tired, her dad said, "Oh, Demi. Now I start again to figure out what to do."

"Don't even think about another arranged marriage for me."

"Chica—"

"No! I am not your property, Dad! You gambled. You made those debts. *You* pay them!"

"Exactly how?"

"As long as it doesn't involve me, I don't care how. Your debts are not my problem. And if you make them my problem again, I will take mom and run so fast and so far, you will never find us. Then you will be forced to deal with some very angry people. The way you should have all along. Except at least the Sokols will only be after money, not blood."

"You would let me lose everything?"

"Are you kidding me? You had no qualm about taking away my life!"

"Liam was a good man! You would have been a queen!"

"It wasn't my choice."

"Choice," he spat. "What would be a better choice for you than to be a queen?"

To be loved. Now that she knew Liam, she also knew love was the greatest thing in this world. She wanted to feel it coming from him.

But he didn't love her. With the long flight to reflect, she'd finally seen the signs that he'd been holding back too. Maybe because he'd been hurt by Lilibet? Maybe because he didn't want to get hurt again? Or maybe because he'd finally accepted his fate as a king? His duty and responsibility and his *life* belonged to his country. He could not give them to someone else. Especially not a wife.

Maybe that was the real bottom line of how she knew he would never love her.

Liam spent the day on pins and needles waiting for Demi to call or just show up. Prewedding jitters was a perfect explanation for why she would throw away everything they had. Why she had talked of love when they both knew love was dangerous.

Basking in the excitement of his upcoming wedding, his assistant brought several newspapers into his office, all of which had headlines about the enthusiasm over his wedding. They were down to five days until he was supposed to marry. The country was going overboard with anticipation and his bride had gone.

He worked late then went to his quiet quarters. He supposed it was lucky Demi had refused to live with him. There were places in his apartment where he didn't see her face, hear her voice. His bedroom wasn't one of them. He could hear her laughter, see her shining eyes, remember the touch of her skin under his eager hands.

He changed into sweatpants and a big T-shirt and stayed in the den, watching television until his eyes drooped.

He still couldn't fall asleep. He couldn't believe a person who loved him would leave him. Her explanation made no sense. If she loved him, she should want to help him, not hurt him.

Eventually, he eased into a fitful sleep. In his dreams, he argued with her. He told her a woman who loved him would have stayed. She'd said nothing.

But how could she? She wasn't real. He was dreaming her. He didn't understand her logic, so how did he think he could make her arguments for her?

The next morning, four days till his wedding, he woke and forced himself out of the den. But he wasn't ready to go downstairs. Not to eat. Not to work. He called the kitchen for a cook and though she made his favorite bananas foster French toast, he didn't have an appetite.

The cook left after cleaning the kitchen and he threw the French toast into the trash.

He should have showered and dressed for work. But he didn't feel like working.

He didn't feel like anything. Even his anger was gone. Replaced by the confusion of not understanding how a woman who loved him thought leaving him was for the best.

Especially when he missed her. He swore his chest had a hole in it.

Twodays till his wedding, there was a knock on his door then Axel entered without waiting for permission.

"Liam! What are you doing?"

Liam ran his hand over his unshaven face. "Brooding. Kings brood."

"Well, stop brooding. I was sent here by Castle Admin to talk to you. Russ thinks you need to cancel the wedding. Now. Like today."

Liam said, "Sure. Sure. Fine." But he didn't move from the sofa.

Axel sat on the arm of the sofa. "You look like hell."

"I'm going through the biggest embarrassment of my life. I have to announce to my country that my bride doesn't want me. Even Lilibet didn't put me through that."

Axel's head titled as he pondered that. "You know, now that you mention Lilibet, you weren't this bad when she left."

Liam snorted. Lilibet leaving seemed like a lifetime ago, almost as if it had happened to another person.

"Really. You weren't. You were hurt, but you were more concerned with keeping up your kingly duties. You worked as if nothing happened. Handled the press like you'd taken PR lessons. But this," he motioned toward Liam. "You're devastated."

"Demi left me with a mess to clean up."

"That's my point. Usually that would cause you to spring into action. To show people you're in control."

"I don't want to hold a press conference and tell people she's never coming back." Even Liam heard the sadness in his voice when he said that.

Axel laughed. "I'm going to go out on a limb and say that's because you love her."

When Liam didn't answer, Axel's laughter grew. "You love her!"

When Liam again didn't answer, Axel rolled his eyes. "Oh, my God, you love her, and you can't admit it."

"Love has never been my friend."

"Just go after her!"

"For what? She refuses to marry me."

"She won't refuse if you admit you love her."

"I'm not sure I do."

Axel picked up a pair of trousers off the floor. "Well, I'm sure you do. Only people who use their floor as a laundry bin and refuse to let housekeeping into their quarters love the person who dumped them." He shook his head and tossed the trousers back the hall toward the bedroom. "Go get that woman. You love her and she's so in love with you she can't handle the idea that you'll never love her."

Liam frowned. "What?"

"That's the bottom line. I think there would be nothing worse than to be married to someone who'd rather give me the world than humble himself and admit he loves me."

"I have no problem humbling myself."

"Then go get her. Tell her what she needs to hear." Axel paused, thinking again. "Unless you're afraid. Unless you thought the legal commitment was stronger than trusting love, and that's why you liked the idea of an arranged marriage—" He snorted. "Oh, my gosh! That's it. You'd rather pretend you don't love her than take the risk." He shook his head. "What a stupid choice."

Liam's head snapped up. "What did you say?"

"I said you had a choice, hang your hat on an arranged marriage or admit you love her, and you made the stupid decision."

All that rolled around in Liam's brain. He'd been so angry

with Lilibet when she'd taken the choice of their relationship out of his hands. He should have been angry with Demi for doing the same, but he'd been too hurt to think of it.

But if what Axel was saying was true, when Demi walked out the door, technically she'd ended their arranged marriage. If he went after her, it would be a fresh start. *His choice.*

And if she agreed to marry him…that would be her choice.

Not an arranged marriage after all.

All these years all he'd ever really wanted was a choice. Now, he finally had one.

Axel shook his head and kept talking. "That woman's your queen and if all you need to do to bring her back is admit you love her, just go admit the obvious. All she wants is your love. Not a signed document. But an emotion she can trust."

Liam started to laugh. "You know what? I think you're right."

Axel's expression shifted. "You do?"

"Yes. If I love her, I should go after her. If she loves me, she should marry me."

Axel frowned. "Isn't that what I just said?"

"Yes…but no. The way I said it was better."

He took an old jet to Hermosa, something his military had classified as decommissioned and on paper it was sold. But it really hadn't been. It was used for clandestine diplomatic trips so that no one could track the person who'd used it.

In case his plan didn't work, Liam didn't want to have been tracked.

A rental car awaited him at the private airstrip. He hopped inside and drove directly to the homeless shelter.

The sounds of the small city hummed around him as he got out of the SUV and walked into the bright blue building—where they were packing boxes of food for the needy.

Wanda saw him first. "Prince Liam!"

The busy warehouse room came to an immediate halt that silenced all the noise of their work.

Demi turned from the shelf she was inventorying, her eyes wide. He saw hope blossom in their dark depths before she shut it down and strode over to him. "You're interrupting our work."

He glanced around nonchalantly. "Yeah. I get that."

"So go."

"You want me to help?"

She gaped at him. "No! You're a distraction."

He peeked at her. "A good distraction?"

Just seeing him and hearing his voice made her heart hurt. Longing tried to form but she stomped it out. It had been hard enough leaving him the first time. She couldn't soften, listen to him, let him stay...only to lose him again.

"Just a distraction. Go. We have work to do."

The crowd that had been packing boxes began ambling over. Freddie liked Liam. So did Oscar. But Wanda was smitten.

"You come to take our Demi again?"

He faced her. "I wish. We're supposed to get married on Saturday."

A general gasp went up in the group, who didn't have enough access to the internet to realize the wedding was so soon.

Undoubtedly having heard Liam's voice, Strawberry and Shortcake came bounding into the room. They ignored

Demi and raced up to Liam. Strawberry head-butted his left shin. Shortcake wrapped himself around the right.

Liam stooped down and let them nuzzle his fingers. "Hey, guys." He looked up at her. "They're probably hoping I brought the twins."

The cats had been restless and bored. Gazing at her with curious expressions. Sometimes looking at her as if she were totally wrong about going home. "Maybe."

Her staff stared at her the same way now.

Exhaustion sat on her shoulders. "Everybody go back to work." She headed for her office. "Liam? Come with me."

He followed her to the little office.

"Still homey as ever," he said.

She waited for him to sit. He didn't.

"Come here."

She almost refused. She didn't want to stand that close to him, to smell his scent, to feel the magnetic pull he now had for her.

But in the interest of getting him to leave, she gathered her defenses and defiantly stood in front of him.

He gazed down at her. "You said I deserved to love someone. Well, I do. I love *you*."

Of all the arguments she expected him to make, that one hadn't even made the list. Though she wanted to believe it, she knew better. "Right."

He put his hands on her shoulders, eased them down her biceps and forearms then back up again. "I do."

"The last time we talked, you were extremely sure you didn't. You told me love was untrustworthy and duty and responsibility were better. Now you're saying a couple of days changed your mind?"

He thought about it. "Yes."

"Then we are in worse trouble than I thought. The night I

left you were very clear that you didn't love me. Now you're saying you do love me. I risked everything to admit I loved you and I ruined what we had. So we can't go back to that."

"Maybe that's the fun of it."

She gaped at him.

"My feelings for you are so strong. Different than what I'd ever felt for anyone else. Stronger than what I ever felt for Lilibet. That's why I think I didn't recognize what was happening between us was love."

Her expression turned skeptical. "Really?"

"Honestly, Demi, if you look at this the right way, my not recognizing what we had was love might mean I never loved anyone before you. That might mean love hadn't been godawful to me...but expectation had."

She leaned back, letting her butt fall to her desk. "What?"

"Think it through. I didn't have a lot of time for reflection when we were together. Everything was happening so fast, but also like dominoes. I persuaded you to keep the arrangement your father made. You came to my country. We made plans for personal appearances that worked. But we also had private time that worked. Every day we felt a little bit more for each other professionally in our respective roles and personally. It worked so well that I never felt the need to analyze it.

"But when Axel came to my quarters to tell me Castle Admin had sent him to get me to cancel our wedding, I couldn't actually take any steps toward doing that." He caught her gaze. "I kept hoping you'd change your mind and decide to keep our deal."

She laughed, but tears filled her eyes.

"I missed you," he said quietly.

"I missed you too."

"I love you. I love everything about you. Even the fact

that you need me a little bit because all this stuff I feel for you makes me need you too."

She smiled at him. "We're even?"

"Is there any other way to form a good arranged marriage?"

She laughed and ran her hands down her face. "I don't know."

"What do you say... Do you want to be a queen? My queen? The love of my life? The person who makes me happy even when things are sketchy?"

"Sketchy?"

"That's an Axel word."

"What are *your* words?"

"I feel so connected to you that I can't imagine that we aren't meant to be partners, lovers, *everything* to each other."

She whispered, "I can't either."

He caught her hands and pulled her up to stand in front of him. Then he kissed her. All her emotions broke free and flooded her and she knew this was what she'd been waiting for, the joy, the happiness, the desire from both. Not just her. Not just him. Both.

"We have a choice... Cancel the wedding and start all over with everyone wanting to know the story of why we canceled one wedding only to plan another. Or—given that Prosperita's over halfa day ahead of us—we can still get to the wedding. We don't have to cancel it, and no one has to be any the wiser."

"I haven't unpacked yet."

He smiled at her. "I never packed at all."

"You were that sure of me?"

He put his arm around her and turned her to the door. "You loved me enough to leave me. That's the kind of sacrifice only a person deeply in love could make. I was counting on that."

She laughed.

They said goodbye much the same way as when he'd whisked her off to Prosperita the first time. They flew to New York, refueled, took a long nap, then showered and got ready to sneak off the plane and race to the Castle, staying under the radar.

The time difference and travel had eaten up most of their precious few hours, but they kept in touch letting everyone know the wedding was on. Castle Admin had sent frantic texts. Rowan coordinated last minute details with Demi. Axel sent laughing emojis. The cats milled around the jet like they owned it. No one in this relationship got a better deal than Strawberry and Shortcake.

They arrived at the private entrance in the back of the Castle at the same time early guests began showing up at the front entrance. Rowan and the twins met them, ready to take Strawberry and Shortcake to the King's quarters to spend the wedding day and month-long honeymoon with the twins.

They raced up the back stairs laughing, then stopped when they got to the door to her quarters.

"I'll see you in twenty minutes."

She frowned at him. "It takes me twenty minutes to do my hair."

"You're saying you're going to be late?"

"Yes. You'll have to stall."

"Or we could say nothing and keep everyone guessing, looking at their watches, wondering if one of us is having second thoughts."

She held his gaze. "Never." Then she smiled. "But I do like keeping everyone guessing."

"You always have."

He kissed her, started walking to his quarters and turned back again. "I'm going to marry you."

"You bet your sweet butt you are."

His laughter echoed down the hall as she walked into her room.

The wedding started only thirty minutes late. Everything was so perfectly, wonderfully, orchestrated that no one would have known that only hours before no one in the castle was sure there would be a wedding.

Demi wore a white gown that was so full Liam wondered how he'd stand close to her. Fitted at the bodice, it happily displayed all her curves, as the sheer veil cascaded from the back of her head down her shoulders and along her body until it hit the floor and trailed at least twenty feet behind her.

When she reached him at the altar and faced him, he took her hands. "You look amazing."

"So do you."

The emotion of it nearly overwhelmed him. He wasn't just marrying a woman who would be a queen, he was marrying the woman he loved and trusted. "This is all I've ever wanted."

She smiled in the way that made his heart sing. "Me too."

They said their vows as two people in love. When the papers began speculating that this had been an arranged marriage, they laughed, sitting on the sandy beaches of the royal family's private estate in Fiji.

EPILOGUE

ALMOST TWO YEARS to the date after Liam and Demi's wedding, Rowan sat with her husband, the King of a decent-sized country, who couldn't handle the hours of waiting required to bring a child into the world.

"I don't remember you being this tense when the twins were born."

Jozef snorted a laugh. "I hid it better."

She caught his hand and squeezed. "And you also knew our children were not the heirs to your throne."

"Not unless Liam and I were killed."

At Axel's pragmatic but perhaps inappropriate comment, Rowan rolled her eyes. "Stop."

Heather sighed. "He's been like this all day. Julian's still not sleeping through the night."

Axel grimaced. "It makes me moody."

Jozef laughed at his son. "Just wait until he realizes he can turn off the alarms to the Castle."

"I'm not giving him a chance to learn. We'll be living at the cabin most of the time we're home."

Rowan pondered for a second. "I wonder if all the traveling you do with him is affecting his sleep."

"I'm sure of it," Heather said. "He's a year and a half. He should be sleeping through the night."

"Maybe you should take three months and not travel,"

Jozef suggested. "Give him a chance to get accustomed to the same bed, the same room. And set a schedule."

Heather said "Hmmm."

Axel leaned around her to direct his question to his father. "You think that would work?"

"I don't know, but I think you're at the point where you should be willing to try anything."

Axel groaned. "We are."

Rowan started to say something, but the doctor walked into the private waiting room. The hospital had an entire floor dedicated to the royals. There wasn't even a button for it on the elevators. Though no one would notice. The numbers in elevator cars ran normally. But the fifth floor on the buttons was actually the sixth floor of the hospital. A private elevator in the back only went to the floor dedicated to the royals. And without a lock sequence, the elevator didn't even open, let alone climb to the hidden fifth floor.

"Your Majesty," the doctor said, bowing slightly. "Your son and daughter-in-law would like to see you."

Panicked, Jozef rose. "What's wrong? Something's wrong! Right?"

"I'll leave the discussion to your son. He simply asked that I suggest you go in alone for a few minutes before the rest of your family."

Heather and Axel rose too.

Jozef motioned for them to return to their seats.

Rowen said, "You're not going in without me."

She caught Jozef's hand, and they walked along the hall to the room where Demi had had the baby. As soon as she stepped in the door and saw the pink blanket on the little bundle, Rowan laughed.

"You had a girl?"

Jozef laughed too. "Oh, my gosh! Our next ruler is a queen?" His laughter grew and he reached out to take Rowan's hand. "You know? It seems fitting. We were the dullest group of royals on the planet until Rowan came into my life, then Heather into Axel's and now Demi into yours, Liam. Women gave our castle life and energy again. Let's see what this one can do for our country."

He walked over to the bed. Rowan wanted nothing more than to hold the tiny bundle, but she knew protocol reined in this family.

Jozef quietly asked, "Have you named her?"

Demi looked at Liam, who nodded once. "We're calling her Monique, after your mother."

Jozef's face fell. "My mother will be—amazed."

Liam laughed. "We're hoping this will make up for not telling her we were getting married."

Demi shook her head. "That's not why we're naming her after Jozef's mother." She caught Jozef's gaze. "We've talked about this, and we think this amazing family all began with your mother."

Rowan nodded. "I think you're right." She paused for only a second. "Now let me hold her."

Demi laughed and handed her daughter to Rowan. The King told the nurse to get Axel and Heather. The nanny brought the twins into the room.

From there everything became noisy and confused. Rowan relinquished the baby to Jozef who held her for a few minutes then gave her to Axel. He held her for a few minutes, crooning to her, telling her her life was going to be extremely interesting, before he gave her to Heather who burst into tears. Rowan suspected she was pregnant again, but wasn't about to announce it on the day Demi had her baby. They'd stolen Demi and Liam's thunder when they announced her first pregnancy the day Demi arrived. Rowan knew they wouldn't do it again. But Heather's uncharacteristic tears were more than a hint.

The nanny took the baby from Heather and stooped down to show her to the twins who were now six.

Rowan stepped back, seeing it all, remembering it all, because someday, when this Monique was being crowned queen, a reporter would want to know about this minute and she wanted to tell everyone that this gregarious, smart, emotional, wonderful family had been overjoyed, over the moon and so in love with the little pink bundle of joy that no one could completely capture the moment.

That was the day she decided to keep a journal.

* * * * *

COMING SOON!

We really hope you enjoyed reading this book. If you're looking for more romance be sure to head to the shops when new books are available on

Thursday 14th September

To see which titles are coming soon, please visit

millsandboon.co.uk/nextmonth

MILLS & BOON

MILLS & BOON®

Coming next month

OFF-LIMITS FLING WITH THE HEIRESS
Rachael Stewart

"Gabe?" She stumbles along with me, her green eyes wide as she blinks up at me.

My jaw is gritted so tight I can't respond. Her perfume is more intoxicating than the whisky, her arm through mine, a heated magnetic field. It takes everything I have to fight the burning connection, to remind myself that she's Aiden's sister—too young, too forbidden, and too much…even for me.

Too clever and wasted on the path she has chosen too.

We break out into the fresh air, and I suck in a breath, release her with a flourish. I need the space, the air to breathe without her in it.

"Get in."

My driver already has the door to my gunmetal-grey Aston open and she gawps back at me, hand propped on one hip, chin at a defiant slant.

"Who do you—?"

"I said, get in!"

I'm already scanning the dark alleyway for unwitting passers-by ready to snap a pic of our standoff. It'll be all over social media in seconds and I don't want to face that kind of the scrutiny. Neither should she. But Avery's been courting bad press for years now. Loves it, by all accounts.

And grief will only get you so far. Sympathy for the daddy's girl suffering the sudden loss of her father has long been replaced by hostility for the rich, spoilt heiress.

Not that I believe the half of it…though faced with the defiant woman before me it's hard to keep sight of that.

"No 'Hello, Avery. How the hell are you?'" Her eyes flash gold under the solitary amber lamp hung over the door we broke out of. "It's been months, if not years…"

It's been three months at most, something she'd remember if she hadn't been so drunk or drugged up. I'm not sure which.

"Hi, Avery. How the hell are you? It's been months, if not years. Now get in."

She folds her arms, doesn't budge and my driver's mouth quirks but he doesn't dare smile. No one defies me. No one save for Avery, it would seem.

"Or do you want me to call your brother and tell him where we are, where you were?"

She blows out a breath, says something I can't decipher and moves. Clambering onto the back seat without a care for the plush upholstery.

I curse the heavens and follow her in.

Continue reading
OFF-LIMITS FLING WITH THE HEIRESS
Rachael Stewart

Available next month
www.millsandboon.co.uk

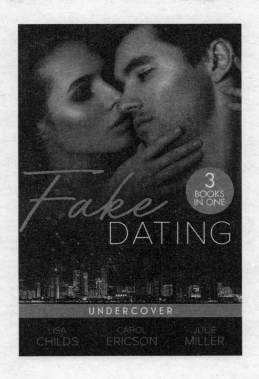

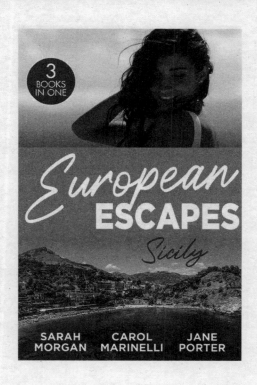

LET'S TALK
Romance

For exclusive extracts, competitions and special offers, find us online:

- **f** MillsandBoon
- **𝕏** @MillsandBoon
- **⧉** @MillsandBoonUK
- **♪** @MillsandBoonUK

Get in touch on 01413 063 232

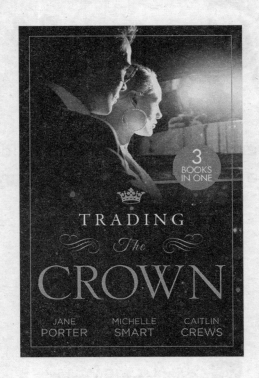